Tales of
Darkness
and Sin

Cover Designer: Opulent Swag and Designs

Interior Formatting: TRC Designs

Aleatha
Romig

Tales of
Darkness
and Sin

Natasha
Knight ♥

Sold to the Highest Bidder

ALEATHA ROMIG AND SKYE WARREN

Chapter One

BRIANA

The helicopter's blades stopped.

A cold chill prickled my skin as I stepped from the helicopter, my sandals sinking in the soft sand. With the sun high, the torches surrounding the landing pad and lining the path were unlit, yet their presence was like breadcrumbs indicating the direction for us to go. From the depth of the foliage, a man in a light suit appeared.

"Welcome to Malaking Kuta."

I'd been told the translation meant fortress. It was a fortress protected not by stone walls but by miles of sea complete with rip tides and currents guaranteed to keep boats away.

The man came closer and offered a nod of his head. When his eyes looked up, they were on me, scanning me from my painted toenails to my dark brown hair, lingering too long on my breasts, visible in the neckline of the dress Curtis had chosen. Yet, when our welcoming party spoke, I wasn't addressed.

"Mr. Kidwell, Mr. Knapp was happy to receive your call." He gestured

toward the path. "Follow me."

"I don't know about this..." I whispered after the man had turned. "He seems...slimy."

Immediately, Curtis's hand went to the small of my back, leading me forward. "He is, but I'm here." Curtis's lips spoke near my ear. "Bri, you can do this."

I inhaled, nodding with the knowledge that I'd promised to do what I could.

How was I to know what he would ask?

How could I know a place like this truly existed?

We moved forward, our guide leading us from the landing pad along a winding path to the group of main buildings we'd seen from the air.

With each step we were surrounded by paradise, from the tropical air filled with floral scents and sea breezes to the crystal blue sea of the South Pacific, glistening in all directions of this private island. After we'd flown for nearly twenty hours in an airplane, we'd boarded a helicopter. Leaving what little bit of civilization could be found, we'd flown by helicopter, watching through the windows as water overtook the world.

Finally, we arrived.

Despite the balmy breeze, I couldn't shake the unease caused by Curtis's request, the way the man stared, or perhaps from my decision to oblige in this farce.

Two days ago, Curtis and I were in our luxury penthouse in the cool and harsh world of Detroit.

With the slivers of sun shining through the dense foliage, my body tried to persuade me to enjoy the warm air and din of waves lapping a nearby beach. However, my mind was awhirl with what was at hand.

To say that our lives—or Curtis's—were in flames would overstate the more concentrated concern that Curtis's company, the one he inherited from his father, was in a low smolder. The markets were in peril and given the correct conditions, his corporation would ignite, causing total annihilation. It was a future he was willing to risk anything to save.

Anything.

Anyone.

Me.

I stilled as the palm trees thinned, looking out at the endless miles of sea.

There was no turning back.

"Mr. Kidwell, Ms. Pierce, this way," the man leading our way said. "Mr. Knapp is waiting."

Well, at least he knew my name.

What choices did I have if I refused to go forward?

Back to the helicopter.

No. The sound of its engines roared overhead as it left the island.

Could I convince Curtis there was another way?

No. Mr. Knapp was waiting.

Mr. Knapp was the man Curtis believed would be his savior in this time of trouble.

I reached for Curtis's hand. "I'm not sure I can do this."

My fiancé's dark eyes simmered with emotions too many to differentiate. Together they created a boiling concoction that had only cooled enough to touch since my agreement to this scheme. He lifted my hand, bringing my knuckles to his lips. "I wouldn't have asked you here if I thought anything would happen. You know that, Bri. Tell me you know."

For only a moment, his gaze disappeared as his kiss brought warmth back to my flesh.

"How can you be certain?" I asked.

"Booker Knapp has a reputation." Curtis's eyes closed as the cords in his neck tightened.

With my hesitation, I was pushing him and I knew it. Nevertheless, I deserved more information. Now that we were here, I wanted reassurance.

"A reputation...?" I allowed the rest to go unsaid, hoping Curtis would give me more than he already had.

A few years ago, Curtis made the bold move to take controlling

9

interest in the family empire, purposely leaving his brother in the wake. It was a coup of sorts. The two brothers had an uneasy relationship.

Personally, I'd always found Cameron more aloof, gruffer, and a bit intimidating. Curtis's charisma attracted me before his good looks. Both brothers were blessed with devilishly handsome appearances.

Curtis's plan for autonomy from his sibling worked and it didn't.

While Curtis was finally free of Cameron's intrusion, the transaction left Curtis in a financial predicament. The liquid assets Cameron acquired, he took with him to a new life in Tanglewood, where he created his own kingdom of sorts.

Determined to make the new arrangement work, Curtis turned to the unlikely investor, the Ivanov bratva, the ruling power in Detroit. Recent events have found Curtis again in need of an infusion of cash. The bratva was demanding payment, payment he didn't have.

I'd suggested contacting another entity, one that could supersede the Ivanov bratva, the Sparrows of Chicago. It made sense that Sterling Sparrow would be interested in a piece of something belonging, at least in part, to the Ivanov bratva.

Curtis wouldn't hear of it.

Instead, he had a plan, a plan that would bring in revenue without relinquishing more of his enterprise—at least permanently.

That was why we were here, on Malaking Kuta, Booker Knapp's secluded island, the place where the rich came to get richer, deals were made, fortunes secured, and dreams fulfilled.

As my steps approached the large white mansion, I questioned whether it would be dreams I found or nightmares.

"A reputation for making dreams come true," Curtis said. "Baby, my company is my dream. Here, we will save it."

Together we climbed the steps leading up to the mansion.

It isn't the only building upon the island, but it is the grandest, upon a hill. As the warm breeze blew the skirt of my dress and the wisps of hair around my face, I found myself mesmerized by the beauty. Upon the stately

large porch, I took a deep breath as the double doors opened.

Beyond where we stood were voices, deep and husky. The scent of cigar smoke wafted toward us.

"Aww, Mr. Kidwell. It's always nice to see a familiar face." The gentleman speaking was younger than I expected, probably not even fifty, with just a touch of gray in his temples, enough that it made him distinguished without saying he'd aged.

And yet he too was sizing me from head to toe until his vile gaze landed upon Curtis.

Again, Curtis's hand came to my back as he encouraged me forward. "Booker, I appreciate you accepting my offer. May I introduce my fiancée, Briana Pierce. She's everything I promised."

"Stunning." Booker Knapp gestured for us to enter. "Please, we want to learn more about this lovely beauty."

Chapter Two

CAMERON

I'm sitting in the corner of the room, my back to the wall, looking out at the suits and the glitter, a glass of scotch in my hand. Ice clinks against the crystal, slowly melting. I'm not planning on drinking what's left. It's for show along with the Bulgari cufflinks and Aubercy shoes. There's endless entertainment on this island. Gambling and women. Street-illegal cars. I'm here for one purpose—business.

"Ground floor," the man in front of me says. His name is Don. Dan? I'm not sure. Beads of sweat line his pale brow. "This kind of opportunity, it doesn't come along every day."

I have a hundred investment opportunities cross my desk on any given day. I'm not interested in ordinary. You don't come to Malaking Kuta for ordinary. "What's your role in the company?"

"Business. I'm the moneyman." He laughs. "It's my job to get us funding because this kind of market opening won't last forever. A small investment, one point five mil, and we'd be global in two months."

It would take closer to three million dollars and six months, but I

don't bother correcting him. It doesn't matter. Gabriel Miller taught me everything I know about investing. *Follow the dream.* Someone in his company might have vision. It's not Danny here. His dream is to cash out. The payday. He doesn't care about the technology or about the lives it would impact.

Which means he's worthless to me.

"Excuse me," I say, setting down my drink and standing. I ignore his startled words and his promises to call me. I hope he doesn't have my number.

There are a few people I came to the island to meet. A woman who rarely leaves her mansion in northeast China. A man who travels so much it's hard to pin him down. A married couple who own an island in the Bay of Bengal. People who can deal with the large volume of cash Miller Industries is ready to invest. With the market tanking, this is the perfect time to build it back up.

Mr. Knapp stops me as I cross the room. A short man who looks perpetually angry. I think he tries to look pleased to see me, but it only comes off as a grimace. "Mr. Kidwell. We're honored to have you here at Malaking Kuta. After our many invitations to Gabriel Miller, we thought he would never attend."

I offer a bland smile. "Your persistence paid off."

"And I'm certain you will be most pleased with the luxuries we have to offer. You must have seen your private cabin. Was it to your liking?"

The porch had been bigger than my first apartment when I moved to Tanglewood. Only feet away from the lapping blue water. Blinding white sand. It would have been an oasis to someone on vacation. For me it held the same appeal as a dimly lit hotel room—a place to rest between making deals.

I'll meet with Jade Changueng and Anand Shah and the Wilson couple. I'll see if anyone else on the island is worth doing business with, and tomorrow, I'll fly back to Tanglewood.

"It was satisfactory," I tell Mr. Knapp.

He frowns. "No no, we want to do better than that. We wish to please you. That's the purpose of Malaking Kuta—pleasure in all its forms. Would you like a woman sent to warm your bed tonight?"

The sexual daring of the island makes it legendary. If I want a woman, I'll find her myself, among the bejeweled women sprinkling the crowd. Maybe it will be Jade Changueng, whose talents have distracted me for an hour or two before. "No, thank you."

"Perhaps a man?" He gives a sneaky laugh. "Or both? Don't worry if you have certain predilections. Our entertainment is well versed in the sexual arts. And tolerant. Very tolerant."

Hell, he's practically inviting me to beat them. "No."

He brushes off my refusal with a pudgy hand. "They are too pedestrian for you, these practiced people. We have something much more interesting tonight for a man of your refined tastes."

Christ. I keep thinking he's going to run out of illicit things to offer. "Such as?"

"Fresh meat."

A little flare of heat in my veins. That is interesting, but it shouldn't be. Nothing matters except signing on the bottom line. Follow the dream. Find the people who will change the world. Give them enough money to do it and then reap the profits afterward. "Fresh meat."

"We're having an auction. Three specimens. All of them new to the island. All of them untrained."

Jesus. The idea of initiating someone into sexual bondage, of that shiver of uncertainty, even fear—it shouldn't be so appealing. I've fought for years to get rid of the desire. Only in the dark, alone, do I admit my wish to control someone. To own them. "I'm not sure I'll attend. There's work to do."

"You must. *You must.* Everyone else will be there. No one will miss it."

No, I doubt the people I want to deal with will miss the auction if it's the entertainment of the evening. There's a reason those people only emerge

to this island—to sate their sexual appetites. Which means I'll have to go along with it. I'll have to watch someone be placed on an auction block, touched and examined, sold to the highest bidder. Lust rages inside me at the thought, but I force it down.

When I left Detroit, I took a job as a clerk under Gabriel Miller. It was beneath me. My brother sure as hell never would have done something so demeaning. But I knew it would be the start of something new. He taught me everything I know about business. I worked my way up and now I get a percentage of the deals I ink. A thick bank account pays for a penthouse apartment that's empty while I work long hours. It's not a warm life, but it's a lucrative one.

I give a short bow. "Then I'll see you tonight, Mr. Knapp."

He smiles, and my blood turns cold. It's not a nice smile. "One more thing."

"I would prefer to rest before the evening entertainment."

"There's someone else I want you to meet. I'm sure you'll agree once you see them."

Keep a cool head. That's the first thing Gabriel taught me when I was young and stupid. Full of anger at my brother. Full of unfulfilled desire for his girlfriend. That's the only reason I don't punch this fucker and his obsequious smile. Rule number one: keep a cool head. Rule number two: follow the dream.

Men in suits and women in gowns move aside, revealing a couple that I never expected to see again. Certainly not here. Not on Malaking Kuta. It's my brother, Curtis. The woman I've loved for years stands at his side, wearing a small but sparkling diamond. Her eyes meet mine, those gorgeous blue eyes that have haunted my dreams. The ones that show up when I'm stroking my cock alone in bed. That mouth that moans my name.

The woman I can never have. She's on the island.

"Cameron," she says, sounding as surprised as me. More.

I struggle to control my emotion, but it's like trying to tame an ocean. Keep a calm head? No goddamn way can I do that now. Follow the dream?

Briana is my dream. "What the fuck are you doing here?"

She shakes her head, as if still reeling from shock. "Curtis brought me."

Mr. Knapp looks pleased with himself. "She's going to be at auction tonight."

"What the hell do you mean?" I snarl past the buzzing in my ears.

"We pride ourselves on the island to fulfill your deepest fantasy, Mr. Kidwell."

She stares back at me, my deepest fantasy, my darkest dream. And she's afraid.

Chapter One

BRIANA

Leaving Curtis and Mr. Knapp in our private cabin, I kicked off my sandals and made my way out onto the sandy white beach. As the sea breeze fluffed the skirt of my sundress, my toes sank into the soft sand, yet I didn't feel the warmth. With the sun streaming down, I wrapped my arms around myself and lifted my face to the sky. No amount of tropical grandeur could make up for what was about to happen. Sun rays, no matter how intense, couldn't bring heat to my chilled skin.

My hands trembled as they had since seeing Cameron Kidwell.

How was he here?

My mind scrambled with the realization that Curtis's brother was not only here, but Mr. Knapp had invited him to the auction.

Closing my eyes, I replayed the conversation Curtis and I'd had before I agreed to this ridiculous escapade.

"Bri, I have it worked out. It's a show." Curtis gently pushed a stray lock of hair away from my face. *"You're beautiful. I've been talking to Booker Knapp. He has the answer for our financial woes."*

"I-I don't know."

His expression turned solemn. "You know what Andros Ivanov will do to me if I can't make this payment."

I shook my head and swallowed my response. I wanted to say it wasn't our financial woe. I wanted to recommend Curtis speak to one of the Sparrow men from Chicago. I knew getting a direct line to the kingpin, Sterling Sparrow, wasn't easy, but I had a connection, albeit distant. As a fashion buyer for a charming boutique in Sterling Heights, I had spent the last few years trying to acquire the license to sell an exclusive brand of women's fashion, Sinful Threads. It so happened that my contact—Louisa Toney—was a good friend of the wife of the kingpin, Araneae Sparrow.

I wasn't sure how it all worked, but it seemed better than Curtis's proposal.

"Is that what you want," he asked, "to identify my body?"

"You know it isn't."

"It's one night. Like I said, it's a show. The bids are taken electronically. It's not like I'm the only man—"

"What the hell?"

"Bri, it's one night, and if Booker can work out the particulars, it won't really happen."

"It? The transaction? Being bid upon and sold?" My voice was getting higher with each statement. "I'm not sleeping—"

"Of course you're not. Yes, there's an auction. You'll stand before a group of people. The bids will come in and Knapp will keep it going until the price is what we need. Then, he'll announce the winner. It's staged. They do it all the time."

"I don't understand how you get the money if I don't...end up..." I couldn't make myself say the word—sold.

"The patrons of Malaking Kuta drop a lot of money to be there. Knapp will spread the word that he has a special auction. I'll get the cut from what he makes. At the end of the night, you will be back with me in our cabin. We'll make love to the sound of the waves, and the bidders will be none the

wiser."

"People go there to...?"

"Everything from business to debauchery. That doesn't concern you. No one will know you."

"Bri," Curtis called from the large front porch. "Booker needs to go over a few items with you."

I didn't move.

A statue in the sand with the warm waves lapping my toes.

Perhaps if I stayed where I was long enough, the tide would take me out to sea.

Anything was better than what I'd heard.

Cameron's voice was a snarl, a growl. "What the fuck are you doing here?"

My words barely formed. "Curtis brought me." I was paralyzed from his stare.

In seconds Cameron had gone from shocked to enraged, yet it was Mr. Knapp who spoke. "She's going to be at auction tonight."

My stomach twisted as my circulation settled.

"What the hell do you mean?"

Swallowing, I lowered my eyes as Mr. Knapp replied, "We pride ourselves on the island to fulfill your deepest fantasy, Mr. Kidwell."

"Bri." Curtis appeared behind me, reaching for my hand.

I spun toward him, my volume low and words sharp. "How. Could. You?"

"Baby, you've got to believe me, the last person I expected to see here was Cameron. Fucking wannabe. He's probably down here as Gabriel Miller's errand boy."

"I don't care why he's here. He's here. You said no one would know me." I tipped my chin toward Mr. Knapp standing on the porch. "He invited Cameron, for some sick game..." I let out a long breath. "I refuse."

Curtis's hand teased the length of my chestnut hair. "Remember, it's only a show. They can't really sell people. That's not legal."

"I have the feeling that legality isn't the rule of this island."

I reached for Curtis's hand. "Listen, I'll call Louisa. Remember, I told you about her. I'll get a connection to Mr. Sparrow—"

With his free hand, Curtis placed his finger on my lips. "Stop it, Briana." His tone cooled, returning the chill to my skin. "I'm not exchanging one mob's money for another's. How fucking hard is it for you to understand this? Hell, I'd stand up there myself if I could make the money, but I can't. You said you would do this. We signed on the dotted line. There's no turning back now."

Letting go of Curtis's hand, I lifted my chin high and walked to where the porch and sand met. "Mr. Knapp. How much money are we trying to raise?"

His thin lips curled. The way he was looking at me made my stomach turn. "Little lady, I am confident that the right price will be reached."

I knew it was a stretch, but if Curtis wouldn't ask for the Sparrows' help, I would. I stood taller. "I don't understand how any of this works, but I want you to know that no matter what the winning bid is, I will not only match it, I'll exceed it."

"Briana," Curtis said my name as a reprimand.

Mr. Knapp's smile grew. "My, she's a feisty one." He looked to Curtis. "Yes, I have no doubt that your goal will be obtained." Before I could speak, Booker turned to me. "Little lady, I'd suspect if you indeed had that kind of expendable capital, you wouldn't be where you are at this moment."

I refused to look away. "I can get it."

He turned to Curtis. "I'll have a dinner brought to your cabin. Have her fully prepared. There is a cape hanging in the closet." He turned to me. "Wearing anything else is your option. Just know, once you're on display, everything will be removed. Our buyers want to get a good look at the merchandise."

"I'm serious," I said. "I have a connection. I can get the money."

The slime winked.

He had the audacity to wink.

"I may have to get in on this bidding. I enjoy spunk, when it's harnessed in the right direction."

Harnessed.

"Mr. Kidwell, assure me that you and Ms. Pierce will be up at the mansion at eight p.m."

"We won't back out on this, I promise you."

I stood silently as Curtis walked Mr. Knapp through the cabin and to the door. When he returned, my head was shaking. "You bastard. You expect me to sleep with someone." I lifted my left hand and pulled the diamond ring from my fourth finger. With a quick spin, I turned toward the water and threw the platinum and diamond symbol that no longer mattered.

"Fucking Christ." He seized my wrist. "Do you know how much that cost?"

"Our future if you choose to go on with this. Get me back to Detroit tonight and we might have a chance."

"Oh, no. You're going to do this. You'll either walk up on that fucking stage with a shred of dignity or I'll carry you up there. Fuck, I'll hog-tie you if I have to."

"Who the hell are you? Why do you care so much that I do this?"

"Because I'm not losing my father's company and I'm not ending up dead courtesy of the Ivanov bratva. I don't give a damn who you have to sleep with. It's one fucking night. Get over it."

I started to walk past him when he again grabbed my wrist and spun me toward him. "What will it be, Briana? Dignity or hog-tied? Either one will work to inflate your price."

The images of what he said went through my head.

"Dignity," I said with an eerie calm. "When this is over, if Ivanov doesn't kill you, I will."

Chapter Four

CAMERON

I make a phone call to the private helicopter company. "Mr. Kidwell?"

"Yes. Please have the chopper brought to the island. I'm leaving early."

"Of course, sir."

"No, wait."

She holds her tongue over the line, probably rolling her eyes at the foibles of the rich. I'm not usually indecisive. Only one person has ever made me that way.

There were many reasons I left Detroit. A floundering economy and the bitter cold. Our father built a tiny empire of appliance stores. He left it to Curtis and me. Two brothers. A lifetime of rivalry. I could say I left when Curtis tried to force me out, but the truth is I could have fought him. He was already unethical then. I had enough to put him in jail if I wanted to. The real reason why I left Detroit wasn't the recession or the weather. It wasn't even my brother. The reason why I left was Briana.

For whatever reason, she chose Curtis. She wanted him. She put his goddamn pawn shop ring on her finger, and I didn't want her heartbroken. So I walked away from my small inheritance, one-half of the appliance shops. I walked away from her because it hurt too much to watch her with him.

"Leave the schedule," I say over the phone. "I'll stay the night."

It would be better to leave now, not to see her on that pedestal. Not to see men bidding on her sweet body. Not to be tempted to bid myself. She wanted Curtis. She chose him. She chose *this*.

Except no woman really would, would they?

Even if she's head over heels in love with my brother, does she really understand what she's giving up for him? There's a stain that can never be fully removed, being sold in a room full of strangers. Having sex with someone who paid for the use of her.

I find myself putting on my tux, donning that costume of the businessman, the billionaire. It doesn't matter if I actually am that person according to my investment portfolio. I'll always be the scrawny kid from the shitty part of Detroit. This is always a part that I play.

Across the white sand and the carefully manicured strip of jungle, the mansion glitters.

Mr. Knapp made it clear that he expected me to purchase her.

I'd have the right to touch her, to fuck her. To do anything I want, even if what I most want is simply to hold her. Unrequited love is a *fuck you* from the universe. And then what? Give her back to Curtis? I'm not sure I could. I'm not sure I *should* if this is how he treats her.

Maybe she's better off with me even if I have to buy her.

A massive staircase leads to the mansion. An upscale Alpine lift brings people from their huts to the top of the mountain because heels aren't made for stone steps. I prefer to walk. I want the burn in my thighs to distract me from what's about to happen.

I might be coming back down the island in possession of a woman.

Half a mile of steps. I'm almost late. Everyone's already crowded into

the ballroom, the men hungry with lust, the women glittering with avarice. They don't mind watching a woman get sold as long as it's not them. The pedestal is still empty.

Mr. Knapp stands at a podium. His eyes narrow when he sees me. He's pleased.

At least someone's happy.

Mrs. Changueng and Mr. Shah are here in the room, ready for me to make a deal with them. Gabriel Miller is expecting me to come back with sizable property and shares. I don't give a fuck about that right now.

I only have eyes on the marble wall at the back and the little black rectangle in the center. That's where Briana's waiting.

Is she nervous? Scared? Excited?

"Now that we're all here," Mr. Knapp says, his eyes meeting mine, "we can begin the auction. I know you're excited to see the precious item we have for the highest bidder."

An appreciative laugh rumbles through the crowd. I want to throw something.

"Please, let's give a warm, appreciative welcome to Ms. Pierce."

Briana steps through the doorway, wearing what can only generously be called a dress. It's more like two strips of silk covering her breasts, wrapping around her waist, and tying over her hips. It covers the space between her legs and falls to the floor. She also has on black high-heeled Louboutins.

She looks like a goddess. For a second the hoots and the applause and the catcalls fade away. There's only her in this room. And me. Her eyes meet mine, and my breath catches. God, she's beautiful. A lily in a goddamn swamp because we're not alone. No, there are a hundred other people in the room, each eager to suck and lick her, to make her suck and lick them. Some of them want to hurt her, to bruise her soft skin. My hands turn to fists. She steps onto the pedestal, exposing her inner thigh, revealing the shadow of her pussy. The collective crowd draws in a breath.

Then she's standing two feet above everyone else, on display in every

sense of the word.

Mr. Knapp looks like a little goblin next to a princess. "You can see she has assets that every fine collector would appreciate. I'm sure the connoisseurs among you recognize first-class merchandise."

"Show us the goods," someone shouts

I curse under my breath. At this rate there's going to be a mob. If Mr. Knapp flashes her beautiful tits, they're going to overpower him. They're going to rape her right here in the ballroom, all two hundred of them. And then I'll have to kill every single one with my bare hands.

Chapter Five

BRIANA

hit.

As I stepped up onto the pedestal, my first goal was to not fall. The heat of the spotlight. The glass of wine in my otherwise empty stomach. The height of the high heels. They all work together, fighting against me.

What if I fell?

What would happen?

Would it save me or would I wake up as someone's property?

I refused to search the crowd for Curtis. I told him what I thought of him when I left the cabin. He'd brought me here to Malaking Kuta, promising me the impossible as he begged for my help. And then, once we arrived, the reality became all too clear.

I'd been deceived.

Instead of being someone special to Curtis, he'd discovered that I could be more useful if he shared. No longer his fiancée—I threw that damn ring into the surf—I was simply a plaything his friends or even strangers

were willing to pay to play with.

My mind swirled with the possibilities the night would hold.

Would I survive?

Not only physically, but mentally and emotionally.

What would be asked of me?

Would it be asked or demanded?

I scoured the crowded room. So many people, male and female. Laughing and nodding. Drinking and eating. This was a spectacle, and I was their focus. A rare statue or perhaps a painting to be assessed and scrutinized.

"Let us see more," a man called above the din.

Some of the others agreed while others simply smiled.

Depraved was what they were. Not one person present appeared shocked or appalled by what was happening.

I lifted my chin in an attempt to look above their heads. I didn't want to remember their faces or their grins. As I did, I found myself bound to an unexpected anchor—to a gaze that steadied me.

It was an unlikely tether, yet Cameron's dark eyes on me were a mix of emotions.

Anger. No, more intense. Rage.

Impatience.

Annoyance.

While also predatory and determined.

And still, there were more.

Could it be desire?

Mr. Knapp's voice barely registered. Even the calls from the crowd were muted under Cameron's stare. With my chin held high, I found myself unable to look away. There was a strange sense of security as well as trepidation in the familiar dark eyes.

I was about to be sold, of that there was no doubt.

What if my fate didn't land at the feet of a stranger but at Cameron's feet?

Mr. Knapp reached for the silk wrap, pulling me back into the present and my gaze away from Cameron.

"Stop," I said, pushing his hand away.

The crowd erupted in laughter. Not everyone. Cameron's expression hardened.

"One million," an older man called out. The woman on his arm nodded.

Did they expect a threesome?

"One million ten," another man called.

My head snapped to Mr. Knapp. "Two million and I purchase myself."

"Oh," he replied excitedly. "I told you she was first-class merchandise. Come now, surely someone will outbid the lady herself."

Time wasn't moving or maybe it was. More bids came and went as others called again for the silk to be removed.

"Two and a half million," a tall man with dark skin said, stepping to the front of the crowd. "And she'll accompany me back to my homeland."

My eyes widened. "What? No. This is one night."

"We have two and a half million," Mr. Knapp said with a grin. "While this was meant to be a one-night arrangement, we here at Malaking Kuta are always willing to make exceptions. As luck would have it, the contract Ms. Pierce signed could be open for interpretation."

My flesh prickled with goose bumps as the room began to swirl.

What was happening?

I eyed the edge of the pedestal. I could make a run for it, but then what?

"My offer stands," the tall gentleman said.

"Going once. Going twice."

"Five million."

A hush fell over the crowd before it erupted, blooming into a symphony of murmurs and gasps. Through it all, only one man came into focus. The man who had just bid five million for me.

He was the same man who'd earlier held my stare. Cameron Kidwell

stepped forward until he was in the front of the crowd beside the other bidder.

His dark eyes were more focused than they'd been a few minutes earlier. He wasn't looking at me, but at Mr. Knapp. In his tuxedo, Cameron was an incredibly handsome man, his shoulders broad, chest wide, and waist trim.

Sometime over the course of the last few years, he'd changed. He was still intimidating, but there was more. There was energy that permeated from him, powerful and steady. His presence commanded the room.

"You heard my bid." Cameron lifted his long leg, stepping up to beside the podium and turning toward the crowd. "Five million for this woman. I would suggest not countering; however, that is the way Mr. Knapp's entertainment is done. Last chance, do I hear any?"

Even the man who had bid before shook his head.

"Mr. Knapp, do your job."

Booker Knapp lifted his hand. "Ladies and gentlemen, remember we have two more excellent specimens yet to be auctioned. The night is still young." He turned to Cameron. "Very well. Five million, going once, going twice." He took a deep breath before bowing graciously at the waist. "Congratulations, Mr. Kidwell, may your deepest fantasy come true."

Cameron offered me his hand. "Briana."

"I—I..." Words didn't want to form.

"Take her away. We have another to take her place."

I placed my hand in Cameron's. His long fingers surrounded mine as he helped me to the floor. Before leaving the spotlight, he unbuttoned the jacket of his tuxedo and without a word, removed it and wrapped it around my shoulders.

The spicy scent of his cologne mixed with the fresh aroma of bodywash filled my senses as the jacket enveloped me. With Cameron's hand at the small of my back, we took a few steps. Before we reached the side stage, another woman passed by wearing a silk similar to the one I had been told to wear. Her eyes were red from tears, yet she continued to walk

to where I had been standing.

Had she been given the same choice, dignity or hog-tied?

The crowd began their cheers and calls.

I was forgotten by all but one patron—the man who arranged my sale.

Curtis stepped from behind the side curtain. Avoiding my gaze, he spoke only to his brother. "Look at this, my little brother is taking sloppy seconds."

Before I could speak, Cameron's fist connected with Curtis's chin.

"Oh," I gasped as my fingers came to my open lips.

Curtis staggered backward before standing straight and rubbing his chin. "Don't give her back broken."

Cameron's neck straightened—tendons and cords coming to life—with the obvious restraint he was enlisting to not hit Curtis again. "Goodbye, Curtis. Go back to Detroit. Briana's condition is no longer your concern. I'm not giving her back."

This time, Cameron reached for my hand and escorted me away.

The black velvet sky sprinkled with millions of stars came into view as the Alpine lift moved farther and farther away from the mansion. It wasn't until we were near the beach that I finally spoke. "I don't know if I should thank you or hate you."

Cameron's lips quirked upward. "There's a good chance that before the night is through, you'll do both."

Chapter Six

CAMERON

She walks around the hut with its fifty-thousand-dollar artwork and profusion of fresh tropical flowers. It's a beautiful place. She belongs in a beautiful place, one without the tawdry undercurrent of Malaking Kuta.

Her gaze studiously avoids the silk-covered bed on the platform.

Slender fingers brush the top of a carved belalu wood cabinet. "What did you mean when you said you wouldn't give me back?" Blue eyes seek mine, beseeching and brave. "Will you take me to Detroit?"

I shake my head without saying anything.

"What about after—" Her confidence falters. "After you use me?"

Another shake of my head. And for emphasis: "No."

"This was only supposed to be for one night."

I push away from the doorframe where I'd lingered, approaching her, feeling like a tiger stalking his prey. She fidgets with the fabric barely covering her luscious body. The strips of fabric only highlight her nakedness. "Is that what you agreed to do for Curtis? You must love him

very much to offer your body for his debts."

"No." A blush tints her cheeks. It spreads down her neck and across her breasts. "He lied to me. He said it was some kind of plan to drum up interest. That I wouldn't really have to sleep with anyone. Only right before did he tell me the truth."

Misery darkens her eyes. Hurt because he betrayed her? There's a lot I'm willing to do for this woman. Comfort her while she cries over another man isn't one of them. I run a hand along her shoulder and down her arm. I push aside the drape over her breast and expose her nipple. It hardens in the cool island air, and I pinch it gently between thumb and forefinger. "I should see what I've paid for, shouldn't I? I should see what you've been giving Curtis."

She shivers, and I pinch harder. I want her to know the danger she was in. The things those men and women would have done to her would have marked her—body and soul. I don't blame her for trusting the man she meant to marry, but part of me wants to punish her for it. After all, she's mine. I own her now. I get to punish her regardless of whether she's done anything wrong.

I tug on the silk, and it unravels in a whisper of assent, sliding down her body.

Then she's standing there naked, her breasts small and high, her waist narrow, her hips flaring, the perfect size for me to grasp and fuck hard. Between her legs she has a small patch of trimmed dark hair matching the curls on her head.

"Are you going to hurt me?" she whispers.

I stare into her luminous brown eyes. "That depends."

"Depends on what?"

Depends on how much it hurts her to fuck a man she doesn't love. To spread her legs while I kiss her and then to open her mouth while I press my cock inside. It depends on how she'll feel back in Tanglewood, my newest and most prized possession. I'm not letting her go. I'm also not fooling myself. She didn't love me in Detroit. It's unlikely that buying her will

change that.

I push two fingers into her mouth, feeling the slick of her teeth and the soft wet of her tongue. She's obedient as she sucks my fingers. Once they're nice and damp, I drag them down the median of her body, down to her pretty little cunt. Her legs are barely wide enough to fit my hand, but I force my way in. I made her lick my fingers so they'd be slick, but I shouldn't have worried. She's already soaked. I press between her legs hard, and she gasps, rising onto her toes. I'll always take care of her, but that doesn't mean I'll go easy on her either. It won't be easy for her to be my possession.

I use the curl of my fingers to drag her close, and her eyes roll back in pleasure. I catch her body with my other arm, lifting her to suck on her nipple. She's so goddamn receptive to everything I do, it's like she was made for me. "It depends on how much you fight me," I whisper against her cheek, finally answering her question. "I'll give you everything you want, anything you want. Travel, purses. I don't give a fuck what you buy or what you do when I'm at work, but when we're in the bedroom, you submit to me. Whatever I say goes."

My thumb brushes her clit for good measure.

She squirms against me, her naked skin against my dress shirt and slacks. She's completely naked while I'm still fully clothed. Well, she had better get used to that. It's how we'll spend much of our time together. Her lids are low but her eyes focused. "Cameron Kidwell. I've known you since you were twelve years old."

And I've loved her as long as that. "Yes."

"You aren't only talking about tonight, are you?"

"You've been engaged once before, Briana." I pump my fingers in and out of her, dragging her mercilessly to the edge. "You should recognize a marriage proposal when you hear one."

Epilogue

BRIANA

As I stared at the text message from my husband and light reflected from my beautiful three-carat diamond wedding ring, a smile crept upon my lips.

For nearly nine months, I'd been Mrs. Briana Kidwell.

Not Mrs. *Curtis* Kidwell.

No, Curtis was back in Michigan, awaiting trial for illegal activity connected to his appliance empire. While I never asked my husband if he had a hand in Curtis's fate, I suspected that he had. Cameron believed in justice. Curtis's financial and ethical downfall was his repercussion for tricking me. Auctioning me was supposed to save his businesses. Instead, it was the cause of their demise. All of his stores were currently tied up in litigation.

Thankfully, I wasn't married to him.

I was Mrs. *Cameron* Kidwell.

The twelve-year-old boy I'd once known did more than save me over a year ago on Malaking Kuta. He used, ravished, and broke me, only to

rebuild me. The result of his both painful and pleasure-filled devotion was evident by the twisting of my core as well as the ridiculous smile upon my face brought on by a one-word text message.

"PREPARE."

Doing what he did for Gabriel Miller sometimes took Cameron away from home. For three days and two nights I'd been on my own with only our house staff, to do as I pleased. That wasn't completely accurate. I could lunch or dine with friends, shop to my heart's content, read or watch TV. I could spend time working on any aspects of the boutique I was about to open in the town where we lived. It would be Tanglewood's exclusive supplier of Sinful Threads accessories and apparel. There was one exception.

My husband was lenient and generous with most things.

He'd set the rules the night he'd bought me.

There was one place where everything was different.

The memory of his deep voice sounded in my mind, scattering goose bumps over my skin as it had nearly a year ago. *"I'll give you everything you want, anything you want. Travel, purses. I don't give a fuck what you buy or what you do when I'm at work, but when we're in the bedroom, you submit to me. Whatever I say goes."*

My sexual pleasure was to come only from him. I wasn't allowed to spend our nights apart with the help of a vibrator or even my own touch. If I did, I'd be punished.

The idea of lying over his strong legs, his erection probing my tummy as he reddened my ass didn't deter me. No, Cameron knew I enjoyed that too much. My punishment would be denying me sexual pleasure. I'd be denied his cock and orgasms. No amount of begging, no matter how demeaning, would change his mind.

The text message I'd just received meant he would be home soon.

With the smile still secured to my lips, I released the house staff for

the night and hurried to our master suite.

Nearly forty minutes later I was prepared and anxiously awaiting his arrival.

My heartbeat kicked up a beat as the alarm system's beep informed me that the time had come. My husband was home.

Would he look for me elsewhere or know I'd obeyed?

I was completely nude, wearing only my wedding ring. The bath I'd taken covered my skin in lavender oils as I meticulously prepared, washing, shaving, and trimming, exactly as he liked. My long dark hair was piled high on my head in a messy bun. And with each passing second, my nipples grew tauter.

It could appear that I was the one making all the concessions.

That would be wrong.

I was simply doing as I'd agreed the night I'd been purchased.

Submit.

Lowering myself to my knees with my toes bent, I sat back on my heels. With my back straight, I placed my arms over my legs, palms up, bowed my head, and waited. Even the opening of the bedroom door added to the growing wetness of my empty core.

My husband didn't speak as he came closer. Only his Italian leather loafers and the cuffs of his designer suit pants came into view.

My breathing hitched as the pad of his finger traced my upper spine and the aroma of his spicy cologne took away the lavender scent. Step by step, he circled. As if they were lasers, I felt his eyes upon me, scanning every inch as I waited, fully exposed. There was no doubt he saw my arousal glistening on my upper thighs.

This predatory preamble was a game he enjoyed, and I did too. With each circle my anticipation built.

Finally, Cameron gently lifted my chin, bringing my gaze to his dark eyes. "You're beautiful."

Warmth filled my cheeks as I released a breath.

No one had ever adored me the way Cameron did. Somehow it wasn't

something I knew I had been missing. And now that I did, I couldn't imagine living without him or it.

"Have you behaved, Mrs. Kidwell?"

I couldn't lie, I wouldn't. That didn't mean I hadn't considered pleasuring myself, but I hadn't.

"Yes, sir. I've been waiting for you."

"That's my good girl." Cameron's smile brought warmth to my exposed skin as he offered me his hand. "It sounds like you deserve a reward. What is it that you want?"

"You, only you."

As I stood, I took him in. Even after an afternoon of traveling, the man before me was incredibly handsome. His toned and muscular body was covered by designer suit pants and a striped starched shirt. While his jacket and tie were gone, Cameron was still completely clothed as his embrace pulled me to him and brought his lips to mine.

My lips bruised as our tongues tangled. My breasts flattened as I pressed closer to his hard, broad chest. Step by step, he directed me, not toward our massive bed, but to the arm of a sofa near the window.

"Bend over, Bri."

Spinning from his arms, I did as he said, folding myself over the plush end of the sofa. With my ass in the air, he gently kicked my feet apart as the sounds of him undoing his belt and fly were barely heard over the thumping of my circulation.

One of his hands pressed upon the small of my back, trapping me.

I cried out as not one but two fingers from his other hand slipped inside my wet pussy.

"You're always so wet. I fucking love your tight cunt."

I didn't need to crane my neck to know that Cameron was still mostly dressed. He enjoyed the inequality as much as I did.

"Please," I managed to whisper as he teased my cunt with the tip of his cock.

My feet shuffled as I tried to back into him, but I couldn't. His hand on

my back was too strong.

His body heat covered my back as the fingers that were inside me gripped my hair, pulling my head back. His warm breath skirted my neck. "Tell me," he growled, "who do you belong to."

"You."

"Whose cock do you want?"

"Yours, Cameron. Only yours."

"Why?"

There were so many answers I could give him. I could tell him over and over that I loved him, that maybe in a way I always had. I have told him that and he'd told me the same. Seeing my wedding ring on my clenched fist as I waited for him to fill me, I could say that I wanted him because he was my husband and I his wife.

However, neither of those were the answer he wanted.

He liked reminding me of how we got where we were.

"Because you were the highest bidder..." My words changed to satisfied whimpers as my pussy contracted and Cameron filled me completely.

The End

Thanks for reading *Sold to the Highest Bidder* by Aleatha Romig and Skye Warren!

To learn more about Tanglewood, check out Skye Warren's *Endgame Trilogy*, starting with _The Pawn_. To learn more about the Sparrows of Chicago and the bratva of Detroit, check out Aleatha Romig's Sparrow Webs: *Web of Sin, Tangled Web, Web of Desire* and *Dangerous Web, beginning with _Secrets_*.

SIGN UP FOR SKYE WARREN'S NEWSLETTER:
http://www.skyewarren.com/newsletter
SIGN UP FOR ALEATHA ROMIG'S NEWSLETTER:
https://www.aleatharomig.com/contact

Stalker

A. JADE AND A. ZAVARELLI

Chapter One

ZANDER

Your car is red.

Your nails are red.

Your favorite kitchen appliance—the one you bought with the gift card your grandmother sent you last Christmas—is red.

The fancy bedsheets you ordered online last week are red.

Your favorite shade of lipstick—the one you stock up on every two months at Sephora—is red.

Yet, when anyone asks you what your favorite color is…you lie and say it's purple.

How do I know this?

Because I know everything about you.

I know that you go for a run at 8:05 am every morning.

I know that you prefer drinking tea over coffee.

But not just any tea—vanilla chai with two splendas and a splash of skim milk—because you're watching your figure.

One must keep up appearances after all.

I know you like to bury your nose in romance books while secretly trying to convince yourself that great loves like those don't truly exist and it's all just fiction.

But that's just another lie you tell yourself.

Because you've always been a hopeless romantic.

However, those hopes were dashed six weeks ago when you caught your husband-to-be fucking your maid of honor in the bathroom at your rehearsal dinner.

He never deserved you, Violet.

You're a rare, exotic flower in a field of weeds.

One that needs to be cherished and taken care of.

You deserve someone who truly values you…the *real* you.

You deserve a man who knows how you like to be kissed, the way you like to be touched.

You deserve a man who knows exactly what you need.

Fortunately, the time has come for you to meet that man.

Again.

Because I'm your new neighbor, Violet Meadows…

And I have every intention of getting what I want this time.

You.

Chapter Two

MONDAY

VIOLET

"Smile for the camera, Nutmeg."

My Bengal cat blinks at me and glances around her new abode with lingering suspicion in her eyes. She doesn't trust this place yet, and I can't say I blame her. All week, I've felt as if something was off. I haven't been able to decide if it's the recent cataclysmic events of my life or something else that has me glancing over my shoulder every few seconds.

When I bought this house, I thought I'd be unpacking all my things in a haze of newlywed bliss. Instead, I'm here alone, screening all my calls and sending my ex's texts straight to purgatory where I'll never have to think of him again.

Shaking off those thoughts, I tap out a quick caption and post the selfie with Nutmeg to my Instagram account. Within seconds, I have hundreds of likes pinging in my notifications. The comments start flooding in from an army of strangers admiring the perfection of my life. They compliment my wardrobe, my smile, my posed snapshots of the few seconds where I can

fake it just for them.

Cringing, I set the phone aside and rub Nutmeg's ears. "It's all going to be okay. You'll see. I think we're going to love it here."

She stands up and swishes her tail in disagreement before walking away. This is what my life has come to. Talking to my cat in an empty house on a Friday night. If only my followers really knew what a disaster everything has turned out to be. I have everything I thought I ever wanted, but I've never felt more empty.

My phone rings while I'm pouring myself a glass of wine and my sister's name flashes across the screen. I've been avoiding her calls a little too much, and I know she'll freak if I don't answer this one. While her intentions might be good, I just don't want to hash out my feelings about the recent dumpster fire that has become my life.

"Hey." I turn on the speakerphone and push open the screen door as I step onto the back patio.

"Hey yourself," Valerie says. "I was about to send out a search team."

"Sorry." I sit down in my comfy new wicker chair and take a sip of my wine. "I've been unpacking all day."

"You know I could have helped you. Just say the word and I'll be there."

"It's okay." I lean my head back and stare up at the stars. "I really wanted to do this on my own."

The line is quiet for a pause, but it doesn't take long for Val to get straight to the point.

"Are you holding up okay?"

"I'm fine," I insist, even though it's a lie.

"You're allowed to have a breakdown," she says. "You know that right? There's nothing wrong with taking some time. The world won't implode if their favorite model misses a few posts on social media."

"I don't need to have a breakdown." I roll my eyes. "I just need… well, to be honest, I don't know what the hell I need right now. But the last thing I want to do is talk about Scott or the wedding."

Val is quiet again, and that can't be a good thing.

A light flips on in the house next door, and I peek over the rim of my wine glass trying to catch a glimpse of my mysterious new neighbor. During the course of my move this week, I've met most of the neighbors except for the one on the left of me. Our houses are only about twenty feet apart, and I've seen a truck in the driveway often, but no sight of who's actually living next door. And yet, the hair on the back of my neck stands up every time I look at that place. I just can't figure out why.

"Were you even in love with him anymore?" Val asks.

"Huh?"

"Scott," she prods. "Did you really want to marry him?"

"Honestly?" I blow out a breath. "I don't know. I thought I did, but now that he's out of my life, I'm not even sad about it. I just feel humiliated and betrayed."

"You want to know what I think?" she murmurs.

"Not really."

"Don't be a bitch." She laughs. "You just hate it when I tell it like it is. Someone in your life needs to."

"Fine." I keep my gaze on the house next door. The TV comes on, the faint sounds of an action movie playing inside. "Tell me what you think."

"I think your entire life has been one big dog and pony show. You've always put so much pressure on yourself to live up to everyone else's expectations. The perfect cheerleader. The perfect body. The perfect clothes and footballer jock boyfriend, even if he was a total douchebag."

"Hey!" I gripe. "He wasn't always that bad."

"Yes, he was. Don't you remember in high school how he used to torment anyone who even looked twice at you? You were always just a possession to him. A trophy."

"Yeah, okay. Obviously, I've figured that out, and I've made some mistakes. But my life isn't so bad."

"Your life is glamorous as hell," Val remarks dryly. "At least, that's how it seems to everyone on the outside looking in. But are you even

happy? Have you ever been?"

Her question feels like salt in an already raw wound. And it's something I've thought about a lot since my life imploded six weeks ago. But I can't admit it just yet. Because without the illusion I've created, I don't know what's left.

"Just give it some thought," she says.

"Thanks." I finish off my wine and set it aside. "I'll do that."

"How are you liking the new place?"

"I like it." I shrug. "But it's strange living alone in a new town."

"Strange how?"

"I don't know." I lean back and close my eyes. "Something just feels a little off. I can't explain it. All week, I've had this weird feeling like someone's watching me. I'm probably just being paranoid."

"Do you think it's Scott?" She sounds alarmed.

"I don't know," I admit. "It could be, but I haven't seen him around since I threatened to mace his ass."

Val chuckles under her breath. "Well, if you ever feel unsafe just call me. I'm only twenty minutes away. We can have a pajama party at your new place."

"That sounds really nice." I smile through the phone. "Maybe once I get everything unpacked."

"It's a date," she says. "Now go get some sleep. You sound exhausted."

I tell her that I will and then disconnect the call, but instead of going inside, I stay out on the back patio until the chill of the plummeting temperature bites into my skin.

The lights in the house next door have since gone out, and the whole neighborhood is quiet and still. But when I glance up at the neighbor's window, my breath catches in my chest.

Either I'm really losing my mind, or I just caught him watching me from his bedroom.

Chapter Three

"Here, kitty, kitty."

It's not long before I have the Bengal cat in my arms, purring away.

I give her a treat for her cooperation and stroke her rusty colored fur. "Good girl."

A moment later, I shoot my gaze toward Violet's house where I catch her pacing the wooden floors, her panic rising by the second.

"Nutmeg," she calls out, opening the front door. "Baby, where are you?"

She looks around the porch, checking every nook and cranny. "Nutmeg?"

Fear mixed with desperation is practically coming off her in waves.

Time to make my move.

Pasting a look of concern on my face, I amble up her driveway with the cat in my arms.

Her back is turned to me when I approach.

"Is this your cat?"

She jumps, her hand flying to her heart as she turns around.

"Oh my God." Almost immediately, her gaze falls on Nutmeg. *"There you are."*

I hand over the little furball. "I found her on my porch." Shrugging, I jut my chin toward my house. "I live right next door. Poor thing must have gotten confused."

Her chest is still heaving, and I find myself grateful for the drop in temperature when I see her nipples peeking through the thin fabric of her t-shirt.

The former head cheerleader's body is still every bit as banging as it was back then.

"Right." She gives Nutmeg kisses and snuggles before focusing on me again. "Thank you for bringing her back."

"No problem."

With that, I turn, intending to head back home.

I'm not sure if I should be happy she doesn't recognize me or disappointed.

Then again, whereas she hasn't changed at all in the last six years, I've changed plenty.

Not only have I managed to pack on forty pounds of muscle, I got rid of my braces and acne.

I also ditched my glasses for contacts.

"This might sound weird, but you look really familiar," she calls out behind me. "Do we know each other?"

I bite back a smile.

"We do actually." Spinning around to face her, I utter, "We went to high school together."

Her eyes widen as she appraises me from head to toe. "Holy shit. *Zander Sinclair?*"

In the flesh.

"The one and only."

We stand there, smiling at one another like a couple of idiots for the better part of a minute before she finally speaks again.

"You look *so* different." Catching herself, she quickly adds, "In a good way."

Notice that, did you?

A smile pulls at my lips. "Thanks."

Laughing, she shakes her head. "I can't believe we're neighbors."

"Small world."

Chewing her bottom lip, she shifts Nutmeg in her arms. "It's good to see you."

The feeling's mutual.

However, I don't want to come off as some kind of creep, so I have to be smart.

If I push too hard, too fast I'll scare her off.

I have to play my cards just right.

"Have a good night."

Giving her a small wave, I excuse myself for the second time.

Then I start the silent countdown in my head.

Five.

Four.

Three.

Two.

One.

I'm on the last step of her porch when it happens.

"I was just about to pour myself a glass of wine. Do you want to join me?" She draws in a quick breath. "I mean it's totally okay if you—"

"I'd love a glass of wine."

Chapter Four

oly freaking crap.

Zander Sinclair got super hot. *When the hell did that happen?*

I can't seem to stop staring at him and I wonder if it's totally obvious. He seems to be at ease, sitting on the sofa as he waits for me to pour the wine. When I join him, there's a lingering note of that same scent I remember from high school. I used to wonder if it was cologne, but now I'm pretty sure it's just Zander. He smells so insanely good I want to lean into him and take a long, deep hit like a fiend.

I can't tell if there's an awkward tension lingering between us or it's just my racing heart. He's watching me watch him, and I can't seem to break the spell. His eyes are as intense as they've always been, and it would be so easy to get lost in those dark orbs all over again. We were friends once. Or at least I thought we were. He was magnetic, even when he didn't look like an MMA fighter sitting in my living room. I remember how he made me feel whenever he looked at me. Like I was the most beautiful

thing in the world, even on my worst days. But then one day, he took his dark, angsty eyes and his poetic smile and he walked right out of my life. He never spoke to me again, and I could never admit to anyone just how much that broke my heart. I still don't know why he quit me like a bad habit. I racked my brain for the next few years, trying to figure out what I did to piss him off. But sitting here now, it seems as if all that history between us has been wiped from his memory.

"So what have you been up to these last few years?" I choke out the words.

A smirk plays across his lips and he shrugs. "I'm a detective for the special victims unit. It keeps me busy."

"Oh, wow." I take a sip of my wine, praying I don't spill it on myself. "You got your dream job after all. I'm so happy for you."

"I've heard through the grapevine you've been pretty successful in your modeling career as well," he observes.

"You have?" I blink, wondering where he could have heard that.

It's not like we have any real mutual friends. Zander was always the broody loner in high school. He didn't hang out with anyone that he'd specifically call a friend. Except for me.

"It's pretty common knowledge," he answers with a slight bite to his tone. "You were the most popular girl in school if I remember correctly. You and Scott were the golden couple. What ever happened to him, anyway? You guys still together?"

I dip my head and lower my eyes so he can't witness the shame burning within them. "No, we broke up."

"Huh, I thought I heard a rumor you were marrying him."

"Yeah, that didn't work out."

"Why not?"

I meet Zander's gaze, and it's so intense I feel it into my soul. "He cheated on me with my bridesmaid."

"Ouch." Zander shakes his head, but he doesn't really seem all that surprised. Scott had a reputation for being an asshole, so I guess the only

person it really surprised was me.

"What about you?" I drain the rest of the wine from my glass and glance at his hand. "Are you married yet?"

"Nah." Zander grins and shakes his head. "I've been busy making a life for myself, as you can see."

"Right."

He finishes off his wine and abruptly dismisses himself to return the glass to the kitchen sink. "It's getting late. I should probably go."

I nod, but inside I'm thinking about how much I don't want that. He just walked back into my life, and there's still so much we have to talk about.

I stand up and he offers me a smile as he rejoins me in the living room. "It was good to see you again, Violet."

My eyes burn with emotions I can't quite make sense of as I close the distance between us and offer him a hug. When he wraps his strong arms around me, a shiver moves over me. Zander has always felt a little dangerous to me, but in the best way. He's terrifyingly beautiful, and his presence is a comfort I would indulge for eternity if he'd let me. But all too soon, it's over when he releases me and I glance up into his eyes.

"It was so good to see you," I croak.

He nods and turns to go, and I don't know what comes over me when I reach out and grab his arm. Maybe it's the wine, or maybe it's just that I can't accept this is it. He might walk out of my life and we'll never talk to each other again.

"Hey, Zander?"

"Yeah?" He quirks a brow at me.

I lean up on my toes and grab his face before I can talk myself out of it. My lips collide with his, soft and warm and so addictive. It lasts for all of about thirty seconds before I realize he's gone completely rigid, and he isn't kissing me back.

"Oh my god." I yank myself away, humiliation burning my flesh as I slap my hands over my face. "I'm so sorry. I don't know what the hell is

wrong with me."

Chapter Five

I've wanted to kiss Violet Meadows from the first moment I laid eyes on her.

And now that it's finally happened all I can feel is…

Confusion.

To say she's royally fucked up my plan would be putting it mildly.

Or has she?

I wanted her to want me…

No, more than want.

I want her to crave me so much she can't think straight.

But the only way to do that…is to give her a taste.

A taste that will leave her wanting more.

Pulling her hand away from her face, I finish what she started.

Our kiss is turmoil and passion.

Hate and lust melded into an all-consuming fireball.

Violet kisses me like she's starving for it and I can't help but wonder if it's because no one has ever touched her like this.

I should tell her all the dirty things I want to do to her body, all the ways I plan to worship that sweet pussy of hers, but I'd rather just show her.

Gripping the base of her neck, I utter one simple instruction, "Bend over."

Shock crosses over her face, and for a moment I think she's going to utter some bullshit about what a bad idea this is and blame the wine.

But while Violet is a liar...she's never been a stupid girl.

And she wants this. Hell, her body is practically begging for it.

Her breaths are shaky as she positions herself over the arm of the couch with her plump little ass in the air.

I don't waste any time tugging her sweatpants down her hips.

"You're not wearing any panties," I note, pressing my nose to where she's slick and warm.

Heat licks over my skin and my balls draw tight as I inhale her heady scent.

"You have such a pretty pussy."

Perfect actually. She's bare, wet, and those lips of hers are so plump I could kiss and suck them all night.

I bet she tastes every bit as good as she looks.

Spreading her open with my fingers, I decide to find out.

She jumps and a noise of surprise escapes her the second my tongue comes in contact with her slickness.

Pulling back, I stroke my knuckle along her swollen lips, teasing her. "So sensitive."

Hand clutching the couch cushion, she whimpers, "Please."

My voice is low and rough. "Please *what*?"

I need to hear her acknowledge what we're doing.

Turning her head over her shoulder, she looks at me down the length of her body. "Please don't stop, Zander."

I hum in satisfaction. "Good girl."

With that, I turn my attention back to her pussy. Feasting on her like a man starved.

And I am.

I've had visions of Violet spread out for me like this—at my mercy—since I was sixteen years old.

A groan tears out of her as I suckle her swollen clit.

Fuck. I groan too because she tastes so fucking good I can't stop myself.

And then there's nothing but her little whimpers and the wet suck and glide of my mouth pleasuring her.

Reaching down, she grasps the back of my head. "Oh, God." She shivers. "Oh my *fucking* God."

I pump my fingers deep inside her and speed up my suction on her clit.

There's a sharp intake of breath right before her body breaks out in a fit of jerks and shudders.

I grab her thighs, holding them steady as she writhes against my face and creams my tongue.

Breathless, she sags against the couch. "Jesus."

Smirking, I stand up.

And then...

I walk the fuck out.

Chapter Six

THURSDAY

ZANDER

Past…

"Question ten," I utter, reading off the piece of paper Mrs. Griffin handed us at the beginning of eighth period. "What do you want to be when you grow up?"

When we first got the assignment I thought it was a joke and a complete waste of time…

Until I got paired with Violet Meadows.

Suddenly the bullshit project requiring us to get to know a fellow classmate before graduation didn't seem so bad.

Hell, we've been so wrapped up in talking to each other, we both decided to stay after class to finish up.

Bringing her pen to her mouth, Violet thinks about this for a moment.

I can't help but notice she's done this for the last five questions.

It occurs to me that chewing on her pen is her *tell*—the thing she does when she's about to give a response she thinks the other person wants to

hear.

Not one she actually *feels*.

"I'm not sure," she says. "To tell you the truth, I haven't really thought about it."

"Violet." Placing the paper down, I cut my gaze to hers. "Don't bullshit me."

Her mouth parts in surprise. "I'm not."

After swiping my bookbag off the floor, I head for the door.

Before dying from breast cancer when I was fifteen, my mother used to call me the human lie detector.

She said I could smell a lie formulating in a person's brain before it was ever uttered.

She wasn't wrong.

"Baker," she whispers right before I walk out. "I've always wanted to be a baker."

To say I'm surprised would be an understatement. Not that being a baker isn't a good profession. It's just that Violet's the captain of the cheerleading squad and I've never seen those girls eat anything more than salad.

"What's your favorite thing to bake?"

"Birthday cakes." Shaking her head, she grins into her hand. "I know, I know. It's so cheesy. Scott is always making fun of me—"

"Scott's an asshole," I bark, returning to the table.

Her boyfriend has been the bane of my existence ever since I stepped foot into Summerville High.

I used to wonder what a beautiful, kind, sweet girl like Violet was doing with a douchebag like him, but it soon became clear when I realized he was the football team's quarterback.

Hell, it would be strange if they *weren't* an item.

Violet blinks, appearing all kinds of uncomfortable. "Sometimes he can be." She clears her throat, changing the subject. "So, Zander. What do *you* want to be when you grow up?"

That's an easy one.

"Detective." I hold her gaze. "For the special victims unit."

Her eyes widen. "That's...I never would have expected that."

Not surprising. Given I'm about 145lbs soaking wet and clumsy as hell, I certainly don't seem like the type.

However, there's something about Violet that makes me want to open up and be honest with her.

"Back when my mom was sick and going through her chemo treatments we used to watch a bunch of detective shows together to pass the time." I shrug. "She told me I'd make an awesome one because of my need to always want to protect those who aren't able to protect themselves."

Protect women from pieces of shit like my father who like to beat and rape them.

I'm not sure what to make of the look on her face. "I'm sorry about your mom, Zander." She reaches for my hand, and it feels like a live wire connecting our bodies. We both jolt at the touch, but neither of us put a stop to the contact. If anything, she squeezes harder. "If you really want to be a detective, I think you should go for it." A small smile unfurls. "I think you can do anything you set your mind to."

Jesus.

It's not so much her words, it's the genuine look in her eye when she says them.

She's the first person to look past my glasses, acne, and skinny frame...and see something more.

If anyone would have told me I'd be sitting in an empty classroom, having such a personal discussion with the head cheerleader and prom queen while she's looking at *me* like I strung up the moon...I'd say they were on drugs.

But this thing...what I feel happening between us right now.

It's real.

So fucking real.

And I don't ever want it to go away.

69

For reasons I can't fathom, the girl is like a balm to all my internal scars

As if she was put on this planet just for me and me alone.

"It's funny."

A crease forms between her brows. "What is?"

I cup her cheek with my free hand. "You're so much more than just a pretty face, Violet Mead—"

"What the fuck is going on here?" someone who sounds a lot like her boyfriend bellows from the door.

Violet quickly releases my hand. "Scott...hey."

"Don't *hey* me, Violet. What the fuck is this?"

"Nothing." She grabs her purse off the desk and stands. "We were working on an assignment."

He turns his angry eyes on me. "You better not be hitting on my girlfriend, you ugly dipshit." He curls a possessive arm around her waist, tugging her to him. "She's mine."

I want to point out that she didn't seem like *his* a few seconds ago, but Violet's a big girl and is perfectly capable of telling him that herself.

But she doesn't.

"Baby, relax." Angling her body towards him, she runs her hand along his jaw. "Come on, let's go grab something to eat."

Almost instantly, Scott's irritation dissipates.

But not before closing the distance between their bodies and kissing her.

Something strong and ugly rolls in my chest.

It's obvious whatever spark I thought we had between us never existed.

Chest coiling, I watch as he takes her hand—the same hand that was holding mine just a short moment ago—and leads her out the classroom.

They're almost out the door when she cocks her head, her gaze colliding with mine briefly...before she's gone for good.

I'm halfway to my house when I hear footsteps behind me.

I stop, and sure enough, so do the footsteps.

An ominous sensation pulls at my gut.

One that gets worse when I turn around and see Scott…with a bat in his hand.

Motherfucker.

The first swing to my ribs brings to my knees.

The second has me seeing stars and crying out in pain as I curl up into a ball on the pavement. "Wh—"

"You can thank Violet," Scott sneers.

Huh? That doesn't make any sense to me.

However, I can't speak because he attacks my legs this time.

A cracking, throbbing sensation pulsates through me. The pain is so intense—so excruciating—it robs me of breath.

"Violet?" I croak out, because I have to know what the fuck he meant.

Reaching down, he snatches a fistful of my hair.

"This is our thing." A sharp punch to my face sends a bolt of rage spiraling through me. Unfortunately, I'm in no position to unleash it on him. "She flirts with guys and then I catch them together and beat the shit out of them to show them who she belongs to." An evil, malicious smile spreads across his face. "Makes her all wet and horny."

My rage quickly turns to revulsion.

It doesn't sound like the Violet I know, but who's to say I really know her to begin with?

Maybe it was all a ruse.

Violet lies to others…who's to say she'd never lie to me?

I don't want to believe it, but it's the only thing that makes sense.

She's the gorgeous head cheerleader dating the star quarterback…and I'm just a nobody.

Scott positions the bat over his head once more. "Flirt with her again

and I'll kill you."

The metal cracking against my skull is the last thing I feel before everything goes dark.

Chapter Seven

THURSDAY

VIOLET

"Oh my god. Oh my god, oh my god, oh my god."

Did that really happen last night, or am I going crazy?

I slap my hands over my face to smother the stupid grin I woke up with this morning. I shouldn't be grinning. Not when Zander just abruptly walked out on me and I'm still trying to make sense of what happened. Does he regret it? Is that why he left? Or is there a more reasonable explanation… like he had to work early this morning?

Tossing the blankets aside, I indulge this insanity even further by padding across the floor to my window. It just so happens that my bedroom window faces his, and I have a direct view of his driveway from here. I know because I peeked out through the blinds last night. But when I try to do the same this morning, I suck in a sharp breath.

Zander isn't at work.

He's in his driveway, washing his truck, and he's completely shirtless. And I'm not imagining that he's packed on a shit load of muscle. I can see every hard line on his body from here. The sunlight glinting off his tatted

frame makes him look every bit the god he truly is. I'm still busy ogling him when he turns his head to the side and catches me. Or at least, I think he does.

I jump back with a screech and pace my floor. Did he see me through the blinds? Is that even possible?

Oh my God, I'm acting like I'm still a hormonal teenager. I need to get a grip. I need to be an adult and bite the bullet and just go over to his house and discuss this like a rational person. That's my intention when I spend the next hour showering and shaving my legs and flat-ironing my hair and agonizing over the perfect perfume.

As it turns out, it's all for nothing. Because when I finally do work up the courage to go talk to him, I stop short in my driveway. His truck is gone, and so is he.

I sigh and shake my head. This is ridiculous. I'm not this girl. I don't chase after guys. They've always chased after me. It's always been so easy because I never really had to think about it. Opportunities presented themself, like Scott, and I took them. But Zander is different. Zander is the secret crush I harbored all throughout high school, even while I dated Scott. I was too blinded by my reputation to see what was right in front of me. He's the one I should have been with all along.

It's a sobering thought, and it hits me like a slap across the face. So many of my choices have led me to the life I always thought I wanted. The glam and the staged moments of perfection. But I never knew what perfection was until I felt Zander's lips on mine last night. His hard body caging me in, protecting me, worshipping me.

I want that again, and I don't care if it means I have to make a fool of myself. As soon as I get a chance, I'm going to lay it all out for Zander. I'm not letting him get away this time.

"Violet?"

I blink out at the street, startled back to reality when I see Scott has pulled up to the curb. He parks his truck like an asshole and squints at me through the open window before jumping out.

"What are you doing here?" I demand. "I told you to leave me alone."

"Violet, come on… don't be like that."

"Be like what?" I glare as he takes a couple steps toward me as if he still has that right.

"A bitch," he spits out. "You've blocked my number. You won't answer my emails. I've been patient, but I'm done fucking waiting. You and I need to talk."

"We have nothing left to talk about." I point a trembling hand at his truck. "Now please leave before I call the cops."

"The cops?" He chuckles as if I'd never dare to do that.

"Yes." I stand my ground and fish my phone out of my pocket. But before I can get the keypad up, Scott is right in front of me, wrapping his fingers around my arm in a punishing grip.

"Put that phone back now," he sneers.

"Scott, what the hell are you doing?" I try to push him back, but it's like pushing against a tank.

He pinches my face between his fingers and tries to kiss me, and when I turn away, he yanks me by the hair toward the house. "No more fighting, Violet. You're going to get this shit out of your system once and for all. Now we're going inside, and you're going to play nice."

"Fuck you!" I thrust my hands into his chest, but it does nothing. His grip on my hair leaves me no choice but to follow as he drags me along into the house. "I'll scream!"

"Go ahead," he snickers. "I like it when you scream."

"Is there a fucking problem here?"

Both of our heads whip to the side, and the breath leaves my lungs on a gasp when I see Zander standing there. When did he get here? His truck isn't in the drive, and I have no idea where he came from. But regardless, I've never been so happy to see him in my entire life.

Scott releases me and glares at my savior. "This is a personal matter. It's none of your business."

"It's my business if you're trespassing and Violet doesn't want you

here."

"Who is this guy?" Scott pins me with his gaze. "Does he know you?"

Zander seems amused that Scott doesn't seem to recognize him from high school. But all I can think about is getting Scott out of my life once and for all.

"Yeah, I know him." I walk over to Zander and tuck myself against his side. "He's my boyfriend. And he's also a detective, who just happens to live next door. So you might want to think about that next time you try to pay me a visit."

Scott's face mottles with red while he studies us, and a shit eating grin splits across Zander's face. If I didn't know any better, I'd say he's taunting him as he wraps his arm around my waist and pulls me against him, gently tilting my chin up to kiss him.

"It's alright, baby. I've got you."

I sigh into him and somewhere in the space of those few stolen moments, Scott disappears. But before I can get too comfortable, Zander untangles himself from my body, his expression morphing into frustration.

"Um…thank you for doing that. I really appreciate it. I don't know what I would have done if you hadn't come along—"

"I have to get back to work," he says abruptly.

I don't get a chance to ask him if we can talk later because he's already walking away. *Again.*

Chapter Eight

FRIDAY

ZANDER

"Come on, Violet." He pounds on her front door. "Open up."

Scott's always been an idiot, and right now is no exception.

Violet's out walking Nutmeg—yes, I know, she actually takes her cat for walks. Although Nutmeg tends to give up about a minute into it, so Violet ends up scooping her off the ground and cradling her to her chest for the next two blocks.

Either way, she's not fucking home.

And more importantly—she has no interest in seeing *him*.

Something he damn well knows after we sent him packing the last time he showed up.

Hopping out of my truck, I stalk toward Violet's house.

Scott's still banging away on Violet's front door, so he doesn't see or hear me when I approach.

A simple gun to the head would put an end to this whole fucking thing, but given the son-of-a-bitch broke my leg and left me with a brain

bleed that put me in the hospital and made me miss my high school graduation, I think I'm entitled to have a little fun.

Since I just got home from work, I have everything I need at my disposal.

Removing my taser gun from my belt, I aim it at his back.

I'd be lying if I said the sight of him falling to the ground in a fit of jerks and thrashes didn't make me smile.

But it's only the tip of the iceberg for what I have planned.

In one fell swoop, I flip him over on his belly and handcuff him.

He tries to fight me, but I'm the stronger one this time around.

"What the fuck—ouch."

Snatching his hair, I pull him to his feet.

And then I launch my fist into his face, landing a sucker punch to his nose.

One that has him staggering back like a drunk giraffe before he falls.

Perfect.

Whistling, I lug his limp body toward my house.

Hopefully he enjoys our little sleepover as much as I do.

But something tells me he won't.

I toss a pitcher of ice water at his face. "Wake up, sunshine."

I currently have the asshole tied up to a chair in my basement.

And let me tell you, it's a sight for sore eyes.

Scott's head lolls to the side and he mumbles something incoherent, but I can't make out what it is because I secured a piece of duct tape over his mouth.

Since the ice water didn't rouse him enough to my liking, I try a different tactic.

I pick up my taser again, only this time, I aim it at his head.

He wakes with a jolt—a very literal one—and the pain that illuminates

his face is like nothing I've ever seen before.

Oh, but I've felt it.

I've felt it every time he pushed me into a locker or punched me in the face.

I felt it with every insult he tossed my way.

I felt it when he kissed her in front of me.

I felt it when he gripped her arm hard enough to bruise her delicate flesh.

And I definitely felt it when he cracked that bat over my skull and left me for dead on the side of the road silently begging God or whatever great being might exist in the world for one more chance to see *her* before I left the planet for good.

Stalking toward him, I grab the back of his head, forcing him to look at me.

"What's the matter, Scott? You don't recognize me?"

He blinks, confusion etching his face.

Leaning over, I hiss, "Want a clue?"

Reaching under his chair, I pull out a metal bat. It's almost identical to the one he used on me.

Only unlike him, I don't plan on using it.

No, what I have planned is much more sinister.

His eyes widen with recognition and a hint of fear.

Good.

However, it's not enough.

I want his tears, his remorse.

I want his motherfucking *soul* right before I send it straight to hell where it belongs.

But, first? It's time to have some fun.

"Do you know what this is?" I ask, picking up the instrument.

Not waiting for a response—given the fucker can't give me one—I hold it up and smile.

"It's a dermatome," I explain, my orbs becoming tiny slits. "It's used

for skin grafting."

The confusion in his eyes changes to terror and he starts rocking back and forth in his chair.

I can't help but laugh because the fucker can rock and roll all he wants it still won't make a damn bit of difference. I've secured him so tight he isn't going anywhere.

Snatching a pair of scissors next, I cut his pant leg off.

I figure we'll start small and work our way up.

Until his outsides match his insides…and he resembles the monster he truly is.

"This—" I utter as I turn the instrument on and angle it over his thigh. "Is for putting me in the hospital."

Sweat pours down his face and his body breaks out in shudders as his skin comes off, now resembling a slice of Swiss cheese.

He tries to scream, but it's nothing but a muffled, obscure sound in the dimly lit room.

Lifting his shirt, I decide to go for his stomach next.

I can't help but notice he's gone soft around the middle.

The douchebag has clearly let himself go since high school.

"Haven't been to the gym in a while, huh?"

And because I want him to hurt even more, I add, "Maybe that's why Violet spent the night riding my face." Positioning the dermatome over where his abs used to be, I narrow my gaze. "Or maybe it's because you're a piece of shit who likes to cheat on women and put your hands on them when they tell you to fuck off."

He spasms, making a whiney, desperate noise in the back of his throat as tears fill his eyes.

"You never deserved her." Ignoring my disgust, I undo the zipper on his jeans. "I figure it's only fair to warn you...this next one's gonna hurt, ass—"

The sound of my doorbell ringing cuts me off.

Chapter Nine

"Violet?" Zander blinks, seemingly startled to find me on his doorstep. "Uh, is everything alright?"

I think I should be asking him the same question. He looks oddly tense, and suddenly, I'm second guessing my plans to come here. But when I look up into his eyes, I can't help but feel like it will be the biggest mistake of my life if I walk out of here right now.

"Why did you stop talking to me?" I blurt. "Why did you get so mad? We were friends, and then you just… ghosted me."

My voice wavers a little, and I try to compose myself, but Zander can still see me breaking inside. His face softens as he studies me, and within a second, he's pulling me inside the house and wrapping me up in his arms.

"I'm sorry," he murmurs into my hair as he breathes me in. "At the time, I thought I was doing what was right. I was pissed at you because of what Scott told me the night he beat my skull in."

"What?" I lean back and stare up at him. "He… *he hurt you?*"

"He beat the ever loving fuck out of me," Zander answers darkly,

"And he told me it was a game you two liked to play. Is it true?"

"Oh my God." I squeeze my eyes shut and shake my head. "No, never. I would never do that to you, Zander. I was… I was in love with you. It wrecked me when you walked out of my life, and I know it was all my fault. I should have had the courage to ditch Scott a long time ago. I should have done a lot of things differently, but I never wanted him to hurt you. If I had known that, I would have dumped his ass immediately. Why didn't you tell me?"

Zander is quiet for a moment, watching me like he's trying to read me. He's always been good at that. He's the one person I could never lie to.

"It sounds like we both made a lot of stupid mistakes," he mutters.

"What do you mean?"

He sighs and releases me, turning away and dragging a hand through his hair. "I knew you were moving in here. That's why I bought this house. I wanted you to know what it was like. I wanted to make you fall for me so I could drop you cold once you did. I only came here because I wanted my revenge."

My heart kicks against my chest, and I'm not sure whether to run or cry. A solitary tear slides down my cheek and I wipe it away. The easiest thing would be to leave and nurse my wounds at home until I can pretend like none of this ever happened. But I'm so fucking tired of pretending. I want to fight for this. I refuse to believe that Zander doesn't feel anything for me. There's too much history between us for that to be true.

"Do you still want that revenge?" I ask.

He turns slowly, his eyes roaming over my body with a heat I can feel even from a few feet away.

"I just want you."

I'm not sure who moves first. All I know is within seconds, we're colliding into each other with a passion unlike anything I've ever experienced before. Our lips clash, and we're a tangled mess of hands and teeth and breaths as we undress each other. Zander discards my shirt and jeans, leaving them in the entryway before he scoops me up over his

shoulder and hauls me down the hallway to his bedroom.

When he spreads me out on his bed, I feel like I feast fit for a king the way he's looking at me.

"You are so fucking beautiful," he murmurs. "I just need to be inside of you, Violet. Tell me you want this."

"I won't let you stop now," I tell him. "Please, Zander. I need you."

He groans and kneels on the bed, making quick work of removing my bra and panties before he yanks down his briefs. His huge, throbbing cock springs free and I squeeze my thighs together in anticipation. I've wanted this for so long I feel like I'll die if he doesn't give it to me right now.

But Zander has his own plans. His palms skate up my thighs and spread them apart as he leans his massive frame over me. He rocks his body against mine and dips his head to my breast, sucking my nipple until I can't think straight.

I'm soaked for him. Desperate and wanting as he slowly tortures me with his tongue. When he's finished feasting on my breasts, he kisses his way down my belly and eats me out again. It isn't until I've come twice when he finally relents and comes up for air.

"Please, Zander," I beg him between ragged breaths.

A smirk plays across his face and he shrugs. "I've waited a long time for this, baby. I'm going to take my time. Hopefully you didn't have any other plans today because I'm spending the rest of it inside of you."

He positions his hips between mine and kisses me. His tongue slips into my mouth and he sighs in content as he starts to push himself inside of me.

I curl my fingers into his back and try to breathe. He's so big it's taking my body a minute to adjust to him, but I don't care. I just want him in me like this forever.

Once he's fully inside, he reaches down to touch my face. It's the most intimate moment I've ever shared with anyone. Staring into each other's eyes while our bodies are skin to skin. He's inside of me, raw, and I don't care. I want all of him. No barriers.

He slowly starts to move, and my head rolls back against the pillow as I take everything he has to give me. Moaning into his shoulder, I breathe in his scent and try to relax as another tidal wave builds up inside of me.

"Holy shit," I whimper.

"Let it happen, baby," he growls into my neck. "Say my name when you come. Say it loud."

I do exactly that. I scream out his name as I shatter around him again, and Zander pumps into me a few more times, grunting out his release and filling me with his come.

Vaguely, in the back of my mind, I think I hear someone grunting in protest. But when I look up at Zander, he's just grinning.

"Probably the neighbor." He shrugs. "Now, where were we?"

Chapter Ten

SUNDAY

ZANDER

I'm balls deep inside Violet for a second round when I hear it.

The sound of something—or rather, *someone* crashing into something downstairs.

"What was that?" a breathless Violet questions.

Shit.

"Stay here," I tell her as I get out of bed and slip into my boxers.

My heart pounds in my chest as I jet out of the bedroom and race down the staircase leading to the basement.

The pounding in my chest grows when I turn on the light.

Scott's still secured to his chair, but it's now tipped backwards.

However, it's the pool of blood surrounding his lifeless body that makes mine run cold.

Upon closer inspection I spot a large gash in the back of his head.

Fucker must have hit his head on the corner of my tool chest on his way down.

Not only did I want the honor of killing him myself, I have one hell of a mess to clean up now.

I can't help but smirk as I tilt my head to the computer monitor I set up earlier. The one that ensured Scott saw every second of me fucking Violet before meeting his demise.

However, my bliss is short lived when I realize.

Violet's no longer in my bedroom.

As if on cue, I hear footsteps scampering down the staircase.

It all happens so fast I don't have time to stop Violet from entering the basement.

"Were you recording us having sex—" The words die in her throat when she spots her lifeless ex. "Oh my God." Eyes wide with terror, she looks at me. "What the hell—"

"I can explain," I tell her.

But I can't. Because how the *fuck* does someone explain a dead body in their basement?

A dead body belonging to the man she was once going to marry.

The muscles in my chest spasm.

I don't regret what I did—not when it gave me a few fleeting moments with her—but I hate the look in her eye.

"I…uh. Yes. I did record us having sex," I start, deciding to tackle her original question first. "After what he did to you, I figured he deserved to watch you screw someone else."

"Okay." I can practically see the wheels turning in her head as she takes this all in. "But how did he end up *dead*, Zander?"

"I didn't do it." I shrug. "Not that I hadn't planned on it…the corner of my tool chest just happened to beat me to it."

Hell, the shit I'm in is so deep I might as well be honest.

I expect her to yell, run away, tell me I'm a murderer and then call the police and turn me in.

But to my surprise, she walks over and kisses me.

As much as I hate to pull away from her touch, I have to know what's

going through her mind. "What—"

"Do you believe in karma?"

"Karma?" I repeat, not understanding.

She blows out a shaky breath. "The way I see it he ruined both our lives. Not only did he cheat on me, steal money from me afterward, and almost kill you when we were teenagers...his lies tore us apart." Anger fills her gaze. "It's only fair the universe sorted things out and got rid of him." She looks around the basement. "Do you have a shovel?"

I never thought it was possible to love someone so much.

But fuck, I *do*.

I love my sweet, kind girl whose soul is as twisted and warped as mine.

And I'm never going to stop.

Epilogue

SUNDAY

ONE YEAR LATER...

Y ou still chew your pen when you're lying.

You still go for a jog every morning and walk your cat every night.

Your favorite kitchen appliance is still the red mixer you bought with the gift card your grandmother sent you for Christmas.

Lately, you have an affinity for making children's birthday cakes.

Your favorite of them being superheroes and alligators.

When the sun sets, you still bury your nose in romance books—only now you know great loves like those do exist.

But your favorite pastime?

Spending your nights getting fucked and worshipped by a man who knows exactly how you like to be kissed…the way you like to be touched.

How do I know all this?

Because I know everything about you, Violet Sinclair.

And I have every intention of keeping what's mine.

You.

The End

About the A. Jade
Want to be notified about my upcoming releases?<u>https://goo.gl/n5Azwv</u>

Ashley Jade craves tackling different genres and tropes within romance. Her first loves are New Adult Romance and Romantic Suspense, but she also writes everything in between including: contemporary romance, erotica, and dark romance.

Her characters are flawed and complex, and chances are you will hate them before you fall head over heels in love with them.

She's a die-hard lover of oxford commas, em dashes, music, coffee, and anything thought provoking...except for math.

Books make her heart beat faster and writing makes her soul come alive.

She's always read books growing up and scribbled stories in her journal, and after having a strange dream one night; she decided to just go for it and publish her first series.

It was the best decision she ever made.

If she's not paying off student loan debt, working, or writing a novel—you can usually find her listening to music, hanging out with her readers online, and pondering the meaning of life.

Check out her social media pages for future novels.

She recently became hip and joined Twitter, so you can find her there, too.

She loves connecting with her readers—they make her world go round'.

~Happy Reading~

Feel free to email her with any questions / comments: <u>ashleyjadeauthor@gmail.com</u>

For more news about what I'm working on next: Follow me on my Facebook page!

BOOKS BY ASHLEY JADE

Royal Hearts Academy (Books 1-4)
Cruel Prince (Jace's Book)
Ruthless Knight (Cole's Book)
Wicked Princess (Bianca's Book)
Broken Kingdom

The Devil's Playground Duet (Books 1 & 2)

Complicated Parts - Series (Books 1 & 2 Out Now)

Complicated Hearts - Duet (Books 1 & 2)

Blame It on the Shame - Trilogy (Parts 1-3)

Blame It on the Pain - Standalone
* * *
Thanks for Reading!
Please follow me online for more.
<3 Ashley Jade

Poisoned Hearts

PARKER S. HUNTINGTON AND GIANA DARLING

From *USA Today* and *Wall Street Journal* bestsellers Giana Darling and Parker S. Huntington comes a steamy, dark mafia romance with a virginity pack and an arranged marriage.

"Come play with the Devil..."

They say the Devil comes as everything you've ever dreamed of.
Mine has a cocky smirk and blackmail that may get me killed.

Enter Francesco Amato.
Made man. Sicilian playboy. Completely devoid of morals.

I'm engaged to Frankie's arch nemesis.
And he'll stop at nothing to ruin my marriage.

Even if it means taking my virginity.

Playlist

"Blue Blood" - Laurel
"July" - Noah Cyrus
"War of Hearts" - Ruelle
"If You're Gonna Lie" - Fletcher
"I Don't Wanna Be in Love" - Dark Waves
"Dead" - Madison Beer
"Bad Intentions" - Migos, OG Parker, Niykee Heaton
"Rome" - Dermot Kennedy
"Die For You" - The Weeknd
"Bad Habit" - Zach Sorgen

To the dark and deviant...
This hate story is for you.

Epigraph

"Because what's worse than knowing you want something, besides knowing you can never have it?" - James Patterson

Prologue

LILY

Dr. Mancini had a tendency to gawk at my vagina like it was one of those macaroon-stuffed cookies from the bakery next to my house.

I shifted as much as I could, given the stirrups situation and the fact that, every time I moved, one of my barely-existent boobs popped out of the flimsy disposable gown. His eyes shifted with me, the tip of his tongue peeking out the corner of his lips. He toyed with his surgical tray of tools, eyes never leaving the center of my legs for more than a few seconds.

If my older sister were here, she would tell me to fuck with his head.

From the other side of the curtain, Papà stopped his phone call long enough to shout out, "Well?"

Dr. Mancini adjusted the height of his seat. "We've just started, sir."

"Hurry. I have a meeting across Sicily."

Hurry.

Easy for Papà to say when it wasn't him getting fingered by someone twenty years older.

I'd been twelve when I'd had my first *check.* One of Papà's night

guards had caught my sister Carlotta, sneaking into the main house from the servants' quarters. The only boy living there that was remotely her age was the gardener's son. Papà had an enforcer execute him while his parents watched.

Meanwhile, Papà accompanied me and Carlotta to an emergency appointment with Dr. Mancini, who stuck his fingers inside us and confirmed our hymens were, indeed, intact.

That night, Carlotta slipped into my room and confessed that she'd given head to the boy's dad.

"He fingered me and called me tight," she whispered between fits of giggles.

On the other end of our estate, they were probably mopping his son's blood from the servants' quarters floors as we spoke.

I pulled the sheets over us. "Did you tell him he was tight, too?"

"Tight as in *narrow*, not tight as in *cool*." She snorted out her laughter and squeezed me to her side. "You're too innocent for your own good, Liliana."

And that's how the world saw me.

Liliana Vitali: innocent, naïve, and official property of the Vitali family.

As soon as Dad resumed his phone call, Dr. Mancini fixed the stirrups to part my legs wider.

Every year, Papà escorted me to the OBGYN.

Every year, Dr. Mancini concluded my annual exam by checking for my virginity.

And every year, he confirmed what we all already knew—I got less action than the fucking Pope.

This was normal when your dad was Paolo Vitali, brother to *il condottieri* of the Vitali family. One day, my marriage will be arranged to some hot shot mafioso, and I'll be forced to lose my virginity during a deflowering ceremony in front of mafia bosses from all of Italy's crime families.

Until then, I had to deal with Dr. Mancini's prying fingers.

He distributed lube across his fingers and spread my lips open, breathing loud enough to pass for Darth Vader.

Stop being so nice, Lil. Fuck with him.

I could practically hear Carlotta goading me on.

But I wasn't nice, and she didn't know me.

Not really.

No one did.

I adjusted a little, so Dr. Mancini's fingertips brushed against my clit. Just to see how uncomfortable he'd get.

He froze for a split second, swallowed, and grabbed the speculum. "This will be cold."

I nodded, like the good girl everyone expected me to be. "Okay."

When he slid the metal inside me, I bit my lip on a barely restrained laugh, made sure Papà couldn't hear above his own voice, and let out a little fake moan. Dr. Mancini's eyes shot to my face before darting to the curtain and back.

I blinked back at him. "Did you say something, doctor?"

He cleared his throat and expanded the speculum. "No." His fingers began their probe. "Your vaginal ring is placed properly. Do you still check its placement and swap it regularly?"

"I forgot how," I lied. "Can you show me?"

"You squeeze the ring between two fingers and slide your fingers inside yourself until you reach the back."

"Is that where your fingers are right now?"

"Yes."

I bit my lip and shifted a bit on the exam bed. "But your fingers are so deep inside me, and I'm so tight."

He froze. "Excuse me?"

"I said—"

Dr. Mancini snatched his fingers back, scratched at his jaw, and pulled back when the lubricated surface met his skin. "Well, you have to

swap your vaginal ring regularly, or we can switch you to another more manageable birth control method."

Papà's footsteps drew closer to the curtain divider. "Jacopo."

Mancini eyed the curtain. "Yes, sir?"

"Take out her birth control."

"Papà!" I clenched my fists and forced myself to be-fucking-have. "I told you, it's for my period. It's not for sex. I'm a virgin. Tell him, Doctor Mancini."

Mancini returned to his seat and prodded inside me for my hymen. I didn't bother messing with him, because this was serious. I had this argument with Papà once a year, and it was probably the only thing I ever won.

"Yes." Mancini pulled out of me, snapped his gloves off, and tossed them into the trash can. "Her hymen is intact."

I moved the curtain just enough to expose my face. "See, Papà?"

His face spoke of a youth he'd never possessed. I swore, Nonna had given birth to Benjamin Button.

"Lily."

My name was Liliana, but Papà called me Lily whenever he wanted to patronize me. I hated the nickname. It reminded me of every moment I was forced to comply. To be weak. "Family above all, including happiness," should have been the Vitali motto.

"Yes, Papà?"

"I just got off the phone with Samuel," he began.

Samuel Bruno was the head of the Bruno family. Maybe I should have paid attention to his call instead of messing with Dr. Mancini.

I tuned Papà out, dread unfurling in the pit of my stomach. I didn't need to hear what he said. I'd seen that face once before. Four years ago, when Carlotta's wedding had been arranged.

That Summer, she hadn't passed her deflowering ceremony.

By the time Fall came, we'd buried her in an unmarked grave in the darkest corner of the Vitali crypt.

A fate I would rather bear than marry whomever Papà's brother had selected.

FRANKIE

"We have a problem."

Don Amato's words weren't especially portentous because of what they meant.

We were *le mafie*, a criminal family deep in the heart of Sicily. We ate problems for breakfast and made trouble for lunch.

So, none of the made men sitting around the glossy mahogany table in the back of Mama Sofia's restaurant in the marina even batted an eye at the head of the family.

But he was looking right at me, black eyes fathomless and narrowed as if *I* was directly correlated with said issue.

Quickly, I thought over my actions the last few weeks and came up blank. Sure, I'd slept with Carlo Moretti's wife, and Marco Umberto's sister and girlfriend…at the same time. But I was discreet, and those women risked more than I did by fucking me.

My deceased father's great uncle continued, his eyes still pinned on me, "The Bruno family plans to marry into the Vitali outfit." The very same family that had murdered and terrorized mine for decades. Just five years ago, they took my brother from me. "By marrying a Vitali, they would ensure a position of power over us. I do not intend to allow this."

Pain burst behind my eyes at the thought of my brother, who should have been sitting beside me at the table. Instead, he was buried in the family crypt, alive in memory only for as long as the people who knew him remembered to speak his name.

On the heels of hurt, came the fury.

"*Cazzo*." I rubbed at my jaw and leaned forward. "Who are they trying

to pawn off?"

"Tommaso Bruno to Liliana Vitali."

I cursed under my breath.

Tom was my age, relatively good looking, and an arrogant *stronzo*. We grew up in Gerosa together, two sons of opposing mafia families playing together in the piazza, our knees deep in the dirt of the cliffs along the coastline, shooting finger guns and sling shots.

It was only when we hit puberty that we understood we were enemies, and the finger guns were exchanged for real guns.

We'd matched each other move for move as we climbed the ranks of our respective organizations. There was no way in hell I'd let Tom marry into the Vitali family and become the golden boy of his family.

No way in hell.

My mind whirred, chasing a fast-forming plan. "Is there a virginity pact?"

Don Amato steepled his fingers and stared at me over the peak. "Don't be slow, Frankie. Of course, there is. The Vitalis are as old fashioned as they come."

"Just fact checking," I countered, ignoring the condescending looks from the other, older men at the table. They assumed the only thing I was good for was seducing the women of Sicily. "What would happen if we made sure the girl didn't arrive at her wedding a virgin? What if someone got there before Tommaso?"

"The girl would be killed, and the unification of the Bruno and Vitali families would be dead in the water." Don Amato cocked his head to the side, peering down his nose at the rest of us. "They'd assume the Bruno family had either deliberately fucked up or that they couldn't even control their own family."

I grinned, the expression slicing across my face almost painfully. "Win-win for the Amato family."

"Assuming we can actually get to the girl. Paolo Vitali locks her in his fortress and barely lets her out of his sight after what happened to the

sister," Uncle Gaetano remarked.

I made a mental note to look into Carlotta Vitali. I hadn't seen her in years, but we never ran in the same circles and I'd never bothered with petty gossip.

"Maybe you can finally put your dick to good use," Angelo sneered, always up for an opportunity to take jabs at me and never succeeding.

He was the same age as me, but that was where the similarities ended. He was stupid and bitter for it, greedy and gluttonous, but without the wherewithal to attain what he desired.

He'd hated me since we were children.

I didn't hate him at all.

Hating him would have implied he was worthy of my notice.

I rolled a pen between my fingers and let a smile tug one corner of my mouth. "Oh, my dick is good for plenty. If you worried about your own sex life as much as you worried about mine, little Angelo, maybe you'd get better results, hmm?"

His fleshy face screwed up, the blood rushing to the surface of his skin as if he were about to pop. "Where the fuck is your respect, Francesco?"

He thought calling me Francesco like the rest of the elders got beneath my skin. It didn't. I went by Frankie, because Francesco was a mouthful for women to scream when I was balls deep inside them.

"You'll get my respect when you earn it." I didn't bother hiding my amusement. "Just like everyone else."

"And what have you done to garner our respect?" Don Amato's words cut through the air with the force of a whip landing across my back. I flinched at the cold anger in that tone. "The Amato family's reckless Casanova and homewrecker. You flagrantly ignore the rules of this family and its men of honor, Francesco. Maybe it's about time you proved yourself worthy of the Amato name."

They obviously didn't understand the irony of their chastisement.

They accused me of being good for nothing but getting my dick wet, yet they were now asking me to prove myself by doing exactly that.

I didn't point that out to them.

They were family, sure, but *le mafie* wasn't about family.

It was about an inbred army. Though these were my uncles, cousins, and brothers, they only saw me as an underperforming soldier.

I'd take this as an opportunity to prove that I was so much more than that.

Than *them*.

The hot swell of anger in my chest cooled and hardened like lava after the flood. I tossed my pen at Angelo, stood, and addressed the room, "Consider Liliana Vitali mine."

And she would be.

At least, her virginity would.

Chapter One

FRANCESCO

S talking Liliana Vitali was dull as fuck.

Usually, I got a thrill from following someone. That animal delight that comes from stalking your prey.

Not so this time.

Liliana was pure as freshly driven snow. As fucking boring, too. She bought produce at the market with her mother once a week, visited her equally vanilla, vapid teenage girlfriends, and spent long hours in her room reading on her bed.

At least she was beautiful, though not in a way I was used to. She was fresh-faced, freckles the only adornment to her glowing, golden tan. She had no curves to speak of, just long, delicate bones that made her seem deliciously breakable.

All that purity excited the darkest recesses of my brain. It conjured images of my big hand around the long column of her fragile throat. Of bruises pressed and punctured into that flawless skin, purple and red around her neck and wrists like exquisite jewelry.

I wanted to bend that little body and sink into her until I broke her mind.

My dick kicked in my jeans.

Directly across from Paolo Vitali's house, I sat on a folding chair on Maria Louisa's roof and watched his daughter through the open doors of her bedroom balcony.

I'd just bedded the plump and deliciously curved Maria Louisa. She hadn't uttered a word of protest when I told her I was going to the roof with a glass of grappa and an after-sex cigar.

Liliana's long spill of black hair caught the dim yellow light of her bedside table lamp. She stood up to accept someone into her room. I watched her smile and take a package from the woman at her door.

The thin thread of her giggles reached my ears like the distant peal of church bells. I wondered what noises she would make when I impaled her on my cock for the first time. She seemed like the breathy moans type.

Liliana bent over her bed to open the large, flat box. Her curtain of hair shielded her expression from my view, so when she removed a white lace corset from the tissue paper, I was not prepared for it.

God, the thought of that little, pristine body in white lace was enough to make any man's dick hard.

She bit her lip and turned to face the mirror in the corner of her room, offering me an unencumbered view of her body as she held the corset up to her chest and posed. A finger touching her pink lips. A hand to the subtle curve of her hip, pert ass jutted out.

Try it on for me. Show me what's under that loose, ugly dress.

As if alerted by my thoughts, her gaze darted out the doors, stopping just shy of my place on the roof. I was in relatively full view of her door. If she looked a bit further, she'd see me.

I didn't bother to make myself hidden. It was a far enough distance that she would have had a hard time discerning my features enough to make me as an Amato. A small part of me wanted my prey to sense her hunter.

She bit her lip again. Then, slowly, hesitating like a virgin on her

wedding night, Liliana Vitali undressed.

A moan caught in my throat at the sight of her little fingers plucking at the buttons on her dress. The material fell to her hips, caught on the flare. Her nipples furled like tightly closed rosebuds, the color of crushed raspberries. I wondered, when I eventually took them between my teeth, if they would taste just as sweet.

She shivered, studying herself in the mirror. A hand slid up her flat stomach over the minute curve of her breast and feathered over the tip. Her mouth fell open on an inaudible gasp as if she was surprised by the sensation of touching her own breast.

Fuck me, she was innocent.

I'd never gone for that before. My women were lush, sensual, and experienced enough to bring me pleasure without coaching.

But suddenly, the idea of teaching the waif unwittingly putting on a show for me was entirely too enticing.

I thought of the way she would look on her knees, big eyes peering up at me as I guided her small hand over my cock, watching her warm to the idea of exploring my flesh until she finally took me past those sweet, pink lips.

My mouth went dry. I pulled my mind away from the fantasy and focused again on Liliana, unwilling to miss a moment of her little strip tease.

She shimmied her hips slightly. The fabric pooled around her waist slipped on the left, then fell away to the ground.

We both seemed awestruck by the sight of her in plain, cotton black underwear. She twisted and turned before the mirror, taking in her almost naked form.

She was more stunning than I'd expected her to be.

Something bestial broke free from its chains in my chest and roared.

I wanted to pin her down and fuck her, teeth to her neck, hands manacled over her wrists so she was helpless against the force of my cruel thrusts.

My cock throbbed against my thigh beneath my jeans. I palmed it through the fabric. Liliana bent over the bed and looked over her shoulder to watch her ass wriggle in the reflection of the mirror.

To think I'd called her boring.

Fuck, she was a temptress just coming into her power.

She reached back to edge the elastic of her panties down the plump swell of her ass until it was totally exposed, the fabric caught around her upper thighs. When she wet a finger and gingerly ran it down the crack of her ass to the crease of her sex, I almost lost it.

A damp spot bloomed on the groin of my jeans from my leaking dick, but I didn't touch myself.

I didn't want even an ounce of my attention off the nineteen-year-old girl I was determined to take for my own.

In that moment, I couldn't remember *why* I was supposed to seduce her, only that it felt tantamount that I slacked my thirst for her between those slim thighs.

She began to visibly pant as she played with her pussy, shivering and arching her back each time she discovered the places that pleased her.

I groaned when she stopped and stood to retrieve the corset. She struggled to put it on, unfamiliar with the little clasps and the garter belt. Somehow, her naiveté made the whole thing more delicious.

When she lay back on the bed to admire herself in the white lingerie, it occurred to me that it was probably her bridal trousseau.

Wicked satisfaction sluiced through me. I loved that I was sullying the virginal set by watching her try it on first, by thinking lusty thoughts too dark for such an innocent girl's head.

What would she do if she knew a grown man was palming his hard cock while watching her? How would she blush and gasp and writhe in embarrassment?

Liliana moved her hands with increasing confidence over her lace-clad body, so I was prepared when she slid her fingers under the edge of her panties and started to touch herself again. Her head fell back between her

shoulder, thick black hair streaming behind her, mouth open to the ceiling.

I wanted to grip that hair, slot my angry red dick between those open lips. My jeans were unbuttoned and unzipped in a flash. Then, my hand was fisted over my flesh, tugging hard.

I wanted to come with her.

Needed to.

Her slim hips began to gyrate as she pleasured herself, her chest heaving and thighs shaking.

When she came, she cried out weakly, like a plea for more even as she hit her climax. Soon, it'd be my name on her lips.

I spilled across my hand, cursing as I came so hard the base of my spine tingled almost painfully.

We both sat panting as we recovered. I cleaned myself up with an old handkerchief embroidered with an 'A' for Amato and tucked myself away. Just as I brought my abandoned glass of grappa to my lips, Liliana stirred on the bed and stood.

I paused, glass suspended, waiting to see what else she had in store for me. She moved to her balcony and lifted her hands to close the doors on her bedroom. Only, before she stepped behind the veiled glass doors, I caught sight of the grin on her mouth, slyly curved and feminine with secrecy.

I slingshotted upright, leaning forward with narrowed eyes as pure Liliana Vitali lifted her gaze to mine across the street separating us and broke into a full-blown smile before she disappeared behind closed doors.

Maybe Liliana wouldn't prove to be so dull or easy after all.

My spent dick twitched at the thought.

Game on.

Chapter Two

LILY

Tommaso Bruno had mushroom hair that reminded me of a misshapen penis head. Excluding porn, it was the closest thing to a real dick I'd seen in my life, wet bangs curtaining the perimeter of his head on all sides.

He'd probably shown up to *La Cucina Della Nonna* with a head full of gel, but I'd arrived late. On purpose. Much to the displeasure of Tommaso, who had stood outside in the rain, drenched and flanked by two hulking Bruno enforcers.

"Liliana." He leaned forward to kiss me, frown deepening when he caught my cheek. "You're late."

Up until this second, I'd held out hope that meeting Tommaso Bruno would spark something within me. Butterflies, maybe? Even a single butterfly would do.

But nope.

Nothing.

The tall build, clear blue eyes, and classically handsome face did

absolutely nothing for me.

"My apologies." I didn't bother with an explanation, only flattening my palms over my dress, which was long enough to make a nun proud.

Beneath it, I wore one of the wedding lingerie sets I'd tried on the other night. When I'd sensed someone spying on me. It happened often enough that toying with the made men sent to gather intel on my family had become a sport.

My lips curved in a smile, which I covered by nodding my head at Thing One and Thing Two. "Will they be dining with us? Papà only made reservations for two."

Tommaso ran a hand through his hair, pushing it back until it no longer curtained his face. "*Lasciami.*"

His enforcers left at his order. We entered the restaurant together. I offered a polite smile to the hostess. She was pretty, so it surprised me when she didn't catch Tommaso's eye.

He had a reputation for sleeping his way through Sicily. I was hoping he'd continue that hobby, so he wouldn't expect anything from me. I'd never been one to attract luck.

"It's perfect weather for yachting, no?"

It's raining, idiota.

"Sure." I slid into the booth, not giving him the space to sit beside me.

He took the seat across, picked up our menus, and handed them to the waitress after she placed a basket of garlic bread on the table. "We're ready to order. Arancini, pasta alla Norma, and cannoli for dessert."

"I'll take a crocchè," I added before the waitress left. I'd take any inch of independence I could get, including meal choice, thank you very much.

Fifteen more minutes of mundane conversation, and I almost kissed the waitress for bringing out the food. This wasn't the type of high-end place I'd expected Tommaso to bring us to, but I couldn't complain. Hole-in-the-wall diners were my favorite. Almost enough to compensate for the bland company.

"As I was saying…" Tommaso fixed his full attention on me after

polishing off the last of his cannoli. "We could go next week?"

"Go where?"

"Yachting."

"I get seasick," I lied. "Are you eating your garlic bread?"

He pushed the plate to me. "You can have it. I need to use the restroom."

"Take your time," I muttered around a breadstick. Hopefully, it had enough garlic on it to fend off a kiss from Tommaso tonight.

"Garlic breath on your first date. What's next?"

I startled at the deep voice behind me. Judging by the arrogance in it, he had no clue I was a Vitali, so I didn't bother muting my personality like I normally did around *le mafie*.

"Yachting, apparently."

"It's the perfect weather for it."

His impression of Tommaso was so spot on, I had to double check that Tommaso had disappeared into the restroom.

"How do you know this is a first date?"

"Would you really go on a second date with that douche?"

Not if I had a choice, but he didn't know that. I bit down on my lip. The bitter taste of blood coated my tongue. I released it, unsure how to respond.

"Fuck," he continued, "you would."

"It's not that bad of a date."

Another lie.

The best part of the night, other than his mushroom hair, was Tommaso leaving for the restroom. How much more mundane conversation could I take? Another minute? A decade? A lifetime?

I needed to find a way out of this engagement that didn't end in my death.

"You hate this place," the stranger said with such certainty, I envied him for it.

Why did he get to be certain while I sat in tortuous limbo, desperate

for a way to escape my fate?

"You don't know me." I bit into the garlic bread. "And I don't hate this place."

I hated a person in it. There was a difference.

"You've been sighing every five minutes," he pointed out.

"No, I haven't."

"In your head."

I didn't answer him, mostly because I couldn't. Who said shit like that?

He didn't relent. "Is the princess used to finer dining?"

"Are you always such a dick?" I moved to see his face, but he stopped me with a *tut*. Like I was a fucking dog.

"I wouldn't do that. Your date is at the register. Wouldn't want him to realize you're more interested in me, would you?"

I swallowed the bread, folded my lower lip into my mouth, and fought the urge to turn and face the stranger. He had one of those deep voices and commanding presences of the heroes I read about in books.

Fuck me.

Seriously, would he fuck me and ruin this engagement? Please?

Kidding. I didn't have a death wish. If I wanted out of the engagement, which I did, it'd be with a well-executed plan.

"Are you always such a dick?" I finally asked.

"Only when I'm breathing."

"What's your name?"

"What's yours?"

"Liliana."

"Lily. Of course it is."

I instinctively jolted at the name, but for some reason, it didn't piss me off as much as when my dad called me Lily. Probably because the stranger had a hot voice.

"Liliana," I corrected. "Not Lily. And what's that supposed to mean?"

"You seem like the type… Lily."

I opened my mouth to respond, but Tommaso returned to the table, hovering at the edge.

"I paid." He rested a palm on the back of the faux leather booth. "Are you ready to go?" His eyes dipped to my lips. "We can stay and talk more."

I slid out of the booth. "I'm ready to go."

"I can walk you home."

"No, thank you." What was with the men in my life assuming I couldn't care for myself? I swung my purse over my shoulder. "I live close enough."

"Are you sure?"

"I can take care of myself."

"For now…"

I bit my tongue, trying not to wince as my teeth reopened the cut I'd made earlier. Tommaso leaned forward for a kiss, which I dodged by giving him my cheek again. The second he left, I turned to face the booth behind mine, looking for the arrogant stranger.

Empty.

The streets of Gerosa resembled a *giallo* flick.

Dark cobblestone roads, dim streetlights, and narrow sidewalks.

When I breathed too loud, it echoed down the alleyways, which was how I heard the soft footsteps behind me as I made my way home by foot. It'd grown dark early, with streets in this wealthier part of town barren of people and cars, which was why Papà had chosen this area to call his home.

I dodged into an alley, reached into my bag, grabbed the tiny Sig Sauer P365 at the bottom, and twisted the custom silencer on it. Whoever it was probably wasn't following me, but if he was, he'd dip into the alley, and I'd shoot him, without remorse, just like Papà had taught me and Carlotta.

My heart fought to escape its cage when the footsteps halted. The

shadowy figure turned into the alley. I couldn't make out a face, but I caught the row of barbs tattooed around his arms. Prison tattoos common among enforcers. One barb for each kill.

And he had rows of them.

"Who are you?" I asked, weapon fixed at my side.

He didn't answer, his footsteps bringing him nearer and nearer until I made out the deep scar across his face. I pulled in my breath, raised my gun, and shot.

Chapter Three

FRANKIE

The hard spit of a bullet exploded from the mouth of the gun held tight in pretty Liliana Vitali's little hands.

I expected the recoil, if not the action, to upset her delicate sensibilities, but she surprised me yet again with her unflappable calm.

Feet braced, arms level, face utterly composed, Lily stared down the barrel of her Sig Sauer and watched as the man who had been following her crumpled to the ground.

The girl had more backbone than I'd originally given her credit for.

The sight of her so bold and brave sent heat bubbling through my veins. I wondered what kind of ferocity she might bring to the bedroom when I finally got between her slim thighs.

I smoothed my hands down the silk of my jacket, tugging it into place so that when I stepped out from the shadows of the alley into the anemic light, I would cut the right kind of imposing figure.

I wanted her afraid.

Not only because it would serve my purposes, but because scaring her

turned me on.

Immediately, she swung the gun to point it dead center at my chest.

Slowly, I raised my hands in a gesture of faux innocence and let a grin curl the left side of my mouth. Her eyes tracked over every inch of my suit-clad form, lingered at the exposed tanned skin of my chest where I'd unbuttoned my shirt a little too low, and soared up to my eyes to lock our gazes.

"You're Frankie Amato," she said, voice strong and confident.

I cocked an eyebrow, surprised and vaguely pleased that she knew of me.

Still, it wouldn't do to let her know that.

"How observant of you. That homeschool education must be top notch."

Her face collapsed into a scowl. I had to bite my lip to keep from laughing at the absurdity of that vicious expression of her sweet face.

"Why were you following me?" she demanded, then paused as something dawned on her. "It was you at the restaurant before."

I ignored her. Even though she was the one training a gun to my chest, it was me with all the power. I needed her to know it.

Instead, I let my eyes fall over her body like warm rain, trickling down her décolletage, sluicing over the golden tanned skin of her forearms and calves exposed in that godawful dress.

"You're grown up," I said, just to watch her inflate with pride before I punctured it, delighted in watching her deflate. "What are you now? Thirteen? It's not possible you've hit puberty yet, surely."

"Nineteen," she bit out. An angry flush spilled like red wine down her neck.

"Hmm…" I let my eyes drop to her small chest once again. "I would have thought you'd have filled out by now."

We both looked down at her slight body. Her brow creased as she caught a glimpse of the small swells beneath the bodice of her dress. I had her flustered, so bemused that she seemed to have forgotten the dead body

slumped against the stained stone wall opposite her.

I gestured to it. "Nineteen years old and a stone-cold killer. Now *that* impresses me."

Lily gaped, head snapping around to stare at the body. "Is he one of yours? If so, maybe I should put a bullet in you, too?"

I didn't respond, walking over to the body and kneeling to inspect it. *He* was a large man, tattooed in multiple places with distinctive mafia symbols, but it was his large gold pinky ring that solidified Lily's question of who her stalker had been.

A ring bearing my family's crest.

I slid it off his finger, swapping it out for the ring I always kept on my person as a reminder of my brother's death.

Then, I held up the offending piece of jewelry so she could see my enemy's insignia. "He's a Bruno. Fighting with the in-laws so soon, Lily?"

Her face went slack with shock before she straightened her shoulders and zipped her lips closed to conceal it.

"How did you know about the engagement? You don't strike me as the type to read the local gossip rags."

"Oh, I'm not. The woman I fucked last night on the other hand…" I shrugged a shoulder and tried not to chuckle at her expression of faint disgust and lustful curiosity. "Or was it the one I fucked this morning?"

"Is that supposed to impress me?" She cocked her hip to the side, gun held loosely by her thighs like it was some designer bag and not a deadly weapon.

I stood up, stuck my hands in my pockets, and rocked back on my heels as I considered her. "The better question, delicate Lily, is whether the murder of this Bruno goon should impress *me*?"

"Why would I want to impress you?" she countered. "Besides, we don't know he's a Bruno."

I tossed her the ring. "He's wearing their insignia. It's not exactly the ring you were expecting from your husband, was it?"

"He's not my husband."

"Yet," I agreed.

She rolled her lips under her teeth, probably an effort to restrain herself from saying something a good Vitali daughter should not.

I nudged my toe against the body and whistled. "To think I believed the rumors…"

"Rumors?"

I smiled as she slid so prettily into my trap. "They say you're a good girl, but I think this proves otherwise. I think you're just begging for someone to corrupt you."

"This was self-defense," she argued, but her breath hitched when I stepped closer. The air between us went static with electricity. "Not some perverted cry for help."

I reached out and caught a loose curl that had fallen over her cheek. The strand was soft as satin between my fingers. I wanted to know what all that silken hair would feel like wrapped around my fist while I broke in her virgin pussy from behind.

"Can't it be both?" I asked softly. Intimately.

She blinked those huge golden-brown eyes up at me, lips parted in a plea her body understood, even though her mind rebelled against it.

"But really," I continued and released her lock of hair to skirt the backs of my knuckles down the soft slope of her cheek. "Why would a man with more important things to do follow boring little you?"

Instantly, her eyes flashed. She stepped away from me, her lips twisted with hatred. "I'm not little *or* boring. He was threatening me!"

"Mhmm. I saw the whole thing, poisonous Lily. The poor man was just taking a post-dinner stroll to digest, and then *bang!* You turn around and shoot him dead."

"He was stalking me," she insisted with a stubborn tilt of her chin. "Would you rather see me raped or abducted?"

I clucked my tongue at her. "You're marrying into the Bruno family. This man was probably sent to protect you." I watched as the color drained out of her face. In this world, blood could only be repaid with blood, and

she knew it. "Now what will you do? Your future husband cares for you so much he sent a man to look out for your welfare, and you kill him? Not exactly an auspicious start to your union."

"He didn't identify himself when he had the chance."

"His orders were most likely to trail you silently and avoid detection. Pretty standard stuff."

"What the fuck is this?" she demanded, tossing her hair like an angry mare. "An Amato defending a Bruno?"

"Ah, but you see, I'm an opportunist, sweet Lily." I smiled, leaning so close to her mouth she swiped her tongue along her bottom lip in an unconscious quest to taste my own. "There are consequences to murder, even for a mafia princess like yourself. Especially when a marriage pact is on the line."

Panic flashed bright as a lightning strike in her eyes. "What do you want?" Her hiss sent amusement through me.

Hook. Line. And sinker.

She was proving herself to be a smart girl and knew this conversation was leading toward a very specific end. Liliana Vitali had killed a man before my very eyes. If she wanted to get away with murder, I was the answer to that prize.

I wrapped my hand around her fragile wrist and brought it up between us, so I could pluck the Bruno ring from her palm.

"I'll keep my mouth shut and help you dispose of the body," I offered as if it was no big thing.

"For what price?" The wariness in her tone contrasted with the hint of an excited flush in her cheeks.

Perhaps there was a dirty girl under all that good girl class, just aching to be beholden to a man who would exploit all those naughty inclinations she secretly harbored at night with her hand between her untouched thighs.

"A date."

Her eyes blew wide open. "Are you serious? You'd hide a body and cover up a murder that could probably serve you well with your family for

a *date*?"

"Don't be naïve, Lily." I captured her chin between my fingers and leaned down to speak against the corner of her pink mouth. "It won't be at all like the farce of a date you just endured with Tommy. In fact, it will be so much *more* than just bland conversation."

She swayed forward, almost subconsciously, her mouth blooming open, breath hot across my skin as she panted softly, desperate for my kiss.

Instead, I angled my head and bit firmly into her bottom lip. She gasped when I drew blood, but I held her still with my hand on her face.

"Do we have a deal?" My cock swelled between us, blood heating at the sight of the blood pooling on her lower lip.

She swallowed hard. "I can clean this up myself."

"Oh really?" My soft laughter brought ire within her eyes. "How?"

She shrugged with the attitude of a child. "I can roll up the body and throw it in the ocean."

"Oh, the sweet idiocy of youth," I taunted. "You weigh one hundred pounds soaking wet, little girl. How do you think you will lift his corpse? Even if you did get to the ocean, the tides will only carry the body back to the shore. Where will that leave you? No…" I smeared the blood over her lower lip with my thumb and watched as she trailed the path with her tongue. "You need me."

"Just one date?" she inquired, breath shaky.

That's all it would take.

"One date." I sucked my thumb, slicked with her blood, into my mouth and watched her lids lower with desire.

The salt tang of her made me hungry for the taste of her untried pussy. The vicious lust this slip of a girl inspired in me gave me momentary pause.

I'd bedded dozens of women, tasted their sex and the blush of their desire, gorged myself on their bodies in ways this girl couldn't even dream of. Yet, it was her who turned my blood to lava and my resolve to volcanic ash.

I moved away before that lust overtook my rationale and bent to deal

with the poor man who'd been playing dead for the last twenty minutes, probably with bruised ribs beneath that bulletproof vest of his.

Because he was not, in fact, a Bruno.

He was an Amato.

My Amato.

A poor cousin of mine, who I'd roped into my nefarious plan to get the lovely Liliana in my debt.

A plan that had gone off now without a hitch.

If I didn't know better, the fake blood pooling beneath his stomach would have fooled me. Lucky for us, she'd gone for center mass instead of a headshot.

"Do you regret killing him?" I asked her, my loud voice muting his soft, pained exhale as I threw his weight up over my shoulder and carried him toward my car.

"Regret is a useless emotion."

And that response should have been my warning. The big red flag that told me Liliana Vitali would be a bigger problem than I'd given her credit for. She possessed a spine of steel hidden in that petite body.

Liliana followed me to the Bugatti I'd parked at the mouth of the road earlier and watched me shove the body into the trunk and slam the door shut.

Her words echoed in the abandoned street.

Regret is a useless emotion.

I doubted she would feel that way when I was through with her.

Chapter Four

LILY

For all intents and purposes, my family appeared normal.

We went to church, watched every Juventus F.C. game that aired in the living room, and ate dinner together every night. The one flaw—the single loose thread among our designer lives—was the empty seat at the dinner table. One we set every night, food piled high on the plate.

With each bite, I felt Carlotta's absence as if it had happened yesterday. It was sad, and depressing, and a reminder of what should be there but wasn't.

But that wasn't what bothered me tonight.

Neither was the threat of blackmail looming over my head.

It was my phone, empty except for a few needy texts from my husband-to-be. Frankie Amato had extorted a date from me, yet he hadn't bothered to ask for my number or give me a place and time.

Was this what crushes felt like? Waiting for a call with baited breath like something out of a teenybopper love song? I was better than this.

"What's wrong, Lily?" Papà's eyes shot to the empty chair. "You've

been silent all dinner."

Everything is wrong. My husband-to-be is duller than an unsharpened pencil. I killed a fucking Bruno. I'm being blackmailed by a man I don't trust not to kill me. A man who probably won't stop at just a date with me, which given my sister's death, is proof history repeats itself.

And, worst of all, I want him to call me.

It's the only thing I'm looking forward to these days.

I didn't say any of that. Instead, I picked at the food on my plate, moving the pasta around without bringing it to my lips. "Just exhausted. I don't feel well. May I return to my room to rest?"

"Yes, darling." Papà nodded to the glass beside my plate. "Take your water with you. You haven't drunk any all day."

"Yes, Papà."

I squeezed my mom's hand, grabbed my glass, and downed it on the way to my room, setting it on the floor just outside my doorway. Frankie Amato was the first thing I saw when I opened the door. The empty packet of Kinder Bueno I kept in my nightstand drawer was a close second.

He laid on my bed, feet crossed at the ankles, flicking through T.V. channels like they were pages in a textbook he never bothered reading. He wore his dark hair messy, brown eyes fixated on the screen. A fitted button-down and designer slacks cased his muscular six-two frame. The sheer size of him consumed my bed.

I wanted to lick the dimple on his cheek. Tie him down on the bed and explore in ways I'd never been allowed to. Or maybe run for my life. I hadn't decided yet.

My pulse thrummed against my neck.

Thrill. Excitement... Fear.

Frankie popped the last of my chocolate in his mouth, turned off the T.V., and tossed the remote on my bed. "People can see you from the street when you leave your window open."

My eyes flicked to the open window and back to him, piecing things together. "I know."

Had he watched me? If so, when?

He sat up, a touch of intrigue unfurling across his features. "You like being watched."

I didn't answer.

He continued, his amusement not dimming for a second, "Why don't you put on a show for me right now?"

I watched as he took his time standing, paraded across my room as if he owned it, and entered my closet. "Why the hell would I do that?"

Aside from the fact that the idea intrigued me.

The Vitalis had made it clear that they expected my virginity. If their demands hadn't sealed it, Carlotta's death did. They say abstinence is the best birth control, but it left me curious, voyeuristic, and perpetually fixated on sex.

Frankie exited the closet, holding up the skimpiest dress I owned. One of Carlotta's dresses, which she'd discarded in my closet and swapped for pajamas after sneaking into my room one night. I couldn't bring myself to toss it or return it to her room.

He toyed with the lace strap. "Or I could go downstairs, join your family for dinner, and tell your dad how great it is that he's passed down his murderous tendencies to his daughter. What's for dinner?" He sniffed the air. "Pasta con le sarde? My favorite."

"Liar." I didn't bother hiding my frown. "No one likes sardines."

"Willing to bet on it?" He dangled the dress between us, getting beneath my skin like only he could.

I snatched it from his fingers, trying to control my errant heartbeat.

Fucking hell, calm down, Liliana.

I was half-convinced Frankie could see my heartbeat as I let my dress straps fall off my shoulders. The fabric pooled to the ground, revealing my braless chest. He stared at my nipples, fingers tapping at his side like he wanted to touch them.

Do it. I dare you.

Disappointment unfurled across my stomach when his hands remained

by his sides.

Maybe I should have hurried and tossed the dress he'd chosen over my body, but I didn't. I couldn't bring myself to. Not when he'd issued a challenge, his arrogant tone suggesting he didn't think I had the nerve to go through with it.

I did.

Proving that to him shouldn't have mattered to me, but here I was, putting on a slow, teasing strip show for him.

I edged closer until my bare chest brushed against his clothed one. Turning around, I gave him my back, bent slowly to pick up the fallen dress, and pretended I didn't notice my ass rubbing against his erection.

When I stood upright again, the heat of his breath met my nape. I tossed the worn dinner dress into my hamper by the door, turned, and pulled the scanty dress over my head and down my body.

Pretending I wasn't affected was, perhaps, the greatest feat of acting ever performed. I tossed my hair over my shoulder and asked, "What are you doing here?"

His lips curved into a half-smile, just one corner, like he couldn't be bothered with the effort to give me an actual smile. And just when I thought he'd respond—when a normal, polite person would respond—he gave me his back and left out my window without a word, as if he knew I'd follow.

What an ass.

I waited for him to reach the ground before I climbed down the trellis. He hadn't extended me the same courtesy of waiting, so I ended up jogging across my yard and into his car, noting he hadn't even opened the door for me.

There were flowers on my seat. It was such an unexpected gesture, I forgot to hide my smile.

He took one glance at me and said, "They're not for you."

I rolled my eyes, sat, and lifted the flowers to smell.

He *tutted* again, his habit of treating me like a dog rearing its ugly head. "I wouldn't do that if I were you... Unless you'd prefer death over

marrying a Bruno…"

I lowered the flowers to my lap. "Excuse me?"

Would you judge me if I admitted that I was alone in a car with my blackmailer, afraid of him, yet in love with the thrill of it all?

Frankie started his car and took off, one hand on the wheel and another on the stick like something out of a James Dean movie. "They're poisonous."

"They look innocent."

"So do you, but the body I cremated would argue otherwise. If he could speak, that is."

I didn't dignify that with a response. "Where are we going?"

He didn't answer me, not like I expected anything different. He could be driving to a deserted area to kill me for all I knew.

When he stopped the car, he grabbed shot glasses and a bottle of Amaretto from the backseat, swung his door open, and got out. "Bring the flowers."

Hidden from his view, I plucked a bud from the cluster, pocketed it, and exited the car with the poisonous flowers clutched in my palm.

Only then did I realize where we were.

A cemetery.

Chapter Five

FRANKIE

I could feel her fear like a tangible thing, cool and diaphanous as the fog blanketing the tombstones in the family cemetery at the outskirts of town.

Her profile was a study in perfect proportions. She stared at the poisonous flowers and swallowed thickly. Once again, I had to bite back my smile.

There was something about the contrast of her. The sweetly naïve and the sassy stubbornness. The purity contrasted to the dark gleam of desire in her eyes when I took liberties with her.

She was complicated as a well-rounded Chianti. My curiosity to know if she tasted just as complex was beginning to overtake my better judgement.

Before I could reach out, pry her legs apart, and dip my hand beneath that scandalously short dress, I exited the car and barked at her to grab the flowers. I moved quickly through the tombstones lining the hill before the crypts began, not once looking over my shoulder to see if Liliana followed

When I reached the door to my immediate family's crypt, I turned only enough to snatch the lilies from her hand before unlocking and opening the heavy stone door.

She followed me into the dark, dank crypt, only the heavy, stuttering sound of her breath giving away her apprehension.

I continued to ignore her, kneeled, reverently brushed the cobwebs away from the face of my brother's tombstone, and placed the flowers at its base.

Manuel Amato
1990-2018

My hand threatened to shake. I unscrewed the cap on the Amaretto and poured out two shots. I plucked a smooth white petal from the bouquet and set it atop the shot glass I placed in front of Manuel's grave marker.

"I thought you said the flower was poisonous?" Lily finally asked, her voice timid under the press of fear and gloom of the tomb. "What if a groundskeeper or someone from your family comes to visit and drinks that?"

I shot her an unimpressed glare as I prepared to drink my own glass of liquor. "Then, they'll die."

The alcohol burned down my throat, leaving bright almond flavor on the back of my tongue.

Lily shifted behind me, obviously impatient with my lack of attention. "You're not going to offer me a shot?"

I swatted her words away like a pesky fly and stared at the stone edifice that housed my brother, the only man I'd ever been close enough with to give a shit about.

He'd be proud, strong in the way of kings and emperors. He was too grand. Too smart to be a mere foot soldier in the Amato outfit. But he was also young and relatively untried.

If only he'd waited…

Bid his time and carried out his orders.

Waited as Brutus did for a time when Julius Caesar was vulnerable.

For a time like right fucking now when the Amato family's very existence could be snuffed out by a union between our arch rivals and the most powerful family in Sicily.

My own blasphemous thoughts surprised me.

I was not my brother.

I was built for sin and pleasure. A creature of hedonism not subterfuge and war.

Yet…there was something to the idea of destroying the hand that fed me and carving out my own path.

Lily distracted me by grabbing the discarded bottle of booze and swinging it up to her lips, where she gulped from it like a woman parched near death.

Seconds later, the bottle went crashing to the ground, breaking with a symphonic shatter that echoed in the tomb. She bent over, coughing, one hand to her stomach and the other at her wet mouth as she struggled to breathe through the burn.

I sighed, feeling the almost ten-year age difference between us.

Without going to her aid, I stood and leaned against the cold stone, staring down at her like I found her lacking. "I hope you'll prove to be better at swallowing other things…"

Lily, barely recovered, gaped at me, her pink mouth slick with almond-flavored alcohol I wanted to clean with my tongue. "You can't speak to me like that! I'm a Vitali."

"Is that all you are? A Vitali?" I cocked my head and raked my eyes down her scantily clad body. "Or are you a woman? One with her own dark dreams and desires?"

She didn't respond.

I pushed off the wall and moved into her space, stopping only when the toes of my leather loafers pressed to her white shoes. My gaze locked to hers. I ran my thumb along her damp lower lip, collecting the Amaretto.

Her eyes blew black with lust when I brought the finger to my mouth and sucked off the moisture.

"I think the problem is that no one has ever spoken to you like that before," I suggested, then dipped down to drag my tongue along the same path my thumb had ventured, tasting the almonds straight from her source. When I pulled back just enough to see her expression, she was flushed and drunk on lust more than the drink. "And Lily? I think you fucking love it."

I pulled back, stepping until I was pressed against the stone across from her. As if the cold air between us would barricade the base desires storming through my body, raiding my thoughts.

I needed space and distance. Some fucking objectivity, or I'd be drunk as her on the headiness of our connection and throw the rule book out the window.

"I bet you're even wondering just how I'd disrespect your body and all the ways I'd make you love that, too," I taunted to distract myself.

My cock was a steel pipe in my trousers. Her eyes darted between it and my gaze, her little pink tongue peeking out in a subconscious quest to explore that bulge with her mouth. I groaned quietly and readjusted myself so my erection wasn't so fucking obvious.

Lily recovered enough to tip her chin up, so much defiance in her eyes, I wanted to break it. To break her. "You're wrong. I was wondering what kind of man brings a woman on a date to a crypt."

My grin sliced across my face, killing my illicit thoughts. "Manuel was my brother."

She frowned, waiting for me to go on. When I didn't, she pursed her lips and fisted her hands on her hips. "Sooo you left your dead brother a shot of alcohol and poisonous flowers? Doesn't seem very brotherly."

"The combination killed him," I said with that cruel smile I'd learned from the other made men in my family. An expression of joy perverted by murder and the acts that led to it. "Lily of the Valley crushed into Amaretto."

"And you're smiling…" She shook her head, eyes flirting between me

and the glass of poison on my brother's grave. "That's evil, Frankie."

"Of course, you wouldn't understand."

She hesitated, thumbing the material of her dress between her fingers. "Actually, I understand more than you think. Why did he die?"

I liked her question and the intelligence it spoke to. Not *how* he died, but *why*? There was always a reason for death in the life of the mafia.

"He made an unauthorized hit against the Bruno family during a turf war a few years ago. The Council gave him the option between two sentences: death or exile."

"He chose death?" she asked, an adorable knot in her brow.

The urge to smile while talking about my brother's death surprised me. Usually, I felt sick with helplessness and frustrated rage, but Lily made me feel... light somehow.

"For a made man, exile is worse than death. What is life without your family, your religion?" I gestured to the sea of graves around us. A sea of men, who preferred death as a made man over death without honor, loyalty, and family. "That is what life is for these men."

"For you," she murmured, almost to herself. She studied me and looked out the barred window to the deepening night beyond. "My sister chose death, too. I'll never understand why. Our cousin Renata would have let her live in America with her."

So that was what had happened to Carlotta. I'd forgotten to look into it and kicked myself for it now.

My heart clenched at the agony in Lily's tone, a pain that matched my own and could only be echoed by the death of a sibling.

I'd meant to woo her tender heart with my sob story, but it seemed Lily had one of her own.

"Manuel chose death to make a point," I found myself explaining, even though I'd never before spoken of it.

"Which was?"

"In death, he could take his life back from the Family."

Lily paused, digesting that. "Somehow, that makes sense. Carlotta

asked my dad to kill her. We spent the entire day together as a family, going to the beach and out for dinner at her favorite trattoria. Mundane shit I'd always taken for granted. That night, when I was in bed, window open to courtyard where they said goodbye, Papà shot her."

I sucked air through my teeth, shocked that they'd let her witness the killing so intimately. Paolo was known for sheltering his daughters, yet in his haste to right the wrong his eldest daughter had done, he'd exposed his youngest to something she should never have been a part of.

I'd take better care of her, I found myself thinking, the animal in me rearing its wild head, snapping its rabid teeth.

I wanted to kill Paolo Vitali for putting her through that.

A dangerous thought to have.

A surprising one, too.

"What did she do?" I demanded, angry but not with her.

She seemed to sense it. If anything, my outrage seemed to endear her further. She stepped closer until the hard tips of her small breasts pressed against me.

"Carlotta had sex before marriage," she murmured, voice husky. "With someone who wasn't her arranged fiancé."

I dipped my head so my nose could slide against the edge of hers. She smelled like lilies. Of course, she did.

One of my hands found the dip of her lower back and pressed her even closer, so she could feel my semi-hard dick against her belly. The other slid into the silken treads of her hair and the base of her neck.

She gasped when I fisted the locks and tugged her head back, her mouth blooming open for me.

"Maybe," I whispered, voice rough as sandpaper, "the temptation was worth the price."

"She was an idiot," Lily insisted, eyes flashing, but her stare caught on my mouth, and she softened further against me. It was my turn for my breath to hitch when her hand slid up my chest and tangled in the short hair at my nape. "But," she allowed as she rocked onto her tip toes, "maybe

you're right."

"Why don't I help you decide?"

My control snapped. I hauled her to me, feet off the ground, tight, young body banded against mine.

And my mouth was on her.

Her soft, supple lips were tender and curious. She opened for my plundering tongue, her movements tentative, reminding me of our age difference.

Lily rubbed her tongue against mine. Her little kittenish mewl vibrated down my throat. I groaned, losing myself in that almond-flavored mouth. Drunk in the potent scent of lilies.

And I knew, whatever game I was playing had just become a hell of a lot more dangerous for the both of us.

Chapter Six

LILY

Tommaso and I sat across from Father Luigi, undergoing the most pointless premarital counseling in history. We barely knew one another. There was no relationship to council. Plus, I couldn't stand Tommaso. He was controlling, spit when he talked, and possessed the humor of a broken condom. No amount of premarital counseling could fix that.

But I'd grown up in this church, a building that had existed since the conception of civilized Italy and would exist long past my demise. So, Papà had insisted on daily counseling until our marriage. His way of ensuring what had happened to Carlotta wouldn't happen to me.

Father Luigi scribbled something into his notepad and leaned back in his chair. "How did you feel when Tommaso didn't give you a ring, Liliana?"

Relieved.

Tommaso interrupted, "It's not that I didn't give her a ring. It was delayed. They're still making it."

We'd stopped by the shop this morning, only for the shop owner to tell us he'd been out sick all week.

I tipped a shoulder up, ready for this to end. "It's not a big deal."

After all, I'd locked lips with another man. At the memory of Frankie, a smile fought its way to be seen. I played it off as agreeability, much to Tommaso's displeasure.

He gestured wildly at me. "It should be a big deal! We're getting married! Don't you care?!"

I've known you for two seconds. Calm your tits.

I couldn't say this, so I feigned patience. "I do care, but I won't make a fuss about it. I can wait."

"It will postpone our wedding for a week."

"There's no rush, right?"

He shifted in his seat, which only confirmed what I'd suspected when he'd texted me last night, asking for a picture—Tommaso Bruno wanted to fuck me. I'd sent him a selfie with my eighty-four-year-old Nonna. Let him jerk off to Nonna's "Grandma of the Year" shirt.

Tommaso shook his head. "You should be excited to marry me. It seems as if you'd like to delay the wedding."

I was too exhausted to answer him, stroke his ego, or whatever handholding my future husband needed from me.

Father Luigi gave me the same look he'd given me five years ago when Carlotta and I had stolen all the communion wine before mass. "I think that's enough for today. I look forward to seeing you both tomorrow."

Tommaso's hand burned my back as we stepped out of Father Luigi's office. He inched it lower. "My car's around the corner. I can take you home."

"No, thanks. I drove here."

"I didn't see your car."

"I parked it near the flower shop." I gave him my cheek before he could try for my lips and went the opposite way when he exited out the back. Making my way past the pews, I fiddled with my phone, wondering if

Frankie had any plans on calling me.

He hadn't mentioned it, and technically, I'd fulfilled my end of the deal with the date, but I'd been expecting... *more*. I wasn't sure what, considering my virginity equated to my life. The idea of more, however, consumed my mind.

So much so that I didn't notice when a hand slid out of the confessional and tugged me inside.

I opened my mouth to scream, but the hand shifted to cover it. Another snaked around my waist, pulling me against a hard, muscular body. Squirming, I fought my attacker's hold, punching whatever I could until my foot connected with his shin.

"Fucking hell, it's me."

I relaxed at the sound of Frankie's voice, enough for him to release the hand on my mouth and shut the door. "What are you doing here? It's—"

"It's dangerous, and you like it." His whispers caressed my cheek. "I bet if I slipped my fingers inside you, I'd find you wet." He lowered his hand from my stomach to the outside of my thigh, just beneath my dress. It slid inward, drawing a heavy breath from me. "Do you want me to touch you?"

"No."

But I did.

More than I'd ever expected.

Maybe it was desperation to escape my engagement. Or maybe it was the fact that we'd connected on a level I'd never expected. Manuel. Carlotta. Two sides of the same coin.

Where did that put me and Frankie?

"Tsk, tsk..." Frankie's fingers inched up. "You're in a confession booth. Surely, it's a sin to lie."

"You're no priest."

He pulled at my panties and released, so the fabric snapped at my sensitive skin. "I'm whatever the fuck I want."

"Forgive me, Father, for I have sinned."

He countered my sarcasm with his own. "I prefer you call me Daddy, but Father works, too."

"I prefer you let me go."

"Another lie. I'm starting to think I'll have to spank that habit out of you." His fingers ran a path across my slit over my panties. "Wet, to no one's surprise."

I bucked against his hand, trying to maintain the conversation. "Why are you here?"

It occurred to me to ask how he'd even found me, but before I could question him, he cupped me and pressed the heal of his palm against my clit.

"For part two."

"Of what?"

"Our deal. I hid a dead body for you—"

"We went on the date. I don't owe you anything."

"Our date hasn't ended." He dug his erection against my ass. "Confess a sin."

My heavy breaths fogged the tiny confessional. We stood on the priest's side, because of course, we did. "And you'll let me go?"

"To be determined."

I tried to fight off his arm. He didn't budge. I could yell, but getting caught in this booth with him would be worse, so I conjured the easiest confession I could think of. "I'm wet for you."

"Already knew that. Try again."

"After our date, I ran to my room, fingered myself, and cried out your name when I came."

"Better," he ground himself against me, "but I figured as much. Try again."

He pinched my nipple through my dress, and I blurted out, "I stole a flower bud from you."

Fuck. Me.

This was the type of torture designed to deliver confessions.

Waterboarding. Breaking bones. Nothing was more effective.

Frankie froze, his fingers still attached to my budded nipple. "Why?"

It was the last thing I should have blurted, but now that I had, I wasn't sure if I was scared or relieved. Maybe both. "Because I wanted it."

"Not good enough. What did you want it for? No one steals a poisonous flower for no reason."

"Well, I did."

"Bullshit. You're forgetting that I know you. I can call your bluffs a mile away." He nudged my panties to the side and brushed my clit with the pad of his thumb, eliciting a moan from me that echoed within the narrow walls of the confessional. His finger gathered my wetness, then rubbed it in a circle around my empty ring finger. "Case in point. You're wet for me, no matter how much you denied it. What's the lily for?"

I couldn't answer him.

I didn't know how he'd react or if I could trust him.

He continued to toy with my slit. "Are you trying to kill yourself, Lily?"

"Why do you care?"

"I don't."

"Sounds like you do."

My heart beat an erratic rhythm at the thought.

Frankie Amato was Sicily's heartthrob. My sister and her friends used to gossip about him after school, whispering about the dirty things they'd do to him when they thought I couldn't hear. I used to latch onto their words, searching them on my laptop in the privacy of my room.

The truth was, I'd let Frankie Amato do all those things to me—and more.

But the idea that he might have cared about me?

I didn't know how to process that, other than an electric spark inside me I couldn't control.

"You're deflecting," he accused. "Is the flower for you?"

I didn't answer.

He slid two fingers inside me with ease, instantly drenched with my wetness. "What's the flower for?" I still didn't answer, not even when he pumped his fingers in and out, a steady and teasing rhythm that left me soaked and panting. "You'll tell me if you want to come."

"Careful," I warned. "Don't break my hymen."

His fingers pushed deeper, so far in, he had to be touching it. We were playing a dangerous game. I loved it. Thrived on it. Had never had this much excitement in my life. "I can break it right now. It'd be so easy. Do you know what the best part is?"

"What?"

"You'd like it." He didn't give me the opportunity to deny it, not that I could. "Now tell me, who is the poison for, Lily? Remember…" He curled his fingers against the most sensitive spot inside me, hitting it over and over again. "Good girls get rewarded."

I was close to coming.

So fucking close.

I moaned, resting my head back against his shoulder, finally catching the shadow of his face in the darkness of the confession booth. He was unnaturally handsome. Sharp lines, high cheekbones, and the type of eyes that ensnared.

"I'm close," I panted. At my words, he stopped his hook movement, pressing his lips against my temple. "Frankie…"

"What's the poison for?"

"Him!" I shouted out, bucking against his hand, so desperate for more. "It's for him. Okay? For Tommaso. Now make me come."

He pulled out of me, unzipped his slacks, turned me so I faced him, and sat us both down until I was straddling him with his cock positioned just at my entrance. "Explain first."

I bucked against him, rubbing his head against my slick slit. So desperate for him, I could barely speak, let alone form a coherent sentence.

"I'm going to kill him during our honeymoon." I reached between us, grabbed his thick length, and rubbed the tip of it against my clit. In the

distance, I could hear some of the clergymen, but I didn't care. I was too far gone. "Then, I'm going to run away."

"Such a bad girl," he whispered against the column of my neck, smacked my hand away, and thrust inside me.

I felt my hymen break at the same time he pinched my clit. My teeth met his shoulders and bit down, transferring my pain onto him. I lost myself in the pleasure with each thrust. We were lust, and recklessness, and heavy breathing, and pain, and pleasure.

And by the time we came together and I realized what this meant for my life, I considered that we were the closest thing to love I would ever have the opportunity to experience.

Chapter Seven

FRANKIE

"It's done."

My voice echoed throughout the silent room at the back of Mama Sofia's restaurant. I'd never seen the Family so silent. Even the fucker Angelo was quiet as a nun at confession, his hands clasped in front of him, head bowed and eyes trained on the surface of the table Amato men had sat around for decades.

For a moment, I thought they hadn't heard me, which was fucking impossible because I'd said the words loud and staccato to punctuate their importance.

"It's done," I repeated. "She won't pass the deflowering ceremony."

Don Amato finally stirred from his old-man stupor. Italians revered things with *age* as if that made them inherently and automatically wise, better than their younger counterparts.

Don Amato, in my humble, never-voiced opinion, was evidence to the contrary.

His bones creaked as he moved back in his chair to fix his beady eyes

on me over the steeple of his joined fingertips. "*Bene*. We can move to propose our own marital union between Angelo and one of the Vitalis when the dust from the scandal settles."

"And Liliana?" I asked despite my best intentions.

Don Amato scoffed, prompting the rest of the men to chuckle. "She won't be viable after she fails the deflowering ceremony. She will be dead... perhaps excommunicated if she is lucky."

Guilt ignited in my belly and raged into a cataclysmic wildfire that razed my heart to ash.

Liliana dead.

Because of me.

There was no way around it. I might as well have been the one to shoot her in her back courtyard instead of Paolo.

Lily would die just as her beloved Carlotta had.

She would die for following her passions, for being too bright to stifle with our antiquated mafia rules.

I struggled to focus on my breathing. In. Out. In. Out.

Fuck. Me. Fuck. Me.

I couldn't let this happen, not without warning her at the very least. She deserved that, didn't she? After what I'd taken from her.

I could still feel the hot blood of her virginity on my cock, the way she'd rippled and clenched around me like an iron vise.

We'd fucked in a confessional like two ultimate sinners, but the feeling that lingered wasn't shame for our actions.

It was a haunting sense of wonder, as a man who has suddenly rediscovered his sight. Lily had colored in my black and white world with her sass and brightness. I found myself horrified that all her goodness would be so unjustly snuffed out.

These were dangerous thoughts, skirting far too close to caring for comfort. But I couldn't stop them if I tried.

"I can attend the engagement dinner tonight as the Amato representative," I offered. "Scout the eligible Vitali women for prospects."

Don Amato's wet black eyes pinned me to a stop, searching me for weakness. I held fast, chin tipped the way Lily did, lips crooked in my habitual cocky smirk.

Finally, he nodded. "Stay away from the spoiled Vitali girl. Your job there is finished."

But it wasn't.

I'd do anything in my power to make sure Lily at least had a chance of making it out of this alive.

The restaurant was empty of civilians and packed to the rafters with mafia families. A cacophony of voices raised in passionate tones was made even more aggressive by the amount of wine imbued, people calling to each other from across the room, and the swell of Umberto Tozzi singing over the sound system.

It was after dinner and its requisite formalities. Everyone was distracted by their own drunkenness and what late night revelries they might indulge in.

I'd bid my time, tucked away at a table in the back with lesser made men than myself. The grunts and wannabes who reeked of eagerness and greed.

To make matters worse, Lily had been out of my reach the entire night, sequestered at the head of the long table in the middle of the room with Paolo and Tommaso. The latter was all over her.

My poisonous Lily delivered only reluctant politeness and a barely acceptable level of impudence in return.

I wanted to touch her.

My cock had been half hard in my trousers all night as I watched the way her thick black hair shone blue in the low light. How her chest flushed that delicious wine red when we caught eyes across the crowded room.

I wanted to sit her on my cock and watch her squirm again.

Tom said something to her. She turned her head away, pretending not to hear, only for her father to chastise her. My Lily furrowed her brows and lifted her wine to her lips. Her future husband clucked his tongue and forcibly unwrapped her fingers from her glass.

I wanted to steal her away from those assholes and break their spines so they'd never bother her again.

Heathen. She was making me heathen.

A man ruled by his base needs, incapable of higher thinking.

And I didn't care.

I needed to see her one more time.

The opportunity came when she made her way to the restroom as people started to say their goodbyes and drifted drunkenly home. I took advantage of the chaos and followed her into the room.

Her startled gaze snapped to mine in the reflection of the mirror, tiny fingers clutching her pink lipstick.

"Don't pretend to be surprised," I scolded her, locked the door behind me, and stalked forward until my front was flush to her back. "You knew I'd come for you."

"You're a fool for taking such a risk," she countered, but she was already melting back against me, rubbing her sweet ass on my groin.

"A fool thinks himself to be wise, but a wise man knows himself to be a fool," I quoted, skimming my nose down her neck and breathing in her floral scent.

"Shakespeare. How erudite you are for a common foot soldier." But she was breathing heavy, probably soaked for me.

"Your homeschooling must really be top notch," I teased, reminding her of how we'd met before sinking my teeth into her neck just to hear her gasp. "Come away with me tonight."

"With such a good education, you think I'd do something so stupid?"

"I think you played the good girl all night, and you're bored out of your fucking skull." Before she could protest, I wrapped a hand around the front of her body and raised the skirt of her dress to expose her underwear.

We both watched as I edged my thumb under the elastic and played it over the edge of her wet pussy. "Come play with the devil for a while."

***

Picking the lock was child's play, but the alarm system took a little more work. I'd always been good with tech. It was the primary way I'd helped the family business in the past, hacking and circumnavigating security systems.

The jewelry store in downtown Gerosa was laughably easy.

"What are you doing?" Lily hissed from behind me.

I tugged her into the store, closed the door behind us, and grinned. "Do you want to see the ring your husband had made specially for you?"

"Not especially," she said dryly as I let go of her hand to let her explore the glass cases and shelves filled with precious jewels. "Definitely not enough to commit a felony to see it early."

Nothing was a felony when we had the police and politicians bought. I didn't say this.

Instead, I shrugged a shoulder, leaned against the wall, and watched her move through the space. "We committed a felony for the fun of it, my sweet Lily. You want to be a bad girl. I figured you needed at least one illegal activity on your record."

Neither of us brought up the murder, which she still didn't know I'd faked. Sweet, naïve Lily. She'd followed me to hell and didn't even know it.

Lily snorted, but a small, thrilled smile teased her lips, which told me she loved the edge of danger. "Thanks for looking out."

I didn't tell her I knew old man Garibaldi or that he wouldn't have cared I'd broken in because he was my deceased mother's favorite cousin.

I didn't tell her he'd left Tommaso's ring out 'for cleaning' on a velvet cushion, so it would be easy to pilfer.

"What is that?" Lily moved toward me when the ring in my fingers

caught the low light from the street.

"Tommy's gift to you."

She reached for my hand to lower it but didn't touch the ring, as if it had teeth and she was in danger of its bite. "God, that's ugly."

It was easy to agree with her. The diamond was large, but garishly cut into the shape of a heart on a rose gold band. It was too gaudy, too girly and sweet for my poisonous Lily.

"It's not you," I told her.

She looked up at me through her lashes and cocked her head. "If you know me so well, Amato, what is *me*?"

I moved away to peruse the glass cases and almost immediately found the perfect one. I picked the lock and hid the ring in my hand before walking back slowly to Lily.

"If you were to get married to the man you love and not the man your family wants for you," I started, stalking toward her, "he would be dark and dashing enough to surprise you constantly, to keep you on your toes. He wouldn't ask Paolo for permission. He would whisk you away in the middle of the night, stolen straight from your bed, and take you somewhere dark and intimate, say... a crypt or a confessional. He'd fuck you senseless before asking the question just because he couldn't keep his dirty hands off your tight body, and in your post-orgasm haze, you'd think it was a dream."

I stopped before her, eyes locked to her dazed, dreamy gaze as I dropped to my knees and produced the ring I'd picked for her. A large, princess-cut black diamond on a white gold band. Simple, dark, and utterly compelling.

Her fingers reached out to touch it, hovering as if asking for permission.

I continued, "You'd think it was a dream because you're living in a nightmare, where you marry the mafia prince instead of the villain."

"What are you saying, Frankie?"

I didn't know what I was saying. I was just giving voice to the impossible dream that seemed to link us like spider webbing, an

inescapable and deadly trap.

"I'm saying, he's not right for you and I'm not either. I'm saying I'm sorry you might die for this."

Lily stared down at me, transforming before my eyes. Chin tilted, hair tossed over her straightened shoulders, face set to benevolence like a queen faced with her subject.

"Well, then," she practically purred. "Let's make sure I go out with bang instead of a whimper."

Her lips swallowed my dark chuckle. She fell into my arms. We went tumbling to the ground, where we fucked for hours, until her pussy was raw and so swollen I couldn't fit a finger inside her, until we were glued together with sweat, wet and dried.

We fucked like convicts on death row.

The metaphor couldn't have been more fitting, because the next day, the day of Lily's wedding, neither of us doubted she might die.

Chapter Eight

LILY

I held lilies between my palms.

Papà thought it would be cute.

Poetic, even.

Lilies for my Lily, he'd said, handing them to me before we were set to begin.

They weren't the poisonous kind, and he didn't realize I thought of death every time I looked at them, especially as I walked down the aisle in my hundred-thousand-dollar wedding gown.

A gaggle of Vitali and Amato children held my train. Papà's arm steadied me, more threatening than reassuring. In front of me, a row of bridesmaids I'd barely spoken to in my life stood at the front of the chapel, hand-plucked by the Vitali elders.

My soon-to-be-husband was a virtual stranger, so much so, I only just noticed the small mole above his eye as I inched closer. And I had absolutely no idea who his groomsmen were or if he'd even been the one to select them.

Each step closer was a step closer to my death.

I'd lost my virginity.

In the very confession booth I'd just passed.

I hadn't even considered the consequences over the fog of lust that clouded me whenever Frankie Amato neared. The same Frankie sitting close to the front with a few other Amato members.

I was so fucked.

I would never make it past the deflowering ceremony, let alone the honeymoon to poison my husband.

The option of excommunication was rarely given, and such benevolence was wasted on Carlotta, who'd dismissed the idea with a fucking laugh. I passed Frankie, swallowed the lump in my throat, and forced myself not to stare at him too long.

I expected him to wink at me. A wicked spark in his eyes or something equally playful. But he appeared serious. More serious than I'd ever seen him.

My final step onto the alter felt like the last I'd ever take.

Tommaso smiled at me while his eyes descended a path to the swells of my cleavage. "You look beautiful," he mouthed.

I swallowed the vomit climbing up my throat and shifted my attention to Father Luigi. The sympathy in his eyes was almost too much. Maybe that was why he kept it short and skipped over most of the vows.

"Liliana Aurora Vitali and Tommaso Roberto Amato, have you come here freely and without reservation to give yourselves to each other in marriage?"

"I have," I lied.

Freely? What a joke.

"I have," Tommaso echoed.

"Will you honor each other as man and wife for the rest of your lives?"

God, I hope not.

"I will," we spoke in unison.

"Will you accept children lovingly from God and bring them up according to the law of Christ and his church?"

Children with Tommaso sounded as appealing as binge-eating rotten eggs.

"I will," I lied. Again.

How many lies did it take to burn in flames on the alter steps? This had to be some sort of blasphemy. At this point, I welcomed the flames. It would happen sooner or later. Better now than during the deflowering ceremony.

"I will," Tommaso parroted.

Father Luigi continued, "Do you, Tommaso Roberto Amato, take Liliana Aurora Vitali as your lawfully wedded wife, to have and to hold, from this day forward, for better, for worse, for richer, for poorer, in sickness and in health, until death do you part?"

Tommaso winked at me. "I do."

"Do you, Liliana Aurora Vitali, take Tommaso Roberto Amato as your lawfully wedded husband, to have and to hold, from this day forward, for better, for worse, for richer, for poorer, in sickness and in health, until death do you part?"

Fuck me. Fuck me. Fuck me.

My eyes shuttered closed. I couldn't say this with them open. No way. "I do."

I tuned out the rest of his words. Father Luigi took his time blessing the rings. I plucked a thick band from a satin pillow and slid it on Tommaso's finger, careful to touch as little of his skin as I could. He grabbed the replacement ring, a thinner band with a smaller diamond than the original gaudy one Frankie had stolen from the jeweler's.

I preferred this smaller one over that monstrosity, but Tommaso's lips turned down with displeasure as he slid it up my finger.

The weight of the ring felt like shackles, binding me to a man I couldn't stand, a life I'd never chosen, a future that ended in my death.

I barely focused in time to hear Father Luigi finish his speech. "You

may now kiss the bride."

The second Tommaso's dry lips touched mine, my eyes shot open. His tongue dove past my lips, stroking every surface it could reach. I drowned in his saliva, wishing it would end. That I could fade away.

Away from my family.

Away from this church.

Away from the hoots and hollers of the made men in the audience.

And finally—fucking finally—when I couldn't take it anymore, my eyes slid to where Frankie sat, his expression harder than the granite lining the church floors.

And I realized, if this was to be my last kiss, I didn't want it to Tommaso's.

I wanted it to be Frankie's.

Chapter Nine

FRANKIE

Watching Lily marry fuck-face Tom was the hardest thing I'd ever done in my life, and that included watching Manuel decide between death and excommunication.

At least Manuel had a choice.

Lily had none.

No one else would have noticed the strain in her delicate jaw. The way her hands strangled the lilies in her grip until the spines snapped and the blooms lilted to the left.

No one else knew what hell she was going through in this holy place, because no one knew Liliana Vitali.

Not really.

Not even me.

But what I did know made me crave her to the point of sin.

My lust consumed me enough to give me a hard on just watching her at the altar in virgin's white.

My envy enough to spur my imagination to morbid daydreams, where

Tommaso's blood was wet and hot on my hands. A murderous baptism as I plunged a knife into his back.

My greed and gluttony were so acute, my stomach cramped and my hands itched to stalk to the front of the church, rip open her expensive dress with a mighty tear, and gorge myself on her sweet body for all to watch.

And I was proud enough to believe I could have her against all the odds.

As I watched her marry a man who was in every way inferior to her, the only sin I followed through on was sloth.

I sat there, and I watched.

By the time the ceremony ended, my heart had successfully corrupted my more highly evolved instincts.

The beast that lurked in the pit of my belly broke free from its bonds, overriding my humanity. I was an animal with hatred. All instincts. No conscious. Wild and deadly.

When Tommaso disappeared behind a door near the altar, I followed.

He was tall, maybe handsome if you liked men with weak chins and weaker minds.

But he was no match for me.

The shadows were deep between the narrow walls of the ancient church, so he didn't notice me until I was on him. My arm banded around his throat like a boa, compressing the scream that rose to a soft wheeze.

"Did you enjoy that kiss with your new bride, Tommy?" I hissed into his ear, raised the knife in my free hand to his belly, and played the edge against the thin fabric of his dress shirt. "I sure as fuck hope so, because it's as close to Liliana as you'll ever get again."

"You're a dead man," he managed to croak before I slammed him up against a wall.

The tip of my knife dug into his side so hard, it tunneled through the fabric and skin. Red bloomed like a flower over his kidney.

"You were a dead man the moment you put your mouth on what's mine," I growled, lost to the dark pleasure of my rage. "Any last words,

Tom? Before I stick you like the suckling pig they served at your wedding dinner?"

"Fuck. You." His weak gasps barely reached my ears.

"I'll pass. But I did fuck your wife, and trust me," I paused, angling the knife so it slid beautifully between his ribs, "if I'm dead like you say, it was fucking worth it to see Liliana's blood smeared on my cock as I took her."

He dragged in a raspy breath of furious surprise. It choked off into a wet gurgle when I plunged the blade into his body and the tip broached his poisonous heart.

I held him close as his struggles weakened, just to feel the life leave his body.

This was the man who was ready to indenture Lily to a loveless marriage just so he could rise in the ranks. This was the man who was willing to rape her on their wedding night, because he felt it was his right.

This was the man who'd insisted Don Amato kill my brother.

And now, in some Shakespearean twist I knew Lily and her dark heart would relish just as much as I did, he was nothing.

Because he was dead.

It was too easy, really.

I disposed of Tommaso's corpse in the crematorium attached to the back of the church and snuck through town into the courtyard of the Vitali home I'd been stalking for weeks.

It was tradition for the bride to lose her virginity in the house of her father. A symbol of her passing from his possession to that of her husband's.

Lily hated the patriarchal cast of our culture. Knowing her and what it was doing to her, I did, too.

Everything I'd ever known and believed in was poisoned by this feeling that bloomed in my chest. Maybe I'd sprung a new organ. One

bigger and stronger than the one that had pumped my heart before.

And with each beat of this new pulse, it seemed one name echoed through my thoughts.

Lily.

I had to get to her.

Because of my mindless obedience to the laws written by my forefathers, I'd manipulated and seduced her like sport. And now, she was going to die for it.

Killing Tom wasn't enough.

I had to ensure she lived, even if it was only for one more day.

The Vitali house was oddly quiet as they prepared for the deflowering ceremony. Servants hustled with heads down, lighting candles and placing flowers in a path leading up to the bedroom.

Lily was the only one in her chamber, sitting on the edge of her bed with the curtains of the four-poster bed tied open on one side. Her eyes fixated out the window, across the street to the place I'd sat and watched her. She was lost to her thoughts, face pale, lips in a thin, pressed line.

Before the bed, a row of padded leather seats had been laid out like the seats of a luxury theater. Within minutes, they'd be filled by representatives from all major Sicilian families. All there to witness her supposed deflowering.

When I padded across the floor and leaned into the bed, Lily didn't stir. My breath wafted over her neck a second before my hand wrapped around it.

"What a pretty fake virgin you are," I whispered, squeezing her throat when she jumped and tried to turn to me. "What a lovely, filthy little liar."

"Frankie," she breathed. A shiver ripped up her spine. "What are you doing here? They see you, and we're both dead."

"Don't you want to live a little before you die?" I breathed, running my nose down her ear and inhaling her fragrant floral perfume that made my dick hard. "What are the odds of either of us getting out of this alive?"

"Tommaso and the Council will be here any minute," she argued, even

as she tilted her head to give my lips better access to her neck.

"Then, we'd better close the curtains." I pulled her farther onto the bed and into my arms.

She gasped at my touch. It occurred to me that, if we died tonight, it would be intwined with lies. It shouldn't have mattered, but it did.

I slipped her silk robe off her shoulders and ran the pad of my thumb across her collarbone. "I lied to you."

Fierce eyes met mine. So strong for a wilting lily. "Why doesn't that surprise me?"

"A union between the Brunos and Vitalis would weaken the Amatos. They sent me to ruin your marriage."

Anger flew across her face before resignation took its place. "They sent you to take my virginity. It was all a game."

I lifted her hand and pressed it to my heart. It beat faster at her touch. "Does this feel like a game?"

"You're such a talented liar, I have no doubt you could convince your heart to lie for you." Her nails scraped my skin, digging into my chest as if she intended to tear it from my flesh. "You're not a good person, Francesco Amato."

"I'm evil, my poisonous Lily, and you like it."

Her eyes flashed with warning, but I was right, and she knew it. "You need to leave. They'll see you. Tommaso—"

"Fuck Tom. The only man inside you will be *me*."

I sunk my teeth into her neck and sucked hard, bringing a bruise to the surface. A physical reminder of my possession. When I was done, I pulled back to study the wet purpling skin and adjusted her small form, so she laid spread out for me on the pristine white bedspread.

I rose to my knees over her and leaned to flick the curtains closed, ensconcing us in warm, sheltered darkness, sheer enough to hide all but the shape of our bodies.

She laid there on her back, slim legs spread, that flush I loved warming her skin to rose gold. Desire rimmed her eyes. She might not have

said it verbally, but with every inch of her body, she told me she trusted me.

And I intended to take ruthless advantage of that.

I fell on her, hands in her hair, tugging and twisting. Her mouth fell open in a gasp for my plundering tongue. She tasted of communion wine and heat so incendiary it sent flames racing through my blood.

Heavy footsteps pounded the old wooden steps leading to the bedroom, followed by low grumbling voices speaking in antiquated Italian.

The Council had arrived.

Lily stiffened beneath me as she heard them too, but I didn't let her protest.

Instead, I reached beneath the hem of her long lace dress and ran my fingers up her thigh until I reached her underwear. I pulled back, so I could see her eyes, and smirked at her as I snapped the fabric between my fingers.

"I own this pussy," I whispered into her ear and played my fingers in her soaking wet folds. "The moment I broke your hymen, you were mine."

"Only because I didn't want my fate dictated by others," she argued, and fuck me, if I didn't love her sass even in the face of such a fucked-up situation.

"And you chose the more charming of two evils," I teased, sliding two fingers inside her and watching her brown eyes blow to black with lust.

"I was damned whomever I chose."

Her breath stuttered when I pulled away and unzipped my pants to tug out my steel cock. It visibly throbbed, weeping a pearl of precum just at the idea of being inside her again. Her little fingers tore at my shirt until it opened.

She brushed the piercing on my nipple, surprised by its existence. We knew so little of each other, but it was enough.

Around us, hidden by the curtain, the councilmen took their seats. A rush of heeled footsteps pattered across the floor, signaling their escorts had arrived.

I slotted my hot crown against Lily's wet entrance and teased her by thrusting just the tip back and forth inside her. "At least this way, you'll

earn your spot in hell."

And then, in one cruel thrust, I seated myself inside her.

Her yelp of lust-tinged pain echoed in throughout the room, prompting a low murmur of pleased voices from outside the curtain and a swell of applause.

Liliana's virtue was long gone. All that remained was the corrosive, dangerous levels of desire swallowing us whole.

"Brace," I warned her, voice low for only her to hear. "I plan to give these old perverts a show they won't ever forget."

Her nostrils flared, but her limbs wrapped around me almost as tightly as her pussy around my cock. "I want them to hear you make me cum."

I groaned, shoving my face in her neck, so I could lick and suck at the salty skin there. My hand arrowed between our bodies, playing and pinching at her swollen clit.

She mewled and arched like a cat into my body, needing more.

I thrust shallowly, dragging the head of my cock against her front wall until she writhed and begged for more.

"You like my cock, don't you, Lily?" Her moans drowned out my low murmurs. I squeezed the raspberry peak of her breast and thrummed my thumb against her clit. "You want to come all over me, don't you?"

In answer, she threw her head back into the pillow, mouth pink and slack as she hissed then scream with pleasure and came apart all around me. I gritted my teeth at her walls clenched around me like a fist, desperate to fuck her hard through the climax while staving off my own.

I wanted to fuck her until that newly broken-in cunt was swollen closed with overuse.

"Bite me," I ordered as she panted after coming. I pressed my wrist to her damp lips. "Do it, Lily."

"I don't want to hurt you."

"Your death would hurt me more. Now, bite me."

Her eyes flashed. She bared her little teeth and wrapped a hand around my wrist. I groaned, cock kicking. She tore into my skin, blood spilling

over her lips.

Quickly, I pulled my hand away and smeared the blood between her thighs, against my dick as I held it halfway inside her wet heat, and across those pure white sheets beneath us.

"You bled for me," I whispered into her ear when I'd finished. Red still glistened on her lips. I leaned down to lick it clean, kissing her deeply. "Now, I bleed for us."

Her moan vibrated through our bloody kiss, her hips surging up against me, already eager for me.

"My slutty virgin," I practically purred, dragging my cock out of her tight folds and savagely beating back into her. Again and again until sweat beaded on her crown and her legs shook. "My poisonous Lily loves to be fucked, don't you?"

"Only by you." She gasped when I hit that spot inside her that made her soar.

"You like my thick cock inside your snug cunt?" I needed to possess her in every way. Needed to hear how much she wanted me. To see if it was anywhere close to as much as I wanted her.

"Yes," she chanted. I planted another bruise against the minute swell of her breast. "Yes, yes, yes."

"I'm going to come with you," I warned and grounded my hips against her, the wet sounds of our joined bodies loud in the cocooned bed. "Deep inside you, so you're entirely filled up with my cum, and when you face the Council, it will drip down your thighs."

"Oh my God," she cried out, so loud, the soft sound of the escorts pleasing the councilmen paused for a brief second. Lily's eyes squeezed shut. She clutched me to her and convulsed with the violence of her second orgasm. "Please, I need to feel you cum inside me."

I was a goner the second those breathy words left her lips. The base of my spine tightened. With a roar like a conquering heathen, I planted myself to the root inside her and came.

Again, our climaxes were met with leering calls and applause from the

old men gathered around the bed, ruining the bliss of our post-coital glow.

"Come, child," Paolo Vitali called from beyond the veil. "Present to us your bedclothes and the evidence of your union."

Lily bit her lip, her eyes wide with panic. I brushed my hand over her forehead into her hair and anchored her with a sharp tug.

"You're fine, my poisonous Lily," I murmured against her lips. "There's blood to show, and no one will be any the wiser. They'll leave the room after you've shown them what they want to see."

"The wrong man is in my bed," she hissed, careful to keep her voice low.

I cocked my head, studying the sweet blush in her cheeks, loving the way she still clung to me even after our fuck. "Maybe, but I think the right man is in your heart. If you want a different kind of life than the one your father has bought you, you'll go on your honeymoon as planned. I will find a way to meet you there."

"Are you serious?" she gasped. "There's no way."

"You let me worry about that," I ordered, punctuating my words with a hard kiss before I rolled off her and started to strip the sheets off the bed. "Now get your sweet naked ass out there. The pervy old guys want to see my cum and your blood on your pretty thighs."

She hesitated for only a moment before collecting the sheets. A thin layer of sweat and lust coated her naked body.

Before parting the veil, she paused to look over her shoulder at me and whisper, "If this is the last thing I do, I'm glad it was with you."

And then she slid out from the curtains, naked and beautiful and mine.

A moment later, a raucous cheer erupted from the men, and I knew it was done.

Liliana was saved from death and disgrace.

Now, I had to make sure I would be, too.

Chapter Ten

LILY

I'd never been inside the High Council's chambers, but the fact that I still had Frankie's cum dripping down my inner thigh as I sat before the Council seemed on brand with the shit show of my life.

Papà sat near the center of the elevated curved benches, right beside Uncle Vanni, my cousin Renata's dad. Growing up, she'd described him as cruel and vicious. I'd never talked to him long enough to confirm her assertion, but gossip ran rampant in Sicily.

Mamma's best friend Luna once whispered about how Uncle Vanni had forced his wife Margot, a frenchwoman who'd had the misfortune of marrying into my family, to have a threesome with them.

The hottest orgasm of my life, Zia Luna confessed over a cup of *Lavazza*.

I'd run to my room and looked up the words "threesome" and "orgasm," falling down the rabbit hole of Pornhub for a solid hour before Papà knocked on the door to check on me. The same Papà currently staring at me like I'd chopped off his arm and fed it to one of Carole Baskin's

tigers.

"Do you know why you are here, Liliana?" Uncle Vanni's voice boomed across the chambers.

Representatives of every major mafia family flanked him on the raised bench, including my husband's and paramour's. The sight would have intimidated me, had I not been so resigned to my death. Maybe that was why I hadn't bothered holding back during the deflowering ceremony.

If it was going to be my last time, I wanted it to feel good.

And it did.

Holy shit, it did.

They say sex follows love.

I wondered what follows sex.

Probably nothing short of a miracle.

I sighed, drawing it out as if it'd change my fate. "No."

"We will ask a series of questions about the events that took place two hours ago in the ceremonial chamber."

"I'm not sure what I could tell you that you don't already know. You all were there with me."

They'd probably enjoyed it, too. I'd heard a few groans and grunts past the canopy. No matter how serious they made the deflowering ceremony seem, rumor still had it that escorts were rushed in and out of the ceremony before the bloodied sheets were offered.

I didn't even have it in me to blush at the thought of these men getting off with me.

The don of the Amato family cleared his throat. "Our vision was blurred by the veil."

Piero Bruno sneered at me. "We couldn't tell it wasn't my son you were fucking."

I wanted to shutter my eyes shut, to fade away into the wall and reappear when it was safe. Instead, I swallowed my reaction long enough for Uncle Vanni to speak.

"Enough, Piero."

He slammed both palms on the table before him. "My only son is dead!"

My jaw nearly unhinged itself. I let it, playing on that shock to convince them of my innocence. I mean, I was innocent. And shocked. But I had no doubt in my mind who would kill Tommaso. Hint: He possessed the filthiest mouth, wielded an eight-inch dick, and had a name that rhymed with Spanky.

I shook my head. "My husband is dead?"

Piero scoffed. "Don't play coy."

"I was just with him in the chamber..."

"You were with Frankie Amato."

How could they possibly know that? They'd left the room before we did. Someone had to have told them, and I doubted it was Frankie.

I feigned shock. "I... I didn't know. It was dark. I thought it was Tommaso. We'd never had... intercourse before. I couldn't have known it wasn't him."

No one was buying my excuses, least of all Piero. "You dirty whor—"

"Enough." Uncle Vanni cast a firm look at my father-in-law. "We're family now, Piero, and we do plenty of lucrative business together. Certainly, you value your relationship with the Vitali, yes?"

He swallowed his retort. "I do."

"I believe my niece." Uncle Vanni lifted a brow. "Do you?"

"I do."

Despite Piero's begrudging tone, I relaxed. This had gone the opposite of how I thought it would. I was safe, for now... but what about Frankie?

Chapter Eleven

I had a plan.

Lily would leave on her honeymoon today with her new husband, only poor Tom was dead, ashes dissolved in the Tyrrhenian sea. I would take his place. It was easy to bribe the pilot to allow me on the plane early, a stow away until the jet took off for Malta.

Then, we'd disappear.

Lily and me.

To a life across the sea in America, where we could carve out our own future.

I already had an in with an old friend of mine, Dante Salvatore, who'd recently set up shop in the Camorra outfit in New York City.

I was ready to leave the motherland and their old customs for the slick shine and more lenient moral bent of the New World.

Hopefully, Lily was, too.

My bag was packed, a small leather backpack with photos of Manuel and a cold million in cash I'd stolen from our cache in the family crypt.

I was seconds from leaving when a knock sounded at my apartment door. Frowning, I checked my 9mm handgun before tucking it back in my waistband and answering the door.

It was the last person I'd expected.

"Angelo?"

A grim smile split his face. "Can I come in?"

I hesitated, opened the door, and stepped out of the way to allow him entry. "What the hell are you doing here?"

Lily's plane was due to leave in three hours. I couldn't miss the window to climb onboard.

Angelo fidgeted with his cuffs, then adjusted the angle of a family photo I kept on the fireplace mantle.

"Angelo?" I prompted, even as my belly clenched with foreboding.

We were not friends.

Not really.

It was impossible to have true camaraderie in a family where you were encouraged to step on the heads of your brothers in the quest for more power. Sometimes, I wondered if that wasn't the problem with the Amatos. If we might've accrued more power like the Vitalis by encouraging our relations instead of pitting them against each other like gladiators.

He heaved out a dramatic sigh and wiped his sweating hands on his trousers, leaving behind slimy trails like a snail. "You need to prepare."

"For?"

But fuck, I already knew.

Something had gone wrong. Something that meant all my well-laid plans would crumble to ash and dust just like Tommaso's body in the flames.

"The Vitalis know you took Liliana's virginity. Now that Tommaso Bruno is missing, they assume you are the cause." Angelo paused, bit his lip, and shrugged. "They want you dead."

I sucked a deep breath through my teeth, struggling for nonchalance to mark my turmoil. "I see. Given Liliana herself was the only person outside

of the Amatos that knew about this, I'm assuming our family had something to do with it?"

Angelo hesitated and nodded. "Don Amato offered them my hand in marriage given I'm one of the last eligible bachelors. He suggested your head on a platter to appease them of this unfortunate situation."

"Mmm," I hummed even as my heart beat like a wild thing in my chest. "So, I'm the scape goat." I noticed the way he shifted uneasily and swallowed the swell of dread that rose with the bile at the back of my tongue. "This was the real plan all along, wasn't it?"

"It seems Don Amato never trusted you again after what your brother did," Angelo admitted. "Two birds, one stone."

"Clever old *bastardo*, isn't he?"

Angelo blinked. "You seem... very unperturbed by this."

"If the same thing happened to you, would you really be so shocked?" I countered, pushing off the wall to stalk toward him. "In a family like ours, do you really feel safe? I am guessing the answer is *no*, considering you're here to warn me and get me out of town despite the fact that you've been jealous of me all our lives."

"You're a prick," he spat.

"A prick who's right," I said with grim satisfaction. "Well, congrats, Angelo. Isn't this what you've always wanted? To best me?"

"Not like this."

"No... It's better to earn your fate than have it force fed to you, especially when it's poisoned like this. Still, I appreciate the heads up, and I hope you get a nice flexible Vitali girl to warm your bed and lay some more rungs on your ladder to success."

"What're you going to do?" He glanced out the window. "They'll be here soon to take you away. I think...I think they mean to offer you the same choice as they did Manuel. The poisonous lily or banishment."

I snorted. "You know, Angelo, I think I'll choose both."

Epilogue

FRANKIE

Three years later.

I fucking loved New York.

She was a woman, and she was a bitch of a female.

Dark, gritty, and ruthless. Wrapped in a flashy dress with good hair, so you didn't notice how savage she could be until it was too late, and she caught you in her snare.

She was good to me, because I respected her.

I carried a gun on my person when I walked the dark alleys at night, doing work for the Camorra that I'd never been given the responsibility of in my first life as an Amato foot soldier.

In the New World with my new school crew, the Salvatores, I was consigliere.

Third man from the top and secure in my position, because I'd fucking earned it.

After I arrived in the city a broken man with a backpack of cash and a chest echoing from a shattered heart, there was nothing for me to lose in joining up with Amadeo and Dante.

And everything to gain, save one thing.

Liliana Vitali.

I fucked my way through New York's glamorous women. The ones that wanted me to use my dirty money to wine and dine them at the best restaurants before taking them home to fuck them senseless with my hands over their throat like the animal they sensed I was.

Each woman was faceless, nameless, and gone from my mind the moment I left her bed.

There were a few who tried to tame me, but the three Salvatore men were confirmed bachelors and infamous for it in a dozen social circles. It was what made us so powerful.

No women to wrap us around their little fingers and twist us away from our prize.

We were powerful and rich, but truthfully, I was *bored*.

"Am I boring you?" Dante drawled, his low voice bringing me out of my thoughts.

I turned my gaze to him, my face infused with ennui. "Would you stop talking if I said yes?"

His big face (he was a big man) broke open into his charming bastard smile. The smile that had secured us many deals over the years and broken even more hearts.

"No. Sometimes you forget, it is me who is in charge of you, *capisco*?"

I tapped my cigar against the crystal ashtray on the table between us and looked out over the New York nightscape again. "Whatever helps you sleep at night, *capo*."

He grunted, but it was amused, and he let it slide. Dante was the boss, no matter that Amadeo, his pseudo-father, was the figurehead of our operation. It was Dante that held the strings of our many enterprises and the fates of his many men in one hand like a master puppeteer. He did it without breaking a sweat and making enemies.

He inspired trust and love, because he was a *good* boss and a good

man if you excused his piss poor morals.

It was no wonder we'd bonded intractably almost the moment we reconnected four years ago.

We were cut from the same cloth.

And we understood, as my dead-to-me family had not, that you could reign supreme without being a complete dickhead.

"I've got to meet Cosima and my brother for dinner, but before I stop 'bothering you,' I've got something for you," D ventured, tone casual.

Too casual.

My instincts prickled, and my eyes narrowed as I looked over at him. "Do you?"

He leaned back in his chair and dangled the sweating glass of whiskey between two fingers. "There's talk of a new player in town."

I scoffed. "New players are a dime a dozen, and their currency goes just as far."

He stared at me implacably, which made my heart drop into my stomach.

"Who is it?" I asked, quieter than I would have liked.

Afraid of my own question.

"I'm not sure. But I think they could be a high-risk rival. I need you to do your stalker thing and find out whatever you can about this woman. She's quickly becoming one of the Romano family's top distributors."

The Romano family weren't our rivals exactly. They dabbled in different enterprises than us for the most part, but they were dangerous nonetheless, and Dante liked to know everything about everyone, so I wasn't surprised.

"I'm on it. Hey, maybe she's hot and I can introduce her properly to New York society."

The woman went by the name of Capulet.

A pseudonym if ever I saw one.

And not even a very good one.

Why anyone would want to bear the moniker of the heroine in one of the greatest romantic tragedies ever told was beyond me.

Though, I had to admit, it was a little badass.

Other than her street name, it was impossible to dig up information on her in the system. And I was good. In the intervening years since I'd come to New York, I'd made tech my bitch. Now I was a hacker in leagues with the best of them.

But this Capulet had no online files.

The only paper trail I could find was for a warehouse apartment she bought in Brooklyn with cash eight months ago.

I made my way there, dodging into the abandoned warehouse across from her. It was in the process of being renovated into luxury apartment like the one she occupied, smelled of wet paint, and possessed no furniture beside the folding chair I brought with me, along with my flask of *grappa* and night vision binoculars.

The lights blazed from the massive square windows, so the latter weren't necessary.

I could see nearly every inch of Capulet's apartment, so I leaned back, untwisted the cap on my engraved flask, and settled in for a boring night of spying.

Steam fogged the small window to the bathroom, so I gathered she was taking a shower. I adjusted myself uncomfortably in my jeans as I thought of the first time I'd watched Liliana in Gerosa, how sweet and innocent she had been in her room.

Three years later, and I still couldn't get a handle on my desire for her. I'd looked her up countless times, but when Dante discovered my obsession, he'd put a swift end to it, calling me weak for lusting after a woman that would never be mine.

He was one to talk. I was fifty percent sure he held a serious torch for his brother's wife, but that was a story even more complicated than my

own.

Last I'd heard of Liliana Vitali, she was about to be remarried to some poor prick in Gerosa.

The woman in the window drew my attention as she turned off the bathroom light and moved into her well-lit bedroom, wearing only a white towel. She had long black hair. Italian hair. It swished in wet ropes over her slim shoulders. I only had the view of her back, but I knew she was beautiful just by the grace of her step.

My mouth went dry as the towel dropped without fanfare. The entire span of her golden tanned back was exposed to my greedy gaze.

Fuck me, she was more than beautiful.

Exquisite.

She bent slowly to retrieve something from the chest of drawers, thin thighs spread, plump ass tipped to the sky, so I could see the dark shadow of her sex even from a distance.

My cock was hard as a steel pipe.

I watched with my heart in my throat as she shimmied into a pair of black underwear that barely covered her ass. As she moved to the side of her bed, I noticed, with a shock like ice water dumped over my head, she had a vase filled with lilies.

Mind numb, I watched as she plucked a bloom and laid back on the bed to trail the silken petals over the small swell of her breasts, then down, down to her pussy, where she swirled the petals the way I was sure I'd once swirled my tongue.

"Holy fuck," I breathed and stood up so abruptly my chair fell over and my flask dropped with a clang to the rooftop.

As if drawn by my expletive, the woman named Capulet, the woman I knew more intimately than God, rolled over on the bed so her face was in full view of the window.

Lily in hand, smile affixed to a face that had somehow grown even more beautiful, Liliana Vitali locked eyes with me across the street, across three years and a lifetime of regret, and erased all of it with a single wink.

LILY

Six Years Later

This was probably the last scene my husband would expect to come home to—homemade food spread across our kitchen island like I was some sort of domestic goddess. He would call bullshit, and he'd be right.

Lucy Black had made it.

My twins were on the balcony, fighting over the attention of her son. She stood in front of the oven, adjusting the temperature, wearing the apron neither I nor Frankie had ever worn in the six years we'd owned this Central Park brownstone.

(In my defense, New York take out is the best. Hands down.)

I cocked my hip against the island and watched her. "Smells good."

"It's lasagna." She moved to the stove and tasted the sauce simmering in a pot. "Asher's favorite."

"I should've added pasta con le sarde to our menu." A smirk curved my lips upright. "It's Frankie's favorite."

Lucy scrunched her nose. "Ew. Pasta with sardines? Really? Sounds like cat food."

"Well, he does like pussy…"

She swung to face me, jaw a little slack, before her head pivoted to the open balcony door to make sure the kids hadn't heard. "Damn it, Lil! This is why I made the kids play outside!"

I tipped a shoulder up and nodded at the empty wine bottle. "I thought it was because you wanted to day drink."

She erupted into giggles. "That, too."

When I'd landed in New York, Renata had hooked me up with the Romano family. They were my suppliers, while I was one of their top distributers. An added bonus—I'd met one of my best friends Lucy. She

was married to their former fixer, billionaire real estate and tech mogul Asher Black.

Frankie and I had carved out a nice life in New York, better than we could have ever imagined. He worked for the Salvatore family. I worked with the Romano family. And every night, we came home to our kids, barely able to keep our hands off one another long enough to feed the girls and help them with their homework.

The front door creaked open. At the sound, the kids sprinted to the entryway. If they could hear the door open, they'd probably heard my pussy comment. In my defense, Frankie wasn't any better at keeping it PG.

"A pussy is a cat!" I yelled out, just in case my kids decided to Google it.

Lucy groaned at the same time Asher said from the hallway, "Did she just say what I think she said?"

My husband, my dearest defender, replied, "Probably."

"We're in here!" I shouted out, stealing a red velvet macaroon from the counter.

Frankie entered, followed closely by Asher. He eyed the spread and nodded at it. "Thanks for the lunch, Luce."

"Hey, I helped!" I picked up a Himalayan salt shaker, thought better of ruining one of the dishes, and gave up on proving my point.

"Sure, you did." He plucked the shaker from my fingers and tossed it on the counter. Then, he folded me into his arms, copped a feel of my ass, and whispered in my ear, "Liars get spanked."

I tipped my head up, rested my chin on his chest, and quirked an eyebrow. "Why do you think I lied?"

He squeezed my ass again and leaned back. "A pussy is a cat?"

"Yes."

"I can't wait to *pet* my cat tonight."

Lucy hip-checked me out of the way and pulled the lasagna out of the oven. "You two are gross and no longer allowed around my son."

She liked to pretend Rowan wasn't a deviant in the making... Or

maybe she genuinely believed it, but it didn't change the fact that he'd had every girl fawning over him from a young age, which always meant trouble.

"Fair enough." I tried and failed to hide my smile, but I couldn't.

I was happy.

Completely, entirely, wholeheartedly… happy.

Because I wasn't a virgin anymore, I served no real use to the Vitali family. They'd released me from a future of arranged marriages. Papà knew I'd be miserable, so he and Mamma had let me leave Italy. They even flew here to visit a few times a year.

I took a bite of another macaroon and tossed the remaining half to Frankie. "How was *fishing*?"

He caught it and ate the rest. "You don't have to say it like that. We were actually fishing."

"Sure." I made quotation marks with my fingers. "Fishing."

A former Romano fixer and an Italian-born made man leave on an overnight fishing trip? Sure… I was certain a dead body was involved somehow.

"Okay, we weren't fishing."

"I knew it was bullshit! Who'd you kill? Another Bruno?"

"Lil!" Lucy waved the cooking spoon at me like she was waving her finger. "The kids are close!"

I shrugged at her, nodded to the sauce, which was two seconds from boiling over, and returned my attention to Frankie. "Well?"

He tugged me against him. "Asher had a hookup with a botanist through Black Enterprises. We drove to Maryland to pick up flowers." When Asher entered, Frankie grabbed a pot of flowers from him and handed them to me.

"Lily of the Valley," I whispered, running my pointer finger down a petal. "They're beautiful."

"Oh, my God!" Lucy threw her hands up. "What is with you two?! Those are a one on the poison scale! As in, deadly. As in, not for kids. Your babysitting privileges are so revoked."

Asher chimed in, "They're genetically modified to not be poisonous."

Frankie plucked the pot out of my hands and placed them on the counter, grabbing me instead. "We brought back enough seeds to fill your rooftop garden with them." He tightened his arms around me, brought my ring finger to his lips, and kissed the ring. The same ring he'd picked out in that jewelry shop we'd broken into. They same ring he'd later proposed to me with. For real, this time. "Happy anniversary, Lily."

I planted my lips on his, ignoring the *ews* from the kids and Lucy's rant about PDA and the parenting books she'd read.

This was us.

Crazy. Happy. Reckless. *Free.*

Our love was venom.

The type you could never purge from your body.

The type that would either kill you or leave your poisoned heart scarred.

The End

ABOUT PARKER

Parker S. Huntington hates talking about herself, so bear with her as she awkwardly toots her own horn for a few sentences and then bids her readers adieu.

Parker S. Huntington is from Orange County, California. She graduated pre-med with a Bachelor's of Arts in Creative Writing from the University of California, Riverside. As of August 2017, the 22-years-old novelist is still pursuing a Master's in Liberal Arts (ALM) in Literature and Creative Writing from Harvard University. *Go Crimson!*

She was the proud mom of Chloe and will always look back on her moments with Chlo as the best moments of her life. She has 2 puppies—a Carolina dog named Bauer and a Dutch Shepherd and lab mix named Rose. She also lives with her boyfriend of five (going on six!) years—a real life alpha male, book boyfriend worthy hunk of a man.

If you liked the book, please leave a review wherever you can! Just a sentence or two makes a huge difference! If you didn't like this book, I'd love to hear why, too! Feel free to reach me at parkershuntington@gmail.com.

ALSO BY PARKER

Cruel Crown
Devious Lies
FT (#2)
TS (#3)

Five Syndicates
Asher Black
Niccolaio Andretti
Ranieri Andretti
Bastiano Romano
Renata Vitali
Damiano De Luca
Vincent Romano
Marco Camerino
Rafaello Rossi

ABOUT GIANA

Giana Darling is a USA Today, Wall Street Journal, Top 40 Best Selling Canadian romance writer who specializes in the taboo and angsty side of love and romance. She currently lives in beautiful British Columbia where she spends time riding on the back of her man's bike, baking pies, and reading snuggled up with her cat, Persephone.

Join my Reader's Group and Subscribe to my Newsletter

f ⓞ ⓐ �𝕐

If you enjoyed reading about Frankie and Lily's forbidden love story, you'll love Cosima's dark love story with her enigmatic Master Alexander.

ENTHRALLED and ENAMOURED are available now!

You can also read her sister, Giselle's story right now for a glimpse at what happens to Cosima and Alexander TWO YEARS after the events of Enthralled! Find out what happens when Giselle takes a vacation before reuniting with her family in New York City, and meets the French billionaire Sinclair. He is everything she never knew she wanted, but he's also taken…

One-click THE AFFAIR now!

5 HOT STEAMY AFFAIR STARS!! Get ready for a hot steamy one week holiday affair with twists and turns. Sexy Sinclair knows what he wants which is beautiful Giselle and he goes for it. These two will heat the pages up and suck you into their story. — Goodreads reviewer 5 stars

slavery… Their epic tale spans across Italy, England, Scotland and the USA across a five-year period that sees them endure murder, separation, and a web of infinite lies.

Enthralled (The Enslaved Duet #1)
Enamoured (The Enslaved Duet, #2)

The Elite Seven Series
Sloth (The Elite Seven Series, #7)

Coming Soon
Inked in Lies (The Fallen Men, #5)
AhiL (Dante's Mafia Book)

The Dirty Bargain

LYLAH JAMES AND CORA REILLY

Prologue

TALIA

The world I grew up in was defined by old-fashioned, ironclad laws, as non-negotiable as time itself.

The Bratva is our mortal enemy was at the top of this set of rules. It was ingrained in the minds of every member of the Italian mafia families from their birth, and they took this irrefutable truth to the grave with them. As a woman, I wasn't allowed to be part of the mob itself, and yet the golden cage of man-made rules determined every aspect of my life.

For a long time, I'd made my peace with it.

Today, I set out to commit the ultimate betrayal.

If I were a man, I'd be faced with the only acceptable punishment for such a crime: torture and death. My cousin Luca, the Capo of the New York Famiglia, may go more lenient on me if he ever found out. Leniency wasn't among his character traits though.

Yet, I didn't regret my decision to slip away from the watchful eyes of my bodyguard and travel to enemy territory. In the Famiglia, nobody would have helped me get revenge on the man who'd destroyed my life

when I was fifteen. He hadn't been the only one, not even the worst, but all the others had been killed. Only he remained alive—my only chance to get a taste of revenge. It was an insatiable hunger I couldn't suppress and had only grown in the five years since my family had been torn apart.

I smiled wryly. How ironic that I was on my way to ask the most notorious Bratva assassin with the telling name "Killer" to end the man I hated, when the Russians had been the reason for my family's fall from grace in the first place.

Fear and nervous excitement fought a relentless battle in my body as the plane finally landed in Miami, the place where life could change for the better or the worse.

Would Killer be my salvation…or my doom?

KILLER

Some called me a psychopath. Some said I was a heartless monster. I had been called many things in my life, and all of them were true.

Psychopath. Monster. Evil. Inhuman. Cruel. A brutal savage… I was all of that. I was people's worst nightmare. They said if I called your name thrice… it meant I was coming for you. For your life and… your soul.

The Grim Reaper was one of my many names. Angel of Death, they'd call me. But I always preferred… KILLER. My given name and the direct meaning of who I was… and what I did.

I killed for sport; I killed for hobby… and I killed for my job.

My hands were tainted with blood and countless deaths. The cage was my home and the screams of my victim? Fucking music to my ears. A goddamn lullaby.

My phone rang, pulling me out of my thoughts. I paused mid-rep as I hung upside down using the pull-up bar. My muscles strained as I closed my eyes and ignored the ringtone, focusing on finishing my workout.

Sweat trickled down the side of my temples as I gripped the bar tighter. I continued with my pull-ups, feeling my muscles burn and tighten with each movement.

The blood rushed to my head as I finished my second rep. The phone kept ringing and I bit back a curse. With a low growl, I released the bar and brought my legs down, landing on my feet without stumbling. I stalked toward the table and grabbed my phone, accepting the call without looking at who was calling me.

I already knew who it was.

"Took you long enough," a nasally, annoying voice said.

"Text me the information," I snapped. He was starting to piss me off with that attitude. I was neither his buddy nor his fucking slave.

He let out a sigh. "This job is important."

Aren't they all?

"They are paying good money," he continued.

"Name. Address. Picture," I growled into the phone. He was wasting my time and I didn't have time for little talks with a pest like him.

He released a small chuckle, but there was a hint of nervousness in it. He was scared of me. Good. He should be.

I hung up before he could say anything else. Two seconds later, my phone pinged with a message.

My lips twitched.

My veins throbbed with fierce adrenaline.

The hunt begins...

Chapter One

TALIA

From the moment I set foot in Miami yesterday, for the first time in my life outside of Italian mob territory, an almost intoxicating sense of freedom overwhelmed me. Maybe this was enemy's land, but it felt like I'd escaped my golden cage and could take my very first flight.

I bought new clothes, way more revealing than anything I'd ever been allowed to wear at home, and set out to the bar *Kazan* in Wynwood, north of downtown Miami. The Kazan was situated in one of the many converted warehouses of the area. If anyone didn't know it was Bratva owned, the majestic mural of a snarling wolf above the steel-door would have clued them in.

Nerves twisted my belly in an unrelenting grip as I entered the bar. The smell of old smoke and spilled beer hung heavily in the air. My heels clacked on the dark stone floor. Graffiti of snarling wolves, flames and Kalashnikovs adorned the walls— martial images that raised goosebumps along my skin. The bar would open in an hour, but as one of the new

waitresses, I needed to be early. The attractive Russian bartender dipped his head in greeting and raised his thumb. "Better for tips."

I flushed and gave him a small smile, realizing he was referring to my clothes. When I'd applied for the job yesterday, I'd been in my usual attire: a modest dress and flats, minimal makeup and a no-nonsense ponytail. Nothing that would fly in a bar like this. Today in my four-inch heels, mini-leather skirt and leopard-print top I fit right in. My brown hair fell in curls down my back, almost reaching my butt, and my skin felt sticky with the amount of makeup I'd plastered on my face. It didn't feel like *me*.

I went ahead to the narrow staircase at the back of the building, leading down to the underground arena. Yesterday, I hadn't been allowed downstairs but today it would be my workplace. My breath caught when I stepped into the dimly lit space. A myriad of disgusting smells hit my nose: piss, blood, vomit and shit. Bile traveled up my throat, but I swallowed it down.

I needed to get a grip if I didn't want to be fired on my first day. Then everything seemed to freeze as I spotted the fight cage in the center. It screamed death. How many people had found their brutal end within those metal bars? Goosebumps covered my skin. Now everything was deserted but tonight the room would be packed with a roaring, blood-thirsty crowd. I'd seen it on TV when my brother-in-law, Growl (my sister called him Ryan but his old name stuck with me) had watched the Darknet broadcasting of Killer's last fight. Growl was the Enforcer of the Famiglia, responsible for the dirty work, and had a penchant for brutality. But I couldn't ask him to help me get revenge since his vow bound him to his Capo and forbade him from a mission in another mafia's territory. He had helped me without realizing it anyway. Immersed in the bloody fight, he'd let it slip who Killer was and where he usually spent his time. Of course, Growl would know.

In that moment, my plan had been set in motion, and now here I was, about to start working for the Bratva to get in contact with their brutal assassin. But as I regarded my surroundings, doubt wormed its way into my

body.

"Natalia!" another waitress named Britt called.

"Only Talia," I corrected her. I'd used a little white lie to explain my Italian name: that it was short for the Russian Natalia and that sadly I didn't speak any Russian because my parents had been worried, I wouldn't learn English properly if they taught me.

Britt showed me how to work the bar and warned me to stay away from the expensive champagne and vodka bottles, which were solely reserved for the high-ranking Bratva members in the VIP glass cabin on an upper level above the fight cage. Soon I busied myself with the hustle of a bar on a Friday night until my nerves were only a distant memory. While upstairs in the official bar, a DJ heated up the crowd with a mix of Latin American rhythms and Russian club sounds from the most popular places in Moscow, in this underground hellhole, Death Metal screeched from the speakers. My skin glowed from sweat as I meandered through the crowd. The odor of sweat pressed in on me, mixing with the pungent stench of foul breath from the men around me. They weren't the kind of company I was used to. Our men mostly kept up an outward experience of normalcy, hiding the monster lurking within, but the guests of the Kazan's underground arena screamed "criminal" from afar. Their leering smiles set my teeth on edge. Luckily for me, a large number of prostitutes kept their attention occupied.

I'd almost forgotten why I'd come to Miami in the first place when, shortly after midnight, the music was turned down for the announcement of the upcoming fight. A hush went through the crowd akin to the silence of the birds of prey when a raptor crossed the sky above their home tree. I froze, my eyes darting to the doorway.

Killer's opponent appeared, a massive man with an unpronounceable name who strode purposefully toward the cage and climbed through the opening. He was a new arrival straight from Saint Petersburg. He looked monstrous, almost grotesque with his scarred, twisted face.

The crowd seemed to draw in a collective breath when, finally, Killer towered before us. My mouth ran dry at the sight of him. Now I got why

they had to import his opponents from Russia. Everyone who'd ever seen him in person wouldn't face him in a cage for all the money in the world.

The tray balanced on my palm became heavy, but I couldn't deliver it to the next customers. My legs were useless.

Killer was even taller and more muscular than his opponent. Every movement accentuated the heavy muscle under his inked skin. He stalked by me on his way to the cage, his eyes capturing mine. My head thrown back to meet his intense gaze, I shivered violently as his arm brushed mine in the barest ghost touch. In the dim light of the patio, his eyes appeared black like bottomless pools. I felt the ridiculous urge to run my fingernails over his dark buzz cut, then slowly down the myriad of tattoos adorning almost every inch of his upper body. He wasn't attractive in the conventional sense. His face too harsh, too many sharp angles and foreboding scars, and yet he oozed raw sexuality that called to a part of me forced into dormancy by the traditional rules of my upbringing.

Sucking in a sharp breath, I backed away, even if he had already passed me and stepped into the cage. My pulse galloped in my veins, a mix of animal fear and exhilarating rush. The referee threw the door of the cage shut with a resounding metallic clang that made me and half of the crowd jump.

He stepped between the fighters, explaining the rules. Then he left the cage, lifted a gun above his head and shot.

What happened after turned my insides to ice. The crowd screamed madly, calling for more blood.

Killer was more monster than man, and I had come here to ask for his help.

Chapter Two

KILLER

The cage had always given me a sense of belonging. I was born to fight, to stand inside this metal cage. Others called it a death pit… I called it home.

I made my first kill at eight years old. In a cage.

I won my first fight at eight years old. In a cage.

And I had never lost a single fucking fight since then. I had a love and hate relationship with this cage.

I loved it because it gave me a purpose.

I hated it… because it was a reminder that I was an addict.

The underground ring… this death pit called to me. My blood sang with the need to maim, to fight… to spill blood. To kill. They were right to call me a monster.

I owned this ring, I lived it, I breathed it.

The moment I stepped away from the shadows, the crowd scattered to make way for me. A path to the underground ring. My arena.

The cheers were loud, almost too loud… it was deafening. The crowd

chanted my name.

Killer. Killer. Killer.

The men thumped their chests with their fists, roaring. The women screamed, wanting to be heard… craving my attention.

They knew I'd pick one of them tonight. After my fight, after my win.

Fighting in this arena built up tension. Adrenaline that would course through my veins for hours, even after a bloody, well satisfied fight. A good fuck usually helped with the tension surging through my veins.

Tight pussy. Round ass. Pretty tits. Yeah, that usually did the job.

The women handed themselves over on a silver platter. Fuck, they crawled to me… with pleading eyes, begging for my cock.

The chants grew with an intensity as I got closer to the cage. The metal door opened and I stepped inside my arena. He was there already. My opponent.

He was big, but I was bigger.

His face looked like someone had fun with a burnt blade. His flesh didn't heal properly, the scars looking like melted skin had been stitched together over his bones. He was an ugly motherfucker as he grinned, showing me his razor-sharp teeth. There was a look in his eyes, a look that told me… this man was absolutely deranged.

My lips twitched and I fucking smiled.

Yeah, this was exactly what I needed tonight. The last few fights, I had a bunch of pussies as my opponents. They barely lasted thirty seconds and they begged for mercy before I spilled their blood.

I eyed him, feeling my muscles tense. My fingers curled around my knuckle duster. My vision became a red mist. My blood roared and my heartbeat echoed in my ears.

My brain stuttered and I exhaled my humanity.

I inhaled…death.

The gun fired; he rushed forward and I grinned. He lunged, going for my throat.

I side-stepped him and elbowed his side. He growled, furious that I

got him first. My opponent had skills... but he was slow.

I ducked as he aimed for my head and my knuckle duster slammed into his rib cage. I felt his bones crack. I swung my left fist and got him in the face.

We danced around each other and I dragged the fight out longer than I should have. He got a few punches in. My face felt swollen, but he was worse.

He got me in the stomach next and I felt my rib cage caving around my lungs. I stumbled back and hissed. He was bleeding far more than me and his moves were getting slower, less skilled, while I was barely out of breath.

Time to end this.

The next time he came at me, I lunged forward and threw my right fist up... the one with my brass knuckles. I slammed my fist into his throat and I felt it... his mangled bones. His throat caved in, his eyes widened, his breathing stuttered and he crumbled.

I saw a broken bone sticking out from the side of his neck.

His blood pooled onto the surface of the arena.

The gun fired again, indicating the end of the fight. The crowd roared at my win. My name echoed as the chants grew louder and louder.

The door opened and I stepped out of the cage. I took in the crowd as they spilled closer toward me. I growled in warning. No fucker better touch me. I was going to rip their arms out of their goddamn sockets. The adrenaline was practically bursting through my veins. I was fucking high – on this place, this crowd, the need to kill... to fuck this out of my system.

I scanned the spectators, looking for tonight's fuck.

My heart pounded for a second. My gaze snagged on her. Like she had been calling to me, as if my body recognized her and told me, *"Look, there she is."*

But she hadn't been calling for me, nor did she belong here.

Long brown hair, round eyes, plump lips and so fucking small, the crowd was practically eating her.

The look on her face... she was appalled at what she had just witnessed. A crowd roaring for blood and death. Me fighting. Me killing that man without a second thought.

She was standing against the farthest wall, as if she was trying to hide in the shadow, to blend in...

She trembled and her face paled as she brought a shaky hand up, covering her mouth. Her eyes flared with shock and... indecision.

This girl looked completely out of place. The innocence in her gaze and in the way she curled against the wall told me she didn't belong here, in this underground death pit.

This little pixie had just unknowingly walked into a monster's lair. It must have been her curiosity.

Too bad, her little curious mind brought her to me.

I took a step forward and the crowd parted for me. She noticed me, walking toward her. Her whole body was shaking and my lips curled, grinning at how frightened she looked.

I cocked an eyebrow, amused.

When I was merely a few feet away, her lips parted with a silent gasp.

Her eyes widened with fear and shock, then the girl turned on her heels and sprinted away.

She ran.

She. Fucking. Ran.

I threw my head back and laughed. *Tsk.*

Instincts kicked in. The animalistic part of me growled at the challenge.

It had been a long time since I hunted someone.

Chapter Three

TALIA

What had I been thinking?

My God.

This man...no, this monster was something straight out of hell.

I didn't stop running until I was upstairs in one of the bathroom stalls. My heart pounded in my chest, my pulse thudding fearfully in my throat. With a choked gasp, I opened the toilet lid and threw up my dinner. My stomach kept constricting. The smell of blood clung to my clothes like the memory of the man's cruel end. How he'd bled to death at Killer's feet who hadn't shown a flicker of pity.

I wanted to return to New York, forget about my daring plan and just go on with my life.

But hadn't I chosen Killer exactly because of his ruthlessness, his brutality? He was good at what he did, and I needed a man like him.

Slowly, I made my way back underground, glad to find Killer gone and a thinned-out crowd. If I wanted to stick to my plan, I needed to keep

this job. It was my only way to get close to Killer.

Only, I was terrified of having him near me after what I'd witnessed today.

Over the next two days, I worked the official bar, deemed too squeamish for the underground service—which suited me just fine.

I didn't see Killer on my shifts, but I couldn't shake off the feeling that someone was following me. I had been asking Britt and a few of the other waitresses about him, trying to figure out how best to approach him with my request, but they had been evasive, only increasing my anxiety about the matter. When I walked home at night, I could feel a presence in the shadows, knew I was being watched by the way the little hairs on my neck stood on end.

I never saw anyone, but deep down I knew it was him. The way he'd looked at me after his fight…like a lion who'd picked out the one gnu out of a herd of thousands that appeared weak.

It was close to midnight on my fourth day, when the atmosphere in the bar shifted, turning frightful. My eyes searched the room until the source of the unease came into focus. Him. Killer.

Tonight, he wasn't shirtless, a tight black t-shirt covered many of his scars and tattoos. It didn't make him appear less imposing, though. His dark eyes settled on me and didn't move on.

My hands began to tremble, the ice cubes in the glass beginning to clank together. I quickly set it down, worried I'd drop it otherwise, and looked down, away from the man who terrified and fascinated me equally.

From the corner of my eye, I saw him approach and the people in his way stepped aside almost reverently. Then he towered right in front of the bar, waiting for me to look up. Bracing myself, I lifted my face with a shaky smile "What can I get you?" My voice was too hushed, underplayed with an anxious tremor.

Killer took in my flushed face. It was a struggle to hold his penetrating stare. "Whiskey. Neat."

A small chill passed my body at his rough, deep voice. Even that

oozed danger.

I nodded hastily and reached for a bottle of whiskey.

"I hear you've been asking about me."

My fingers clenched around the bottle. I set it down on the counter and busied myself pouring it into a glass, considering what to say. "I did," I got out and shoved the glass over to him. He ignored it, his entire focus on me.

"Why?"

The word was demand, not question.

I looked up and was immediately captured by his intense gaze. Everything about him screamed danger.

Lie. Make something up. Anything.

I opened my mouth but he braced his arms on the counter between us, bringing us closer. The muscles in his strong arms flexed and beneath the ink on his forearms, countless scars glared at me, telling his story of death and brutality. His musky scent hit my nose. "The fucking truth."

It was too much. The situation. Him. Being away from home and my bodyguards for the first time in many years. But especially him.

I shook my head. "Nothing." I stumbled back and hurried through the backdoor toward the staff room, leaving the bar unattended. Only one of the bouncers sat at the worn-down table inside, having a smoke, despite the non-smoking rule.

He raised one brow, but a moment later, his expression flashed with anxiety. I knew why without turning around.

"Out," Killer growled and the bouncer didn't hesitate. He practically fled the room, leaving me alone with Killer. What was I supposed to do now?

The door clicked and then the lock turned.

Running was no longer an option.

My heart hammered wildly as I faced Killer. He simply stood there, his expression hard. "You need something from me," he muttered.

I shook my head mutely. He took a step closer and I backed away. Something flashed in his eyes, as if I'd awoken the hunter, and he stalked

toward me.

I stumbled into the wall, terrified of him. He stopped right in front of me, so close, that if he took a deep breath his chest may have brushed mine. "Tell me."

I had to crane my head all the way back to meet his gaze. It had been years since I'd been this close to a man and that hadn't been by my choice either. I swallowed, tipping up my chin to feign bravado. "I told you it's no—"

He reached out and tugged at one of my locks, his knuckles brushing my cheek in the process. I sucked in a shocked breath. His closeness was overwhelming in so many ways, my breathing came in sharp exhales.

"Tell me what you need, Little One." The name sounded like an insult coming from his harsh lips. His eyes mocked me.

And I lost it. I'd been scared out of my mind before, had watched my father getting shot in front of me, had been given away like a piece of furniture. I had survived and wouldn't let anyone treat me like a stupid child ever again. "I need you to kill someone for me," I blurted.

Chapter Four

KILLER

When I asked her what she needed from me, *that* was the last thing I expected her to utter through her plump, red lips.

She needed me to kill someone? For her? Was this a fucking joke?

"What did you just say?" I asked, my voice rough and grating to my own ears. I tugged onto the lock of hair wrapped around my finger. There was something about her nearness, her warmth… her sweet fucking smell that made my cock throb.

They called me an animal for a reason. *I sleep. I eat. I hunt. I kill. And I fuck. Hard.*

Talia smelled of innocence and I wanted to rip it away from her; I wanted to bathe her in my depravity; I wanted to show her why little girls like Talia shouldn't step foot into *my* world.

She swallowed hard, her pale throat bobbing with the action. I stepped closer, forcing her back… trapping her against the wall and my body. Her whole body trembled against mine and her teeth sunk into her bottom lip.

Talia held my eyes for a mere second before she dropped her gaze to my chest. "I need you to… kill someone… for me."

A little whisper, her sweet fucking voice, candy breath and brown eyes filled with uncertainty and fear – Talia had absolutely no idea what she just walked into.

"Why?" I demanded.

She struggled to speak and her chest rattled with a harsh inhale. I tugged on her hair, a little harder than before. A silent warning. Talia shuddered, almost violently. She seemed to want to cower but couldn't, since she was trapped.

"Because he's a bad man," she whispered.

Little one, so innocent… so young…so trusting… so fucking naïve.

"Because he's a bad man," I said aloud. Talia nodded, not realizing that I was indeed mocking her words.

If *he* was a bad man – whoever he was – *then what am I?*

"Why is he a bad man?" She squeezed her eyes shut and swallowed hard. I saw her fighting for composure. Hmm, interesting.

Bringing my other hand up, I grasped her chin and tipped her head up. Her eyes opened and our gazes locked. Her pupils grew larger, a look of fright in her eyes. But there was something else…

"He hurt me and humiliated me," Talia confessed, her voice so soft that I almost missed her words. "He doesn't deserve to live."

"How did he hurt you?" I don't know why I asked the question since I never cared before. When offered a job, I never needed or asked for details. I only needed a name and location, then I made my kill.

Talia flinched but responded to my question anyway. "He…treated me like dirt, like I was less than a human to him, he hit me… and threatened me…. To hurt me…"

I let out a small, dry laugh. "Do you know who I am, Little One?"

"Killer," Talia whispered my name.

"Do you know *what* I am?"

She bit on her lip, her shaking becoming worse. Poor girl was so

frightened she was practically mute. She shouldn't have come here. She shouldn't have put herself in my path... or asked for my help.

Talia let out a low exhale and her shoulders squared, as if she was getting ready for a battle. A battle she already lost.

"I can pay you. Money, that's what you need, right? I have money."

I clucked my tongue, a merciless taunt to her words. Talia wasn't a smart girl. If she were, she wouldn't have walked into my territory, looking for a man like me to help her. Or... maybe she was just that desperate. A desperate maiden, falling right into the arms of the villain. What a lovely, fucked-up fairy tale.

"You can't afford me."

She seemed taken aback by my words. "What?"

I ducked my head to her level, leaning closer to her face. The top of her head barely came up to my shoulders. Her small frame trembled when I spoke, my voice low and provocative. "Do you know how much I'm offered for one job? Millions, Little One."

"Millions?" she stuttered, sounding almost indignant.

"How much are you worth?" I enjoyed mocking her, reminding her that she was at my mercy. I enjoyed watching the fear flashing in her brown irises. I fucking loved the way she was vulnerable and open for me... to take, to tease... to taunt.

"Not millions..." Talia muttered, regretfully.

"Then, you're worth nothing to me." Her eyes watered as she flinched at my sharp, cold words.

"But... but, I will do anything. I'm sure there's something I can offer you," she rushed to say. "I can offer you... I mean, my sister's got money. I could ask her and find a way to get the money."

Chuckling, I rubbed my calloused thumb over her full lips, smearing her red lipstick. "You have no idea who and what you're messing with. You don't know the outcome of this. Too young, too innocent to understand my world. Yet... here you are, trying to bargain with me."

Talia let out a choked sob, desperation masking her pale face. I was

a sick, sick fucking monster. My cock grew harder at the sound of her soft cry.

"Go," I said. "Run back to where you've come from and hide before you make a very, very bad decision."

Her hand came up and she circled my wrist with her small fingers. "No," Talia uttered, her voice coming out shaky despite trying to sound confident, in control.

"No?" I taunted. Blood pulsated through my thick, heavy length and I throbbed at her small defiance.

Her eyes pleaded to me. "I know what I'm doing. And I know what I want. Please, I'll give you anything you want. Money... I'll find a way... but if it's not enough... Just name your price... I'll give you anything. Please, *please*."

Desperation clung to her words and I knew... she'd do anything, like she vowed.

"Anything?" My chest rumbled with a low growl at the possibilities. *Careful, Little One.*

Talia nodded. "Whatever you want," she rushed to say, almost breathless. Realization at what she just said, what she just offered, dawned in her pretty eyes and she then snapped her lips shut.

I pushed closer, bringing our bodies together. Touching. My hands curled around her hips, my fingers digging into her flesh. Her lips parted with a silent gasp and her cheeks flushed. I pressed my thigh between her legs, forcing them apart.

Talia looked completely scandalized. She blinked; her surprise evident in her expression, but fear quickly masked it. She made a panicky sound at the back of her throat and her eyes widened, in both terror and... a ghostly curiosity.

From her reaction alone it seemed she was quite a sheltered princess. Her pussy was most likely untouched. Pure and ripe for taking. Fuck, I'd guess she probably never even had a man this close to her. But her need for vengeance brought her to me. Away from her safety net, away from her

home… and all the way to me.

Young and forbidden…

"What if you can't give me what I want?" I brought my face to the crook of her neck and I inhaled. Goddamn it, she smelled sweet. Sweet like fucking candy. I'd bet her cunt tasted like it too.

"What do you want?" she breathed. Hmph. Brave and stupid. But how far was she willing to go?

My hands slid up, my fingers brushing over her flat stomach and her rib cage. Her chest rattled with a harsh breath as my palm came up to her breast and I cupped the heavy weight in my hand. She wasn't a big girl, her tits a size too small for my preference but fuck it, she felt good. Soft and full.

Talia gasped, turning into a frozen statue in my arms. She looked paralyzed in the moment, her lips parted, her eyes wide, her face pale. Her heart pounded, almost erratically. I gave her tit a soft, but firm squeeze, watching for her reaction. Her eyes grew darker and her face flushed a deep red. My thumb circled her stiff nipple and she bit down on her lower lip, her body quaking.

I lowered my head, my lips brushing against hers. Barely a touch. Barely a kiss. Her knees threatened to buckle and she grasped onto my forearms, her nails digging into my skin.

I waited for her to push me away, to run away, to scream. She did nothing but stayed pliant and submissive in my arms.

How desperate was she? How… much was she willing to give me?

My teeth grazed her wet lips and I gave her a sharp nip. "I want to bend you over, slide right into your virgin pussy and hear you moan my name as I fuck you… then watch you bleed on my cock."

Chapter Five

TALIA

For a moment I was sure I hadn't heard him right.

But the way his eyes undressed me and he pressed into me, there really was no doubt about the reality of his words.

Shaking out of my shock, I gave a sharp shake of my head. "No. Never."

He brought his face even closer, smelling my throat. "So, it's true, you're a virgin?"

My pulse throbbed fiercely in my veins and I wondered if he could see it, if my fear turned him on. Probably. After what I'd witnessed in the cage, his depravity shouldn't surprise me anymore. "Of course. That's how I've been brought up." I pressed my lips together, shocked by what I'd almost revealed. If he found out who I was, everything was over.

"So fucking innocent," he murmured, his tongue darting out to lick over my pulse point. Slowly he raised his head and the eager look in his dark eyes thrilled me in a terrifying way. "Your virginity for a life taken, that's what I want."

I brought my palms up against his chest, wanting to shove him away, needing to, but he didn't budge. The mocking gleam in his eyes intensified and his smile turned darker. The muscles in his chest flexed against my hands, and a small shiver shot through my body. Despite my terror, I narrowed my eyes at him. "You can have everything, but not that."

He stepped back with a cruel twist of his mouth. "You don't have anything else I want, Little One. Either you bend over and offer me your pussy or nothing at all. Unless you have a few million bucks to spare?"

I stared at him. Maybe my sister could give me a few thousand dollars, maybe even more. After all, her husband earned plenty of money as Enforcer. And my cousin as Capo of the Famiglia was one of the richest men in the States. Of course, talking to Killer was already a betrayal.

"I don't have that much money, but I could try to pay it off in rates?" I realized how stupid that sounded. How long would it take to pay off millions of dollars?

He laughed cruelly, his eyes sliding over my body. "I'm not a fucking bank. I want my money all at once and before the job. I'd say you're a lucky one. It's more than anyone else ever got. I can have all the cunts I want. That I offer you my services for a simple fuck is a bargain."

"I'm not a whore," I said with forced bravado.

"Then you'll have to find someone else to kill for you. I don't hand out freebies."

I swallowed. He turned. I grabbed his arm. He looked down at my thin fingers around his muscular forearm then up at my face. "Wait. Please. Help me."

His expression turned mocking. "I made you an offer. Take it or leave it."

"I can't. You don't understand."

He shook his head then shocked me by grasping me and pulling me brutally against him, his mouth pressing against my ear. "I don't want to understand. I don't give a fuck. You can either give me what I want and get your biggest wish or you don't. I won't be waiting on you forever. Decide

now what you want."

Part of him wanted me more than he wanted to admit and the knowledge gave me a surprising sense of power. "Who said it's my biggest wish?"

"If it wasn't, you wouldn't have asked for a man like me. You crave revenge. You crave it more than anything else."

I looked away from his penetrating stare. He was right. I wanted Pasquale dead. Even after all the years, I still remembered how he'd dragged me through his house, how he'd thrown me to the ground at his feet and spat down on me, calling me a traitor, when it had been my father and not me who had betrayed his oath. Remembered how he'd told me what he'd do to me, how he'd brutally fuck me once he got the okay from his Capo. I had been fifteen and if Growl hadn't saved me, I probably would be dead by now.

I wanted revenge. I needed it.

But sleeping with Killer would ruin me in my world. Maybe the Bratva followed different rules, but the Italian mafia was still ruled by old-fashioned traditions, and that included that girls needed to lose their innocence on their wedding night. If I gave Killer what he wanted, I'd be shunned once I returned to New York. Unless I managed to hide the truth. I wouldn't be the first woman who faked her virginity on her wedding night to appease the traditionalists.

Killer watched me with a dark smile as if he could feel my resolve slipping. My eyes took in his tall frame, his scarred hands, the harshness of his expression. I was terrified of him. He didn't strike me as a man who was gentle in bed.

He'd said it himself. He wanted me bent over so he could take me from behind like an animal. That wasn't how I wanted my first time to go. I shook my head and backed away. "No. I can't."

"Scared?"

Yes. He scared me senseless.

"Then run, Little One." This wasn't an endearment. He was *taunting*

me with the pet name. "Run."

And I did. Again, I ran from him, from his offer. But I couldn't run from the part of me that wanted to consider it.

Chapter Six

KILLER

Talia didn't realize that every time she ran away, she was driving me insane with lust. It was my instinct to chase her, to hunt after my prey. This was basically foreplay before the fucking.

Run, Little One. She could run, but she couldn't hide from me.

Talia tempted the monster inside of me.

A few days ago, she ran away from me. I'd say it was shocking, since I truly thought she was desperate. And she *was*. But not desperate enough to bargain her virginity to a savage beast.

I told myself to slow down, to give her time to think about my offer. After all, I was the only man who could help her. Talia would have to crawl back to me… I was her only option.

For two days, I watched her. From afar and in the shadows. Stalking her like a hunter would stalk its prey. Sometimes, I'd make my presence known. Just to annoy her. To watch her eyes widen in fear. She'd bite her lip, nervous and wary of me.

Like today. Day three and Talia was still just as overwhelmed by my

presence as the day she had watched me fight in the cage.

I sat alone in the corner of the bar, *watching* her. Talia worked silently behind the bar, but I didn't fail to notice the way she sneaked glances at me. She tried to act like I wasn't here, like I didn't matter... but her nervousness was palpable.

Talia struggled with her principles and beliefs. She needed me, but she couldn't have me. She needed me, but she was... scared of the outcome.

So, I didn't approach her. *A skilled hunter is always patient.*

"Killer." A breathy voice forced me to look away from Talia and I focused on the woman who had succeeded in forcing herself into my personal space. Candy – a Kazan's whore – placed her hand on my shoulder. Just like I belonged to the cage, she belonged to the Kazan. Passed around between the champions. She was fifteen when she first stepped foot into the bar and begged for our protection. And so, we gave it to her.

Some people – the decent, lawful people – would call us evil for taking 'advantage' of Candy.

Some would say it was immoral. Many would belittle Candy for her choices. But fuck it, she was safe, fed, protected, happy... and well-fucked.

"You haven't visited me in a while," she said, her voice husky.

I grunted. "Busy."

Candy let out a small laugh and placed herself on my lap. She tucked a long strand of blonde hair behind her ear and licked her red lips. Tempting, very tempting. "Too busy to visit your favorite? Don't lie, Killer."

She pushed her ass against my crotch, grinding a little. "C'mon. Don't sit here like a loner. Let's go to my room."

Candy leaned forward and her lips met mine. I spared Talia a quick glance as Candy kissed me and our eyes locked. Her brown eyes flared with something unreadable and even with the distance between us, there was no mistaking the flush in her cheeks.

Hmm.

Candy let out a low whine as I pulled away from the kiss. I turned her around in my lap, so she was facing Talia, with her back against my chest.

She straddled me that way and I spread my thighs, forcing her legs open. Candy was wearing a mini-dress that barely covered her ass. I pushed the hem up around her waist, keeping my eyes on my prey – Talia.

Her shocked expression was quickly replaced by a look of disgust as I shoved my hand into Candy's panties, rubbing her pussy in an obvious manner that couldn't be mistaken.

My lips twitched with a smirk as Talia looked completely affronted by the act of me bringing Candy to an orgasm in front of her, right in the open for anyone to watch.

Talia couldn't seem to look away from my eyes. She was completely ensnared as I silently pushed my message across. *I don't need you. I got all the pussies I want. YOU need ME.*

She seemed to understand my unsaid words. Talia squinted at me, nudged her chin high and stalked away.

I hadn't expected her to be so... stubborn.

She was firm on her principles and beliefs. After all, I was forbidden to her. Talia was disgusted, frightened, overwhelmed... but there was a hint of something else. Surprise and curiosity. She could be as rigid as she wanted, but I had caught her reaction in the staff room three days ago. It was slight and if I hadn't been paying careful attention, I wouldn't have noticed it. It wasn't exactly lust... but she didn't *hate* my touch as much as she wanted to.

Candy came on my hand, her choked moan bringing my attention back to her. She looked back at me; her eyes hazy. "Let's go to my room."

"I have unfinished business." I nodded toward the man staring at us with avid hunger. "You can satisfy Pike's needs tonight. He won last night's fight."

Candy glanced at Pike and grinned, her smile seductive and inviting. "Of course. He deserves some extra love."

She got off my lap and Pike lunged forward, curling his arm around her hips in a possessive manner and practically lifting Candy off her feet as he stalked away.

I downed the rest of my whiskey and in the same moment, Talia walked

out of the staff room, dressed in her coat. Her night shift had ended. I chuckled as she kept her head down and practically sprinted toward the exit.

I pushed away from the table and followed her.

Talia didn't notice me. I kept a distance between us, blending into the night as we made our way to her apartment. She didn't know that I knew where she lived. She didn't know that I had been *inside* her apartment.

Talia didn't know a lot of things.

The walk was about twenty minutes to her apartment. We were halfway when something else caught my attention. Talia and I weren't alone. Someone else was following... her.

I paused. I crouched low, hiding in the darkness. I waited.

My instincts kicked in as he grew closer to her, but I... waited.

He grabbed her. She screamed. My blood roared between my ears. Fury pumped through my veins. I. Waited.

She struggled, her tiny fists beating at the man who dared grab her. Talia screamed again, his hand muffling the sound as he dragged her into a dark alley.

Tick. Tock.

I counted the seconds in my head.

One. I moved away from the shadows.

Two. I stalked forward.

Three. Four. Five.

I stood at the entrance of the alley.

Six. I found the man on top of Talia. He had ripped away her coat and her shirt was in shreds.

Seven. She was crying, struggling, fighting.

Eight. A growl rumbled from my chest.

Nine. His head snapped up and he finally noticed me.

Ten. Talia's tearful, frightened gaze met mine. There was instant relief in her brown eyes at the sight of me.

I lunged forward and grabbed the man by his throat, throwing him off her. Talia let out a small frightened sound and curled into herself.

My fist made contact with his face, without any mercy. Bones crunched. He screamed and clawed at the filthy ground, trying to get away from me. I punched him again. And again and again. The sound of mangled bones and wet flesh filled my ears until he was unrecognizable. He was barely breathing, his face bleeding, swollen and broken.

My hand wrapped around his fragile neck. My fingers dug deep until I broke through his skin and practically ripped open his throat with my bare hands.

He bled and bled until his chest stopped moving and my job was done.

Turning around, I faced Talia. Her eyes were wide, her cheeks tearstained and she swallowed back a cry.

I took a step toward her and she flinched. "I'm not going to hurt you," I spoke gently, to soothe her.

She was completely shaken. Talia looked so vulnerable in that moment. My chest… tightened. A fathom of an ache.

"Are you hurt?" I asked, crouching in front of her. I wrapped her coat around her shoulders, protecting her modesty and I knew she needed to feel… safe right now.

Her chin wobbled, but she didn't answer. "Little One, I need to know if you're injured."

She gave me a small shake of her head. Bullshit, I didn't believe her. Her cheek was red and swollen and I knew he must have struck her. Talia was clutching her ribs and her face twisted with pain.

I reached for her, but she flinched away again. I pulled my hand back, clenching it into a fist so I wasn't tempted to try to touch her again. Talia struggled to her feet but let out a soft, pained cry and her knees buckled.

Fuck!

I grabbed her before she face-planted into the ground. My arm curled around her hips and I swung her up in my arms. She gasped, a protest on her lips, but I cut her off with a low growl. "Don't ever lie to me again, Talia."

She swallowed and blinked away. "Where are you hurt?" I demanded again.

"My ankle," she whispered, her voice cracking.

"And?"

"My ribs…"

I carried her out of the alley, leaving the dead man behind.

"You're covered in blood," she breathed, her lips so close to my neck.

My arms tightened around her. "I just killed a man to save your life. You're worried that I'm getting blood on you?"

"Put me down, Killer," she choked. "I can walk. Please."

"No." Fuck that. The only way she was getting home was if I carried her.

She had no other option. But *me*.

Chapter Seven

TALIA

My heart was a frantic flutter in my chest, terror crippling my limbs. My ribs ached fiercely. I gave up my struggle against Killer and relaxed in his hold, oddly soothed by his presence. He oozed strength and confidence. He had *killed* a man for me.

My head against his shoulder, I peered up at him. Blood splatters dotted his throat and chin. He'd viciously beaten my attacker to death. Without hesitation or mercy. Brutal efficiency combined with lust for bloodshed. A deadly combination that should have driven me into hysterics.

And yet, I felt almost safe as he carried me. A dark, angry part of me wondered if Pasquale would find the same brutal end if I hired Killer. Would he be beaten to death and drown in his own blood? It was a thrilling thought.

I tensed when Killer stopped in front of my shabby apartment building without me giving him my address. "You know where I live?"

He gave me a brief smirk. "Of course. I scout possible business partners."

My lips snapped shut. I had refused his offer. His impossibly, rude offer.

My virginity for a kill. It was immoral. But wasn't I being a hypocrite judging Killer when I was the one who wanted to hire him to kill a man?

"Talia, keys. I don't have all night. Or I'll kick the door in."

"No," I said quickly, fumbling in my coat pocket for my keys before handing them to Killer.

A few minutes later, we entered my tiny studio apartment. It was sparsely furnished. Only a narrow bed on the right, a tiny kitchenette, an old sofa and an ancient TV. Killer barely spared his surroundings a glance, instead he carried me over to the bed.

Tension radiated through my body, realizing we were alone in my apartment and remembering what he wanted from me.

"Don't get tense," he said gruffly.

Easy for him to say. "Maybe you just killed the guy so you can finish what he started." My voice shook. He set me down on the bed and brought his face very close to mine. "I don't *fuck* unwilling women, Talia. When I'm balls deep inside your cunt, you're going to be *begging* me."

I flushed at his crude language. His gaze lingered on my flushed cheeks, still so close he could have kissed me.

"Let me check out your injuries."

He pushed down my coat, revealing my ripped shirt and my flimsy white bra beneath it. I jerked my arms up to cover my modesty. He gripped my wrists and shoved them down. "Let me." His voice allowed no argument.

I let my arms drop to my sides.

He touched my ribs with his big, blood-covered hand. I winced at how tender the spot felt. A shiver passed my spine when he pushed my tattered shirt aside to get a good look at the blooming bruise. His touch was surprisingly gentle, something I hadn't expected from a man like him.

"Not broken," he said. "Your ankle?"

I lifted my hurt foot and he carefully slid off my heels, causing me to flinch. His touch became even softer as he felt my ankle with his fingers then moved it slowly.

It was obvious he tried not to hurt me. "I didn't think someone like you

could be gentle," I whispered.

His eyes darted up to my face and I bit my lip at the intensity of his expression. "If the situation requires it, I can be *careful*."

I had a feeling he wasn't referring to treating my injuries. Heat shot into my face.

His thumb traced the bare skin of my calf and goosebumps rose all over my body. Swallowing, I averted my eyes from his.

"This should heal on its own. It's only twisted." He fell silent, regarding me in a way that made me feel too warm. He straightened without warning. "Sleep now. I'll check on you tomorrow and tell Igor you can't work tomorrow."

Before I could fully register his words, he was gone.

Stunned, I lay back and then everything overwhelmed me. The attack. How Killer had beaten the man to death. The bargain.

I cried myself to sleep.

I spent the next day at home, wondering if Killer would stop by, half wishing he wouldn't, half eager for his appearance. I was lonely. Not just since I'd come to Florida. Living in a golden cage like I did made it difficult to meet new people, much less men. Killer's attention, no matter how immoral and terrifying, thrilled me.

A knock startled me out of my reverie. I limped toward the door, but before I could look through the peephole, Killer's voice boomed. "It's me."

I unlocked the door and opened it. He towered over me, holding a bag with takeout. "Food."

I backed away, making room for him. He slipped past me and put the bag down on the counter. Slowly I closed my door. His eyes took me in. It was exceedingly hot today so I was only in shorts and a tank top. Again his gaze sent a wave of heat through me. Suddenly shy, I cleared my throat and looked away. "Thanks."

I limped toward him.

"You like Chinese?"

I nodded then jumped when he nudged my chin up. He registered my puffy eyes. "He's dead. Not worth a single tear."

Why was he being this considerate? This gentle? It made me crave more of it.

"Will you eat with me?"

Surprise flickered in his eyes. He wasn't the only one who was surprised. He gave a sharp nod.

We settled on the sofa and I ate a few bites. He kept looking at me. "What's your real name?" I blurted eventually when I couldn't stand the silence anymore.

"Killer."

"That's not a name."

"It's the name given to me when I was groomed for the cages."

"Like a caged animal," I mused.

Something flashed in his dark eyes. Anger, maybe even a flicker of hurt. "I know what it feels like to live in a cage."

"Many strict rules in your world?"

I searched his face, wondering how much he knew about me. Did he know who I was? Who my cousin was? "Yeah."

I allowed my eyes to take him in, his muscles and the harsh lines of his face. "I've been thinking about your offer..." I trailed off. Was I losing my mind? But did I really have any other option if I wanted revenge? He'd said he could be gentle if necessary. Would he be with me?

He narrowed his eyes. "My offer stands. I don't barter."

"I know," I whispered, digging my nails into the sofa. "I...I accept."

The second the words were out of my mouth, a wave of shame washed over me. I'd been brought up traditionally. Bartering my virginity away was the worst crime in my world.

Silence fell over us. Killer regarded me closely, a hint of triumph in his eyes.

He had won, but I would too, once he killed Pasquale for me.

He leaned closer and I held my breath, thinking he wasn't going to waste any time, but he only let his gaze trail over my body, the hint of a smirk on his face. He touched my ribs, his thumb at the underside of my breast. I shivered. "Not today. Your ribs need to heal before I fuck you." The smirk got wider. "I can't wait, Little One."

It made me furious how he used this pet name to taunt me, but I had accepted and I wouldn't back out now.

After he left, I still sat motionless on the sofa, shocked that I'd really agreed to his offer. What had I done?

Three days later, my ribs weren't as tender anymore. They still hurt when I put too much pressure on them, but I wanted to get the bargain over as soon as possible *before* I freaked out completely. I had considered returning to New York every second of the day, but my wish for revenge was too strong, stronger even than my pride.

If I was being honest, a flicker of curiosity played into my decision. I had always been shielded from male attention and once I returned home, I'd have to wait until my wedding night to be close to a man. Here in Florida I got a taste of freedom. Nobody would have to know what I'd done.

When I opened the door to Killer's imposing form, trepidation overwhelmed me. In my silly dreams, I'd always imagined a loving, gentle first time. Looking at his hungry expression and scarred hands, I couldn't hope for consideration. This was his payment and he'd take whatever he desired from me without a care for my emotions.

He closed the door, advancing on me, and I couldn't stop myself from backing away. Suddenly, he was upon me, wrapping a strong arm around my waist and jerking me against his muscled body. His mouth pressed against my ear. "It's too late to change your mind."

"I haven't," I choked out, even as my brain wanted to scream yes.

His lips crashed down on mine, his tongue claiming my mouth without mercy. I gasped, completely overwhelmed by the sudden intimacy. He pressed me backward until my calves hit the bed and I fell down. Disoriented I only registered a heavy weight settling on me and for a moment panic settled in.

He cupped my cheek so I met his gaze. "How far have you gone?" His voice was low, drenched with startling desire.

I blinked, trying to get my bearings. My heart pounded wildly in my chest. "Gone?"

He smirked. "You're a virgin, I got that. What have you done?"

"Nothing."

He let out a dark laugh. "Right."

"You gave me my first kiss," I admitted. Maybe he didn't know who I was after all. The rules of our society were known by our enemies.

He became still, his eyes searching mine. He pressed his mouth against my collarbone and chuckled darkly. I wasn't sure what was so funny. I was about to ask him when he trailed his tongue over my skin down to the swell of my breast and I became still, like a doe hiding from a hunter. "Relax, Talia."

His rough fingertips slid below my shirt, over my belly, pushing up my shirt. Before I could feel embarrassed, he'd removed my shirt and bra, and I was topless. My nipples hardened. Of course, he registered it and terrifying hunger twisted his face. I released a small breath, feeling my face burn fiercely. He took his time taking me in, then he lowered himself.

His rough palm cupped my breast, squeezing gently before he flicked his thumb over my nipple. I gasped, surprised by the flicker of pleasure. He smirked and kissed my mouth harshly. My tongue met his hesitantly, even as I felt him smile in triumph against me. He ripped away and sucked my nipple into his mouth, making me arch against his face.

"Ohh," I pressed out. His teeth nicked me lightly, and I moaned in the most embarrassing way.

His palm slid down my belly and into my waistband. I tensed. This was going too fast. I wasn't ready, but I couldn't stop him, not if I wanted

to uphold my part of the bargain. He licked my throat as his fingers slipped inside my panties. Holding my breath, I waited for him to plunge his fingers into me before he moved on to the actual deed. A moan left my lips when the pad of his thumb swiped my clit. He sucked my nipple into his mouth once more and kept up his torturous caress between my legs. His body was tight as a bowstring, his chest heaving as he obviously fought for control.

"I told you I'm going to be careful with you," he growled.

I didn't understand him. "Why?" I whispered.

He bit down lightly and I cried out in surprise. Instead of replying, he pushed up on his arms and moved down my body. He hooked his strong hands into my waistband and pulled both my panties and shorts down. Completely exposed, I trembled. He knelt over me, broad, muscular and dangerous, watching me like something he wanted to devour.

My eyes darted to the very prominent bulge in his pants. I swallowed.

"Not yet, Little One."

He touched my knees and pushed my legs apart. Acute embarrassment cut through me as he regarded me and actually licked his lips. "What…what are you doing?" I asked, half-terrified, half-excited.

He stretched out between my legs, shoving my thighs farther apart with his strong shoulders. "Eat you out until you're ready to take my cock."

"I—" His tongue licked a hot trail from my back entrance to my clit. I arched, my fingers gripping onto his head, my eyes rolling back. What? He hummed and licked me as if I was an ice cream cone and he was a starving man. I wasn't supposed to enjoy this. It was payment for Killer…but this… this…

My God. I let out an undignified moan when he sucked my clit into his mouth. I couldn't keep the sounds in and he wasn't trying to be quiet about what he was doing either. I'd never felt this out of control, as if Killer knew exactly what buttons to push. "Your pussy is so fucking sweet," he growled. His voice and the firm flicks of his tongue sent a flood of pleasure through me. My back bowed as I gasped. My fingers scraped over his scalp, overwhelmed by the sensations.

Killer groaned against me but he didn't stop. I dug my heels into the mattress, sure I'd lose my mind any moment if he kept up the torture. He pulled away, pressing a kiss against my inner thigh. His fingers brushed over my opening and I knew what was coming. He caught me by surprise when he bit the sensitive skin on my thigh the moment he breached me. I stiffened, my muscles clenching tightly around his fingers, my breathing coming in quick bursts. His own breath was harsh. "Fuck."

He began to fuck me with his fingers, slowly, gently, until the twinge turned into a low hum of pleasure. When his mouth cupped my clit, my body exploded again.

I was still coming down from my high when Killer straightened and got out of his clothes, and then everything seemed to stand still as reality set in. This was it. I was going to lose my virginity to the enemy in exchange for his services. If someone found out, I'd be ruined. This dirty bargain could be the end of me.

Fear tightened my chest when Killer climbed on the bed. I'd never seen a naked man, much less one like Killer with scars, bulging muscles and an erection that was going to rip me in two. He braced himself on his arms over me and lined himself up. I flinched, from the expected pain, from the inevitable consequences, from my possible ruin.

Killer lowered his head until our lips brushed. "There's no going back now, Talia." He held my gaze as he pushed into me. I dug my nails into his shoulders, choking on a gasp. To my surprise, he lowered himself until our bodies were flush together and slowed even further. It felt like he was tearing me apart despite his slow pace. His muscles quivered with the effort to be gentle. The struggle shone on his face. He wanted to slam into me like a savage. I could see it plain as day in his eyes, so why wasn't he?

When he was finally sheathed all the way inside of me, my eyes squeezed shut. My body struggled to accommodate him. The pain was intense, and yet in a strange, disturbing way having Killer's body on top of me, having him inside of me felt good. Exhilaratingly forbidden.

"Open your eyes. I want you to see who's fucking you."

I looked at Killer. His expression gleamed with triumph. He gripped my thigh and draped it over his muscular ass. I couldn't look away from his fierce eyes as he began to move. He was slow and gentle, his chest heaving, his breathing low and harsh.

His movements grew faster and occasionally a flicker of pleasure lit up beneath the dark pain of his claiming, but it was gone before I could chase it. Soon Killer's control was at its limits. I clung to him, trying to meet his thrusts, and finally his body tightened, his face flashing with unguarded pleasure.

It was an astonishing sight, as if for a brief moment Killer allowed me to glimpse behind the walls that he'd built around himself. I marveled at his brutally handsome face.

His eyes met mine, and the brief connection was gone.

Chapter Eight

KILLER

Her pussy clamped around my cock and I let out a groan. Her plump lips were parted, her eyes hazy and her thighs tightened around my hips. Goddamn it, my dick was ready to go for a second round. She was so fucking tight, felt so fucking good.

A shudder rolled down my spine as her tight heat pulsed, practically begging me for more. I throbbed; my thick length still semi-hard but I knew it was best to give her some time to recover. After all, Talia had been a virgin. She was probably really sore and aching right now.

I rolled off her and sat down on the edge of the bed. Talia remained in the same position, looking completely spent, her body limp and she blinked up at me, almost sleepily. I could see her mind turning, trying to come to terms with this situation but she simply looked… a little lost and thoroughly fucked.

"If you keep looking at me like this, don't blame me for turning you over and fucking you like I *want*." The roughness in my voice surprised me.

Talia flushed at my words. My lips twitched and I couldn't help but

smirk at her red face.

"Like you want?" she whispered, pushing her hair away from her sweaty face. "Didn't you just do that?"

Chuckling, I raised an eyebrow. "I just did you a favor, Talia. No, I didn't fuck you like I wanted. I fucked you like you needed me to. You were a virgin and so, I had to be… *tender*," I said. The word 'tender' sounded foreign on my tongue and I was disgusted by it and the meaning behind the word. I was neither gentle nor tender. "Consider this a charity."

"Are you always an asshole?" Talia mumbled more to herself than to me. She hadn't meant for me to hear it.

"Now, now. That's not how you speak to your savior."

Her eyes darkened at the mocking tone of my voice. "You used me to your advantage. I wouldn't say you're my savior."

I stood up, reaching for my discarded clothes. Talia's gaze lingered on my body, far longer on my cock before she quickly blinked away. "You seem to have some memory problem. Let me help you remember," I taunted. "You came here because you needed me. You didn't have enough money to pay for the job, so I offered you an easy way out. Which was quite… considerate of me. I could have asked for something more debase. I only asked for your virginity. Then, I saved you from getting assaulted and raped. I killed a man for you… free of charge. And I'm about to kill another. So? What do you have to say for yourself?"

"I think… I think that's the most I ever heard you speak." Of course, she'd divert my question and the whole conversation. Slick little Talia. I guessed she wasn't as stupid as I thought. Maybe naïve and a little too trusting… but hmm, not stupid.

My chest rumbled with a dry laugh. She was silent as I quickly dressed. Once I was done, I grabbed the glass of water on her nightstand and offered it to her. She licked her dry lips and took it without question.

"Thanks," I said.

"For what?" she asked, confusion lingering in her eyes.

I looked back to where she was still sprawled, legs opened. There was

a wet spot on the bedsheet underneath her. My cum was starting to dry on the inside of her thighs. Her cunt looked red and swollen, covered with my semen. There was no mistaking the hint of blood there.

I nodded toward her. "Thanks for the payment. You look just as filthy as I imagined you would after I'd take your virginity."

Talia followed my gaze and she gasped, closing her legs as she finally realized how indecent she looked. Tsk.

She pulled the covers over herself – as if to hide the proof of what we had just done. Her nakedness. My cum, still dripping out of her cunt. The fact that she bled for me. What we had just done... *this* could ruin her.

But there was no hiding it.

It was a cruel reminder of what she sold and bargained for the death of her enemy. Talia had to live with this night, ingrained in her mind, for the rest of her life. *Er, well...*

I grabbed the empty glass from her hand and placed it back on the nightstand. "Good night."

Not waiting for a reply, I walked out of her bedroom and closed the door behind me. Maybe it was my mind playing tricks on me, but I swore I heard her whisper *goodnight* back to me.

Right, Talia was about to have a good night's sleep. No nightmares, like the last few nights.

Not after the sleeping pill I had slipped into the glass I offered her.

Two days later, I walked into her apartment and found her sitting on the couch, cuddled up against a bunch of pillows and staring at the TV. She gasped as I walked through the door and jumped to her feet in alarm. Only to end up back on the couch with a loud cry.

I walked over to her and crouched to her level. Grasping her lower leg, I placed her injured foot on my knee for a closer look. I probed her ankle with my thumb. "It still hurts?"

"You need to knock. This is my apartment. You can't just come and go as you please."

I raised my head and speared her with a look, cocking my head to the side. Really? We fucked... I was about to kill a man for her and she was worried about me coming into her apartment without knocking?

She swallowed and averted her gaze. "How did you get in anyway?"

"I have my ways," I said, not elaborating. Meaning...I had a duplicate key made, but she didn't know that. Or maybe she guessed it now. My words were cryptic, but I was starting to learn that Talia wasn't as stupid as I thought she was.

Talia let out a low hiss and crossed her arms. "Well, you can't just walk in like that!"

"I can and I have." I placed the plastic bag on the couch. "Food. Eat."

"I already had a sandwich," she replied, but gave the bag a longing look. She was practically salivating at the smell of the Chinese food.

"You lie. I checked your refrigerator and it was empty. Eat."

Talia made an agitated sound in the back of her throat. "Maybe if you tell me nicely instead of *demanding* I eat..."

I kept my expression blank and stayed silent, waiting for her to give in. And she did. Not even a minute later, her stomach growled and she reached for the food, practically digging in like a desperate, starving little thing.

She shoved a spoonful of rice into her mouth and chewed almost aggressively as she kept her eyes averted. It was kinda... cute.

I watched her as she ate. Until I couldn't *just* watch anymore. My hands twitched with the urge to touch her and so I did. My hand came up and tucked a lock of hair behind her ear and my thumb brushed away the grain of rice that was stuck to her lips. Talia inhaled sharply and her gaze landed on me again.

"What are you doing?" she whispered.

My head lowered and my lips slammed against her, stealing her breath and swallowing her gasp. Her tiny fist thumped against my chest for a mere second... before her touch became less of an effort to escape me and more...

Her fingers dug into my shoulders and her body slid closer to me. I groaned into the kiss, my tongue sliding across her lips and demanding entrance. She let me and I fucking devoured her. Talia pulled away, breathless. Her eyes hazy, her lips red and swollen and her cheeks flushed.

"What...?"

My cock throbbed. "You're getting better."

"Huh?"

"Kissing. You're getting better, but I think you need a little more practice." I had known Talia was a virgin, but I hadn't expected I would be her first kiss. She was so goddamn innocent and so fucking inexperienced.

And here I was. A bastard who was taking advantage of it all.

Talia's eyes flared, growing darker. I didn't give her a chance to refute me before I claimed her lips again.

Fuck, she tasted so sweet.

Three days later, Talia sat next to me on the couch, wringing her hands. She was less nervous in my presence now, but still somewhat fearful.

Yesterday, she said I was unpredictable. Which was... true, I'd give her that. She even went as far as saying she couldn't let her guard down around me... or trust me.

Yeah, Talia was finally learning.

But no, she was still quite...innocent. Not stupid, she had brains – I found out. She also had a sharp tongue when she wasn't too frightened.

I bumped my knee against hers, bringing her attention back to me. "I asked you a question."

"Yes, my ribs are feeling better now. My ankle is fine, the sprain wasn't too bad."

"And your sleep?" I continued to push. Talia looked a little reluctant to answer my questions. Not because she was scared. Because she was confused by the attention I was giving her.

"Surprisingly, I'm sleeping better," she confessed.

Because of the sleeping pills… unknown to her, of course.

"When…" She broke off when her voice cracked. "When will you…"

"Do you want him to have a quick death? Or do you want him to suffer?"

Talia swallowed. "Make him suffer."

"Please."

"What?"

"Say please." There was outrage in her brown eyes. I curled a lock of her hair around my finger, tugging her closer to me. I leaned forward, rubbing my nose along the column of her throat. Talia responded with a small shudder. "Beg me to kill him."

"*Please*, make him suffer."

My dick hardened. "Say it again."

"Please," she breathed.

I pulled back, a grin on my lips. "I quite like you like this. Submissive." And at my mercy.

Talia was provoked and she squinted at me. She opened her mouth, but I placed a finger against her lips, stopping her tirade of words. "Careful, or I might decide to continue our kissing lessons right now."

Her jaw snapped shut. I knew exactly how to shut her up.

"I can kiss just fine." Talia glared with no heat.

I chuckled at how affronted she appeared. "You're getting better."

She nudged her chin up and looked away from me. I stood up and straightened to my full height.

"Once the job is done, I'll collect the second half of my payment."

Talia paused. Her eyes lost the mirth and were now replaced with caution. "Second half?" she sputtered. The color drained from her face as she finally came to the realization. "Wait, I thought this was a one-time thing. You wanted my virginity and I gave you that. The payment has been made."

"No, the payment is done when I say it's done. You gave me your virginity… but I had to hold myself back," I growled. "I'm not satisfied with your service, Talia."

Her eyes widened and she jumped off the couch, taking a few steps back. "You... you mean..."

I stalked to her, moving forward for every step she took away from me. Her back slammed against the wall and I crowded into her space. "You struck a bargain with the Kazan's Devil. You're out of luck, Little One. I'll be back to collect the rest of my payment."

I pushed away from her soft, tempting body. Talia brought a hand up to her heaving chest and silently gasped.

"If you run," I warned. "I will find you. And you won't like the consequences."

Chapter Nine

TALIA

After all these years I'd finally get my wish. Killer would kill Pasquale, would dole out the revenge I'd only ever dreamed about. It was an exhilarating feeling. Even knowing that Killer would make him suffer, I didn't feel a hint of guilt.

I'd gone through my work shift in a trance today, thinking about Killer, about what he'd do, about what *we* had done.

Nerves tightened my belly. I'd really slept with him. From an early age, girls in my circle were taught to protect their virtue because it determined their worth. It was something deeply engrained in me, and yet I'd given it up to Killer. Not just anyone, but the enemy. If my family or my friends found out, they wouldn't understand. Maybe Cara would understand. My sister herself had been with Growl before marriage, but her situation had been vastly different. She had been a captive, trying to make her situation more bearable. My mother, she'd be terribly disappointed, even heartbroken.

They'd condemn me for my choice, and maybe they would be right to do so.

I hadn't offered myself to Killer to protect someone or for some other virtuous reason. I'd done it for simple revenge, to still the hunger for blood humming in my veins.

I glanced at the door for what felt like the hundredth time, waiting for Killer to return. I didn't know when that would be, how long he'd need to end Pasquale for me, to end him *brutally*.

Sighing, I closed my eyes. Images from our time together flashed through my mind, vividly, breathtakingly. I tensed when heat pooled in my belly, remembering Killer's imposing body, the feel of his muscles on top of me, the pressure of *him* inside of me. It had been painful, and yet I'd felt the teasing hints of something more beneath the ache. Something I was dangerously curious about. But worse than my kindling desire was that gentle flutter in my chest when I thought of him, of how carefully he'd treated me. I hadn't expected him to be gentle. To know that there was more to him than brutality made me want to discover all of him, peel back all the layers of darkness to the man hidden beneath.

I wanted to spend more time with him. But how would that ever be possible? Our time was limited. Eventually I'd have to return to New York. Not yet though. We still had time. I had time to coerce more out of Killer, to make him realize that it was okay to be gentle with some people, with me. We had tonight, and tomorrow, and maybe…

…maybe I could stay in Florida for a bit? Was anyone really missing me in New York? Cara perhaps, but she'd understand if I stayed here to find happiness. My mother wouldn't approve but she was caught in the past, in her sad memories, and barely paid attention to me most of the time.

Florida meant freedom. The chance to explore who I was without the restrictions of tradition. I could date, could be with someone…

Maybe I was foolish for thinking that someone could be Killer.

The lock turned. My eyes flew open as Killer unlocked my door with his spare key and stepped in, looking like a demon straight out of the deepest pit of hell. His hands, his arms, his upper body were covered in blood, proof of a life taken. I stood slowly, my heartbeat speeding up. Then I registered

Killer's face, the lingering brutality and bloodlust…

And worse than that, the dark, relentless hunger in his eyes.

KILLER

The moment I had her against the wall, Talia went limp in my arms. She didn't struggle, but her eyes shone with uncertainty and… strange interest. Curiosity. Need. Hunger.

Anticipation poured out of her and I could taste her lust on my tongue.

"Are you scared?" My words spilled out like a growl. I was covered in Pasquale's blood and the pungent smell of death still lingered on me. Adrenaline coursed through my body, making it harder for me to think. My dick was hard as granite and I wanted to push her legs open and slam right into her cunt, take what was mine, claim what belonged to me.

"Yes," she breathed.

I pushed my face into her neck, inhaling her scent. Sweet. So fucking sweet. My nose trailed up, along the column of her throat. My teeth grazed the skin right below her ear and she trembled in my arms.

"Do you want to run away?"

I was giving her a way out… or maybe I wanted her to *think* she could escape.

Her hands came up and she grasped my forearms. She clung to me. Oh, little Talia kept surprising me on every turn.

"Will you hurt me?" she asked quietly.

"Maybe," I confessed, my voice taking a deeper undertone. "It depends on your definition of hurt." Lust fired up through my veins and all I wanted to do was throw her on the ground and fuck her like the savage I was.

I grasped her hand and brought it to my lips. Talia stared at me, our gazes locked in that single moment. I gave her index finger a sharp nip and her eyes flared. "Pain and pleasure are the same to me. I indulge in both."

Talia shook her head, looking a little scared…a little…eager. "Pain is

not pleasure."

Another nip and she flinched. "So innocent. So naïve."

So fucking restraint, I wanted to push all her buttons. I wanted to strip her bare, discover all her hidden desires, force them out of her and show her what it truly felt like to be mounted and claimed by a man like me.

"Will you be collecting the rest of your payment now?" she whispered, her voice shaking.

I didn't answer. My hands landed on her waist and pulled her hard into my body, my fingers digging into her hips. I waited for a reaction.

Talia didn't push me away. Instead, in a small gesture of submission, she tilted her head to the side. The slightest and smallest movement, something I'd miss if I wasn't so in tune with her body and her reaction. Talia gave me full access to her lips, a silent permission.

To take, to devour, to hurt, to ruin.

I made my kill.

And now I needed to fuck the aggression... this *need*...out of my system.

Carnal lust licked through my veins, like gasoline added to an already out of control fire. With a low snarl, my lips crashed against hers.

I kissed Talia.

I devoured her lips.

I breathed her. Inhaled her. Fucking kissed her like I needed to.

She gasped; her knees weakened and her legs gave out.

Her hands came up to my shoulders and she clung to me, almost in a desperate attempt... to push me away... to pull me closer. Fuck! FUCK!

I growled into the kiss, shoving my tongue into her mouth. She cried out softly but kissed me back. Her tongue tasted mine, a little tentative... inexperienced, but she didn't pull away.

Lips. Tongue. Teeth.

Blood roared between my ears and I lost sense of everything. Talia owed me. This was her payment to me. And I was going to take... until she had nothing left to give.

Grabbing Talia by the waist, I kept our lips locked and walked us to the opposite wall. A soft moan came from her throat when I pulled away from the kiss and turned her around. With her back against mine, I pushed her front against the full-length mirror that was attached to the wall.

Talia gasped as she took in our reflection.

Her lips swollen and red from my kisses. Her chest heaving. Her hair in disarray. And I still had dry blood on me. My arms curled around her and I grabbed the front of her dress. Her eyes widened and she cried out as I ripped it open, her bra coming along too until she was fully exposed. I crowded into her back, forcing her against the mirror. Her tits pressed against the cold mirror and her nipples hardened.

Her neck and cheeks flushed red.

Talia looked scandalized.

She was at my mercy.

I pulled her dress up and shoved my hand into her black, cotton panties. She was...fuck, she was soaked. I ripped her panties away, not giving her a chance to react. My fingers slid over her wet pussy lips before my teeth sank down into her bare shoulder. Talia screamed and rocked against my hand as I speared her with two fingers. Her cunt clenched around the intrusion, her juices soaking my hand.

Oh fuck. She was already primed and ready.

I fucking ached to be inside her. My fingers kept a brutal rhythm, thrusting in and out of her cunt as I pulled my sweatpants down enough so I could pull my cock out. The tip of my hard length rubbed against the crease of her ass, before sliding against her wet lips.

Our eyes met through the reflection. Her pupils were dilated, eyes blazing with a mixture of fear and something carnal. And I looked crazed, completely fucking deranged.

I pulled my fingers out and she let out a choked moan, which turned into a desperate cry when I slammed inside. My cock thickened and throbbed as I thrusted inside her, all the way to the hilt until she was full of me.

Talia fed the beast in me.

And she fucked the monster like she was born to submit to me.

Talia rocked against the mirror, her lips parted with a silent moan and her back arched. I kept a hand on her hip, keeping her anchored to me as I pistoned in and out, forcing myself harder and deeper inside her. Her pussy clenched around me every time I thrust inside. She whimpered every time I pulled out. My other hand curled around her nape, feeling her submission bleed through her and into me.

"Killer," she whimpered as I pinned her against the mirror.

"Fuck," I grunted.

I rutted inside her like a beast. There was unwavering obsession coursing through me. The need to defile her… to show her the depraved side of pleasure was strong.

A ripple ran down my spine and my muscles tightened. Talia was close, I could feel it.

My hips drove forward, again and again.

Harder. Faster. Deeper. The sound of our fucking filled the room. Her moans. Her little whimpers. My grunts, that sounded more animal than human.

"FUCK!" I slammed inside her one more time and stilled, buried so deep. My cock pulsed as I spurted my cum inside her, until Talia was full of me. Until I was everywhere. Inside her. Outside her. In her mind. Around her.

I reached around, shoving my hand between her thighs. I tugged at her clit; her body clenched; Talia screamed and spasmed around my cock.

I didn't want to leave the warm clasp of her pussy but I had to. My eyes went to where we were still connected and I slowly pulled out, watching my length slide out of her pink hole as she leaked my cum.

Her legs finally gave out and she sunk to the ground, her body shaking with the aftershock of her orgasm and our fucking. I wasn't done… just yet…

I bent low and wrapped her hair around my fist, my knuckles digging into her scalp. Talia looked at me with hazy eyes, lost somewhere far away…

She knelt in front of me. I pushed a hand between her thighs and gathered the mess I left there with two fingers, rubbing it over her folds. I

brought my fingers up to her tits and smeared my cum on her nipples. Talia gasped softly and my lips twitched.

I grasped my semi-hard length. "Suck me."

Talia blinked as I brought my dick to her mouth, rubbing the wet tip against her lips. "Suck me clean, Talia. Taste yourself on my cock."

Goosebumps speckled her flesh. Her lips parted and she took me in her mouth, sucking me clean. Good girl, doing as she was told.

There was pleasure.

There was pain.

There was everything filthy and depraved...

I slipped out of her mouth and crouched to her level. My thumb rubbed along her swollen lips and her eyes... grew soft.

"Killer," she whispered.

My chest tightened.

When Talia first bargained with me... she didn't know what to expect, she didn't know what it'd mean to belong to a savage, unhinged man like me. Now, she knew.

Too bad, this wasn't going to last. Too bad, Talia had been too naïve. Too innocent to realize the consequences of her bargain.

If only she had paid attention to the warning signs. If only she hadn't stepped foot into my territory.

If only she hadn't been my target... all along.

Talia Barese was my job.

My prey.

My kill.

Our eyes locked...

And I broke her heart.

"You have twenty-four hours to live, Little One. Any last wishes?"

Chapter Ten

TALIA

It took me a couple of moments for Killer's words to penetrate my dazed mind. "What do you mean?"

I had trouble focusing after what had just happened. When Killer had said he'd wanted a second time, I hadn't expected this unhinged fucking. Even if the word made me squirm, it was the only term fitting for what Killer had done to me, for what I had let him do to me. I was sore, could feel my sensitive flesh throb with a strange ache I couldn't explain.

Killer smirked, his eyes suddenly harsh and cruel. "You've got twenty-four hours to live before you *die*."

I shook my head slowly.

"I was paid to kill you, Talia. That is the only reason I even bothered with you, with this bargain." He snatched up a strand of my hair, letting it glide through his scarred, glistening fingers. Glistening from our joined releases, from his...cum, and suddenly I felt dirty.

He'd used me, had betrayed me. "So, the bargain was a charade so you could *fuck* me?" I whispered harshly, feeling the proof of what we'd done

trickle out of me, feeling tainted and degraded because of his words.

Killer straightened with a cruel smile. "That was an added bonus."

"Did you even kill Pasquale? Maybe that, too, was a lie." I put up a brave front even as fear quickly spread in my chest.

"I killed him as brutally as you asked me to. It was fun, but not as much fun as your cunt."

I stumbled to my feet, stark naked, sore, and heartbroken, but I fought the urge to cover myself. I didn't want to show any more weakness in front of Killer, not after what he had just revealed. Never again.

Never isn't going to be long...

My heart squeezed tightly at the realization.

Twenty-four hours. I searched his face for a flicker of softness, for a reason to hope for pity. There was nothing.

Was I such a bad judge of character? I'd thought Killer had showed me his gentle side for a reason, an emotional reason, not to trick me, not to play with me.

I staggered toward my cupboard even as my legs shook wildly. Killer had ruined my clothes so I needed to grab new things to cover myself, and I needed time to think, to figure out a way out of this. Grabbing jeans and a shirt, I quickly got dressed, my back to Killer, even if it raised the little hairs on my neck. I wanted to school my face into an expression of calm, wanted to hide my hurt from him. He didn't need to know how shaken and heartbroken I was.

Slowly I turned. Killer leaned against the kitchen counter, arms crossed in front of his chest, looking relaxed and at ease, when he'd just shattered my entire world. "Who—" I cleared my throat, hating how shaky my voice was. "Who paid you to kill me?"

I was the cousin of the Famiglia's Capo, the sister-in-law of his Enforcer, but that was all there was to me. I wasn't important. Who'd hate me enough to want to kill me? Who'd spend so much money on it?

Or maybe Killer had taken sex as payment from whoever wanted me dead. That thought made me feel even dirtier. In my silly, naïve mind I'd

thought maybe I was special but I was a job and a pleasure object, nothing more.

"Maybe I'll tell you as a last wish tomorrow," he said, again with that horrible smirk.

I rushed toward the door, hoping to escape, but his steps thundered close behind me and his arms wrapped around my middle, lifting me off the ground as if I weighed nothing.

I struggled like a madwoman, clawed and kicked, but he carried me over to the bed and dropped me unceremoniously. Then he crouched over me, his body holding me down.

"Don't touch me!" I hissed.

"Only a few minutes ago you squeezed my cock while you came around me, and now you play hard to get?"

He was being cruel on purpose, and it was having an effect on me. Tears sprang into my eyes. "You aren't any better than the man you killed for me. You are a monster. You don't deserve to touch me ever again, not after betraying me."

He laughed darkly. "Betrayal?"

I glared, even as a tear slid down my cheek. I was fighting so hard to be strong but it was too much. Killer's eyes followed the descent of my tear.

"How will you kill me?" I asked softly. "Will you make me suffer because someone paid you to do it? Or will you make it quick?"

Something shifted in Killer's eyes and for a heartbeat it gave me hope, but hadn't I misinterpreted his actions before? He was playing with my emotions, maybe that was part of the torture leading up to my death.

Killer pushed away from me and straightened, looking away. He smirked again. It looked wrong on his face. "Twenty-four hours, Little One, then you'll find out."

Chapter Eleven

KILLER

Part of me knew that I did her wrong. Whatever humanity was left inside me, pitied her. Ached for her.

I didn't remember much of my childhood before the cage... before the insistent *need* to kill... before the bloodlust and the vicious anger inside me. For a long time, I forgot to be human. I forgot what it felt like to be... human.

I was owned. A slave. An animal.

A fearsome beast – and I had been treated as such.

A monster who slaughtered.

I was... KILLER.

But in this moment, I actually *felt*... bad for Talia Barese. I might have been the Grim Reaper... but I guessed, I was still human, after all.

Too bad, I had been paid to kill her. She was my job and there was nothing I could do to save her. Even if little Talia had crawled under my skin, her death clock had started ticking the moment someone paid for her blood.

Goddamn it. She was a temptation I was weak against... a forbidden

fruit I craved to taste. An obsession I couldn't possibly deny.

When she had walked right into my territory, I thought she would have been an easy kill. I didn't have to hunt her down, she had unknowingly walked right into her death. I had been pleased with the outcome.

Until I saw her.

Until I touched her.

Until I tasted her.

Until her cunt had squeezed my cock like her life depended on it.

FUCK!

Talia whimpered and her eyes fluttered open. She winced with a pained groan. I watched as she came back from her little sleep, as she fought to stay awake. A cough ripped from her throat and she groaned again, appearing to be just as disoriented as I expected her to be.

She had been sleeping for over twelve hours.

Talia slowly grasped onto her consciousness and the moment she was finally awake enough to realize her predicament, she thrashed to get free. A loud wail escaped her.

"Noooo! No! Let me go!!"

The chains clanked as she kept thrashing, fighting to get free.

There was no point. She was trapped.

Trapped for another twelve hours before I end her life…

I stepped out from the shadows. Her head snapped toward me and her wide, fearful eyes met mine. They glistened with tears. Tsk, poor Talia.

Minutes passed in strained silence before she finally let out a choked sob. "Why?"

I cocked my head to the side, waiting.

Her chin wobbled as she held in another cry. She sniffled and her watery eyes narrowed on me. She was refusing to break down in front of me. Strong and fierce. If it was any other time, I would have appreciated that.

Talia pulled on her chains, the sound of metal clanging against the wall loud against the silence. "Why are you doing this? Why did you use me? Why not just… kill me? WHY?"

"I do what I want." I grinned. "I'll kill you when I want and how? I will decide that too."

She spat on the ground, looking incensed. "I hate you."

My jaw locked, my eyes hardened and I took a step forward. I didn't know why those words irked me, especially coming from her sweet fucking lips. My fists clenched. "Good. I've heard those words a thousand times."

I crouched to her level, bringing our faces closer. "Hate me, Talia. It won't change your fate. You are meant to die at my hands."

Our noses touched as I gripped her jaw in my hand. My thumb stroked her soft skin, feeling her twitch under my touch. "Hate me, Little One," I taunted.

She wretched her face out of my grasp and my lips curved with a smirk. My head dropped to the side as I studied her. I had undressed her, only leaving her bra and panties on.

Talia was... beautiful.

Small and dainty.

Vulnerable.

Seeing her like this, fragile and weak... at my mercy... my dick hardened. I was a sick fucking bastard.

I have had my fair share of beautiful women, but there was just... *something* about this one.

A sudden rage consumed me. Talia was my kill. Fuck, I had to remember that.

I stood up to my full height and took a few steps back, taking a seat on the single chair that was facing her. "You're confused. You have a lot of questions, I see. Let's say I'm feeling very generous today. Ask me your questions and I'll give you the answers you're looking for."

Talia glanced around her, taking in the semi-finished basement. It was just one large room. Four drywalls. Two metals chains, where Talia was currently trapped by her wrists. A small caged window. Cold, cement ground. A flickering lightbulb. And a single chair, that I was sitting on. There was nothing else. It was an empty jail.

"Where am I?" she asked through gritted teeth.

"My home."

Her head snapped back toward me. "Your... home? You brought me to your house?"

I shrugged. "I couldn't possibly let you escape. This is where I can finish... my job."

Her chest rumbled with a helpless, kitten growl. "You're an asshole."

"That wasn't a question. Try again."

Talia tugged on her chains again and she winced, her eyes screwed in pain. The metal must have been biting into her skin since she was pulling at it way too much. She took in a shuddering breath and opened her eyes again, narrowed on me.

"Why did you use me?"

My teeth scraped across my bottom lip. "Because I felt like it."

"Who ordered you to kill me?" Talia whispered, ignoring my previous answer.

"Cutillo," I replied honestly.

She looked confused for a moment until finally realization set in. She let out a sigh, letting her head thump back against the drywall.

I raised an eyebrow, curious. "Why does he want to kill you?"

"*She,*" Talia hissed. "Old enemies. She stole my sister's fiancé and then he got our father killed. And when my brother-in-law dished out his vengeance, Anastasia ended up losing everything. It makes sense... why she'd want me dead. She wants to hurt my sister... through me."

Her breathing was shaky and she curled into herself. "I shouldn't have left home..."

"I would have found you either way," I growled.

Talia shook her head. She didn't say anything. A stab of something strange, an unknown feeling twisted my stomach. I quickly shoved it away and braced my elbows on my knees, nodding toward the tray in front of her.

"Eat." One word. A single command. She hissed, her eyes narrowing on me.

"Is this my last meal?" The plate was filled with pieces of roasted chicken, garlic bread and vegetables. There was fruit on the side with a mango smoothie. And a brownie.

My jaw locked and I didn't answer. She shot me a look of distaste. "How long do I have left to live?"

"Hours," I said. "Or days."

She looked at the plate, a resigned expression on her face. "But you said I only had twenty hours?"

Pushing the chair away, I stood up. "Maybe I changed my mind."

Talia bit on her lip, her brown eyes boring into me... as if she was trying to dig into my soul. "You... won't kill me?" Her question had been so quiet I almost missed it.

"No, I *will*." My chest tightened as the words spilled past my lips.

"What do you mean then?"

My lips twitched and my dick throbbed. "I'm not finished with you... yet."

Chapter Twelve

TALIA

I wasn't sure how long I'd been in Killer's basement, chained to the wall. The hours blurred together. I shivered again. I'd been alternating between freezing and burning up for a while now. A fine sheen of perspiration covered my bare skin.

I tugged at the chain once more, wincing as the metal dug into my sore skin. My head was throbbing and I just felt…off. I leaned my head back, squeezing my eyes shut. I was coming down with something. No wonder really, considering I'd been trapped in this dank basement in my underwear for God only knew how long.

The lock turned, but I didn't bother opening my eyes.

Steps rang out. "Trying to ignore me, Little One?"

I still didn't react. I felt dizzy and tired. I wouldn't waste my energy on the man who wanted to kill me. Clothes rustled and suddenly his palm pressed to my forehead. My eyes shot open, staring into Killer's face. For a second, I was sure I saw worry in his expression. Maybe he didn't want a fever to kill me off and ruin his specific plans for me.

"You're burning up."

I smiled wryly. "See, you can let nature run its course. You don't even have to kill me with your own hands."

With a frown, he unchained me and picked me up.

"What are you doing?"

"Shut up for once," he snapped.

The motion made me sick so I had no choice but to lean my head against his chest, hating how I still felt comforted by his strength, even though he was my killer. He carried me up a narrow staircase into what looked like the master bedroom. Was it his bedroom?

He set me down on the king-size bed then hovered over me. Conflict showed on his face before he straightened and disappeared through the door. I sat up slowly, even as my vision swam. This was my chance. I stumbled to my feet then plopped right back down.

Killer entered with a tea. My eyebrows shot up.

"You can't run, so don't waste your energy." He set the cup down on the nightstand then pushed me back down and covered me with the blanket.

"Why do you care?"

"I don't."

"Then why can't you just let me rot in your basement? Why bring me up here and give me tea if you're going to kill me anyway?"

"Because it's no fun killing someone this weak," he growled before he walked over to an armchair in the corner next to the window and sank down. I lowered my head to the soft pillow, confused by his strange behavior but also oddly comforted that I wouldn't spend my last hours in the basement.

Shuddering, I closed my eyes.

"Drink the tea," he ordered.

That night my fever broke. My teeth clanked together as I shivered wildly, my skin hot to the touch. My underwear and the sheets were soaked

by my sweat and I must have looked an absolute mess with my hair stuck to my forehead.

Maybe my pitiful sight was why Killer stayed at my side, foregoing sleep. He pressed a cold washcloth to my forehead, brows pulled together. He hadn't said anything in hours, only watched me with this intense expression. It didn't make sense for him to take care of me like this…unless he cared for me a little.

I doubted he generally felt pity for his victims so it was the only explanation why he took care of me. Maybe our time together had stirred something in him like it had in me. A longing for a connection, for a meaning in his life that went beyond killing.

"Don't look at me like that," he growled.

"Like what?" I croaked.

He shook his head and dropped the washcloth on the nightstand. "As if I'm your fucking savior. I just want to make sure I fulfil my contract."

I laughed weakly. He stalked over to the armchair and sank down.

Two days later I was feeling much better. I finally managed to get out of bed and take a long shower, washing off all the grime. When I emerged from the bathroom with a towel wrapped around my body, Killer sat on the bed. Slowly I made my way over to him. Something in his eyes gave me hope and more importantly, courage.

I stopped right in front of him. His nostrils flared and his gaze lingered on the edge of my towel, right over the swell of my breasts. "No matter what you say, I know you don't want to kill me. If you did, I'd already be dead."

"You know nothing," he snarled.

I didn't let his anger deter me. I moved even closer between his legs. Even with him sitting and me standing, we were at eye-level. He grabbed ahold of my hips, the touch possessive and threatening at once. I touched his strong shoulder then slowly trailed my fingers up his tattooed throat,

surprised he allowed me to touch this vulnerable spot. But I wasn't really a threat to him, was I?

I leaned forward when my palm touched his cheek and kissed him softly. The look in his eyes was thunderous. My towel fell to the floor with a soft swoosh. "If you let me live, I could be yours."

With a growl, he pulled out of the kiss and grasped my wrist painfully. "Run, Little One, run. And don't let me catch you, because when I do, it's over."

He released me and I staggered back, naked and stunned. Then I whirled around and started running. I knew he'd catch me, knew running was futile, and yet I did. He caught me in the hallway. This was his game, his hunt, and I was only the prey.

His fingers clamped down on my wrist, but I was done being toyed with. I whirled on him, tried to jerk free. We started struggling and suddenly I was falling. The back of my head collided with the edge of a cupboard. I hit the ground hard. Before my vision turned black, Killer came into view, towering over me.

Not the savior I'd wanted him to be, but my ultimate doom.

Everything faded to black. Would Killer's face be the last I ever saw? Were these the last seconds of my life?

Epilogue

KILLER

Three months later

I was seven years old when I was sold to the devil and became a slave... a cage fighter.

I was number 781. That was my identity.

At eight years old, I made my first kill.

At thirteen, I became KILLER.

At fifteen years old, I was declared a champion in the cage.

I had been my master's favorite. The best of the best.

When I was twenty-two years old, I murdered him...and his wife... and I became a free man.

For ten years, I took odd jobs here and there. I hunted, I kidnapped, I killed. I was the Bratva's assassin.

Until *she* walked into my life and tested my loyalty.

Talia Barese was my job. I was paid to kill her...

It didn't matter if she had wormed her way into my heart or that her

vulnerability called to me… she had to die.

I remembered her face that night. The look of pure terror in her eyes as she surrendered herself to her fate before she lost consciousness. She knew there was no escaping Death…

I was the Grim Reaper and I had called her name three times.

And so, Talia died.

At my hands.

Her death was easy… and fuck, it was painful to watch.

I inhaled the salty smell of the ocean as my yacht moved with the waves. Standing next to the railing, I watched the dolphins swim along in the vast body of water. I was in the middle of the ocean, in the middle of nowhere. Far away from my reality.

Closing my eyes, I breathed in. *This* was freedom.

I turned around and my gaze slid over to her. She was sunbathing, in her very indecent red bikini. Fuck me, she was a temptation I couldn't resist.

She pushed her sunglasses up, revealing her pretty brown eyes and smirked. "Are you going to just stand there or join me?"

My chest rumbled with a chuckle and I joined her, laying next to her on the towel. She rolled her eyes and climbed on top of me, straddling me. My hands curled around her hips and she smiled.

"Are you hungry?" she said.

"Fucking starved."

She giggled and leaned in for a kiss. My lips captured hers and she moaned.

Three months ago, I had been too fucking selfish to let her go.

Talia died…

Nova took her place.

Nova Armani. My wife.

TALIA

When I'd lost consciousness three months ago with Killer's brutal face over me, I'd been certain he'd kill me. Images of my life hadn't played out before my eyes. And even if they had, few of them would have been happy. All my life I'd felt as if the future was on hold, as if I was living with the brakes on. Always controlled by others.

Maybe everyone had that moment of no return. A pivotal instance that changed everything. For me it was the moment of my death.

I promised myself to live, take more risks, be free, and in the same instant, I worried I'd never get the chance.

Talia Barese died that day.

But I had eventually opened my eyes, my head throbbing with a fierce headache and had stared at Killer who perched on his bed beside me.

"You couldn't let the cupboard kill me, you need to do it yourself?" I croaked.

Killer didn't crack a smile. "I won't kill you. But you must die."

My brain was still too fuzzy to make sense of it.

"You can live if you let Talia die. I'll tell everyone the job is done. They won't doubt me. I'm the fucking Grim Reaper. But you'll have to go into hiding. Leave everything behind. Your family. Your name."

I sat up slowly. "You'll let me run?"

"I never said I'd let you run from me." He leaned close and kissed me harshly, completely catching me by surprise. When he pulled back, he searched my face.

I nodded, even though he hadn't asked. "We can run together. You aren't free here. We both have never truly been free. Maybe together we can finally discover what true freedom tastes like."

"The only taste I want now is your pussy."

We'd packed everything that same day and Killer had declared me dead to his client. I didn't exist anymore.

He bought a yacht from his savings, blood money all of it, but as a mafia princess, I'd grown up surrounded by dirty riches. The next day, we set out in our boat. I wrote a letter to my sister Cara, telling her I was safe but couldn't return to New York and the mafia. One day, I'd see her again. She had found happiness with Growl, and now it was my turn to find my own.

Killer got new IDs for us, new names we'd come up with on a late night with too much wine and even more sex. Nova and Nero. A new beginning and a man who burnt down a city. Both names oddly fitting for us. Our last name was the result of Killer's insistence that I needed to start drinking vodka.

As I stared down at Killer now, straddling his hips, feeling his hard cock digging insistently against my pussy, I couldn't help but grin. "Nova and Nero Armani. It can't get any more extra than that. We'll never make important decisions with vodka again."

Killer nudged up his Armani sunglasses with a smirk, letting me see the hunger in his eyes. Those glasses were our own personal inside joke and they still cracked me up after all this time. Killer shoved my bikini bottom aside and slipped a finger between my folds then pushed the digit into his mouth. "Never thought my wife would taste so sweet."

I leaned down. "I'm only your wife on paper. We never got married officially."

"Who gives a fuck about official. We're the rulers of our fucking lives. No one else. You are mine. End of story."

Killer freed his cock from his swim shorts and plunged into me with a vicious upwards thrust. I gasped, throwing my head back with a smile. The sun warmed my skin. The breeze tugged at my hair. The ocean whooshed in the background. I felt free. For the first time in my life, I tasted freedom.

Killer's hands on my hips tightened until I looked at him again. My smile widened. I rotated my hips. We were in the middle of the ocean. Without a destination. Adrift but not lost. We were each other's home.

I was reborn. We were both reborn. Nova and Nero Armani. Finally free.

The End

ABOUT LYLAH JAMES

Lylah James uses all her spare time to write. If she is not studying, sleeping, writing or working—she can be found with her nose buried in a good romance book, preferably with a hot alpha male. Writing is her passion. The voices in her head won't stop, and she believes they deserve to be heard and read. Lylah James writes about drool worthy and total alpha males and strong and sweet heroines. She makes her readers cry—sob their eyes out, swoon, curse, rage, and fall in love. Mostly known as the Queen of Cliffhangers and the #evilauthorwithablacksoul, she likes to break her readers' hearts and then mend them.

Connect with me!

Did you enjoy THE DIRTY BARGAIN? Come and join my reader's group:
Lylah's Lovelies Therapy Group
or Like my author page to make sure you stay in the loop!

Or you can sign up to my Newsletter

BOOKS BY LYLAH JAMES

Tainted Hearts Series

The Mafia and His Angel: Part One
The Mafia and His Angel: Part Two
The Mafia and His Angel: Part Three
Blood and Roses
The Mafia and His Obsession: Part One
The Mafia and His Obsession: Part Two

Truth and Dare Duet

DO YOU DARE? (Book one)
I DARE YOU (Book two, the conclusion)

Standalone

A VOW OF HATE

ABOUT CORA REILLY

Cora is the USA Today bestselling author of the Born in Blood Mafia Series, the Camorra Chronicles and many other books, most of them featuring dangerously sexy bad boys. She likes her men like her martinis—dirty and strong.

Cora lives in Germany with a cute but crazy Bearded Collie, as well as the cute but crazy man at her side. When she doesn't spend her days dreaming up sexy books, she plans her next travel adventure or cooks too spicy dishes from all over the world.

BOOKS BY CORA REILLY

Born in Blood Mafia Chronicles:
Bound by Honor
(Aria & Luca)
Bound by Duty
(Valentina & Dante)
Bound by Hatred
(Gianna & Matteo)
Bound By Temptation
(Liliana & Romero)
Bound By Vengeance
(Growl & Cara)
Bound By Love
(Luca & Aria)
Bound By The Past
(Dante & Valentina)
Luca Vitiello (Luca's POV of Bound by Honor)

The Camorra Chronicles:
Twisted Loyalties (#1)
Fabiano
Twisted Emotions (#2)
Nino
Twisted Pride (#3)
Remo
Twisted Bonds (#4)
Nino
Twisted Hearts (#5)
Savio
Twisted Cravings (#6)
Adamo

Coming 2021

Mafia Standalones:

Fragile Longing
Sweet Temptation

Mr. Foster

K. WEBSTER AND SAM MARIANO

Chapter One

CHELSEA

Coming to a sudden stop on the bustling NYC sidewalk, I shield my eyes and look up at the towering building before me. It's slate gray with plenty of windows, the reflection of the sky bouncing off and making the building appear blue and sleek.

"I think this is it," I murmur to myself.

There's no way to tell, but the PR firm I'm looking for is so elite and exclusive, they don't need a sign. I know it's on the top two floors, so I take a quick look all the way up at the levels I'll be spending my days on.

I could be spending my days on a beach in the Hamptons with my family, but I chose this instead. I've spent the last eighteen summers at the Hamptons house—I figured it was time to do something else.

An internship at Dunbar Foster may not sound glamorous, but come fall when I start my first semester of college, real world work experience at one of the most prominent PR firms in New York City is bound to serve me better than a flawless tan.

Most people who know me would probably guess I'd take the flawless

tan over hard work any day, but that's not an image I want to carry with me in the fall. I want a fresh start in college. I want to show all the people who underestimate me that I can be so much more than a blonde bombshell in a party dress.

I mean, I'm still going to wear kickass cocktail dresses—but now I'll get paid for it.

I smile as I make my way inside the building to get out of the sweltering summer heat. I'm nervous—but also really excited—to start my first day of work.

I make my way to the elevator and press the button. On the way up to my floor, I smooth down my skirt and straighten my outfit, then I grab my iPhone out of my Chanel bag and double check the details in the "welcome to Dunbar Foster!" email they sent to prepare me.

It's a stodgy email with a lecturing tone telling me all the dos and don'ts of the workplace. For example, *do* show up fifteen minutes early to work. *Don't* fraternize with co-workers or anyone in any kind of management position. There's even a fun graphic with faux-handwritten type and clipart to support the most important tenants for anyone who decides to skim the long-ass PDF attachment.

I didn't skim. I read every single word. I know what a great opportunity this is, and I'm not going to blow it over something trivial.

When the elevator doors open, straight ahead of me is an empty wall with only the company name emblazoned across it.

DUNBAR FOSTER and ASSOCIATES.

My heart skips a beat as I read it, lingering on Foster.

Seeing his name there on the wall, so bold and imposing...

Well, it reminds me there's one more person I have to prove myself to.

William Foster, co-founder of this company and good friend of my father's. I guess they met in college and, both of them being smart and ambitious, became fast friends.

Their lives took different paths, though. My dad accidentally knocked up my mom junior year, so they decided to get married and go the family

route.

William Foster isn't the sort of man who does anything accidentally. He didn't make any mistakes or let himself get distracted. He pursued his goals relentlessly until he had what he wanted.

It's only because of their friendship I was able to score this position. Daddy didn't blatantly tell me his friend was reluctant to give me a shot, but I could tell in the careful way he told me about the position and the responsibility it would entail.

You're taking this position in place of someone who worked really hard to qualify for it, so you have to take it seriously.

Like it was a stretch of his imagination to think I could take anything seriously.

Oh well. Shaking off everyone else's doubts, I take a left and head over to the reception desk.

Greeting the chilly-looking woman who sits there with a sunny smile, I tell her, "Hi, I'm Chelsea Parker. Today's the first day of my internship—"

The lady thrusts her palm up to halt me and I realize she's wearing a headset. "No, she isn't in today, but I can forward you to her voicemail box and she can get back to you tomorrow."

"Oh. Sorry," I whisper, falling back a step and looking around awkwardly as I wait for her to finish her call.

After taking three more, she finally gets to me. I was here fifteen minutes early, but after standing here for ten minutes, I'm getting a little nervous about being late by the time I get to where I'm supposed to be.

Surely they're a little more lenient on the first day, but they did send me that email…

Sighing as she switches off the headset, the woman shoots me a brief, apologetic smile. "Sorry, I'm a little busy over here. I am not a receptionist."

"Oh." I frown slightly, looking around, but I don't see anything that looks more like a reception area than this. "Is this… not the reception desk?"

Her eyebrows rise with familiar annoyance. "Oh, no. It is—I'm just not a receptionist. I'm an assistant pulling double duty until we can get someone in here Foster doesn't hate. A temp showed up this morning and he fired her on the spot. It may not surprise you to hear the last receptionist quit, so…" Suddenly struck by an idea, she eyes me up and asks brightly, "Have you ever worked the phones?"

I shake my head quickly. I don't want her getting any ideas, so I quickly light up my phone screen and flash her the time. "I'm almost late and that's probably not the first impression I want to make, so…"

"Oh! Yes, you need HR." Finally, the woman directs me to the appropriate office on the same floor, so I make my way to it.

Orientation is a bit tedious, but it breezes by. In fact, the whole first half of the day does. I'm introduced to the people in my department and shown the ropes. Then—since his assistant is preoccupied at the reception desk—I'm handed off on a temporary basis to an associate named Ryan. He seems nice enough, but he doesn't ask a lot of me. Basically, I'm just fetching him coffee and drafting emails that he reads before they're sent, anyway.

I get the feeling there is much more to the job that he's just not putting on me, because he's running around all morning and seems as overwhelmed as the front desk girl.

Just before lunchtime, I head into his office to see if I can order him something. I've never been an assistant, but I have seen assistants on movies and TV shows order out for the person they're assisting. Seems like it might be helpful.

When I step inside, I see Ryan standing at his desk, leaning down to type on his computer with the phone wedged between his ear and shoulder to keep it from falling.

"I hear a fax coming through right now, that's probably it," he says into the phone.

I see the fax machine, so I run over to grab the paper it's spitting out and walk it over to him.

He flashes me a grateful smile as he grabs it and starts skimming so he can sound more prepared than he is for whatever conversation he's having.

I don't know what else to do, so I wait for him to finish his call. When he finally does, he drops into his office chair and sighs. "Is it time to go home yet?"

The poor man looks exhausted. "I wish I could help. I can help, but you need to let me do more. I'm not useless, I swear."

In a half-hearted attempt to be nice, he tells me, "You have been helping."

I cock an eyebrow at him. "Helping enable your caffeine dependency, maybe. I know it's only my first day, but I'm here to assist you. You don't have to take it easy on me, Ryan. I'm a big girl, I can handle a little hard work."

My words do seem to have a relaxing effect on him, but I'm not sure it's in precisely the way I intended. I only meant he could take me seriously and give me actual responsibilities, but his gaze travels over my body in a way that makes me wonder if *he* has read the no-fraternization policy.

"I bet you can," he murmurs.

I straighten, glancing away from him so he'll think I didn't notice.

Ryan is an attractive man—a good build underneath that gray suit he's wearing, golden blonde hair he spends time styling, an easy smile and an endearing dimple to top it off. He has nice eyes, too, and I'm a sucker for nice eyes.

I've read the rules, though, and there's only one man in this building who could possibly tempt me to break them.

The man who never would.

Ignoring the way Ryan looks at me, I ask if I can order him some lunch. He has a meeting directly after that he's not prepared for, so he probably won't be leaving the office today.

He thanks me and gives me his order, so I head off to place it and get him a fresh cup of coffee.

As I'm walking back to the office, I spot a gaggle of assistants

gathered together, whispering about something of apparent urgency. I wonder if I should poke my nose in and see if there's anything I should know about, but I want to get Ryan his coffee first.

When I come back, Ryan is in his office chair with his back to me, rifling through a drawer of files. Without interrupting, I make my way over and go to sit the coffee down on the coaster atop his desk.

Ryan spins back around and knocks into me. I lose my balance, dropping the coffee mug and grabbing the edge of the desk to keep from falling. The mug hits the desk and falls over—spilling piping hot coffee directly onto Ryan's lap.

"Oh, my God," I say as he shouts, jumping up out of the chair. My heart skitters to a stop, then starts racing, my face heating with a mix of horror and embarrassment. "I'm so sorry!"

I turn around and look for anything I can find to clean it up. What I need is a clean towel, but all I find are some brown take-out napkins.

Ryan can only think to get the hot liquid off his body, so I'm not all that surprised or alarmed when he rips open his pants and shoves them down to get the soaked fabric away from his skin.

"Here, let me help," I say, rushing forward with my fistful of napkins.

I think he starts to object, but before he can, I thrust my hand forward and start dabbing.

His skin is red and irritated where I spilled the coffee on him so I try to rub carefully. "I'm so sorry. Does it hurt?"

Ryan swallows and throws his head back as I dab. He makes a noise low in his throat that makes me think it probably does hurt, but before I can ask again, I hear my name uttered in such a sharp tone, I nearly forget about Ryan's ailment.

"Miss Parker."

My heart falls straight to my feet.

I know that voice. Deep and masculine, entirely commanding—but not loud. He doesn't have to be loud.

It was his voice that I first noticed at the Hamptons house a couple

of summers ago. Mom was throwing one of her famous summer soirees, and Foster happened to be in town, so he stopped by. I actually had my eye on someone else—one of the waiters Mom hired to work the party—but Foster stole my attention away. One minute I was helping myself to a flute of champagne I was too young to drink and trying my best to captivate the cute cater-waiter, the next... Foster happened.

As soon as he spoke, my focus was his. I turned around to see who was speaking to me and met the familiar, piercing blue eyes of Daddy's best friend.

It wasn't long before I'd completely forgotten about the waiter. Foster captured my attention in that moment, and as the night wore on, he definitely kept it.

I was only a passing amusement for him, though. A casual flirtation that meant absolutely nothing—especially when he realized who I was, how old I was...

William Foster may have forgotten about me, but he always lingered in my mind.

It's daunting given the position I'm in at the moment, but when I raise my gaze to meet his beautiful blue eyes, it's just like it was at the party—all thoughts of any other man evaporate in a puff of smoke.

His face is perfect. As if sculpted lovingly by an artist who regarded the task as his life's work. His granite jaw is locked, making him appear almost... irritated. His piercing blue eyes are locked on me, pinning me to the spot. I want to move, but I can't.

I can't look away.

Then his perfect lips lift the tiniest bit—in amusement or disdain, I can't tell.

"Kindly remove your hand from my employee's dick and come with me. It appears we need to talk."

Chapter Two

FOSTER

I knew this was a terrible fucking idea.

But how was I supposed to tell Mason I didn't want his daughter interning for me?

"Sorry, man, but your little girl's ass is a tempting distraction I absolutely don't need in my life right now."

Hell no.

I'd wanted to tell him no—even had the two-letter word sitting on the tip of my tongue—but he fucking begged.

Mason Landon Parker pleaded for a *simple* favor.

I owe him so much and he's never once asked for anything in return. He's a good guy. Wears charisma better than the ten thousand dollar suits he dons each day. Smart and business savvy and a fucking go-getter if I ever saw one. For most of our friendship, I've aspired to be as well-rounded as he is. I'd promised myself if he ever needed anything, I'd find a way to give it to him.

Except this.

Fuck.

Of all the things he could ask, this was the one that was almost too much.

Chelsea Parker.

The same stunning little temptress I'd flirted with when she was barely old enough to drive. Stupid and out of character. Yet, my dumb horny ass thought there was no harm in teasing the smiles out of her.

It's not like I planned to kiss her or fuck her.

Harmless.

But it wasn't harmless because I couldn't get her out of my head. Two years later and my dick still reacts to the gorgeous young woman.

She's untouchable, though, for a multitude of reasons. Not only is it against company policy to bend the hot new intern over my desk, fucking her until she screams, but she's also Mason's goddamn daughter.

"I, uh, it's not what it looked like," Chelsea croaks out, her cheeks flaming pink and her neck turning splotchy red. Her sea green eyes plead for me to understand.

I've never seen eyes that color green. Exactly like the Caribbean Sea that surrounded Saona Island in the Dominican Republic. The color, when I'd visited seven years ago, stood out to me. I took the time to really appreciate the fruits of my labor, enjoying every detail of that trip, even down to the color of the water. When I was a kid, I would have never imagined I'd leave Dad's scummy apartment in the Bronx and one day be sitting on a boat marveling over the most beautiful scenery I'd ever seen— probably in the world.

And, yet, there I was.

Hard work and perseverance got me there. I'm not weak. I won't allow myself to be sidetracked by a gorgeous socialite with a nice rack and legs that go on for a mile.

"Mr. Foster," Ryan grumbles as he pulls his pants back up. "She spilled my coffee. It's not whatever it looked like."

I narrow my eyes, darting my gaze between the two of them. Ryan

wilts under my stare while Chelsea simply seems mortified.

"Why don't you run home on your lunch and take care of your situation?" I suggest, gesturing at the horror show that are his slacks.

Ryan sighs but nods. "I don't have time for this, but I guess it's out of my hands."

"I'm sorry," Chelsea blurts out as he passes.

His irritation melts away when he walks past her, unable to keep his lecherous eyes out of her cleavage. The urge to grab hold of his tie and yank him to his knees to remind him he serves me in this company is strong. Instead, I allow him his creepy peep show. Then, he's gone, leaving nothing but the scent of cheap cologne and hazelnut in his wake.

"Mr. Foster—"

"We'll discuss this in my office."

I turn on my heel and storm out of Ryan's office. Several women who are gathered nearby smirk at Chelsea. Unfortunately, I work in a den of vipers. Each female at this firm make up for their lack of cocks with razor-sharp fangs that are always poised at each other's jugulars. I tip my head at the group, earning a few starry-eyed gazes in return.

Chelsea's designer heels clack furiously behind me as she rushes to keep up with my intense stride. Her long legs had no trouble keeping up with me at that soiree as we walked the sands of Georgica Beach in the East Hamptons.

I guide her to the office with the best view. Mine. It's encased in glass so everyone can see what real work looks like. I'm at the office before everyone and am the last to leave. Hell, I've even crashed on my leather sofa a few times when my workload was too much.

Pushing through the door, I step aside to grant her entry. She's quiet as she takes a seat in front of my desk. Her back is ramrod straight— posture that's long been perfected from years of playing the princess in her daddy's wealthy world.

I walk past her, noting a hint of a sweet, fruity perfume that seems to fill the air. Like an idiot, I inhale the scent, memorizing her smell like a

pathetic creep. With great difficulty, I remind myself I'm in charge here.

"So," I say as I take my seat. "Here you are."

She's unsettled and flustered. At her mother's summer soiree, she was the perfect socialite, polite and friendly and fucking flawless. Now, she's older, somehow even more stunning, but her poise is gone. The girl is out of her element, swimming with the biggest shark in Manhattan, the tiny cut to her self-esteem in Ryan's office quickly becoming a gaping, hemorrhaging wound.

I lick my lips, salivating for the opportunity to drag her into the deep end and remind her she can't swim.

And fuck if her eyes don't track the movement of my tongue.

"It's been quite a day," she finally utters, tearing her stare from my mouth as she lifts her chin and meets my intense scrutiny head-on.

"Quite." I pause because watching her squirm has been the highlight of my day. "First you were late, then you pranced around running coffee to my associate as if he needs anymore goddamn caffeine, and you ended your morning by possibly giving him third-degree burns. I agree, Miss Parker, it's been *quite* a day."

She scoffs, her nostrils flaring in outrage. "I wasn't late and your associate was too busy to find anything of actual use for me to do."

"And what exactly did you expect to do on your first day?" I challenge, cocking a brow up at her. "You're an intern at Dunbar Foster, not an influencer on Instagram or TikTok or whatever it is you *children* waste your time on these days."

She flinches, gaping at me as though I've struck her. Sure, it's rude as fuck, but if I don't put her into the appropriate box—best friend's little girl—where she belongs, she'll end up in my bed and I can't have that. Not ever.

"Foster—"

"*Mr.* Foster," I correct, flashing her a wolfish grin.

Rage flashes in her pretty eyes making them seem to explode with electric slivers of dark blue. It'd be mesmerizing if I weren't telling my

dick to sit the fuck down. I wait for the onslaught of bitchiness I know is itching to come out based on her enraged expression. But, like the practiced puppet she is, she sucks in a deep breath of air, relaxes, and plasters on her Barbie smile.

"*Mr.* Foster." The way she purrs my name should be illegal. I should send her ass to HR and have them write her up for being so goddamn tempting. "Lucky for you and your impressive..." She trails off, her lips quirking on one side in a flirty way I remember from Georgica Beach. "Firm." A pregnant pause as she smirks. "I am a woman of many, many talents."

My dick is aching and throbbing, threatening to tear through the fabric and make an appearance. I clasp my hands together, resting them in my lap and nod at her to continue.

"I can make coffee and answer phones," she continues, "but I can also do other things. All you have to do is show me once." Her dark, mascara-painted lashes bat innocently at me. "I'm a fast learner."

Irritation burns through my veins, chasing away any lust lingering. She knows exactly what she's doing. Matching my dickheaded behavior with a bratty, seductive taunt.

Focus, Foster.

"Fine," I clip out, returning to business mode. "While we wait for Ryan to return—so you can get back to wowing him with your multitasking abilities—let's discuss your future."

A genuine smile graces her lips and goddammit, my unruly dick takes note.

"I'm not like my mother," she says carefully, as though she's walking through a landmine and doesn't know where to step. "I have ambitions outside of my country club gal pals."

Jesus. It's like she's auditioning for Miss America or some shit.

"Mhmm," I grunt, turning my attention to my computer to check my emails. "Continue, Miss Manhattan."

She starts her spiel, one I tune out as I send Evan Swanson—a model

who blew up in the acting scene last year and someone I represent—a reply to let him know I'd love to see a Broadway show with him but I'll have to check my schedule and get back to him. Next, I send out some more emails pertaining to a few meetings I have lined up with new clients. Chelsea continues to talk about God only knows what while I offer her the occasional nod.

"I've seen it all," Ryan says from the doorway.

I snap my attention to him, noting his new pair of slacks with the price tag still hanging on. This guy's drowning in so much work he couldn't even lose the time it took to go home, instead stopping off at Armani on Fifth Avenue, if I know my designer labels—which I absolutely and completely to my horror do.

"What?" I bite out, harsher than necessary.

Ryan's predatory grin is one that sold me when hiring him, but now it just annoys the fuck out of me. "You, boss man. I stood here for a full five minutes listening to her name every nail polish color Dior makes, mentioning at least fifteen times that Tra-la-la is her favorite because it's so unassuming."

I blink quickly trying to make sense of his words.

"He wasn't listening," Chelsea says with a shrug. "Ready to put me back to work?"

"I'm kind of enjoying this," Ryan teases, chuckling as he crosses his arms over his chest. "And here I thought this guy was subhuman. Turns out, he's just like the rest of us."

"Not every guy gets bored to tears when talking about nail polish," Chelsea argues, her blond brow hiking up high.

"I'm going to have to beg to differ, Chels," Ryan tosses back, clearly amused at her words.

Chels.

The shortened nickname annoys me for reasons I can't begin to fathom.

I'm about to tell them both to get the fuck out of my office when I see

it. Behind the glossy façade of a prissy girl is a viper. She's in the right den. And her fangs are bigger than Ryan's dick could ever be. Poor guy doesn't realize she's about to school him. Leaning back, I wait for her to strike.

She rises from her seat, taking a moment to smooth out the wrinkles of her skirt. I skim my gaze over her juicy ass and then to her fingernails that are flawlessly painted in what must be Tra-la-la.

"I know one guy who could talk about nail polish all day long," she says, tapping one of those painted nails on her pouty pink bottom lip. "You might know him."

Ryan, the idiot, just stares at her, fixated on her sexy mouth.

He *does* know him.

Schmoozed the hell out of him in March at the SAG Awards after party. If he'd listened for half a second rather than running his mouth, he'd have learned this too. Question is, how does she know?

"Evan Swanson." She cocks her head at him. "You know him?"

Realization dawns on him, causing his brows to pinch together. "Of course I know him. He's a great client of Dunbar Foster."

"He's *the* Harry Styles of this year," I cut in so he doesn't make an idiot of himself for not knowing such a small yet important detail of one of our clients. "Worldwide fashion icon as you know. Despite his blossoming acting career, he continues to be a spokesperson for Dior. Their makeup line exploded in popularity when he wore Tra-la-la to the Grammy's and gave them a shoutout, saying—"

"'Boys can love pink too,'" Chelsea finishes for me. "He's been quoted to say Tra-la-la is such an unassuming color and is his favorite."

She grins my way, proud as fuck at her victory. The girl knows her stuff. I'll give her that. And because I'm not a total asshole, I reward her with a small smile.

"Right," Ryan clips out. "It's just been a helluva day." He motions at his dick. "Ball burn and all. But, if you're ready, I have a bunch of work to do."

Her confidence flickers as she nods and starts to follow him toward the door.

"Ryan," I call to him, making him stop before he makes it out of my office. "Don't underutilize our intern. Anyone can make coffee. Not everyone can name all twenty-nine shades of the Dior Vernis polish line."

"Loud and clear, boss man," he grunts out, stalking out of my office.

Sea green eyes meet mine and she shoots me a sweet-as-sin smile. I wink at her because apparently I don't know how to keep from fucking flirting with her. She leaves, but her fruity scent and the surprisingly good impression she made remain.

This girl is going to fuck up my world.

Chapter Three

CHELSEA

Turning to see more of my reflection in the full-length mirror, I scrutinize my appearance. My off-the-shoulder leopard print blouse is flowy and comfortable, but paired with this tight black pencil skirt and a classic pair of pumps, it's what I'm going to call business sexy.

I know I shouldn't be worried about sexy at work, but Foster oozes sexiness just by existing. As hard as it is to focus on anything else when he's in the room, it's only fair I tempt his gaze in my direction as well.

Satisfied that at the very least his gaze will be drawn to my ass in this skirt as I'm leaving the meeting today, I leave home super early so I'll have time to wait in line for coffee on my way to work. I'm still working with Ryan and I've come to believe the man can't function without equal parts blood and caffeine running through his veins.

Me, I don't drink coffee. Don't like the taste, and I don't particularly want the teeth stains, either.

It's a busy morning. Ryan has phone call after phone call, email after

email, text after text. I can't help noticing how much busier he is than the rest of the associates. They're all working hard and keeping busy, but not one is as bombarded as Ryan.

I really wish he'd let me help more. Even Foster told him to. I don't understand why he keeps giving me mindless busywork instead of letting me lighten his load. He might as well pat me on the head and tell me to spend the day popping bubblegum and painting my nails.

He doesn't take me seriously.

I shake it off, refusing to let it get me down.

Another call comes in for him, but I glance in his direction and see he's still on the last call I sent him.

"I'm so sorry, Mr. Wilkes is on another call right now, but if you'd like I can take a message and catch him up before he calls you back?"

The woman on the other end is not pleased. "You know, this is not what I expected when I hired Dunbar Foster to handle my PR shit show. It's not what I was pitched, it's not what I was promised—I'm seriously considering firing you guys and taking my business elsewhere."

Dread pools in my gut. I freeze for a split second, then I cut a look in Ryan's direction, considering whether or not I should interrupt his call. He told me never, ever to do that, not even if the building caught fire, but this... well, it's a fire of another sort.

"I'm so sorry, Ms. Winston, you're absolutely right. Your problems are very important to us and I'm going to personally see to it that you get the help you need right now. Tell me what we can do for you."

Her tone relaxing slightly, the client continues. "Ryan told me I needed to write up a note of apology, that way when I deliver it, I already know what I'm going to say and I don't say anything I shouldn't."

"Right," I offer supportively.

"He wanted me to send it back once I finished so he could go over it himself."

I cradle the corded phone between my ear and shoulder, reaching for a pen and grabbing a piece of paper so I can write down any pertinent details.

"Perfect. Did you want to go ahead and email that over to him right now? I'll have Mr. Wilkes review it right away and email you back. If you have any questions, call back and I'll make sure to put you straight through."

"Okay, that will work. Thank you."

"Of course. We know what a stressful time this is for you, we're so glad we can help you through it."

Once I get off the phone with the temporarily mollified client, I glance back at Ryan. He's still on the phone, his face seeming to get older by the moment from the stress of the conversation.

Definitely can't interrupt that one.

That's all right. I may not be a fully trained associate like he is, but I *do* know apologies. I know bad ones—like Brad from junior year trying to foist off the blame on me after he was caught getting a blowjob from another girl—and good ones. All I have to do is read over the email myself and make sure the client's apology falls into the latter category. In fact, since she said he sent her a sample to follow, if I pull that from his sent emails, I might be able to handle this entirely by myself and get one thing off Ryan's plate.

Satisfied with that plan, I log myself out of my temporary employee email and type in ryan.wilkes@dunbarfoster.com instead. His password is on a slip of paper his old assistant wrote down and slipped into her desk. He didn't tell me about it—I found it myself—but it stands to reason if she was allowed to access his work email, I should be, too.

The password works and a split second later I'm in. I go to the sent folder first to find Ryan's emails to and from the client so I can catch myself up.

By the time I've finished and printed off the sample email he sent for reference, there's a new email in the inbox. I mouse over to it, expecting to find an email from the client I just spoke to, but it's something else. From an Aaron Elman—not a name I recognize from the client list. The subject line reads "Swanson" and the content simply reads, "Is he onboard?"

Evan Swanson? Has to be. I frown, wondering what they could be

talking about. I shake off my curiosity—I'm not in here to snoop—and back out of the message.

Luckily, the apology email comes through a moment later. I read through it, but it's bad. Rambling and mildly ranty, underhanded attempts to shirk responsibility, trying to avoid even mentioning what she's apologizing for—all kinds of bad.

I don't even bother consulting Ryan since it's such a mess. I print out her email, grab a red pen, and brutalize the text. I leave helpful, upbeat comments about the structure and content, explaining that she needs to stop shying away from what happened and own it. An effective apology can only happen once you've acknowledged the mistake. I tell her what she needs to do step-by-step instead of sending her a lame template like Ryan did to take all the personalization out of her speech. She could be a president who got a blow job or "oops! There was a typo in that coupon we sent out" and the language would barely differ with what he sent her to model her long-winded apology after.

It's probably not my place, but I want to talk to Ryan about this. If this is the template he's sending out to other clients… I don't want Dunbar Foster to look bad just because he's overwrought and trying to half-ass his job with boilerplate templates instead of one-on-one attention. I know Dunbar Foster's rates; we charge way too much for service like this.

I know Foster wouldn't like it.

I don't want to get Ryan in trouble just because he's overwhelmed though, so I'll talk to him instead of Foster.

At least, that's my plan until I go back to the inbox and the "Swanson" message is gone. My gaze darts across the screen to the folders. There's one for each of Ryan's clients to keep everything organized, but when I click on Swanson, the email from that Aaron guy isn't there.

Covertly, I glance over my shoulder into Ryan's office. He's still on the phone, but he's moving the mouse, also focused on his computer monitor.

I refresh the inbox and one new email pops up, but not in the inbox.

There's a file folder labeled "fantasy football," the only non work-related file folder. The new message is in that folder, so I click it.

None of these messages seem to be about fantasy football. Briefly skimming all the names and subject lines I see a lot from Aaron Elman, but there are others, too. Smaller clients of Dunbar Foster responding to a vague, "Have you thought more about what we talked about?" message Ryan sent them first.

That seems fishy. Why keep them in a dummy folder? The Swanson email is in this folder now so Ryan must have checked it and rerouted it after I read it. I click it again to see the new messages on the thread. Ryan answered back, "Not yet. I have to move carefully with him. It's complicated. He likes Foster."

Aaron wrote back, "So make him NOT like Foster."

My eyes narrow on the screen. Ryan types back, "Working on it," and Aaron responds one more time with, "Keep me posted."

Working on it?

That feeling of dread settles in my gut again as I sit back in my computer chair and stare vacantly at the screen, trying to piece together what I read in a way that doesn't sound like subterfuge. It can't be. That would be crazy. For one thing, how could anyone be stupid enough to discuss something like that in their *work email*? Sure, he's being vague, but not vague enough if *my* suspicions are aroused and I've only worked here for four days.

Feeling the need to dig a little deeper, I open the Swanson folder to see what he and Ryan have been talking about in their most recent emails.

Ryan's last response is, "That's too bad. You know Foster though, such a workaholic. Work smarter not harder, I say! When it comes to my favorite client, there's always time. I'd love to catch a show with you this weekend if you're still free."

I narrow my eyes at the screen, scrolling up and reading the rest of the emails. Apparently, Evan asked Foster to see a Broadway show with him and his boyfriend this weekend, but Foster's schedule didn't allow for it.

Now Ryan is trying to weasel his way in.

I bet this is part of his "I'm working on it" plan. Sour Evan on Foster and ingratiate himself... but why?

I don't know exactly what to make of all this, but I know who will.

I guess it's a good thing Ryan never gives me any real work to do, because it means I have all the time in the world to print off every last email in his "fantasy football" folder and slip each one into a pretty, color-coded file folder to present to Mr. Foster.

Once I have everything I need, I poke my head into Ryan's office. Shooting him a hopeful smile, I ask, "Everything going okay?"

Nodding impatiently, he says, "Yep."

"Can I get you anything?"

His gaze drifts lower to my cleavage—which makes him a bit nicer—and he offers back a tired smile. "Another cup of coffee would be amazing."

With an indulgent giggle, I assure him I can take care of that for him, then I go grab him a cup of coffee to keep him from leaving his office while I'm away. When I come back, I poke my head in and ask if he'd mind if I take an early lunch. I start boring him to tears telling him about my friend Betsy and the terrible time she's having with her boyfriend, how she needs a little girl time.

Ryan can't bear to feign interest a moment longer and can't get me out of there fast enough. I shoot him a grateful smile, tell him, "You're the best!" and head back to my desk.

Then I gather up my files full of all the incriminating emails, slide my purse strap over my shoulder, and make my way toward Mr. Foster's office.

It's my fourth day at Dunbar Foster and this is only the second time I've been to his office. The first time Foster brought me himself so there was no gatekeeper, but today when I go to see him, I have to wait for *his* assistant to let me in. She doesn't socialize with the other assistants much. There seems to be a clear hierarchy that sets her above the rest of them even though they share the same job title. She's older and more serious, the kind of woman who looks like she's been passed over for promotion one time

too many and now she's permanently pissed off.

Personally, I think Foster should have a friendlier assistant. Someone more like me. But maybe on a subconscious level, I also just feel a little jealous that she gets to spend so much time with him each day while I have to settle with glimpses from my desk as he strides through the office with purpose, or meetings where I get to hear that incredible voice of his.

Shaking off my fruitless mooning, I look up as the assistant calls out, "Mr. Foster will see you now."

Straightening my skirt and clutching the files against my chest, I thank her with a polite smile and make my way into his office. It's all glass walls so there's no real privacy, but I'm pretty sure everyone at this company has already written me off as a ditz—they won't expect me to be in here stirring up any trouble. If anything, they'd expect to find me under his desk with his cock in my mouth—and I'm sure that despite the strictly enforced no-fraternization policy, they would all know better than to pay any attention to that.

Foster's gaze travels down over my body in a quick perusal before landing back on my face. "Can I help you with something, Miss Parker?"

Stepping forward and closing the door behind me so no one overhears us, I tell him, "Actually, I think I may be able to help you."

Curiosity flickers across his handsome features. He leans back in his chair, interlacing his fingers and resting them over his taut abdomen. "Really? How so?"

I approach his desk, dropping my file folders and opening the top one. "This is an email I intercepted today between Ryan Wilkes and someone named Aaron Elman. Any idea who that might be?"

Foster's perfect lips curve up, an unmistakable glint of amusement in his gorgeous blue eyes. "Intercepted? Are we in a spy movie, Miss Parker?"

I shoot him a look to let him know I don't appreciate being made fun of, but otherwise, I ignore his comment and pass him the printout. "It sounds like they're discussing something shady. Something disloyal."

The amusement I saw a split second ago flickers, giving way to

interest. He sits forward again, his posture no longer making it clear he regards my presence as playtime. "What do you mean?" he murmurs, sliding the paper closer and directing his gaze to the text.

I give him a moment to read it, then I go on. "I think Ryan Wilkes is up to something. I found a dummy folder in his email and it's full of messages like these. I printed all of them off for you, just in case he catches on and deletes them. Some are from Dunbar Foster clients expressing interest in some vague…" I take a breath and let it out, looking him directly in the eye. "It sounds like he's trying to poach clients. It sounds like he plans to leave and he's hoping he can undermine you and take Evan Swanson with him."

Foster doesn't say anything right away. He spends a few minutes going through the emails I organized for him. With each message he skims and sets aside, the irritation on his face escalates.

Once he's read all of them, he does what he did the other day when I was in his office—suddenly ignores me. It's hard not to feel a little annoyed by his drifting attention, but I shake it off. He's typing something on his computer, so maybe he's not intentionally ignoring me, just checking into something or contacting someone from the emails I gave him.

Suddenly breaking the silence, he asks, "What are you doing tomorrow night?"

My eyes widen and my stomach drops. "Uh… me? Nothing."

He cocks an eyebrow and regards me as if unconvinced. "It's Friday night and you have no plans?"

My cheeks warm under his scrutiny. I shrug my shoulders. "I wasn't sure what my first work week would be like. I thought it would be busier and I would be exhausted so I wanted to give myself time to relax if I needed to."

His amused gaze drifting back to my face, he asks dryly, "And are you exhausted, Miss Parker?"

I shake my head. "Nope. I can definitely come in this weekend and help you ferret out the extent of Ryan's duplicity."

"Not precisely what I had in mind." His attention returns to the computer monitor as he finishes up whatever he's typing, then drags his mouse and clicks.

Now he sits back in his chair again, appearing almost relaxed. I can't imagine a man looking relaxed when I've just handed him the information I have, but this time it's not because he's dismissing me and whatever I might bring to the table. It's simply because he has handled the situation already—or he knows he will and he's not worried.

I love his confidence.

Smiling a little more fondly than I mean to, I ask, "Then what do you need from me?"

"Well, considering it appears I'll be catching a Broadway show with Evan Swanson, after all... I'm going to need a date."

Chapter Four

FOSTER

It's a work thing.

That's what I told Mason when he texted to ask how Chelsea's first week went. I'd somehow tattled on myself that she was going with me to schmooze a client. Of course, unlike when I told her I needed a date, I told him it was a work thing and I wanted her to shadow me.

Thank fuck he wasn't standing in front of me.

Mason is one of the few who can read my poker face. Hell, it was him who taught it to me. He taught me a lot of shit, so he'd be the first to call me out.

It is a work thing, though.

Evan Swanson is my client and Chelsea is an intern at my company.

Explain the state of your dick, Foster.

I glance over at Chelsea while I wait for the light to turn green. When I picked her up a bit ago, I was not at all prepared to see her all dressed up. At work, it's practically torture seeing her prance around in her tight skirts and tall heels. But, she does dress professionally.

Now, though, she's dressed like a goddamn movie star.

I'm thoroughly impressed at her ability to throw together such a glamorous ensemble on such short notice. Tonight, she's wearing a silky, gold wrap dress that dips low, revealing more cleavage than is acceptable for work. Rather than her modest-length skirts, this dress is daring with the hem ending high up her smooth, tanned thighs. Her gold strappy shoes give her a few extra inches on her already tall frame—something I've realized I've come to enjoy this week being nearly eye level with her.

"The light's green," she says, a playfulness in her tone.

A taxi driver honks at me and I gas it, feeling like an idiot for getting caught staring at her sexy ass thighs.

This was a bad idea.

Besides the fact she's my best friend's daughter, she's only eighteen. Barely eighteen. Girls that age are clueless as fuck. I'm not interested in regressing in the dating world from successful women my age to young, naïve women just because they're an energetic lay. No matter how tempting Chelsea Parker is, I can't ever go there.

The car in front of me slams on their brakes and my arm flies out in front of her on instinct like it'll do more than her damn seatbelt. Her breath rushes out in surprise causing me to jerk my hand back, grumbling out a half-ass apology.

"I'm looking forward to tonight," Chelsea says, shifting in her seat, causing the hem of her dress to ride up farther.

My dumb ass can't help but sneak a peek.

"Oh yeah?" I rumble. "A fan of Broadway shows?"

"Not really." She chuckles. "I was more interested in *who*'ll be there."

"Evan."

"Of course. And I saw on Instagram, Heather Caviche is going to be there with her on-again-off-again boyfriend. She could really use Dunbar Foster. I looked her up and Celebrity 911 represents her."

I cringe at the name. They're the equivalent to ambulance chasing lawyers in the PR world. Only after the wild clients because it keeps their

name in the press and keeps the paychecks coming. Our firm focuses on rejuvenating and rehabilitating our clients' images. We're in the business of helping rather than throwing kindling on the reputation dumpster fires they tend to start.

"I'm going to see if I can talk to her," she tells me, practically thrumming with energy. "She's a great actress and with the right public relations team on her side, she could leave the front pages of the negative tabloids and help her acting career with more reputable PR."

I'm impressed that she clearly does her homework. I'd misjudged her the first day. And, after what she brought to me about Ryan, I realize she's sharp and doesn't miss a thing, much like her father.

"Slow your roll, Jerry Maguire, you're only an intern," I remind her. "Why don't you let me talk to her?"

Chelsea scoffs. "Because I'm confident I can get her over to us. Celebrity 911 has flimsy contracts. I know Dunbar Foster has an entire legal department dedicated to finding holes in contracts so we can rightfully take on clients like her." She points at a crowd gathered around someone, camera flashes going off, as we arrive in front of the building. "Besides… you have your work cut out for you with Swanson. You need to do damage control with him. Let me do my magic."

She's green and I've yet to see hard proof of said magic aside from a few instances at the office. Anyone else and I'd shut them down. But, Chelsea's confidence reminds me of my own when I first started out. She believes she can do this which probably means she can.

"And if you don't land this client?" I ask, arching a brow at her as we wait for traffic to move in the valet line.

"All I need is the meeting, and then we can land her together." She grins at me. "Right?"

That smile would have me agreeing to anything.

"If you can get her in the building, I can get her to sign on the dotted line." I roam my gaze down her delicate, exposed throat. Her blond hair has been pulled up into a sleek ponytail that incites many filthy fantasies

inside my dirty mind. My eyes land on her cleavage for a long moment before I pull them back up to her face. "What happens if you don't get the meeting? Should I let you go?"

She rolls her eyes, reminding me of how young she is. "I'll get the meeting. I'll indulge you, though. If I don't get the meeting, you can make me grab your coffee for a week or take your suits to the dry cleaners. I honestly don't care because I'm going to do this."

"So confident," I murmur. "And if you get the meeting with Heather?"

"Then you have to go dancing with me after this."

"I'm not going dancing."

"If I win you will."

"Chelsea," I growl. "I don't dance."

"Liar." She smirks. "I have seen plenty of tagged photos of you dancing at parties."

I lift a brow at her. "Been stalking me?"

"I stalk everyone." She lets out a laugh that makes my dick twitch. "Evan Swanson loves to dance. He'll go with us. I promise. Remember, you're still trying to woo the guy to keep him from switching teams."

"He switched teams long before me," I throw back.

"Are you always this difficult?"

"Always. And you have yourself a deal. I hope you don't break a nail carrying all my suits back and forth to the dry cleaners."

"Sounds like a job better cut out for Ryan. Hope those shoes are good for dancing."

As Evan and his boyfriend, Quincy, preen in front of the cameras in the lobby, I stand unnecessarily close to Chelsea. Whatever perfume she's wearing fucking calls to me. I'm distracted each time she laughs and her tits jiggle or the way she smiles with her whole face.

"Mr. Foster," Evan says, finally done with his mini photoshoot. "So happy you could make it after all."

We shake hands and I introduce Chelsea as my intern. She doesn't sit back, meek and unsure. No, this girl was born for this, immediately chatting Evan up. He and Quincy are charmed by her, both of them grinning as she speaks. Pride swells up inside me. Last time, when I had Ryan with me, Evan didn't wear such an unguarded, interested expression.

"Sorry," Evan interrupts, "but I can't wait another second, Chelsea, without asking. Your dress. Is it—"

"Dior?" She does a little spin, showing off the ensemble. "It was a race to get to Hudson Yards and back before tonight's show, but I just knew you'd appreciate the extra effort."

"Indeed," Evan says with a wide grin.

Quincy chuckles. "Delilah was probably on shift this afternoon. She's my favorite salesperson at Dior. No one recognizes me when I show up to buy prezzies for Evan, but just in case, she always makes sure to have a stack of things he might love ready for me in a private room when I show up."

"Yes!" Chelsea nods her head, her blond ponytail swinging. "Delilah was a doll. We have a date for sushi soon."

As she continues to chatter to the guys about their common love for Dior, my eyes skim the room. I notice Heather Caviche around the same time Chelsea does.

"Excuse me, boys. I just saw Heather Caviche and on her Instagram, she claimed she was going to try and smuggle her dog Pootsie in. I'm going to go say hello. Catch you in a few before the show starts." She blows a kiss to them before prancing through the room, completely unaware of all the hungry stares of each male she passes.

"Intern, huh?" Evan asks, leaning in.

"We're *not* dating," I blurt out, dragging my gaze back to him. "She's my best friend's daughter."

Quincy laughs and then excuses himself to go greet someone he

knows.

"I was *going* to say, she's a helluva lot more qualified than that. I was *going* to tease and say she would be taking over your job soon." Evan's sculpted brow arches high. "But, with how quickly you jumped to the defensive, I'd say you *wish* you were dating."

I groan, rubbing at the back of my neck.

"She's beautiful," Evan says clutching my shoulder as if to comfort me from my internal ass whipping. "If you didn't notice, I'd say you were dead inside, Foster."

As soon as I see her laughing and chatting it up with Heather, I realize my ass is totally going dancing later. Evan is right. She's more than qualified. A helluva lot better at this damn job than Ryan ever will be.

Speaking of Ryan, I'm going to deal with his ass and soon. But first, I need to know exactly what it is he's doing with my clients.

"Beautiful indeed," I admit with a sigh. "But, as much as I'd love to discuss Miss Parker's charming ways, I actually wanted to talk to you about something else."

"Come dance with me," Chelsea yells over the club music. "You owe me."

Quincy grins at me while Evan waggles his brows. I shake my head at them, biting back a smile. They were Team Chelsea from the moment they laid eyes on her. When she brought Heather over to meet Evan before the show and managed to easily incorporate that we were his PR firm into conversation, I'd gotten on Team Chelsea too. She's smart and charismatic. There's an energy about her that draws people in, myself included.

"A deal's a deal," I say, taking her hand, allowing her to lead me onto the dance floor that's crowded with moving bodies. "You know I'm the oldest guy out here, right?"

Her slender arms wrap around my neck as her sea green eyes light up

in a mischievous way under the flashing lights. "Sorry, couldn't hear you."

Our hips move in tandem with the beat. Now that I'm allowed to touch her, I quickly become greedy, grabbing hold of her narrow hips and pulling her flush against me. I dip my head to her ear, letting my lips brush against the shell.

"I said, you look beautiful tonight."

She turns her head slightly, so her mouth is near my ear now. "Thank you. And, for the record, you're not old, Foster."

With her young, ripe body grinding against me and my eager dick shamelessly pressing into her, I feel anything but old. It's easy to forget who she is and how old she is or the fact she's my intern when my palm is dangerously close to her ass.

It's my turn to speak into her ear. The urge to nip at her earlobe is strong.

"You were spectacular tonight," I rumble, no longer able to keep up with the beat. We slow our dancing to a sway. "My client loves you and you've already hooked another one who desperately needs Dunbar Foster. You're a natural."

She turns, pulling slightly away to look at me. "You seem surprised."

"A little." My gaze drops to her pink, pouty lips that are glossy and so fucking tempting. "I knew you were clever and sociable when we talked that night at the beach, but I didn't realize how driven to succeed you are. And not in a ladder climbing way. You genuinely want to do this job, and not just for any company, but for *my* company. Chelsea, you impressed me, and I wasn't expecting it."

She licks her plump lips. "There's a lot more to me than meets the eye."

"So I'm learning."

Her fingers thread into my hair as she pulls me closer, her lips slightly parting as if waiting for a kiss that will rock her fucking world.

And it would.

My mouth would decimate hers and it would be just the beginning.

I would devour her inch by inch, tasting every sweet part of her until she screamed for mercy. Together, we could be fantastic in bed.

But...

Oh, fuck me, there always has to be a but with anything good.

But, she's Mason's kid. Eighteen. My damn intern.

I take my hand off her ass where it had slowly crept to and press my thumb to her lips. With a quick peck to her forehead, I release her, though it takes every ounce of willpower in my body.

"I should get you home now, Miss Parker."

Her crestfallen expression hits me right in the chest, but ever the poised socialite, she straightens her spine, affixes a pretty, fake smile and nods. "I think you should, Mr. Foster."

Chapter Five

CHELSEA

I think I know how Cinderella felt when that dreaded clock struck midnight and she knew everything had to go back to the way it was before she danced with her bonehead prince.

Tonight was fast-paced and extremely public just like I knew it would be, but deep down I had hoped there might be a chance to get a little alone time with Foster after the business was concluded and there was no one left but us. Like a dreamy idiot, I'd imagined a night like the one in the Hamptons when we walked the beach, only this time, we would walk the streets of New York. Even in the city that never sleeps, it's easy for a pair of lovers to walk hand-in-hand beneath the glow of the lights, talking and getting to know one another better.

But we're not lovers—and if I leave it up to Foster, we never will be.

I suppose that's right. Appropriate, even. But there's nothing appropriate about the way he looked at me tonight. Every time I turned around, I could feel his gaze boring into me, keeping an eye on me as if to make sure I didn't wander too far from his reach.

Even now as we stand on the stoop outside my house, I can see his gaze is tempted to flicker down at my cleavage. He doesn't let it, though. Not this time, not with the privacy of my empty house just on the other side of this door.

He knows the rest of my family is at the Hamptons house. He knows it's only me staying here right now.

God, I wish I were immune to those gorgeous blue eyes. I wish my stomach didn't twist up when he gazed at me the way he is now.

That, or I wish the man would just make a damn move.

Standing here on the stoop outside my house, looking at his handsome face bathed in little more than moonlight, I make a decision.

He's not going home just yet. He's coming in the house with me. Whatever happens or doesn't happen after that, fine, but I'm at least getting him inside.

"I have a confession to make," I tell him, looking up at him through my long eyelashes.

Already onto me, he narrows his eyes. "What's that?"

"I'm afraid of the dark."

He's skeptical, but plays along to see where I'm going with this. "Is that so?"

I nod earnestly, mustering all the big-eyed innocence I'm able. "Not once I know I'm safe, of course—I don't sleep with a nightlight or anything like that. But walking alone into a dark, empty house... now, that's spooky."

"Spooky?" he deadpans.

I nod again, my eyes widening imploringly. "Oh, yeah. Creaking floorboards, shadows behind every door—it doesn't take much to convince me there's a serial killer hiding in one of the rooms I haven't walked into yet."

I pick up on the reluctant amusement in his husky tone, so he must not be working too hard to hide it. "Sounds like you have quite an active imagination, Miss Parker."

"Oh, I do," I assure him, my eyes glinting with mischief. "The fact

remains, though..." To really sell it, I sigh dramatically and look off to the side as if forlorn. "If I have to go inside this house all by myself, I might have a heart attack."

Foster shifts his weight and looks at the front door of my house like it's a beast I'm asking him to vanquish. Not to play along with my "I'm so frightened! I need a big, strong man to protect me" scenario, but as if *he* is the one afraid of what's on the other side of that door.

For a split second, I think I read it wrong and my game won't work, but after a longer pause than I was prepared for, he finally responds and sets my mind at ease.

"Well, we can't have that, can we?"

I grin, grabbing my purse and fishing out my keys so I can unlock the door.

I lied on the doorstep; I'm not afraid of the dark. I'm not afraid of spiders or heights—I'm not really afraid of anything. I don't continue the game once we're inside, but he doesn't expect me to. Foster knows the score. He knows that was merely my way of getting him through the door.

I take a step back and close the door behind him. I lean closer than I need to, so close my breast nearly touches his arm. Our gazes lock and linger for a few seconds.

"Would you like a drink?" I ask softly, careful not to disturb the moment.

"Perhaps. Are we talking lemonade or something stronger?"

I smile, reaching down and twining our fingers together. His whole body tenses when I do. My heart swells at my boldness, then begins to race. I don't say anything. I simply lead him down the hall to Daddy's study.

He lets me.

Emboldened by his cooperation, my mind searches for what to do or say next, but I must admit, I'm feeling a bit flustered. I felt like I had a handle on things when we were still outside, but here in my house... it's different.

Memories flood back to me of years past. Foster only spoke to me at

the party two summers ago because I looked like a woman that time, but I'd noticed him long before that. He was a friend of my dad's, so occasionally he would stop by our house to visit with him. I remember one year close to Christmas he came over. I was twelve and awkward, he was grown and gorgeous. To him, I was nothing more than his friend's kid, but to me, he was the most handsome man I had ever seen. The year I turned fourteen he came over again. I was so eager to greet him when Daddy said he was coming... only to learn when I answered the door, Foster had forgotten my name.

I didn't care, and I certainly hadn't forgotten his.

My mom picked up on my little ill-fated crush and teased me about it, but since he didn't come around often, by the time I saw him in the Hamptons, Foster was little more to me than a childish crush I was mildly embarrassed to remember... until he smiled at me.

He does it again now, knocking me off kilter.

When Foster smiles—a real smile—he doesn't start with his mouth. It starts with his eyes. A warm glint of fondness in his gaze seems to transform his whole face, softening granite slopes and giving him the hooded look of a lover. That alone weakens my knees, but then when his perfect lips tug up and every bit of his attention is focused on me... God, I can scarcely stay on my feet.

Foster is comfortable in Daddy's office, so he makes himself at home. With Daddy gone, Foster takes his seat behind the gleaming mahogany desk. I see him behind a big, impressive desk all the time at work, but it's different here. There's no office noise in the background, no glass walls... no one but us.

I fetch him a drink from Daddy's beverage cart and walk it over to him, hoping he doesn't notice the slight way my hand trembles. There's something about serving him like this...

Without looking away from my face, he takes the drink. "Thank you."

I flash him a little smile, taking the opportunity to look away as he takes a sip. My whole body feels so hot, I'm tempted to flee the room and

check the thermostat. Surely it's been cranked up by mistake.

His voice, sharp and searing as the crack of the whip, brings me back. "Sit."

My eyes widen slightly at the bite of command in his tone. He's a guest in *my* home, but with a single word uttered by him I am somehow so scattered, I can't even think where to sit. I feel like I'm in his domain instead of the other way around. "Where?"

He pins me with his gaze, inciting a swarm of butterflies to break loose in my belly as he sits his drink down atop my father's desk. Then, with a firm pat of his hand against his thigh, he says simply, "Here."

My heart is thumping so loudly I can hear it in my ears. My skin is on fire. I want to rip my dress off and lie down in a pool of ice.

Instead, I look down at his lap.

Big mistake. Huge.

And my mistake is not the only huge thing in the room.

There, between Foster's spread thighs, the impressive bulge of his cock strains against the expensive fabric of his trousers. Liquid desire pours through my veins at the unexpected sight and it puts to bed any doubts I may have had about his interest earlier tonight.

Yes, Mr. Foster most certainly wants me.

I can scarcely breathe as I take the few steps between us. Even though my steps are soft, the room is so silent that each clack of my heels against the hardwood can be heard, and each one makes my heart beat faster.

Despite him being the one to start this, I almost expect him to stop me. He doesn't.

I sit gingerly, keeping my heels firmly on the ground as I look over at him, not even trying to hide my curiosity.

As if this is normal, as if I'm his, he bestows a wicked little smile on me and casually rests his hand on my bare thigh. "Did you have a nice time tonight, Miss Parker?"

The way he calls me that—*Miss Parker*—puts me even more off-kilter. It's so at odds with his private smile, with me sitting on his lap, his

fingers lightly caressing my smooth skin.

It feels wrong, but I'm still dreadfully hopeful.

I'm not sure I can speak without making a fool of myself, so I'm relieved when I manage to answer evenly, "I did. Thank you for taking me along."

His fingers move along the inside of my thigh, drifting an inch higher and robbing some of the breath from my lungs. As if unfazed, he says, "No thanks required. You were magnificent." He waits a beat, but not long enough for me to think of anything to say with him touching me the way he is. "Is your position at my company everything you expected it to be?"

I want to answer him, I really do, but then he slides his hand so high up my thigh, the tip of his fingers brush my panties.

My heart skitters to a stop. The breath freezes in my lungs. The whole world seems to stop moving for the span of a single missed heartbeat.

This is what I wanted, so why doesn't it feel right?

It's his demeanor. He's still completely in control of himself—I haven't awakened some ravenous beast inside him, he's not passionately giving in to some fierce desire for me...

Then it hits me, and it's horrible.

He's toying with me.

Maybe he isn't. Maybe I'm reading it wrong. I've never been in an intimate situation with him before, so maybe my fantasy of what it would be like between us is totally wrong.

I hope I'm wrong.

I couldn't bear to be toyed with, not by him.

Instinctively, I reach down and cover his hand with mine, stilling it against my thigh so it doesn't go any farther. It's not as effective as I want it to be, though. He doesn't resist, he allows me to stop him, but I want so badly to be wrong that my gesture is half-hearted. "What are you doing?" I ask softly.

"Giving you what you want," he says simply, leaving one hand trapped beneath mine, but drawing the other up to play with my hair. First

he caresses a chunk of silky gold hair between his thumb and forefinger and it's almost tender, but then he suddenly wraps my pony tail around his fist and tugs.

I gasp as he pulls me backward, but I notice his grip on my thigh tightens as if he knew he would startle me and wanted to ensure I didn't fall.

He brings his lips so close, I feel them brush the shell of my ear. "This is what you wanted, isn't it? You reached into your pretty little bag of debutante tricks to coax me into the house—you want me to fuck you, right? If there's one thing I know about you, it's that you always get what you want, so let's get on with it."

His words are like little knives being thrust in my heart. It's not just what he says, but how he says it—like he still views me as some spoiled little rich girl and he thinks wanting him is just my latest whim.

Prying his hand off my thigh and reaching back to free my hair from his tight grip, I murmur, "No, Foster, this isn't what I wanted."

He cocks an eyebrow as I launch myself off his lap and turn to glare at him. "No? Could have fooled me."

"No," I repeat, more heated with each passing second. Gesturing wildly between us, I repeat myself with more emphasis. "*This* is not what I wanted. Yes, I tricked you to get you in the house—but you knew I was tricking you; you were hardly defenseless against my wiles. I wanted to spend some time together just the two of us. I wanted to spend time *with you*. I don't see what's so wrong with that."

Foster stands, his dark gaze narrowing on mine as he takes a step in my direction. "And why is that, hm? None of my other employees feel the need to spend alone time with me outside of the office."

I take a step back as he advances, but I'm still angry so I fling back, "Maybe that's because they all think you're an asshole and you'd say no."

His lips curve up faintly as he takes another step toward me. His reluctant amusement always gets to me, but paired with the way he's backing me toward the wall… it feels deliciously dark and dangerous.

"I think it's because the rest of my employees know I'll never fuck them—but not you. Why do you think that is, Miss Parker? Because you don't think the same rules apply to you?"

I've backed myself against a wall—literally. I stiffen as I feel the hard surface pressed against my back, but I can't help noticing that Foster is right on top of me. He could have made his point without getting close to me.

He's close to me because he wants to be. Because no matter how much of a bastard he's being right now, he wants me.

I bet he hates that.

He says I'm the one who always gets what she wants, but what has he ever wanted that he couldn't take?

Maybe just me.

With my confidence renewed, I look him straight in the eye, far from intimidated as he brings his body so close to mine I can feel the heat rolling off him.

"Why is it Miss Parker again all of a sudden? I was Chelsea just an hour or so ago, wasn't I?"

His stormy blue eyes seem to darken, but he doesn't say a word.

"I think I know why," I tell him smoothly, affecting a tiny, knowing smile. "You're afraid. I spooked you. You *wanted* to come inside tonight, Foster. You called it a date when you could have called it a work function, you picked me up when we could have met there, you couldn't keep your eyes off me to save your life—you *want* me, but you can't really have me… and you must hate that."

Reaching out and grabbing a fistful of my necklace, Foster pulls me close. "You think I want you?"

He startled me grabbing me like that, but I don't show it and I don't even try to break free. "I know you do."

His grip on my necklace tightens. I tilt my chin up to let him see his scare tactics aren't working. Actually, all it's doing is turning me on, and if that's not all kinds of fucked up, I don't know what is.

Rather than try to break away and flee like the fickle little debutante he accuses me of being, I double down. I push my back against the wall to make room for my hand between our bodies, then I reach down and caress the bulge in his pants.

"I have proof," I purr as I curve my fingers around him, lightly scoring the fabric so he can feel my nails.

Foster goes completely rigid. He drops my necklace to brace a hand against the wall behind me, closing his eyes and taking a couple of slow, deep breaths.

Despite my bold gesture, my heart is fixing to beat its way out of my chest. My hand is still on his cock and he didn't move it or tell me to stop, so maybe... maybe he doesn't want me to.

I swallow down my uncertainty and start to caress him through his pants. He reacts immediately, grabbing my wrist to stop me.

"Don't," he practically growls.

I lick my lips and swallow again. I open my mouth to speak, but before I can he cuts me off.

"Don't," he says more forcefully.

I close my mouth and look up at him. His harsh features tell me he isn't playing with me right now, that the warning is real.

"Don't... what?" I ask softly, my gaze trained on his handsome face.

He was looking down while he carefully got himself under control. Now he looks me dead in the eye as he releases my wrist and takes a cool step back.

"Don't play a game you're not ready for, little girl."

I don't know if it's his words or the way he suddenly retreated from me after being so close, but as hot as I was only moments ago, a chill sweeps over me now. I wrap my arms around myself protectively, not looking away from him, maybe waiting for him to say more.

But he doesn't.

He doesn't say another word.

I want to tell him I *am* ready, I *do* want this, but the words are trapped

in my throat.

It doesn't matter, though. He doesn't wait for me to answer. Foster has already made up his mind about how tonight will end.

With me standing here alone, feeling like an idiot, in my father's study.

Chapter Six

FOSTER

S he's pissed.

Really pissed.

But at least she's a professional.

Last week, after my serious lapse in judgment where I nearly fucked Mason's daughter on his own goddamn desk, I expected some sort of workplace drama. Monday morning, I worried myself to death over it, nearly giving myself an ulcer. But Chelsea Parker once again proved herself to be the adult in this situation.

Fuck, what was I thinking?

I wasn't thinking with my head, that's for damn sure. No, after a night at the show and then dancing, I was drunk off her scent and thirsty for her taste. When she invited me in, I wanted it. So. Fucking. Badly.

She has a sense of self-preservation, though, and backed off the moment shit got real.

I was such an asshole to her. Hence her frostiness all week. It's better this way.

"Mr. Foster," Chelsea says from my office doorway. "A word?"

My brain may have decided she was a bad idea, but my eyes are traitorous as they roam down her classy office attire that somehow looks sexy as fuck in a demure way, cataloging every detail about her. Her blonde hair has been straightened, giving it a smooth, silkiness I'd love to run my fingers through. Plump lips are pursed together, glossy and utterly lickable. Though her high-waisted black pencil skirt is long, hitting just below her knees, it's still hot as hell, especially with her too-tall pointed toe pumps. She could wear a muumuu and still look ravishing.

"Yes, Miss Parker," I clip out, careful to keep the husky desire out of my voice.

She bristles slightly at my tone. "I need to leave early."

"It's only two. Hot Friday night date you need to get ready for?"

Not your business, dumbass.

"Something like that." Her cheeks redden. "May I go?"

If it were anyone else, I'd let them go without question.

She's not anyone else.

She's Chelsea Parker. The girl holding my thoughts hostage. Sweet and sexy and so fucking capable. Intelligent and charismatic. Everything a man like me could ever want in a woman.

Which is why I can't erase her from my mind and keep her safely in the untouchable box. Because, goddamn, I want to touch her. Every single damn part of her. With my fingers and my dick and my tongue.

"You may if you tell me where it is you need to run off to," I state as I rise from my office chair.

I get a dark thrill that she's just as affected as I am. Her sea green eyes skim down my front before she casts her gaze out the window behind me.

"I have important *things* to do." She bites on her bottom lip, eyes unable to meet mine.

I walk over to her, frowning. "What sort of *things*?"

"Fine, it's a date," she mutters, finally meeting my stare, unable to hide the sketchy look in her eyes. "Are you happy?"

Yes, because I know she's lying. If it really were a date, my jealous ass wouldn't be happy at all which makes no sense.

Either you want her or you don't, Foster, but you can't have it both ways.

"I'll walk you out," I tell her, gesturing for the door.

Her eyes roll, giving me a brief glimpse at her sassy personality behind the glossy businesswoman she's become. "I can walk myself out, Foster."

"Nonsense," I grit out.

I stride through the office, nodding my head to the occasional person passing by, pleased at the clacking of Chelsea's heels behind me. When we're in the elevator and the doors close, she shoots me an icy glare that has me smirking.

We stop at another floor where six people crowd inside. Chelsea is forced into my corner, her shoulder brushing against my chest. This close, I'm reminded of the way I inhaled her last weekend. Of how she felt rubbing against me on the dance floor. The way she boldly grabbed my dick in her daddy's office as though she'd even know what to do with the thing.

"Leaving early can't be a common occurrence, Miss Parker," I murmur, my breath near her ear making her shiver. "You have a job to do and you can't do it while doing other *things* during work hours."

"It's just something I have to do. Now. It won't happen again, though." She turns her head up, searching my eyes and licking her lips. "I promise."

I've never wanted to kiss someone as much as I do her in this moment. Her juicy lips fucking call to me. Beg and plead for me to taste them. Unable to stop myself, I lift a finger and stroke it along her jaw. Green eyes widen and her mouth parts.

She's shocked I'd touch her in an elevator full of people.

They're all distracted by their phones. No one cares that I want to kiss the pretty girl in the elevator. No one but she and I.

"Good," I rumble, tearing my gaze from her mouth. "I need you…to work."

More people squeeze into the elevator with us. On instinct, I wrap an arm around her, pulling her against me to make room. Her breath hitches when my palm settles just above her ass.

"Foster…" She tilts her head up again, confusion flickering in her eyes. "What are you doing?"

Touching you.

Craving you.

Wanting you.

I study her up close. The barely visible freckles hidden beneath her makeup. Tiny slivers of navy cutting through the sea of green in her eyes. A cute nose that suits her. And those lips. Goddamn those lips. Full and glistening pink.

"Nothing." *Fucking liar.* "Just being a gentleman and walking you out as promised."

The elevator doors open at the ground floor, spilling people out into the lobby, leaving the two of us with her trapped in my grasp. I reluctantly release her.

We step out of the elevator and she starts forward before she glances over her shoulder at me, disappointment gleaming in her eyes.

"Goodbye, Foster."

"Enjoy your *things*, Miss Parker."

Unbelievable.

She told the truth…just not all of it.

Chelsea really was going on a date. It's the who with that has my blood boiling with fury.

Ryan.

She knows he's screwing me over and yet here she fucking is, looking

ready to *screw* him instead.

Calm down, asshole, they're just talking.

I attempt to quell my anger as I sip on a glass of Sullivan's Cove single malt whiskey, watching Chelsea laugh from afar at whatever it is Ryan's saying to her. The whiskey only acts like an accelerant on my flames of rage.

Earlier, after she'd left, I did what any good employer would do when his employee left. I accessed her Outlook calendar to find out where she really was going. Imagine my fucking surprise to see tonight was blocked out with "drinks with Ryan."

What she failed to add in were…

Laughs with Ryan.

Flirty smiles with Ryan.

Frequent touches with Ryan.

A goddamn date with Ryan.

"Sir?" the bartender asks, interrupting my fiery thoughts. "Another?"

I grunt and nod. When he returns, he lingers, pity on his face.

"What?" I growl, pinning him with a glare.

"Want to talk about it?"

Is he fucking kidding me right now? Does this look like a therapy session?

A laugh tumbles out of him, clearly sensing the vehemence rolling off me. "Chill, man, I'm only trying to help. Is she your daughter? Trust me. Mine is only thirteen, but sometimes you gotta let them make their own decision or they'll end up hating you for it."

My daughter?

"I don't know what you're talking about," I clip out, tossing back the contents of my glass. "She's not my daughter."

Unshaken by my surly attitude, he continues on with a wide grin on his face. "Ex-lover? In that case, go rip that guy's balls off for kissing your girl."

I snap my gaze Chelsea's way, ready to explode. She's not kissing

him, though. They're hugging. After a wave of her fingers at him, she walks away from the booth they were sharing. The motherfucker checks out her ass long enough I have the urge to ram my fist through his lying face.

I toss down a wad of bills, mutter out a thanks to the bartender, and then slip through the crowd on a mission to find Chelsea.

We need to talk.

I'm dying to know why in the hell she would go out with that asshole knowing everything he's done to me.

Is this all to get back at me for dicking her around?

My brain can't wrap its head around that thought. She's smart and sassy and sweet—certainly not the vindictive type. Yes, I've been an asshole, but she wouldn't stick it to me with Ryan just to piss me off.

Why then?

I need to know.

Once outside, I catch a glimpse of her hurrying down the sidewalk. Men of all ages stop to gawk at my pretty girl. Tonight, she's more than pretty, though, she's a fucking goddess. She really did do *things* after work and *before drinks with Ryan* because her hair is in soft golden waves, unlike the sleek tresses earlier at work. She exchanged her business attire for a sexy, fitted black dress that shows off every damn curve on her young, tight body. The black pumps she's wearing make her tower over most average-height men and make her legs seem a mile long.

Fuck, I want this girl.

I need her, goddammit.

Would I still want and need her if I discovered she betrayed me by telling Ryan I'm on to his duplicitous ways?

Yes.

I'm such a fucking chump. I'd want to smack her bare ass until it was good and red for punishment. Bend her over the closest car and fuck her brains out. But, yes, I would still want her, even if she told him what I know.

She wouldn't tell him.

My heart is screaming at me—pleading its case.

I want to believe it, but it's at war with my mind. I didn't get this far into my career and become this successful for being a dumbass.

As soon as she hails a cab, I hunt for my own. One whips up to the curb next to me.

"Where to?" he asks, eyeing me in the mirror.

"Follow that cab," I bark out, pointing as the one she's in passes by us. "Go."

He guns it, cutting off a car, earning a honk. I'll tip extra for that move. When her cab gets lost in a sea of cars, I tell the driver her home address. I'm hoping like hell she's going home and not meeting Ryan at his place.

The familiar rage is burning hot like an inferno. I can't get the imagined vision of him on top of her, rutting like a fucking barnyard animal. I've never been a violent man, but right now, I could beat that twerp's ass until he stopped breathing.

What the hell is wrong with me?

I'm obsessed.

And, apparently a fucking stalker too.

The normal, smart me would tell the cabbie to take me home so I could sleep off all the whiskey I drank. To think rationally once more.

She ruined the normal me.

Long ago with a tempting, forbidden smile that lured me over, I was enraptured by a girl too young to be fooling with. Back then, my moral compass worked. I flirted with Chelsea Parker, but never made a move. Now that she's no longer forbidden as far as the law goes, I'm tangled up for other reasons.

Mason's daughter. Barely legal. My employee.

Those reasons seem like a stupid hurdle I jumped the moment she stepped into my office on her first day. I didn't look at her as my friend's daughter or someone too fucking young for me or an employee. I devoured her in one glance. Staked a claim on her in an instant. Inhaled her scent,

knowing good and damn well I'd become addicted to it.

I'm going to find out what she was doing with Ryan.

And then I'm going to…

"This is it," I grunt out, pointing out the window. "Thanks."

He chokes out his thanks when I hand him a few hundreds. I step out of the cab, making a beeline for her front door. She better fucking be here and not at Ryan's. Pounding on the door, I wait impatiently as my blood burns through me, a mixture of anger and lust.

"Who is it?" she asks through the door.

"Foster," I bark out. "Now, open the fucking door."

The locks begin unengaging and then the door wings open. Chelsea Parker stands there, no longer wearing her tall shoes, a frown of confusion on her gorgeous face.

I step into her personal space, gripping her jaw and tilting her head up. Her green eyes are wild as she searches my face for answers. My thumb strokes along her jaw line, making her lashes flutter and her lips part.

I'm here to demand answers.

To confront her.

Soon enough.

For now, I crash my lips to hers for a searing kiss. All plans to interrogate Chelsea and make her tell me the truth take a back seat to the need to claim her. Seeing Ryan's paws on her bred a feral, animalistic need to mark her as mine.

She *is* mine.

She was since that first smile…I just didn't realize it yet.

Chapter Seven

CHELSEA

I don't know if it's the brutality of his kiss or the feral look in his stormy blue eyes that knocks the breath from my lungs, but whatever it is… this kiss is lethal.

I grab onto him thoughtlessly, like he's the life raft that will keep me afloat instead of the storm that shredded my sails. I stumble as he walks me backward, slamming the front door shut behind him without tearing his lips from mine.

I don't know what I expected to find on the other side of that door, but not this.

Not that I'm complaining.

It takes a moment for my shock to dissipate. He's still walking me backward like he knows where he's going, but he stops just outside Daddy's office and pushes me up against the wall.

My heart pounds, my tummy twisted up with a mix of nerves and excitement. I only got here a minute or so before he did, so I turned on the light in the foyer, but it's pretty dark where we stopped.

His gorgeous blue eyes gleam, even in barely any light. "Where were you tonight?"

"I… at a bar."

"You know that's not what I'm asking."

I swallow and look away from him. I didn't want to tell him what I was up to earlier because he'd been a dick to me last time we were alone together and I didn't feel like playing spies with him anymore.

I still had to crack the case, though.

"I met Ryan for drinks."

His jaw locks. I note the way it ticks, his irritation growing. "Why?" he clips out.

Instead of telling him, I fire back, "Why do you care? It wasn't during work hours, so it's none of your business."

"I disagree," he returns, leaning close and angling his head like he's going to bury his face in my neck. He doesn't, though. He merely lingers, his voice low. "I think everything you do is my business, especially drinks with fucking Ryan."

"Well, I disagree," I say, mimicking him.

"Dunbar Foster has a strict no-fraternization policy," he reminds me huskily.

I tilt my neck just a little to give him better access as his lips hover close to my skin. "Ah, right. Of course. You're just enforcing company policy."

"Exactly," he murmurs, his lips finally touching the shell of my ear and sending a shiver down my spine. "I wouldn't want to have to fire you."

My lips curve up faintly as I wind an arm around his neck to tug him closer. His lips find the curve of my neck and a thrill shoots straight through me.

I almost forget what we're talking about, but I force myself to focus and murmur back, "You're not going to fire me."

"No? Why not?"

"Because that would be stupid, and you're not stupid."

He pulls back to look down at me, his gaze probing. "I don't know," he says more seriously than I expect. "I felt pretty fucking stupid tonight."

I don't know why, but hearing that makes my heart hurt. "Why?"

Putting his hands on my hips and creating a little more distance between our bodies, he demands, "Why did you go out with him?"

My gaze softening, I reach up to caress his granite jawline. "To gather intel—why else?"

His dark brow furrows. "Intel?"

I nod, giving him a look of exaggerated patience. "That's spy-speak for *intelligence*. It means I was collecting useful information—"

Cutting me off before I can finish, he grabs me around the waist and pulls me snugly against him. "I *know* what intel means, you infuriating little temptress. If that's all you were doing, why didn't you tell me?"

"I was going to loop you in tomorrow. I wasn't positive my plan would work, but I don't know why I doubted myself. Ryan thinks I'm a moron. All I had to do was wear a boob dress and giggle at him a few times and that numbskull was ready to tell me anything I wanted to know. I was duly impressed," I assure him, batting my eyelashes and placing a hand against my chest with all the cartoonish drama of a southern belle. "Why, he must be a *genius* to come up with such a clever plan." Dropping the act, I flash him a smile. "I know where he's going, who gave him the idea, and who else he's planning to talk to but hasn't made it to yet. I figure we should obviously reach out to those clients right away. If he's confident enough to try to flip them, they must not be one hundred percent happy—"

"Chelsea."

I pause and look up at him. "Yes, Foster?"

"Stop talking."

"But you—"

He grabs my jaw, tilting my face up to look at him again. "Stop. Talking."

I open my mouth to toss back a saucy retort, but before I can get it out, the distance between us vanishes and his face inches closer to mine.

My lips have barely parted when his brush mine. He cradles my face in his hand to get a better hold on me, tugging me closer so our bodies are pressed together. My heart swells in response to the tenderness. It's the best feeling in the world.

Or I think it is until the intensity of his kiss escalates. I felt the rough passionate kiss when he barged through the door and kissed me, I felt the tenderness just a moment ago, but when they both combine... it's indescribable.

I'm plastered against the wall with Foster pressed firmly against my front—the most pleasurable prison I can imagine. His hands are rough, his mouth greedy and demanding. He grabs my thigh and lifts it, pushing himself between my legs as his lips devour mine. The material of my tight black dress has slid all the way up so it's barely even covering my panties.

He's too busy kissing me to look, but when Foster slides a hand between my thighs and his fingers reach the barrier of fabric, he tears his lips from mine long enough to ask, "What kind of panties are you wearing?"

A little breathlessly, I answer, "Black. Lace."

His dark gaze locks onto mine. "When I peel them off you, they'd better be soaked."

I reach down to guide his hand between my legs, pressing it a little harder against my pussy so he can feel how wet I am. "They already are."

"Jesus Christ, Chelsea."

I smile, nipping lightly at his jawline as I leave a few little kisses there. "Maybe you should take them off me now and check."

Curving his hand and gripping my pussy more firmly, he says, "Maybe you should get them so wet I don't have to."

His firm grip between my legs makes me throb with need, but to my disappointment he releases me a moment later. I'm not disappointed for long, though.

His mouth claims mine again as he wedges his thigh between my spread legs. "Ride it," he murmurs against my lips, pressing his thigh

against my pussy. "Grind that sweet pussy against me. Show me how much you want me."

Christ.

I couldn't refuse him if I wanted to. I'm aching with need and even though it's not the friction I'm craving, the moment I rub myself against his strong thigh, an intense shudder moves through my whole body. I have to grab onto his broad shoulders to keep myself upright.

"That's it," he murmurs coaxingly, kissing the side of my face with so much tenderness I could explode. "Rub that needy pussy against me, Miss Parker."

Oh, God.

The way that sexy voice of his caresses the name he calls me at work. He makes it sound so dirty in the most delicious way.

My voice is breathy and needy, but I want to play along so I purr back, "Yes, Mr. Foster."

His grip on me tightens, like my words have the same effect on him.

I never thought dry-humping could make me so hot, but as I rub myself against him over and over, my need ramps up and I *need* to get out of my clothes. I need him out of his. I need what's inside those Armani pants of his.

I stop grinding on him, but his thigh is still pressed against my pussy, dampening his pant leg. I reach for the bulge between his thighs and rub as he tilts his head and starts kissing his way down the sensitive column of my neck.

"Tell me to leave, Chelsea," he says between kisses, making my heart skip a beat. "Tell me to leave or I'm going to drag you into this study, bend you over your father's desk, and fuck you on top of it."

His naughty words send a delightful shiver of anticipation dancing down my spine. My heart beats a little harder with excitement as I loop my arm around his neck and sway back just enough so I can look at him, a gleam of mischief in my eyes. "Promise?"

He shakes his head, a gleam of fondness in his as his lips tug up in a

tiny little smile.

I give him a soft kiss as I reach down to twine our fingers together, much more confident this time as I take his hand and lead him into Daddy's study.

Chapter Eight

CHELSEA

The sight of Daddy's desk makes my tummy flutter. We shouldn't even be in here, let alone doing *this* in here.

I want to be bad with him, though. Just to make sure he doesn't change his mind, I let go of his hand and reach behind my back, drawing down the zipper.

Foster's gaze follows, drinking in the glimpse of my bare skin. I pull the zipper down slowly, watching his eyes darken when it finally reaches the small of my back.

"Let me help you with that," he murmurs, moving up behind me.

He spreads the fabric all the way open and slides the straps down my arms, bending to place a soft kiss to my shoulder once it's bare. Then he tugs the fabric down past my hips. The dress falls to the ground, leaving me standing here in nothing but a black strapless bra and my lace panties.

Foster's gaze roams over my body as he moves to stand in front of me, a gleam of appreciation in his eyes. "Stunning."

His praise makes me flush with pleasure. I can't quite stifle a small

smile. "I'm glad you approve," I say, a note of playfulness in my tone.

His gaze meets mine as he advances on me, reaching for my face. He caresses my jaw, then pushes his fingers into my hair and pulls me close. I wrap my arms around him as his free arm loops around my waist. He kicks my dress out of the way, then slowly begins walking me backward, his eyes never leaving mine. "Do you know what I'm going to do to you, Chelsea?"

I lick my lips, holding his gaze as I shake my head no.

"I'm going to make you forget every boy, every man you've ever let touch you."

I take a shuddering breath, biting down on my plump lower lip.

"And do you know what you're going to do to me?"

I shake my head again.

"You're going to blow up my fucking world." He buries his face in the crook of my neck. "Every last fucking corner of it," he says, his kisses punctuated with light little bites that make my toes curl.

He doesn't stop devouring my neck and driving me absolutely crazy until we're behind Daddy's desk, then he tears his lips from my flesh and reaches around my back. He easily unsnaps my bra and tosses it off to the side, his gaze dropping to my now bare breasts.

A languid feeling hits me the moment he catches them in the palms of his massive hands. "Perfect," he murmurs, just before running his thumbs over my nipples and drawing a gasp of pleasure out of me. "I'm going to devour every inch of you, Chelsea. I hope you're ready."

"Oh, I am," I murmur right back, reaching for his suit jacket. He has me stripped down to my panties, but he's still completely dressed.

He toys with my breasts until he has to stop to shuck his jacket, then he grabs them again. He teases my nipples, seeming to enjoy every small noise he drags out of me. My fingers move unsteadily as I slip each button through its hole. Finally, his dress shirt falls open.

A chord of arousal is pulled so tautly within me, I need to come like I've never needed it before, but dammit, I want him naked. Maybe it's the unsteadiness of my fingers, a gleam in my eye, or the flush in my cheeks,

but he seems to understand my need so he decides to help me. The stark white undershirt he wears beneath his suit is still obstructing my view, so he drags it over his head and tosses it.

I sigh with relief, placing both of my hands on his hard, muscled chest and drinking in the sight of him shirtless. Looking isn't enough, touching isn't enough—I need to taste him. I need to feel his warm skin beneath my lips.

I wrap my arms around his waist, pulling our bodies close enough to touch while I tilt my head and kiss every inch from his neck to the ball of his shoulder. God, he tastes so good. His hands make their way to my hair and he slides his fingers through the carefully curled tresses. I start to kiss him lower, desperate to run my tongue over his nipples, but he stops me before I can. His grip on my hair tightens and he uses it to pull me back, then he looks down at me and chides, "Ah, ah, ah. Someone's being greedy. It's my turn to have a taste."

He walks me backward, grabbing the office chair with his free hand and turning it. He wheels it just a little closer and I feel the soft material against the backs of my legs.

"Sit."

I release a breath and sit carefully since he still has a fistful of my hair. He releases it once my butt settles in the seat, tenderly caressing the spot he'd been holding as if to make nice after the teeny bit of roughness.

I don't know what he's going to do, but I keep my eyes locked onto him, my breath baited because I can't wait to find out.

Foster kneels on the ground, his gaze never leaving mine as he does. He pulls my legs apart so he can climb between them, then slowly rubs my outer thighs.

Anticipation causes my heart to pound wildly in my chest. He slides his hands up toward my hips and hooks his fingers in the waistband of my flimsy lace panties. "Lift your ass."

I release a breath, bracing my feet against the cool floor and pushing my butt up so Foster can drag my panties down my legs. My skin heats

349

even though he can already see most of me.

Now he can see *everything*.

When he draws the panties off, he doesn't toss them along with the other clothes like I expect him to. He stuffs them into his pocket, giving me a wolfish grin.

"I'll be keeping those."

My face heats even more. I feel a twinge of embarrassment but much more pleasure at the thought of him keeping my panties. Looking at them later and remembering this.

My heart jumps as he suddenly pulls me forward until my ass hangs over the edge of the seat. He crawls forward and drapes my long legs over his shoulders. His hand snakes behind my body, brushing my bare lower back and then pressing lower as he positions me where he wants me—with my exposed pussy right in front of his mouth.

Oh, God, is he going to…?

He does. I cry out as his mouth latches onto me and instinctively try to pull my legs closed. His strong arm locks around one thigh, catching it before I can. He spreads my legs wider, keeping that thigh trapped and wrapping his other hand around my hip to hold onto me.

It's a good thing, too, because when he pushes his tongue into me, I nearly fly off the chair.

"Foster," I say on a gasp, grabbing onto the padded arms of the office chair.

He's gentle at first, exploring this new area of my body, listening to the way I respond to him so he knows his way around. He, too, is a fast learner. It takes him maybe a minute to figure out just where to lick to make my legs shake, to master the exact right speed and pressure. He dominates my pussy the same way he dominated my mouth when he kissed me.

I was already so wound up from riding his thigh, I can't hold on for long. He doesn't let me. He drives me straight over the edge, grabbing my hand and holding it as I cry out his name and come apart in Daddy's office chair.

My body is boneless in the aftermath. Foster unlatches and looks at me, but I close my eyes, soaking up the incredible feeling.

He doesn't let me rest for long. He pulls me to my feet but I don't have all the strength back in my legs yet, so I wrap my arms around him and rest my head against his firm, muscled chest.

"Thank you," I murmur.

I feel a rumble as he chuckles, tenderly petting my hair. "Such good manners."

"Mm-hmm. Keep an eye on your mailbox; you'll be getting a card, too."

Foster kisses my head, then he gently tugs me away from him, his gaze traveling down my body. Once he's sure I'm steady on my feet, he lets me go.

I'm still feeling a little spacey, but some of my focus comes back when his hand drops to his waistband and he begins unbuckling his belt.

I thought I was sated, but the sight of him undoing his pants triggers a new strain of desire. I don't know if he wants me to suck him first or not, so I look to him for direction. "Do you still want me on the desk?"

He nods as he draws his belt off, tossing it behind him. Then he steps forward and starts gathering my hair in his hand, making a ponytail to wrap around his fist. My heart skitters with excitement and nerves as he uses it to guide me closer to the desk. He pushes me forward until my tummy and breasts are smashed against the cold, hard surface, then he lets go of my hair. He grabs my hips, running his hands down them before commanding, "Hold onto the edge of the desk."

I do as he says, grabbing the front edge of the desk as he smoothes a hand over the curve of my butt and gives it a little squeeze. I love feeling his hands on me. I close my eyes and sigh a little.

I get so caught up in the gentle, lovely feeling of him caressing my ass, I'm not at all prepared when his fingers slide inward and graze my slit. I take a deeper breath and let it out, but he does it again and again. The feather-light caress feels incredible. A shiver shoots down my spine every

time he touches me that way.

Two blunt fingers delve deeper, seeking access. I sigh happily when they push inside me. I'm already soaked, just the way he wanted me, so even though it's a tight fit, his fingers sink deeper without much resistance.

I can't believe this is finally happening. I've been fantasizing about what it would be like between us for so long, and now he really has me bent over Daddy's desk with his fingers soaked in my arousal.

He withdraws them, but only to get out of his pants. I wait, spread out on the desk for him, trying not to feel awkward knowing he could be looking at every intimate inch of my body.

I hear the telltale crinkle as he rips open a packet and I know he's putting on a condom. Then his hands are on me again. He moves up close behind me, aligning his cock against my entrance. I gasp as the tip of it pushes into me, my grip on the edge of the desk tightening.

"Foster, wait."

I feel the tension in the air as he stills. "What?" he demands, his deep voice made even huskier as he struggles to keep himself from pushing deeper.

I feel so vulnerable asking, but I can't shake the desire even knowing it's a little crazy. "Will you... will you take the condom off?"

Dead silence. My heart pounds so hard in my chest, I'm certain the mahogany wood I'm draped across can feel it. Finally, his voice cuts through the silence like a whip. "Why?"

"It's our first time. I... I don't want anything between us."

He doesn't say anything right away, but finally he says, "I've never fucked anyone without a condom before. It's reckless."

I peek over my shoulder at him. "That only makes me want it more."

His eyes narrow and I can see him considering it. It's a crazy request and he'd be crazy to grant it, but man, I hope he does. I want to feel every bare inch of him straining to fit inside me. I don't want a layer of protection getting in the way.

"Come on, Foster," I say, a little playful teasing in my tone. "Be crazy

with me."

Foster sighs, shaking his head at me and pulling out. Despite his grumbling, he reaches down and peels the lubed up rubber off his dick. "Your father's going to fucking kill me."

I grin at him. "You're the best."

Still shaking his head, he takes my hip in one hand and his dick in the other, pushing the tip back into me. "Hold on tight."

I barely get my hands on the edge of the desk before he drives into me. I cry out in surprise. I expected he'd take his time and go slow, but instead he claims me with one long, deep thrust. He pauses there for a split second and lets out a growl, reaching down and grabbing a fistful of my hair.

"Jesus Christ, Chelsea," he mutters, like it's my fault—whatever *it* is. "You're so fucking tight."

I don't know if I'm so tight or he's just so… massive, but I can definitely feel him filling me all the way up. He pulls on my hair and tugs me off the desk a few inches as he eases back out, then he thrusts forward again. Another low sound emanates from his throat as he mutters another curse.

The friction is delicious as he does it again and again, picking up the pace with every thrust. He keeps cursing at me, but I kind of love it.

He finally has to let go of my hair to hold onto my hips because even though I'm holding on as tight as I can, the force of his thrusts keeps throwing me around the desk. When his hands lock onto my hips, I don't move again. He holds me where he wants me and fucks me so brutally I know I'll be sore tomorrow. And God, I can't wait. Every time I move, I'll feel the evidence that he was inside me tonight.

The friction of his bare cock rubbing against my walls as he fucks me is incredible. There's no feeling in the world like being possessed by Foster. Nothing that even comes close.

I'm coming close, though. I didn't expect to come again, but as he angles his hips and drives into me at a slightly different angle, I feel him

driving me closer and closer to the edge. I grip the desk until my knuckles turn white, my body straining as I meet him thrust for thrust.

"Oh, God. Please, Foster." I cry out senseless pleas for pleasure he's already going to give me, but every sense feels like it's on fire.

I lick my lips and taste the salty tang of sweat I've worked up from being fucked. His cock hits the spot where I'm most sensitive and a strangled cry slips out of me. He hits it again and again, his thrusts coming faster and harder. I can't stop crying out, my legs shaking as he drives into me.

"Foster!" I scream his name as he plunges me over the edge into ecstasy.

A growl rips from his throat as he buries himself as deep as he can and lets go. When I feel him come inside me, I sigh with a strange kind of relief, like all is finally right in the world.

I can't move. I feel bad that he has to stand. My legs couldn't do that right now if my life depended on it. For a split second, I wonder if I should scoot over and he could lie down on the desk with me.

My face is smooshed against the desk but I'm too fulfilled to care about looking stupid. "That was incredible."

Foster runs a gentle hand over my ass as he carefully pulls out of my body. Mimicking what I said earlier, he murmurs, "I'm glad you approve."

I grin, finally moving my head so I can look back at him. "I like you."

A short laugh escapes him. "I fucking hope so."

"I do," I murmur sleepily, filled up with happiness. "And I want to do this again. Can you stay a little longer, or do you have to go straight home?"

"I can stay, but I'm going to need a few minutes," he tells me, gesturing vaguely to his dick.

"That's fine."

I finally peel myself off the desk. I'm all sticky from sweating and my body left an imprint on the glossy surface. I make a note to clean it the instant Foster leaves... but I hope that's not soon.

He's bending to collect his clothes when I hop down off the desk

and look at him. I'm feeling very lovey in the afterglow of that second orgasm—somehow it was even more intense than the first—and I move closer, pushing my fingers through his hair and curling my body close to his.

Foster drops the arm full of clothes off to the side and wraps the other around my waist to hug me back. He's sweaty too, but I don't care, I just want to hold him.

"I think for round two we should move to my bedroom," I tell him.

"Your bedroom?" He pulls back to look down at me, his dark eyebrow cocked skeptically. "Your father's already going to kill me, now you want to defile your bedroom, too?"

I shrug. "If you're going to die, we might as well make sure it was worth it."

His lips curve up in amusement, his eyes glistening with tenderness. "You make a good point."

"I usually do." I flash him a smile as I move out of his embrace. I collect my own clothes off the ground, then I walk over and take his hand.

This time, I lead him up the stairs to my bedroom.

And he lets me.

Chapter Nine

FOSTER

Mondays are typically hell.

But not this Monday. After having Chelsea Parker in every way I could twist her young, flexible body over the weekend, I'm feeling invigorated, eager to tackle the day. It took everything in me to watch her walk into Ryan's office this morning rather than following me into mine. My dick has been uncomfortably stiff in my slacks. Annoying considering only hours ago, I had her up against the wall in my shower. After sinking into her hot, perfect body Friday night, I knew I couldn't have a taste and move on. No, I was addicted. And if I didn't want my ass shot by her father, I had to get her back to my place where we were free to fuck without interruption.

"Sir," my secretary says from the doorway, "you have a call on line one. Mr. Parker."

I try not to cringe. All morning I've been avoiding Mason's calls to my cell. But the man is relentless. If I don't take the call, he'll show up unannounced and I can't have him witness firsthand the way his daughter

morphs me into a feral, hungry beast.

"Send the call to me. And will you ask Ryan to come see me as well?"

She nods. "Sure thing, Mr. Foster."

I pick up the receiver on my desk. "Hello, Mason."

"He *does* know how to use a phone," Mason says with a chuckle. "Asshole. Why have you been avoiding my calls?"

"Busy," I lie. "What's up?"

"I wanted to talk to you about Chelsea."

The line goes quiet. Guilt claws up my throat, choking me. I'm unable to find words to reply back to him with. How the fuck does he know?

"I, uh, Mason let me—"

"That bad, huh? Fuck." He huffs out a breath of air making the line crackle. "She's been tightlipped about the job. I'd really hoped she'd work out."

The job.

Oh.

That.

"I'm sorry," I say, composing myself and finding my voice. "I'm a little distracted with another employee at the moment, who I'm about to send packing. Chelsea, though, is working out great. She was made for this job. It becomes clearer each day. In fact, she's saved this company from crumbling right in the palm of my hand."

Ryan lingers outside my door, chatting it up to my secretary, not at all onto the fact I'm about to hand his ass to him.

"No shit?" Mason says with a chuckle. "She's always been a go-getter and we're proud of her, but I know you're harder to please."

Your daughter pleases me endlessly.

"I…Mason, she's a great employee. Truly." *Grow some fucking balls, man, and tell him what you did.* "Chelsea is an incredible woman. Smart, sassy, *beautiful.*"

"Young," he adds in a gruff tone, quickly interpreting the direction of my words. "She's young, Foster."

"I understand that."

"Tell me you aren't…" he trails off.

"Mase, I need to ask you something."

"I'd rather you didn't."

I can almost imagine him on the other line, frowning much like his daughter does when she's unhappy. A bloom of warmth swells inside my chest. "Do you trust me?"

He sighs. "Unfortunately."

"Have I ever purposefully hurt you or done anything without regard to your feelings?"

"No."

I pause, wondering if I want to take this step. This past weekend was filled with great sex. It was also filled with laughter, long conversations into the night, and affection, all of which I've never wanted or been a part of in my miserable existence. Chelsea breathes life into the husk that I was, reanimating the man I always craved to be but never knew how to. She makes me yearn for a life where she remains in it. For a man who has only ever truly loved his best friend, Chelsea makes me believe I have room in my heart for more.

"Foster," Mason urges. "Just say it already."

I thought I could stay away from her. And, while at work, that may be true. However, once I tasted of her forbidden fruit on Friday, it became impossible to ignore her any longer.

I want her.

Plain and simple.

For how long?

It'll have to be more than just a weekend fling. She's too sweet and unique and a fucking catch for anything other than something serious. I'm not sure I'm even capable of giving a girl like Chelsea Parker what she deserves. But I sure plan to try.

"I'd like for you and Helen to have dinner with me this week. To meet my…*girlfriend*."

Though it sounds foreign on my tongue, it feels right, growing teeth and latching onto my heart. My girlfriend. *Mine.* Yeah, mine sounds a helluva lot better.

"For fuck's sake, man. Girlfriend? The William Foster I know doesn't seriously date."

"This is the William Foster you don't know. Turns out, I think you'll like this guy."

"That remains to be seen," he grumbles and then curses again. "Fine. You want to go this route, then we'll go this route. Friday night let's meet up for dinner. If I haven't punched you in the face by the end of the meal, then I guess I'll let it go." A sigh of resignation. "She's not my little girl anymore."

No, indeed she is not.

"You know I love you, Mason," I say with fierceness. "I always have. You've saved me from every low point in my life. Every time I lost sight of who I was, you were there to put me back on track."

"And now?"

"She has your strength and loyalty. Your fire."

"I'll teach her my right hook too. Just in case."

"I won't fuck up," I vow, my words threading through me in a binding way I feel down to my marrow. "I swear to God I won't."

"You can't." His voice cracks. "You *can't* fuck up. Not now. Not this time."

"I *won't.*"

After a long pause, Mason finally says goodbye and hangs up. I'm pleased to have navigated the minefield with my best friend, our friendship not blowing up in the process. Now, onto my second order of business.

"Come in," I call out, motioning to Ryan.

He walks in, a smarmy smile on his face. "What's up, Boss?"

"Close the door." My voice turns icy cold. "We have much to discuss."

I remember the day Mason told me he was in love Helen. It was a cool evening in November and he'd invited me out for drinks. As we shared a basket of wings and downed a couple of beers, his sea green eyes turned soft, the bar lights above making them almost twinkle. He told me she just did something to him. Knocked him off his axis. Distracted him. Consumed him. Being his logical best friend, I'd had concerns. Grilled him about his swift fall into the infamous love trap. I couldn't comprehend the term other than the platonic way I loved him. My bedroom conquests were almost cold. There were no sparks other than the general heat of lust for a warm body to sink into. No fire, not even an ember.

As Mason described—the most passionate I'd ever seen him—how she got inside him, burrowing her way right into his heart, I felt sorry for him. My levelheaded friend seemed naïve and so hopeful.

Every year after, I waited for the dreadful call. For him to tell me he was sleeping with his secretary or that they'd split up. But he always had this way about him when he spoke of her. And seeing them together, it was obvious how much he cared about her. Even now, nearly two decades later, I'm surprised he still talks about her with the same affectionate shine in his eyes and the same goofy-ass grin on his face.

Tonight, at dinner, my best friend attempted to play the protective father role. All of five minutes. Soon, however, Chelsea had worked her magic to smooth over the uneasiness at the new roles we played. I'd stared at her fondly, amazed that I'd somehow tripped over my own rules of how I run my life and stumbled into her. When Mason caught me smiling as she laughed at something Helen had said, he nudged me with his foot to grab my attention.

His green eyes flickered with understanding. Acceptance drew up his smile that is so similar to Chelsea's and he gave me a nod. It was then, I realized he would never question my intent with his daughter again or worry over her wellbeing while she was with me.

But why?

He saw in me what I saw in him all those years ago.

Where his was a fully bloomed rose, mine is yet a bud, yearning to open up and flower, proudly showing the world I am capable of such an emotion too. With time, I know I'll fall completely over this girl. Hell, I'm halfway there and we've only just begun.

Now that we're back home—since she's officially mine, I'm not letting her go back to her place anytime soon—I can't take my eyes off her. Her blond hair hangs in silky, golden tresses around her pretty face, a smile teasing one side of her full lips, as she texts someone. She stretches one of her long legs out over my lap, oblivious to the fact she maddens me with such an innocent move. The navy dress she wore to dinner seems to dance up her thighs, giving me a tiny peek at the nude-colored panties she's wearing beneath it. I splay may hand over her tanned thigh and ease my palm further up her leg.

"I thought we were watching a movie," she says, a blond brow arched.

"Nah, I prefer to watch you work."

"How do you know I'm working?"

"You're making your work face."

She laughs, such a sweet fucking sound, setting her phone down on the couch beside her. "I have a work face?"

"You do." I smirk at her. "It's sexy as fuck, too."

"What's this face?" she purrs as she sits up, repositioning herself to straddle my lap. She bites on her fat bottom lip, gently grinding against my aching dick.

"It's not fucking innocent, no matter how hard you chew on that lip. This is your 'I want dick face.'"

Her sea green eyes flash with amusement. "You're good."

"I know." A wolfish grin splits across my face as I push her dress up her thighs. "I know all your faces now."

She flutters her eyes closed when my knuckle grazes over her clit, the thin barrier of the material of her panties only serving to aid me in my effort to bring her pleasure. I'm transfixed by the way she rocks her hips and her tits jiggle as she works with me, chasing her orgasm. As she gets closer, I

pull my hand away, pleased at the way her eyes pop open, flickering with annoyance.

"That's your spoiled little girl face," I say with a dark chuckle. "That one gets me really, really hot." I go back to massaging her just the way she likes on her needy clit. "Don't worry, beautiful, I enjoy spoiling you."

She rolls her eyes making me laugh but then her breathing intensifies as she gets closer to the edge. As I draw her nearer to pleasure, I reach behind her to unzip her dress. It slides down her shoulders, revealing her nude bra to me. While I continue to rub at her clit, I peel her dress off her arms letting it pool at her waist. With a quick flip of my fingers, I unlatch her bra, tossing it away too. Her young tits are perky and round, but not too big. I'm addicted to the way her small nipples are always erect for me, hard like tiny rose-colored pebbles, always begging for my teeth.

Leaning forward, I suck on her nipple hard enough she yelps. Her fingers latch onto my hair, tugging in the animalistic way of hers that drives me mad with the desire to pin and claim her.

"Oh God," she cries out, her body trembling with ecstasy.

I bite down on her peaked nipple, pulling back, my eyes drifting up to meet hers. Sea green mixed with flicks of navy seem to glow with overwhelming need for me. Once her body stops quivering, I cease rubbing at her clit and nibbling at her tit to lean back against the cushion. Always in tune with my thoughts, she sits up on her knees while I unfasten my slacks. She tosses her dress away, remaining only in her nude panties. I barely mange to get my pants and boxers yanked down my thighs before she's back on me, rubbing against my length, the material of her panties an annoying barrier now.

"Move those," I growl, my fingers biting into her thighs.

Her smile is seductive and confident as she hooks a finger into the side of the material, dragging them aside to reveal the most perfect, pretty pink pussy I've ever seen. She takes hold of my throbbing dick and teases her opening with the weeping crown of it. Then, with her eyes churning like an angry sea, she sinks down over me, her pillowy lips parted.

"Good girl," I croon, once again leaning forward to feast on her tits. "Now fuck me like you think you're capable of conquering me."

I don't tell her she already has.

Her hips move like she's dancing, smooth and rhythmic. Everything about her movements enraptures me. I want to taste her and see her and smell her and fucking feel her. All of her. All at once. She's cutting through years of indifference and hardness at the world, sliding her sweetness into every nook and cranny of my entire being, not at all fucking sorry she's invading me mind, body, and soul.

Gripping her ass cheek, I pull roughly on it, enjoying how she clenches around my cock and yelps. I urge her to fuck me faster, harder, hungrier. My girl obeys, changing the erotic dance to another one that seems to drive me crazy with need.

I pull my head back to look at her. So fucking beautiful with her neck exposed and lovely sounds escaping her. With a claiming grip on her jaw, I draw her mouth to mine so I can taste all the moans and whimpers to see if they're as sweet as they sound. She devours me with urgency, equally consumed by me. Male pride clouds around us like a protective fog, keeping us locked away in our feral lovemaking.

Mine.

Mine.

Mine.

I've never wanted to claim and keep anyone. Ever. Chelsea morphs the man I was into the beast I'm quickly becoming.

I know I won't last long, especially because her moans are growing louder and more ragged indicating she's close to orgasming again. All it takes is a hard smack to the ass and for her pussy to clench from the shock of it for us both to find our release. She cries out my name, ripping at my hair. I'm drunk on pleasure and high on this girl, spinning off my axis as I try to bury my dick inside her forever. Finally, with her pussy full of my cum and my senses finding their way back to reality, I relax, pulling her against my chest.

She sighs against the side of my throat, in no hurry to slide off me and clean up. That's another thing I like about Chelsea. Each time we're together, she lives in the moment. Enjoys the wildness of the fucking but is content in the quiet of the after. Not needy or clingy, but instead, simply pleased. It never fails to stoke a fire inside me with the desire to please her every day until the end of time.

"You're awfully intense today," she murmurs, kissing my jaw before pulling back to meet my stare. "What's going on inside that brilliant mind of yours?"

"Brilliant?" I smirk. "Someone is gracious with their compliments when she's been fucked raw and been given a couple of orgasms."

She laughs. "Don't ruin it. Be serious."

"Just thinking about how one day, I'll own every part of your body." Leaning in, I sweep her hair aside to expose her neck and kiss the sweet flesh. "Even here, Miss Parker."

A gasp escapes her as I lazily run my finger up and down her ass crack.

"And if I resist?" she challenges, lifting her eyebrow in the sexy defiance that never ceases to make my dick turn to stone. Even now. Even after I've come deep inside her young, ripe body. She has my body convinced I'm a man closer to her age than her father's. My dick twitches inside her, ready for another round.

"Hmm," I rumble, taking hold of her wrists and wrenching them behind her back, glancing down at her tits that now jut into my face. "I think I'd quite like it if you resist actually. Scream a little." I meet her amused stare and flash her an evil smile. "While you're at it, call me Daddy, too."

"Mr. Foster!"

The End

ABOUT SAM MARIANO

SAM MARIANO loves to write edgy, twisty reads with complicated characters you're left thinking about long after you turn the last page. Her favorite thing about indie publishing is the ability to play by your own rules! If she isn't reading one of the thousands of books on her to-read list, writing her next book, or playing with her adorable daughter... actually, that's about all she has time for these days.

Feel free to find Sam on Facebook, Goodreads, or her blog—she loves hearing from readers! She's also on Instagram @sammarianobooks, and you can sign up for her totally-not-spammy newsletter <u>HERE</u>

If you have the time and inclination to leave a review, however short or long, she would greatly appreciate it! :)

ALSO BY SAM MARIANO

Contemporary romance standalones
Untouchable (bully romance)
The Imperfections (forbidden romance)
Stitches (MFM ménage romance)
How the Hitman Stole Christmas (unconventional, a pinch of mafia)
Mistletoe Kisses (student-teacher romance novella)
Coming-of-age, contemporary bully duet
Because of You
After You
If you're a **series reader**, be sure to check out her super binge-able Morelli
family series! It's dark and twisty mafia romance, and the first book is
Accidental Witness.

ABOUT AUTHOR K WEBSTER

K Webster is a *USA Today* Bestselling author. Her titles have claimed many bestseller tags in numerous categories, are translated in multiple languages, and have been adapted into audiobooks. She lives in "Tornado Alley" with her husband, two children, and her baby dog named Blue. When she's not writing, she's reading, drinking copious amounts of coffee, and researching aliens.

Keep up with K Webster

BOOKS BY K WEBSTER

Psychological Romance Standalones:
My Torin
Whispers and the Roars
Cold Cole Heart
Blue Hill Blood
Wicked Lies Boys Tell

Romantic Suspense Standalones:
Dirty Ugly Toy
El Malo
Notice
Sweet Jayne
The Road Back to Us
Surviving Harley
Love and Law
Moth to a Flame
Erased

Extremely Forbidden Romance Standalones:
The Wild
Hale
Like Dragonflies

Taboo Treats:
Bad Bad Bad
Coach Long
Ex-Rated Attraction
Mr. Blakely
Easton

Crybaby

Lawn Boys

Malfeasance

Renner's Rules

The Glue

Dane

Enzo

Red Hot Winter

Dr. Dan

KKinky Reads Collection:

Share Me

Choke Me

Daddy Me

Watch Me

Hurt Me

Play Me

Contemporary Romance Standalones:

Wicked Lies Boys Tell

The Day She Cried

Untimely You

Heath

Sundays are for Hangovers

A Merry Christmas with Judy

Zeke's Eden

Schooled by a Senior

Give Me Yesterday

Sunshine and the Stalker

Bidding for Keeps

B-Sides and Rarities

Conheartists

Cocksure Ace

No Tears with Him

Stroke of Midnight

Paranormal Romance Standalones:

Apartment 2B

Running Free

Mad Sea

Cold Queen

Delinquent Demons

Hood River Hoodlums Series:

Hood River Rat (Book 1)

Little Hoodlum (Book 2)

Campfire Chaos (Book 3)

Hood River Zero (Book 4)

War & Peace Series:

This is War, Baby (Book 1)

This is Love, Baby (Book 2)

This Isn't Over, Baby (Book 3)

This Isn't You, Baby (Book 4)

This is Me, Baby (Book 5)

This Isn't Fair, Baby (Book 6)

This is the End, Baby (Book 7 – a novella)

Lost Planet Series:

The Forgotten Commander (Book 1)

The Vanished Specialist (Book 2)

The Mad Lieutenant (Book 3)

The Uncertain Scientist (Book 4)

The Lonely Orphan (Book 5)

The Rogue Captain (Book 6)
The Determined Hero (Book 7)

2 Lovers Series:
Text 2 Lovers (Book 1)
Hate 2 Lovers (Book 2)
Thieves 2 Lovers (Book 3)

Pretty Little Dolls Series:
Pretty Stolen Dolls (Book 1)
Pretty Lost Dolls (Book 2)
Pretty New Doll (Book 3)
Pretty Broken Dolls (Book 4)

The V Games Series:
Vlad (Book 1)
Ven (Book 2)
Vas (Book 3)

Four Fathers Books:
Pearson

Four Sons Books:
Camden

Elite Seven Books:
Gluttony
Greed

Royal Bastards MC:
Koyn
Copper

Truths and Lies Duet:
Hidden Truths
Stolen Lies

Torn and Bound Duet:
Torn Apart
Bound Together

Books Only Sold on K's Website and Eden Books:
The Wild
The Free
Hale
Bad Bad Bad
This is War, Baby
Like Dragonflies

The Breaking the Rules Series:
Broken (Book 1)
Wrong (Book 2)
Scarred (Book 3)
Mistake (Book 4)
Crushed (Book 5 – a novella)

The Vegas Aces Series:
Rock Country (Book 1)
Rock Heart (Book 2)
Rock Bottom (Book 3)

The Becoming Her Series:
Becoming Lady Thomas (Book 1)
Becoming Countess Dumont (Book 2)

Becoming Mrs. Benedict (Book 3)

Alpha & Omega Duet:
Alpha & Omega (Book 1)
Omega & Love (Book 2)

Elizabeth Gray Books:
Blue Hill Blood
Cognati

Not a
Dirty
Little
Secret

GIANA DARLING AND SIERRA SIMONE

Chapter One

JAMES CALDRON

Frankly, he looked ridiculous.

Which was really the only reason he was still occupying my incredibly precious time while blathering on about something I had absolutely no care about. I was running Her Majesty's Government, not a charity, and the issue of archaeological preservation wasn't even a blip on my radar. Unfortunately, strings had been pulled by the aristocratic pains in my arse, and now here I sat being advised on the importance of historical integrity.

I was more enraptured by the lad than the issue at hand.

I simply couldn't fathom how a grown man—though admittedly, he seemed to be on the awkward, somewhat endearing precipice between boy and man, somewhere in his early twenties at a guess—could present himself in such a way.

He wore a thumb ring.

Bright gold, thick, inset with a glittering sapphire.

As I said, ridiculous.

Yet I couldn't seem to unfix my gaze from it and, subsequently, from his hands.

To my knowledge, I had never actively studied someone's hands before, let alone a man's. But that silly ring locked my gaze to those long, nimble fingers and broad palms. The contrast of his white skin faintly marbled with blue and mauve veins against the black of his velvet jacket was oddly attractive. Though the man himself was tall, he still carried the coltishness of youth, but his hands were graceful, more eloquent than his speech.

Looking at the rest of him, I decided there was nothing spectacular about him. With foppish blond curls spiraling haphazardly into an open, earnest face eclipsed by eyes as blue and delicate as Spode china, he was fairly handsome, but not enough for me to take a second look at.

Particularly as I didn't make it a habit to look twice at any man.

I narrowed my gaze at those flapping, animated hands as he dithered on about the importance of historical preservation and decided that regardless of his ridiculousness, he really did have beautiful fingers.

"There really is no reasonable way to defer the archaeological mitigation of such a large site, particularly when the Roman settlement of Londinium was a mere two kilometers away… Excuse me, Prime Minister, but are you listening to a word I say?" Tobias Talbot-Ullswater's bright voice broke through my ennui and roped me back into the conversation that should have ended as soon as it began.

"I've heard you quite well," I assured him. "In order that the football area for the new Kings Cross United team be built on the proposed site, you need six to unforetold months to properly survey the site, which will cost the government and unwitting taxpayers to spend millions of pounds on this project. I hear you, Mr. Talbot-Ullswater, but you have said nothing to convince me this isn't a waste of time and money. The Battle Bridge Stadium stands to bring the city enormous economic growth, not to mention a neighborhood that fell into significant disrepair in the 19th and 20th centuries. We do not want to hinder or, God forbid, completely arrest the

project based on your guess that there *might* be some bones of some kind beneath the ground."

I arched a brow coolly as I leaned back in my chair and crossed one foot over the other knee. My best mate, Alexander, called it my 'affected professorial posture,' but I didn't let him teasing deter me in its use.

I found it intimidated people into getting to the point or getting out of my sight entirely.

It seemed to have the opposite effect on Mr. Talbot-Ullswater, who braced his feet farther apart and crossed his arms over his pastel pink paisley button-up.

"I am not here to waste your time, Your Excellency," he said with a sweet smile masking his mawkish tone. "The issue of archaeological survey at the proposed site in Kings Cross is crucial to maintaining the history of the area. *No!* Of the city itself."

"I wonder, Mr. Talbot-Ullswater," I mused. "Are you always this dramatic? If so, it must be a characteristic of your age."

Mona, my senior advisor and friend of twenty years, stirred in her seat beside me. It was an innocuous movement, but I knew she was startled by my show of personality and the simple fact that I'd let this meeting continue beyond the allotted five minutes.

I was efficient, calculated, and stern.

Not immature and irascible as I was now.

Something about the bratty cast of Talbot-Ullswater's full, dimpled bottom lip irked me irrationally.

"I highly doubt you were ever anything close to dramatic," he countered easily. "You'd have to be somewhat animated to manage that, and clearly…" He tossed his hand in the air as if the idea of me that way was utter rubbish he was throwing in the bin.

"That's the first clever thing I've heard you say this morning," I countered, idly adjusting the angle of the iron Barbary lion paperweight on my desk so it was precisely perpendicular to my computer on its leather matt. "Perhaps, in the remaining two minutes I'll allot you, you might

endeavor to continue in that same manner."

"There is nothing clever about erecting a monolithic structure on the grounds of what could be a massive archaeological discovery." There was a flush in his cheeks now, rose petals trapped beneath white wax that was oddly becoming.

"We have invested over twenty-one billion pounds in transportation infrastructure at King's Cross. Placing the new stadium there is an obvious choice both in economic value and ease. Football spectators can catch the tube to St. Pancras Station and be seated in the new Battle Bridge arena in five minutes."

"Of course, it goes without saying that the easiest option is always the wisest," he snarked, fisting his hands on his hips.

The robotic tune of a ringtone cut through the rising tension.

"Excuse me," Mona said, tucking a springy lock of her black hair behind her ear as was her habit when she tried to hide a smile. "I've got to take this. Please, try to be civil. We are talking about archaeology, not the fate of all mankind."

Talbot-Ullswater rolled his eyes before offering her a cheeky grin. "Tell that to your prime minister."

"He's your PM too," she reminded him before closing the door after her.

"It would do you well to remember that," I said dryly, standing up because, suddenly, my inactivity felt dangerous. I didn't want this witty, quick-minded creature to trap me so easily.

"Oh, trust me," he said, hands taking flight like twin birds. "I do. Seems a man can't turn on the telly lately without hearing about the fab PM and his heroic deeds bringing down all sorts of bad guys. Are you a politician or Batman?" He cocked his head, ringed thumb rising to rub at the absurd swell of his lower lip. "Although, I always fancied Batman would be sexy."

"And I'm not?" It took years of studied restraint to keep my voice mild.

Why did I care what this foolish boy thought of me?

I was the Prime Minister of England. A forty-three-year-old man who glad-handed global political leaders *weekly*.

Talbot-Ullswater was just a boy.

Admittedly, a very pretty boy.

"I'm fairly easy to please," he admitted with a rakish grin. "But no, I don't typically find obstinate, antiquated men attractive."

"All this because I won't give you what you want." I clucked my tongue as I rounded my desk and leaned against the front, tucking my hands into my trouser pockets so I wouldn't give in to the insane compulsion to wring his lovely neck. "You're acting your age, I'm afraid."

I felt caught, tangled in the golden snare of his cast net, and as any captured mammal will do, inevitably, I fought against that hold. While no one would have ever called me genial before, the panic of my startling infatuation soured me. My own tongue felt pickled, too acidic in my mouth as I engaged in ceaseless repartee with a youth too silly and too whimsical to reason with.

"God forbid someone shows passion about something they believe in," he countered, stalking forward until he was in my space, the tips of his leather trainers against my loafers. "Until this moment, I didn't know lack of personality could be such a danger to our nation's history."

Heat welled in my belly, bubbling up my chest to sizzle at the edges of my refrigerated heart until it burned. Even my eyes felt warm in my head, my hands aching with it as if they were held too close to a flame.

It was the heat of madness.

Of the passion Tobias Talbot-Ullswater had so eloquently decided I was lacking.

Quite honestly, until that moment, my blood fevered and pulse pounded as I stared into that delicately constructed face, I hadn't felt it in years.

Which was why I allowed it to move me to insanity.

I would prove to the git exactly how emboldened and daring a man

such as I could be.

I would take charge of this preposterous situation and bend it—*him*—to my will.

Something changed in his expression as I something morphed in mine, echoing the predatory glint in my eyes with a shocked, thrilling, and fearful excitement in his.

A moment later, my hand was at the long, swan-like column of his throat, my thumb at his jugular so I could feel the alarmed pulse of my prey.

At the moment after that, I was kissing him.

Kissing a man.

Kissing velvet lips until they parted and then a silken tongue. His mouth was so lush it could have belonged to a woman, but the strong, lean throat under my hand and the rough-edged moan in my mouth said differently.

I was kissing a man I found utterly ridiculous just to prove I wasn't so passionless as he claimed.

Only, as the rigidity of his surprise leeched from his body and he grew supple against me, his soft belly against the hardness pressing insistently at my trousers, I knew the only person I had truly shocked was myself.

Chapter Two

TOBIAS TALBOT-ULLSWATER

His hand on my throat.

His lips on mine.

His erection stiff and urgent against my belly.

Even now, two days later, I was dogged by the memory of that kiss.

That kiss.

The prime fucking minister had kissed me in his office. And not just kissed me but kissed me like he wanted me on my knees or bent over his ridiculous antique desk. He kissed me like I was about to know what his cum tasted like.

And oh, I would have tasted it. All he had to do was ask me.

Or command me.

But he didn't ask or command. Instead, he'd torn away from my mouth, staggering back and looking wholly horrified.

"Get out," he'd uttered hoarsely as if *I'd* been the egregious one. As if *I'd* been the one to turn a meeting about archaeology into a snogfest. "Get

out."

I'd been about to protest—I was something of a connoisseur of kisses, and that had been a really good one, the kind of kiss that could land you on your back with your ankles by your ears if you played your cards right— but then he did something so unthinkingly vicious that I'd been robbed of speech.

He'd swiped at his mouth with his forearm as if trying to scrub away the kiss with the sleeve of his jacket. Trying to scrub away *me*.

Feeling as though I'd been shot full of arrows, I turned and left—fled, more like it—wheezing for air the whole way out of his office and out to the curb, where I hailed a cab and panted all the way back to the Ullswater family townhouse in Mayfair.

He's a bastard, I'd tried to console myself. *A jackass. A pillock with internalized homophobia.*

It didn't help. I'd still been hurt and horny all that day and the next— and hurt and horny was my *least* favorite combination of feelings!

And now it was Sunday, and I was at Ullswater Cottage in Wiltshire to have brunch with my new stepfather and his son. I hated brunching with strangers, and I still hadn't shagged through all this pent-up frustration gifted to me by James fucking Caldron, and ugh, ugh, ugh—

"Darling, you must stop fidgeting," Mum said to me, gesturing with her champagne flute as she leaned against the kitchen counter. "Nigel is going to think I raised a little beastie instead of a son."

I took a deep breath, forcing myself to still. I loved Fiona Talbot-Ullswater-Oldershaw—better known as Figgy to her friends (and Mummy to me)—more than anything, and I wanted to make her happy. And if having an exorbitant brunch in the countryside with me and her new husband's son made her happy, then by Jove, we would have the best brunch the realm had ever seen.

Be happy. Stop thinking about James Caldron and his kissing. And his giant cock. And how he held you by the throat when he—

"Nonsense," I chirped to Mum, interrupting my unproductive train

of thought. I flashed her my *I love you, Mummy* grin while I snagged a miniature quiche off a platter. "Everyone loves me."

I said this last with a mouth full of quiche right as Nigel Oldershaw happened to walk into the kitchen. As usual with my new stepfather, I wasn't given a verbal response, only a single, raised eyebrow. I wasn't deterred, though—I was very rarely deterred.

(It's one of my most excellent traits.)

I merely swallowed and grinned again. "Isn't that right, Nigel?"

He cleared his throat, glancing over at my mum, who was obviously choking down her laughter with another sip of her mimosa. Nigel's face softened then. It did that a lot around her. As if he'd spent the day in the cold and she'd just given him a hot cup of tea. Like she was the living embodiment of warmth and joy.

To be honest, I'd had my doubts about him at first—they'd met during a polo match at Cowdray Park and were married within a month—but after meeting him and seeing how lost he was for Mum, I decided he at least had good taste, if nothing else. And for a man in our social strata—nearing his seventieth year at that—he seemed remarkably comfortable with my cheerfully brash brand of pansexuality, which was a pleasant surprise.

Good taste + not a homophobe = welcome to the family, Step-papa!

Anyway, after losing my father, Mum deserved to be happy. I was sad that it had taken her so long to meet someone, but now that she'd found him, I was determined to help her make the best possible go of it. Even if they had only known each other two months. Even if he was taciturn to the point of silence. Even if it did mean blended-family brunches and a new stepbrother—whom I still hadn't met.

I glanced down at my watch. "Where is our missing brunch guest? What did you say he does for a living, Nigel? Surely whatever it is, he's free on Sundays?"

"He's in government," Nigel said. "He's normally very punctual. Perhaps there was some business holding him up..."

Which is when we heard the knock on the door.

"Goodness," Nigel said. "I told him to come right in—"

"I'll get it," I volunteered, trotting through the kitchen and down the short hallway to the front door. My mother renovates Ullswater once every five years it seems, but the front of the cottage remains traditional. A low-thatched roof with a wide wooden door set into a century's worth of ivy and wisteria.

I swung the door open and ducked to step out into the cool autumn morning.

A man waited on the flagged walk just outside, and I had a glimpse of wide shoulders, a narrow waist, and muscular legs—all clad in a crisp tailored suit—as I greeted him.

"Hullo, new stepbrother!" I exclaimed. "Welcome to Ullswater—"

He turned, and suddenly, I couldn't feel my fingers. Or my toes.

It was the prime minister.

James Caldron.

The man who'd rather build a stadium than preserve the past.

The man who'd kissed me and then shoved me away like I was poison.

He was my new stepbrother.

An hour later, I was sitting shell-shocked and sober at the small table outside, watching my mother make small talk with her new son. Her new son, who'd worn a bespoke suit to a damp alfresco brunch in Wiltshire. Her new son, who was the *prime fucking minister.*

He hadn't said a word to me since he'd arrived either. Once he saw my face, he'd blinked once, hard, as though I was a ghost here to haunt him for his past sins, and then he'd simply nodded. Not at me, but almost at himself. Almost like he was saying, *This is my unfortunate reality, but I shall persevere.*

And then he'd pushed past me and entered the house, where he

proceeded to greet my mother with all the cool civility he was so famous for.

It became very, very clear that he was pretending we had never met before. That the kiss had never happened.

That I didn't know how his tongue felt, silky and searching against mine.

It became very, very clear that he still felt the way he had when he'd ordered me from his office. Like I was the last person in the whole of Britain he wanted to see. Which was ironic, given that our parents were now married, and we might be seeing rather a lot of each other.

It was warm for late November, but not so warm that I couldn't excuse myself on the pretense that I needed to warm up by the Aga for a moment— and so as the brunch was eaten and the cold, stilted conversation was entering a lull, I did excuse myself and hurried inside.

After a moment, Mum drifted in after me, searching for a fresh bottle of bubbles to take outside.

"You didn't tell me Nigel's son was the prime minister," I said weakly. "That was a shock."

"It must have slipped my mind, darling," Mum said, giving me a quick kiss on the cheek. "Nigel is quite proud of him, but we do talk about more than just our children. And politics is—well, it's quite gauche to talk politics, don't you think?"

"You're not debating international fishing privileges, Mummy. His son is the head of government! That would be worth mentioning, I'd think!"

She gave a one-shouldered shrug, already nudging open the glass bifold door that led to the garden and the brunch table. "Well, you know now, I suppose."

"But Nigel's last name is Oldershaw," I said, a little desperately. "Not Caldron—"

"Caldron was James's mother's name," Mum said. "She and Nigel were never married, and she was frightfully modern about that sort of thing. Are you coming back out, or do you need another minute to warm

up? I did tell you to wear that Merino jumper of yours. This cashmere one is much too thin."

"I need another minute," I said, forcing a smile and then giving a shiver for good measure. "I'll be back out soon."

She blew me a kiss and then went back outside, and I went back to brooding at the Aga. I didn't know if I could go back out there and pretend. I didn't know if I could trust myself not to notice how his shoulders tested the seams of his suit jacket or how his throat moved when he swallowed. I didn't think I could stop myself from staring into those icy blue eyes or fantasizing about that firm, sculpted mouth.

I needed to leave. Yes, that was what I needed to do. I'd make my excuses to Mum and then drive home. In fact, I could simply call her after I'd already left and say it was...I don't know, some kind of archaeological emergency. My firm specialized in rescue archaeology—that is, excavating sites earmarked for commercial development so we could preserve what we could before the inevitable concrete truck of progress rolled in and began pouring—so she was accustomed to me leaving abruptly for work.

Sorry, Mummy.

I was in the hallway ready to fetch my bag from my bedroom when I heard a voice behind me. Glacial. Elegant. Precise.

"There you are."

I turned and glared. "Yes. Here I am."

He strode toward me. He strode tragically well—the kind of striding that was made for powerful, confident men—and it made me want to slump against the wall. The silver at his temples, the stern brackets around his mouth. The large hands, the leanly muscled frame, the *stride*—

Fuck me, but there's something about an older man. I was used to men my age—just out of college, still rowdy and fumbling—but when confronted with James, so crisp, so *contained*, it was obvious what I'd been missing. I decided I needed to jump age brackets next time I was on my dating app.

"We have some things to make clear," James said, and I shook my

head.

"Uh-huh, Your Right Honorable Excellent Dickhead. Everything's been made clear enough to me. Which is why I'm leaving."

A muscle worked at the side of his jaw. He looked as though he was thinking of taking me over his knee, which was a thought I liked a lot.

Which was stupid! He hated me! I shouldn't be turned on by his Suit Daddy vibes!

I turned, determined to go to my room and get my bag, and that was when I felt his hand on my arm. But instead of pulling me close, he pushed me against the wall.

My chest heaved against the plaster...and even more so when he stepped behind me. Trapping me. I could feel the beat of his heart against my back, and against the curve of my arse, I could feel—oh. Oh, *fuck*. That was his penis—thick and hard as granite, digging right into the muscles of my backside.

He was hard for me, and knowing that made blood rush straight to my cock. So fast it made me dizzy.

"It's a bad idea to walk away from me, Tobias," James said. He was taller than me, just a little, so he had to angle his face down to murmur in my ear. "A very bad idea."

"You wanted me gone two days ago."

"Things have changed."

"Like the fact we are now stepbrothers?"

He stiffened against me. "We are no such thing," he growled.

"Oh, come on," I said, half-irritated, half-too-horny-to-care. "You don't want to play stepbrothers with me? While Mummy and Daddy are outside and they can't see? Maybe you want to break in your new toy. Maybe you want a taste before the holidays when we'll be staying in the same house, and you can use me every night. Maybe you're just so fucking hard that you don't care who gets it, and so it's going to be me. You're going to pull down my trousers right here and use me until you feel better, and then send me back outside dripping. Is that it?"

His hand slid to my throat as I spoke. His thick organ throbbed against me.

"You're goading me," said James.

"And you were cruel to me. Fair's fair."

"You're just a boy. You don't know what cruel is."

I licked my lips and whispered, "Does that mean you want to show me?"

His hand tightened on my throat. His exhale was ragged in my ear.

But he didn't answer.

I took his hand—the one currently braced by my shoulder—and slid it down my stomach to where my erection strained against the placket of my tight magenta trousers. The inhale he gave as his fingers closed around me would haunt my wanking dreams for years.

"You want this?" I murmured, pressing back against him hard enough to make him gasp again. "Then take it, Prime Minister. Take anything you like."

"A dangerous invitation, Tobias," answered James.

"That's the fun kind."

He hesitated. I could feel that hesitation everywhere—in the hand wrapped around my shaft, in the hand wrapped around my throat, in his very breath... T W O H O U R S A G O

And then I viscerally remembered what it felt like to have him push me away. What it felt like to watch him wipe his mouth clean of our kiss.

This was a man who didn't know what he wanted.

This was a man who wanted to hide.

I pulled his hand from my erection and then from my throat. I could feel the moment he let me. I could feel how much he wanted to hold on.

I turned so I could meet that cold glare of his. "If you want to fuck me, then do it. But own that you want it. You can make me dirty. You can make me little. But don't make me your dirty little secret," I said.

"We could never be anything else."

"Then I guess," I said, pushing past him, miserable and still so, so

horny, "we'll never be at all."

And I left him there, alone in the hallway.

Chapter Three

JAMES

They called him Tally.

A silly name for a silly boy.

And like that boy, oddly charming.

It was weeks after the shocking kiss and even more shocking reveal that Tobias Talbot-Ullswater was not only an irritational mistake but an irritating *stepbrother*.

It should have been enough time to purge myself of my poisonous infatuation with him. Instead, I found my mind drifting in the middle of debriefings with my senior advisors, thinking about the surprising petal softness of Tally's lips, wondering what ridiculous thing he might be wearing the same day I greeted the prime minister of France and hosted him for dinner with his astonishingly beautiful wife who did absolutely nothing for my errant libido.

The thought of Tally in those magenta trousers painted on to his lean limbs and that damnable thumb ring with the sapphire the same dark, glittering shade as his eyes, of course, made me hard as stone.

I palmed my erection as I sat in my poorly lit office at half past eleven at night in 10 Downing Street because I'd wasted away the day fantasizing about a boy of all people.

The thing was, I'd surmised with a shiver of unadulterated shame, it was his very youthfulness that entranced me so. I was suddenly acutely aware of why Zeus fell in love with Ganymede or Apollo with Hyacinth. Tally's energetic, almost bouncy energy invigorated me, filling me with a passion for life I'd forgotten over the long, toiling years in politics that had perhaps aged me before my time.

I did not remember a time when I was not serious. My mate, Alexander, often poked fun at my solemnity, but I'd always assumed it was just a matter of my character.

Now, even thinking of Tally and his brattish personality made my heart leap and my lips twitch with reluctant amusement.

I felt as Eurydice must have following Orpheus blindly up into the light, awed and terrified in equal turn.

The infatuation wasn't enough to change my mind about doing something brash like dating a man before I was even sure I would like one beyond Tally and even like him beyond one kiss.

I was a logical man.

A man of reasoning and philosophy.

So my only conclusion as I was frustrated and stretched thin by fatigue alone in my office—so bloody alone—was to conduct an experiment.

Before I could debate the issue with myself, I pulled up my father's text message history. He had passed on Tally's number with the fruitless suggestion we might want to "bond as brothers."

Unfortunately for my father, nothing was brotherly about my obsession with my new stepbrother.

"Hullo?" Tally answered the phone jauntily.

"I'd like to conduct an experiment." I cut straight to the point.

He didn't ask who was on the other side of the phone. He knew, and by the change in his breathing, he was intrigued by it.

"I told you before how I felt," he reminded me, but his voice was soft, pliable like warmed butter.

He was not at all resolute.

But I was.

"If I am going to suddenly be attracted to me, I want to know how I might react to doing more than kissing," I explained perfunctorily.

Tally gasped dramatically. "My, my, Prime Minister, are you calling in the middle of the night to have *phone sex* with me?"

"I am." I adjusted in my chair, getting comfortable. "Indulge me in this."

"Why should I?"

"Because you're curious about me, about what I might want to do to you, and you seem like a man who lets his curiosity rule him."

"Hmm, that seemed like a backhanded compliment, but you aren't wrong," he agreed easily with a note of amusement in his posh voice.

"Are you in bed?" I asked gruffly, already imagining him there.

I was too turned on to use a deft hand or subtlety. My pulse had quickened the moment his voice came through the phone, the heavy beat of it in my groin where my cock was hardening.

There was a slight hesitation, the feather-soft stuttering of a breath caught in his throat, then, "No."

"Go to your room and undress. I'll give you a moment to wrestle with those ridiculously tight pants of yours." I paused. "If I was there, hard as I am, Tally, I'd cut them off you to avoid the issue entirely."

I was rewarded with a hiccough of breath and a silky sigh before he sassed me back. I was beginning to understand he rarely abandoned his impudence, but I was looking forward to distracting him enough to rid him of it. I wanted to see what it might take to make Tobias Talbot-Ullswater pliant beneath my puppeteering touch.

"If you ruin a pair of my GUCCI trousers, I'm more likely to twist your balls off than play with them," he warned lightly.

I chuckled, warm with contentment as I sat back in my chair, cock an

iron pole pressing ruthlessly against my fly. It was, quite probably, the most fun I'd ever had in my office.

"Hush, boy." Tally groaned at my words, and the sound pierced through my chest so profoundly I ached. Not with pain, but with *rightness*. "Do as I say."

My order was met with a faint rustling on the other end as he did as I bid.

"It's bloody cold in here," Tally finally said, and I could perfectly imagine the curl of his lower lip into that audacious, delicious pout.

"Pretend I'm there to warm you," I suggested idly as I squeezed my length and allowed myself to imagine what I might do to him. "My hands are hot on your chest, my tongue molten as I part your lips and devour you with my mouth."

"Christ, you're good at this," Tally breathed. "Are you quite sure you haven't done this before?"

"With a man or over the phone?"

"I'm not sure, both?"

"No to either," I admitted. "I've never wanted someone enough to take them any way I can. Even if it is only over the phone."

"That's the first time you've admitted you want me," he pointed out. "Progress."

"Well, that *is* the entire point of this exercise."

"I thought getting off was the point," he countered playfully.

I bit off the edge of my grin. "That too. Now, stop distracting me. Where was I?"

"We were snogging."

"Yes, we were. But now, I'm not feeling as kind as I did before your glib comment. If you insist on exercising that smart mouth of yours, I can think of a much better use for it." My own voice felt deeper than ever before, velvet crossing over my tongue, dark even in the taste of it on my palate. "I could order you to your knees, couldn't I, boy? But I don't have to because you want my dick in your mouth just as much I do. Maybe even

more."

"Yes," Tally hissed. "I want to know if you're cut, if you're too thick to fit in my hand or too long to take down my throat. I don't have much of a gag reflex, you know?"

"Is that so?" I hummed casually as if I wasn't filled with the fire of his words and the imagery they invoked. "I believe I'm thick enough to stretch those pretty, pouty lips of yours. Long enough to wedge down your throat and disciplined enough not to come the moment you hollow your cheeks around me."

"Oh, I think I would test that iron control, Prime Minister," he cooed wickedly. "I think the sight of a grown man on his knees before you, licking up and down your shaft, then sucking you back like he can't get enough…I think that would prove too much for you."

"Maybe," I admitted, panting now, cock leaking through the tweed of my trousers. I unbuttoned the clasp, pulled down the zipper, and freed my pulsing flesh. A groan rattled through my lungs as I gave it a proper stroke.

"Seeing the way I stretch my lips around you, looking up at you as I take you to the back of my throat so easily, so *eager*. You'd like that, wouldn't you?" Tally suggested, an edge to his voice that hadn't been there before.

He wanted to break me, obliterate the iron will I'd encased myself in all these years.

He didn't understand I wouldn't break.

It wasn't in my nature.

But breaking him?

That seemed to be exactly in my wheelhouse.

"Too eager," I said, voice harsh. "I'm the man in charge, Tally. If you cannot remember that, I'll have to show you."

"How?" he breathed, a little too keen and curious.

Power surged through me. To have a young, wicked man under my control and waiting anxiously for my orders sent desire reeling through me until I was almost dizzy with it.

"I want to make you come apart for me."

"Oh, yes please," he said in a way that made me shiver.

"What…" I sucked in a bracing breath, shame dancing at the edges of my yearning. "What turns you on?"

"When you call me boy," he responded instantly, and beyond that, I could hear that soft sound of skin slapping as he stroked himself for me. "Until recently, I wouldn't have said this, but I almost came in my trousers when you choked me a little in the hall. I think I'd like more of that."

"Mmm, you like being bossed around."

"You like bossing," he retorted.

I did. In all aspects of my life, I was in charge. I didn't know how to be any other way, but I had never allowed myself to dominate in the bedroom.

I was raised by a staid, old-fashioned Brit who believed gayness was not to be remarked on, sexual deviancy was for the low born, and any bodily topic should be avoided.

I carried that learned shame at the heart of me without ever realizing it.

But now, I did, and now, with Tally's stuttering breath and the slap of skin across the phone line, I was going to carve it out of my chest.

"But mostly," he continued slyly. "I love having my arse played with."

My throat constricted, and sweat broke out across every inch of my skin.

He pressed on, purposely driving brutally through my discomfort. "I love having a tongue on my hole and fingers stretching me open, readying me for a nice hard cock."

"Lord," I muttered as I dabbed the condensation on my brow and took a stranglehold on my jerking cock, struggling not to come based on his words alone. "You're filthy."

"I'm lying back on my bed now, Prime Minister," he drawled. "Wanking my hard cock while I suck on my fingers and pretend they're yours. If we were properly together, we would need lube, but for now, spit

will do."

He released a jagged sigh as he played with himself.

I struggled to swallow. "What are you doing now?"

"Teasing my hole," he said thickly. "Christ, it feels good."

"My fingers would feel better," I asserted instantly. "If I was there, you wouldn't dare to touch what's mine. Your pretty dick and your arse."

"How do you know it's pretty?"

"You're the prettiest creature I've ever seen," I admitted, unable to hold myself back from properly masturbating now. The sound of it, the wicked sharp snap of flesh on flesh, joined Tally's. "I've no doubt you have a pretty cock."

"And my arse?" he coaxed, so breathy.

I imagined him splayed on the bed, pale legs rucked up against his chest to reveal his marbled dick and full balls, the pink hole like a punctuation mark beneath it all. My dick jumped in my hand, spitting pre-cum down my shaft.

"Even prettier," I croaked. "Finger yourself for me, boy. Tell me how tight you are so I can imagine I'm fucking you and not my fist."

Safely locked in my office without the threat of discovery and absconded far away from him, I felt safe imagining it and even facing the reality of having intercourse with a man.

While I was submerged by his voice, the fantasy was vivid enough to obliterate every other thought.

"Bloody hell, James," he hissed. "You're going to make me come."

And that did it.

My name in his masculine voice absolutely savaged by lust.

Lust for me.

I was going to come harder than I ever had before, alone in the highest governmental office in the land acting like a heathen all because of one blithe, ludicrously tempting young man.

"Do it," I bit out. "Come all over your hand for me."

The sounds that followed were ripe with sex, heavy breaths,

threadbare sighs, and exclamations to God.

It was, to my ears, even as I spilled hotly over my fist and up onto my spotless linen shirt, the sweetest music I'd ever heard.

We were silent in the aftermath as our breathing de-escalated through the phone. I didn't want to ring off, tidy myself up, and make my way home to a cold, dark house.

I wanted, inexplicably, to go to Tally, clean him of his cum, and tuck him up cozily in his bed. Even if I couldn't join him—and I told myself I never would—I couldn't curb the desire to take care of him after he had so aptly cared for me.

"How was it, then?" he ventured, flippancy hardening the edges of his tone. "What is the conclusion of your little experiment?"

I sighed as I wiped my cum off on a silk handkerchief the French Prime Minister had gifted me. "It's safe to say, I liked it."

"Liked it?" he echoed dully.

"Well, rather, I loved it," I corrected myself even though the truth deeply unsettled me. "But I'm still the heterosexual prime minister with an upcoming election next term. I can't very well uproot my very identity right now."

"Even though pretending as you have been makes you a curmudgeon?" he snapped back.

"Even though the thought of you haunts me," I whispered roughly, cupping my hand over the cell phone as if the hard plastic was his angular cheek. "Even though I want to do all of this again in person."

"Seems you have some serious issues to figure out then," he said haughtily, almost coldly, and it shocked me because it was so unlike the Tally I'd come to know.

"I just need time," I offered—reasonably, I thought—even though I didn't expect him to agree. "This is a big deal."

"I won't be a secret, James," he reminded me sharply. "They never last long. Thanks for the wank and the orgasm. I'll be seeing you."

I swallowed once, twice, and then whispered, "Right, good night,

boy."

He sucked in a harsh breath but didn't reply.

Instead, he hung up and left me once again alone.

Chapter Four

TOBIAS

It had been two weeks since James had called me in the middle of the night and made me toss off to the sound of his voice. Two weeks since the best orgasm of my life.

And two weeks of absolute radio silence after.

You did the right thing, I reminded myself. *You set boundaries. You're not going to be some politician's secret booty call.*

I understood that James was from a different generation; I understood the intense visibility of his job. But hell, if hyper-Catholic Ireland could have a gay PM, then surely the nation that pioneered all-boys boarding schools could? And more importantly, I wasn't interested in hiding. Jesus, I didn't know if I *could* hide at all. All the usual British subtlety and repression genes seemed to have skipped my queer little zygote at conception. For example, I informed my mother I was gay at my seventh birthday party...in front of my grandparents and the entire grade 1 class of Little Langford's Boys School.

And then to re-come out to Mum as pansexual seven years later, I

baked her a cake with blue, pink, and yellow sprinkles. It was supposed to be in the shape of a rainbow, but it definitely looked more like a penis after I'd glommed a bowl of icing on there and tried to spread it around. I also sang her a song of my own invention called "Oops! I Came Out Again" as she ate her slice of accidental penis cake.

My point was that I was both unhappy at the idea of hiding *and* incapable of hiding anyway. I'd been really lucky to have supportive parents and the best therapists money could buy, so I intended to use that privilege well.

Mostly by living a horny, fabulous life—but also by letting other people like me know they weren't alone. I figured the more people lived their lives however the bloody hell they wanted, the more it destabilized The Heterosexual Agenda, which could only be a good thing.

So then *why, why, why* was I still pining—and wanking!—for The Heterosexual Agenda's poster child? One James Caldron, PM?

Fuck, maybe those therapists hadn't been the best money could buy, after all.

And so, after two weeks of this, and determined to wipe James and his deliciously cool voice from my memory, I decided to invite a date to my mum's annual Christmas party.

It was someone I'd met through a mutual friend—the kind of sunny, boozy, regatta-sailing boy whom I typically dated—and I told myself I was going to have a good time with him. I was going to laugh and talk and flirt with him, and then maybe I would invite him to stay in my childhood room instead of the room we let at the village pub, and then I would have sunny, boozy sex and forget all about James.

There was one fatal flaw in my plan, however.

I'd assumed James would be too busy to attend his new stepmother's Christmas party, especially seeing as it was all the way out in the country. But when Oliver and I walked through the door—we were late on account of a train fuckup near Salisbury—James was the first person I saw, scowling in the hallway with a phone pressed to his ear.

Even scowling, he looked unnervingly handsome, and even worse, he'd dressed down from his usual suit, wearing a pair of trousers that did nothing to hide his narrow hips or his powerful legs. His thin jumper clung to his muscle-clad shoulders and his flat stomach, and with his arm raised to hold the phone to his ear, I could see a large watch glinting on his wrist. The kind of watch that announced power and money—and precisely the kind of watch I could imagine flashing beneath his jacket sleeve as he took me over his knee and punished me for my disrespectful mouth.

When he saw me, his eyes flashed, and he took an instinctive step forward. His hand flexed once as if he wanted to grab me and haul me close. My body responded immediately, my traitorous cock stiffening against my mint green trousers, my mouth already watering for his kiss. As he came closer, the light from the sitting room caught his face, and I could see that his blue eyes were rimmed with red, and that the scowl on his face seemed less his usual *everyone is beneath me* frown and something more— well—*sad*. If I didn't think he was incapable of feeling anything other than irritation or lust, I might have suspected he'd been crying.

But as James's stare moved over to my date, his expression changed utterly.

No more sadness. No more hints of vulnerability.

Right now, he stared at Oliver like he could burn down the entire world and not shed a single tear.

James turned on his heel without a word to us and went upstairs.

"Wow," Oliver said after he'd gone. "I can't decide if I'm more surprised that the prime minister is at your mother's party *or* that he's actually a giant bellend."

I gave a weak laugh, fighting the urge to go up the stairs after James. What did I care that he looked like he'd been crying? What did it matter that his obvious jealousy was still swelling certain parts of my anatomy?

It didn't.

Right?

I tried to focus on Oliver for the rest of the party, I really did. I fetched him punch, I laughed at his jokes, I introduced him to the many Ullswater cousins. (Which may have been a mistake, since they were all as adorable and as charming as me, and Oliver seemed to be getting less picky about who he took back to the rented room with each fresh glass of punch I brought him.)

I definitely tried not to notice when James returned to the party without his phone but with a jealous glower that did strange things to both my cock and my heart.

I definitely tried not to notice that his eyes were still red along the insides, that I heard someone telling his father that James was such a dear for celebrating Christmas when it was at Christmastime when he'd lost his mother two years ago.

I definitely tried not to care that he looked sad and lonely and hot and vulnerable, and did I mention hot?

Yes. I tried.

In fact, I was trying so hard that I was about to break one of my top five rules (to be fair, I've broken it before) and had decided to kiss a boy even though my mum was around. Because Oliver happened to be lingering under the mistletoe, quite shamelessly flirting with an Ullswater cousin, and I had made up my mind to remind him whose date he was and also remind *myself* that I was here to have fun with Oliver.

Not to covertly watch a mopey, possessive prime minister glare at me all night.

I came up to Oliver and gave him my brightest smile. "You know," I said coyly. "The Romans hung mistletoe during their winter Saturnalia festivals. They used to fuck under it."

Oliver's answering grin was all the consent I needed. I leaned in to kiss him, my eyes fluttering closed—

—only to be abruptly yanked back by my elbow. I staggered back into a firm chest, suddenly surrounded by the scent of crisp pine and leather.

James.

"I apologize," my new stepbrother seethed quietly. "But I must steal Tobias away for a few moments. Family business. You understand."

And then he hauled me into the hallway and into the small library, kicking the door shut and backing me into the cozy, sagging bookshelves.

I held up a hand. He ignored it, stepping so close that his shoes bumped mine.

"Listen, stepbrother dearest, I wasn't about to make a scene at my mum's party, but what the fuck do you think you're doing?" I asked. "That was weird. And rude. And weird."

The room was dark except for the moonlight streaming in through the window, and it made James's eyes something more than blue, something almost like silver.

"You were about to kiss him," James said. He sounded like he wanted to throttle me or kiss me himself; I couldn't tell. "You were about to kiss that boy right in front of me."

"He's a date. Dates are for kissing, James."

"No, they aren't. Not for you."

I valiantly attempted to ignore the shivers that ultimatum sent skating down my spine. "And what is 'for me' then, if you're to be deciding these things?"

James narrowed his eyes. "Are you saying you want me to decide?"

"I'm saying that you clearly already have, and so you might as well—"

His mouth was on mine before I could even finish speaking, his big hand in my hair, pulling my head back so I had no choice but to surrender to his kiss. To the hot, searching plunder of his mouth. His tongue swept across mine; it stroked, it probed, as if I wasn't allowed to have any secrets from him. As if even my kiss would need to belong entirely to James Caldron, along with the rest of my body.

It was infuriating how hot that was. I pushed him off, glaring up at him.

"Oh! This is just typical!" I huffed. "I am trying to be mature by

setting *boundaries*, and then you show up being all deliciously possessive and vulnerable, and now I don't know what to do!"

"I'm not vulnerable," he ground out, but I'd noticed how his mouth had flattened when I said it, and I was already shaking my head.

"You are. Tonight has fucked you up, and you know it, and you know I know it, so don't make us both into idiots by pretending otherwise."

He didn't answer, but he did rub his forehead with his hand, a gesture endearingly uncertain. Almost shy.

I softened my tone. "Is it your mum?"

I expected him to bark at me, rebuff me, or maybe even mock me. I didn't think he liked being vulnerable and even less having his inner life be anything less than utterly, insanely private. But he surprised me.

He looked at me as he dropped his hand. His eyes were dark silver pools, and his mouth was made of shadows. Seeing him so unbearably gorgeous and sad made my heart feel all sorts of stupid things.

"Yes...I suppose it is. I miss her. Very much."

"I miss my dad," I offered after a minute. "All the time. Even after loads and loads of therapy, I still cry about him."

"Are you suggesting therapy or crying?"

"I dunno, both? All I'm saying is that it's okay to have a shit night. You know?"

"I suppose I don't have any choice."

"You could always go out there and have more punch. Mum always puts way too much rum in it. A cure for any ailment."

He almost smiled at that. "Oh, really."

The moment lingered between us, nearly soft, nearly sweet, and I found I didn't want to ruin it by arguing with him.

I wanted to leave it like it was now; I wanted to leave it good between us. But when I said, "I should go check on Oliver," and stepped forward, I found myself pressed back against the shelves. One hand collared my throat while the other slid through my hair.

"Where are you going?" James asked. He sounded confused, like a

child having his toy taken away without his knowing why. "You're not going anywhere yet."

"And why is that?" I breathed, my body tingling at his touch. With that hand on my throat and his eyes on me, my erection was unbearably hard now. When he shifted closer, I could feel his swollen cock brush against mine through our trousers, and I let out a tattered moan.

"Because you're going to be my boy right now, aren't you?" James said, the hand playing with my hair dropping to my zipper. Moments later, he had me unfastened and throbbing in the cool air of the library, and I was shuddering as if he'd already wrapped a fist around me.

"Is that what you want?"

"It is. You see, I can't stop thinking about that hole of yours. The one you say is so needy. For the past two weeks, the thought of this hot, greedy part of you has taken over my mind. I want it, Tobias. I want it."

Pre-cum was beading on the tip of my erection now, and I was nearly past the point of rational thinking.

"So are you?"

"Am I what?" I asked dazedly.

"Going to be my boy? Or are you going to go back out to Oliver and spend your night having tepid, ten-minute sex with that human rowing trophy?"

Well. When he put it like that.

I took his hand and guided it to where I wanted it. Right to where I loved being kneaded and invaded. He hissed at the first touch of his finger to my hot entrance, his Adam's apple working up and down his throat as he struggled to go slow.

He pushed me back against the bookshelf again and bit at my neck as he explored me. When he started kissing me—his tongue fucking my mouth as his finger finally breached my outer ring of muscle—the line between my cock and my heart sizzled dangerously.

And when he lifted his head and stared at me like I was a work of art—his mouth swollen and his eyes like pools of molten mercury—and he

said, "You are so beautiful, Tobias," that stupid line caught on fire.

This was trouble. I was in trouble with him.

"James," I whispered. "James."

He stilled his caresses, looking down at me.

"I'll be your boy. Just...please be something for me too, okay? Don't let me fall alone."

He stared down at me, a muscle working in his jaw. After a moment, he said, "No, Tobias. You're not alone. I'll be whatever you like."

"Just be here. That's what I'd like. I'll be your boy and you'll be here, and that will mean we're together. We're not alone in falling."

He gave a short, jerky nod as though he was roiling inside, and he spun me around to face the shelves. "I'll be here. Now hands up," he rasped. "Be still."

He tugged my trousers down to my thighs, and then he knelt behind me and spread my bottom. The moment he touched his tongue to me, I started chanting his name. I started squirming back against him while at the same time squirming forward to get away from him because the silky invasion of his tongue was too much. It felt too good; it stirred my impending climax too fast.

He growled when I squirmed away, and he wrapped his hands around my hips, dragging me roughly back to his mouth. "I said *still*," he told me. "This isn't for you. It's for me. It's for every minute of every hour of every day that I've spent obsessed." He licked me again, and then he stood.

"Get my cock out and then bend over that desk. Be quick. I've waited two weeks for this."

Hands shaking, I did as he asked, my neglected erection bobbing painfully in the air as I pulled him free. And my God was he everything I'd fantasized about. A thick eight inches, straight and proud, with a big, flared tip and dark, silky curls at the base leading up to his navel. In fact, when I ran my hand over his hard, muscle-etched stomach, I felt a light dusting of hair all the way to his chest.

He was all man—all mature, hardened man—and I thought I could

spend the rest of my life nuzzling against the hair on his stomach and thighs.

"I'm only dating older men from now on," I murmured to myself, and that earned me another fierce growl of displeasure.

"You are *my* boy," he said unhappily. "*Mine.* Only I get you. Only I get this."

"Yes, James," I said, too horny to argue. Because it was true, and I knew it was true. James had snared me—heart, mind, and cock. For better or for worse.

"Tell me you have a condom."

I let out a small laugh as I pointed him toward my trouser pocket. "You really are new at this, aren't you?"

"Hush," he said. "I'm a busy man. I haven't had time for...trifling."

"I'm also busy, James, but I always find time for trifling. It's what makes me such a magnificent slut."

He hauled me close and kissed my lips before bending me over the desk. "You're my slut now, though, aren't you? Can't even make it through our parents' Christmas party without offering your hole to me."

His filthy mouth was going to be the death of me. Or of my poor, aching cock. I dropped my hand and started rubbing myself. "James," I whispered. "Hurry."

I heard the condom packet tear open, and after a minute, I heard him tear open the second thing he'd found in my pocket: a small packet of lube. He painted my entrance with it, making me slick all over, and then he pushed a finger inside. Then two.

I saw stars.

"Please," I murmured. "Please, please, please..."

He removed his fingers, the vacancy nearly as uncomfortable as the initial penetration was, and then I felt the blunt, latex-covered tip of his erection at my opening.

"Waited so long for this," he murmured to himself, and then he pressed. And pressed. Tunneling past the tight rim into my soft heat beyond.

"Since the day we met," I agreed, my voice choked with the intensity of his invasion.

"Christ, Tobias," he muttered when he pushed all the way in and bottomed out inside my channel. "Christ. I never—if I'd known…"

"If you'd known, what?"

"If I'd known," he replied in a hoarse voice, "that this is what having my cock inside you would feel like, we would have done nothing but this for the past six weeks. Every day. Every hour. I would install you in my office so I could fuck you whenever I wanted. I would have you ride in every car with me so I could fuck you in the back seat before every meeting. I would have you tied to my bed so I could use you all night long."

My erection swells even more in my hand, responding to his dirty words and his even dirtier longings. Longings I shared. To be his plaything, to be his toy, his possession.

"James," I managed. "I think I'm going to—"

"Not yet," he ordered, finding my cock with his hand. Instead of moving my hand out of the way, he wrapped his fingers around my own and squeezed. Stroked. Made me fuck my own fist as he fucked my ass like a man returned from war. "I want to feel it. I want to feel the minute you come for me, Tobias."

He didn't have to wait long. With that thick rod stroking my prostate and his big hand guiding mine, I didn't stand a chance. With a low cry, I collapsed against the desk and emptied my cock in heavy, jolting spurts, sullying the side of my mum's antique desk and dripping onto the rug.

I didn't even care. It felt so good, and James's reaction was enough to keep my cock jerking with more and more spend.

"Beautiful boy," he breathed, his voice ragged in my ear as he pumped and pumped and pumped into me, rutting with short, vicious thrusts. "So fucking beautiful. I saw you, and I knew—I just fucking *knew*—you would ruin me, and so you have. I'm ruined for this, Tobias, because I never want to do anything else. We're never doing anything else, do you understand me?" He gave me a series of slow, deep thrusts that left me gasping. "You

are coming to bed with me tonight after our parents go to sleep so I can do this again, and when we leave tomorrow, you are coming to my house, and you will let me finger you and fuck you until you literally can't stay awake anymore. You will let me play with this hole whenever I want, and I am going to see how many times I can make you come. You'll be just as addicted to me, and you deserve it because *you've ruined me—*"

His orgasm seemed to come at him like a wave he thought he could ride. He braced his feet, his hands tightened on my body, and then he realized all at once that he was wrong, that the wave was dragging him under, and he let out a series of guttural gasps as he pounded me hard against the desk. Hard enough to move it across the rug, his low roar of primal triumph going straight to my semi-erect cock as he drove his release into me. As he pumped his condom full of his release and throbbed his way finally, finally to relief.

Even though he'd just fucked me—his nearly twenty years younger stepbrother—at our parents' Christmas party while calling me *boy* and uttering all sorts of outrageous filth, James was a rather swoony gentleman about helping me clean up. After he gave me his handkerchief, he took care of the condom and helped with my clothes. By the time we were both dressed again, we were already hard and ready for a second round.

"Tonight," he said, making me promise to meet him in his bedroom. "I'll be quiet. But I need you again."

"Tonight," I consented.

"And Tobias…" He paused a moment, pulling his firm lower lip into his mouth and then releasing it. "Thank you. For what you said about grieving. I will take it into consideration."

"The only things that should be stiff around me are cocks, not upper lips," I quipped, and he actually *laughed.* A deep and happy sound that somehow sounded more like Christmas than all the carols I'd heard

415

tonight. A sound encompassing comfort and joy.

"So much I'm learning from you," he teased, and then he gave me a smile that I felt carving itself into my heart.

Oh, God.

I swore I wouldn't be a secret. I *swore*.

But how was I supposed to resist raunchy sex *and* that smile? That fantastic cock *and* these rare little moments when he opened up for me? When he let me see how he truly felt?

He had been right that I'd ruined him.

But unfortunately for me, he had also been wrong.

I was already addicted.

Chapter Five

JAMES

I was infamous in politics for my unflappable composure, rational manner, and the cool wit I used to harness errant naysayers.

This was James Caldron, the prime minister.

Tobias Talbot-Ullswater, pretty and golden-haired like an angel with the heart of a sinner, had revealed to me a very different beast entirely.

James Caldron, the man.

A man with a voracious appetite and an untapped hedonism that revolved like the earth around the sun of a single boy.

A man who was, undoubtedly now after two weeks of ruckus, salacious sex, *gay*.

Gay.

Me.

It should have been harder to wrap my head around. I'd never been much for sex, but I'd always believed myself above it somehow. It seemed to be the bane of all intense intellectuals, chained in their minds so the desires of the gut and the heart went long unused and atrophied.

Obviously, this was untrue.

In fact, I felt feverish with my need for Tally, overcome by the wickedness of my thoughts as they seized my mind at all hours of the day.

He was a hazard to my profession.

But he was a balm for my lonely soul.

I couldn't get enough.

Which explained why I was taking such a horrific risk at that very moment with Tally folded in half over the grand expanse of my antique desk, his glorious bottom raised and parted by his own hands to reveal the pinkish apex of my entire universe.

I licked my lips, saliva pooling on my tongue as I took in the depraved sight of him like that. But it wasn't enough.

The more I had of him, the more I wanted. His submission was a drug I'd never find my way back from. I kicked his feet open wider and casually circled his asshole with my lubricated thumb.

His pale legs trembled deliciously.

"So eager for my cock, boy," I said in the new voice I'd developed in these moments, as coarse as gravel and so deep it rumbled. "I might just have to keep you here, ankles cuffed to the desk, so I can use you whenever I want throughout the day."

Tally groaned and jerked slightly against the desk in a futile attempt to create friction against his cock.

It was pointless because I wouldn't let him come without consent, but also because I'd used the ridiculous purple bow tie he had been wearing when he came in to tie around his balls in a pretty bow.

"I require more than just your cock to live, James," he sassed, as he always did, topping from the bottom like the brat he was. "I need food, wine, and conversation, too. The occasional cuddle wouldn't be unappreciated either."

"Really?" I practically purred, fisting the base of my condom-covered cock that glistened with lube in the light from the same Edwardian fixtures the likes of Churchill and Atlee had sat under.

Far from disconcerting me, it stoked the flames of lust, warming my gut even higher.

I rubbed the tip of my prick up and down Tally's clenching hole, teasing us both. Only when he loosed a frustrated groan and wiggled his lean hips did I clamp a hand on his waist and drive myself deep into his channel.

Our groans twined together in the otherwise silent room, a symphonic coupling that made something in my chest crack.

It was a sensation I was all too familiar with now that I was spending most of my spare time with or inside Tally.

He was decimating the arctic tundra beneath my skin, an archaeologist courageously uncovering what lay beneath the crust of my body. So brave, my boy, and so reckless.

I curled over his prone body as I began to cant my hips, tunneling in and out of his clasping body slowly, drawing out our pleasure until we both shook with it, primed by the same tuning fork.

"Christ, James," he moaned again and again, loving to say my name and knowing how I loved to hear it. "I'm going to come all over your desk."

The thought spiked desire through my low back and contracted in my heavy balls.

I tugged his head back, fingers curling through his silk hair so I could whisper harshly in his ear. "You do, and I'll take you over my knee, boy. When you come, you'll do it in my mouth so I can have the taste of you on my tongue when I leave to go home without you. I wish I could spend myself in you, see the cum drip from your loosened hole when I was done with you. I wish we could both be filled with each other."

"Do it," he gritted out, voiced nearly pained with ecstasy as he thrust back against me. "Take the condom off. I'm clean, and you're the bloody PM, not to mention *you*. I'm sure you're fastidious about your health."

I froze, the head of my cock wedged between his round cheeks. I stared down at it, imagining the sight and feel of taking his sweet arse bare.

"You're sure?" I croaked, moved sexually and emotionally by this act

of trust.

Its significance felt absolute, an act that propelled us further into an intimacy from which I wasn't sure either of us could recover.

"Yes," he whispered back, softer with an aching vulnerability in his sweet voice. "Please."

I didn't hesitate a moment more. Fisting my cock, I carefully left the warmth of his body to peel off the condom, wrap it in tissue, and toss it in the bin before I re-lubricated my straining dick and tapped at the entrance of his body again.

"I'm going to take you hard and fast, boy," I warned as I watched the nearly purple head of my cock dip in and out of him, a bare tease of the intensity that was to come. "I'm going to fill you up with my seed, and afterward, you're going to stay prone over the table so I can see your sweet hole filled with me, do you understand?"

Before he could fully gasp his answer, I seated myself balls deep inside him. My head reared back, tendons so taut in my neck I thought they would snap, and I groaned to the heavens in some blasphemous thanks for the glory of the moment. The sensation of Tally all around me was almost excruciatingly good, searing heat gathering at the base of my spine, tightening in my balls so painfully I knew I would burst within moments.

So immersed in our joint pleasure and the way my boy shuddered and keened beneath me, I didn't notice anything outside my narrow view of him, of us.

Not the clink of a key thrust into a lock or the tell-tale creak of the old oak door pushing open nor the draft that followed.

I only knew the heat of Tally, the wonder of being inside him, of having his trust and his body entirely under my control. My chest ached with the acuity of the moment. Seconds later, Tally groaned and spilled himself, cock untouched, all over the side of my desk. Thoughts of punishing him for disobeying my orders by spanking the porcelain swell of his arse sent me into my own earth-shattering climax.

So, you see, I did not notice the man in the door until all was too well

said and done.

Even then, it was Tally who cottoned on first, stilling so completely beneath me that I was horrified I'd injured him at first.

But then, I too noticed the third set of breaths filling the suddenly quiet chamber.

My head turned by minute degrees, my brain already scrambling for purchase, desperate to devise an excuse for the erotic tableau we presented to whichever unfortunate staffer was suddenly privy to our relationship.

My eyes shuttered closed the moment they landed on Gregory Plume.

The same Gregory who had the political bit between his teeth. Gregory who had tried to elicit promises that I would support him as the next Tory leader when I decided to retire my position as leader of the party.

Tally moved suddenly, carefully separating our bodies so that he could silently, efficiently pull his trousers up from around his ankles and fix his hair. Then he turned to me, the same calm expression on his face, a deadness in his eyes as he put me to rights as well.

All the while, Gregory stared at us, blinking, blinking, blinking, and all I could think was 'does he have astigmatism?'

"Chin up," Tally whispered softly as he adjusted my collar. "You're still the PM, James. This isn't the end of anything."

"Isn't it?" I croaked.

Something dark flashed through his expression before it dissipated. "Good evening, Prime Minister," he said louder, almost jaunty once more as if nothing untoward at all had occurred between us. "Thanks ever so much for agreeing to the archaeological survey of the Battle Bridge Stadium site. I'll make sure everything is in order to proceed smoothly."

I watched dumbly as he smiled widely, a fake, laminated excuse for his normally beautiful grin, and then as he strolled casually past Gregory to whom he inclined his head regally before stepping outside and closing the door.

"Gregory," I said on a heavy sigh. "Please, take a seat."

It was only a facial tic, a micro-expression most men might not have

seen, but I knew it for what it was.

A clenching of the jaw, a flickering of one eye as if he had bit fully into an unripe lemon.

Gregory would not support a gay PM.

An unfortunate and nightmarish reality given the now irrefutable fact I was unquestionably homosexually and deeply, quite ridiculously really, in love with my much younger stepbrother.

"Let's discuss this," I continued tiredly as I leaned against the front of the desk to obscure the splash of Tally's pearlescent seed from Gregory's hateful gaze. It might very well be the end of my life and livelihood as I knew it, but some small part of me still felt it was important to shield my Tally from the light of scrutiny.

"Yes," Gregory agreed darkly, almost triumphantly, as he sat in the offered chair. "Let's."

Chapter Six

TALLER

S tupid. So completely and stupidly *stupid*.

All of it. Including me.

I sat at home in the dark, my knees curled up to my chest with my arse still aching from James's rough fuck, and I tried to think. I tried to be rational with myself. I tried to tell myself it would be okay.

But somehow, I knew it wouldn't. Even if that knobhead MP didn't use what he'd seen as leverage, James would still know he knew. And for James, *anyone* knowing he was anything other than straight as a ruler seemed to be a point of quiet terror.

I hated that, I really did. I hated that we fucked in secret, that I had to sneak around like some kind of mistress, I hated that no matter how much I missed him, ached for him, *felt* for him, there would never be a future for us. Not when he wasn't ready to be out.

It turned out being surprise stepbrothers was the least of our worries. Who knew?

I told myself a bunch of logical things. That James was from a

different generation. That he was a public figure in a country with plenty of homophobia still clouding the air. That my experience of being queer—cushioned by lots of money and wonderful parents and finding my tribe very early on—was not at all universal. Hell, it wasn't even universal to my socio-economic cohort, which was the most privileged in the world.

I reminded myself that it could be more than unpleasant for James to come out. It could be dangerous. So it wasn't my place to push him on it.

But...

But.

A part of me just couldn't understand. If he felt for me even a sliver of what I felt for him, then I had no idea how he was tamping it down and pretending that what we did was separate from the rest of our lives.

Because it wasn't separate for me, not at all.

I woke up and thought of his face; when I worked, I imagined his touch the entire time. I ate dinner and longed for his pine and leather scent. He *consumed* me.

I exhibited a level of self-restraint hitherto unknown to me and didn't call or text him that night. But when I woke up the next morning, I couldn't stop myself. I had to hear his voice and so I dialed him, not knowing what I would say.

Sorry that MP saw me spray jizz all over the side of your desk? Hope you're not being blackmailed right now?

But it didn't matter. James didn't answer my call. Nor the next one I made at lunchtime. Nor the text I sent that afternoon.

A cold, grasping kind of anxiety wrapped its fingers around my throat and refused to let go, choking me for the rest of the day.

It's over.

He's done with me.

He blames me.

I refused to be *that* boy. I'd never been clingy, so I wasn't going to start now. But God, it hurt. It hurt feeling cut off and discarded. It hurt knowing I'd cared more about him than he'd cared about me. It hurt

knowing I was good enough to fuck, but I wasn't good enough to claim.

By the time late evening had rolled around, I was drunk on winter-themed cocktails. After drafting ever longer and ever more dramatic monologues to James in my head, I had progressed to acting them out in my kitchen, waving my arms and everything. Which is when the doorbell rang, of course.

I was in a short silk robe and nothing else, but still, I belted it with great dignity and walked to the door to see who it was. And from the official-looking black car parked just outside my window, I thought I had a pretty good guess.

I flung open the door, ready to deliver one of my scathing diatribes. "If you think you can just show up here—"

I was abruptly cut off because James took one look at me wearing nothing but that silk robe, and suddenly, the door was kicked shut behind him, and I was slammed against the wall, his mouth hot and searching on mine.

"James," I gasped.

"Boy," he growled back, bending down to bite my neck.

"We shouldn't—I'm very cross with you—"

"I need you," he breathed into my ear. He shoved his hips against mine so I could feel how much. "I need you."

My own cock was already responding, announcing itself through the part in my robe. "Okay, but not here—"

He swung me up into his arms like I weighed nothing—which, despite multiple lemon juice cleanses, was just not true—and carried me into my sitting room, where the windows only faced the rear garden and not the street. He dropped me onto my back on the sofa and then followed me down, all muscles and silky, bespoke wool as he crowded over me and slanted his mouth over mine.

As he kissed me, his hand dropped between us to free his giant erection, which dropped on the part of my stomach my robe had exposed.

His cock was velvety, hard, scorching. It bumped against mine, and

we both emitted twin grunts of choked need.

"The end table," I panted. "Lube."

"We'll talk about why the fuck you have lube there later," he rasped, lifting to his knees to get it.

"It's only in certain strategic locations in case a date goes well," I protested, although why I thought I could successfully defend my honor with my robe shoved to the sides and my cock bobbing against my stomach, I had no idea.

His eyes glinted cold and blue in the dark light of the room as he slicked lube around his thick organ. "Are you trying to infuriate me?"

"Dates happened before you, Prime Minister. They'll happen after you too."

The growl he gave then wasn't playful nor was it teasing. It was pure animal anger and need. Raw possession. He gave my hole a cursory anointing and then mounted me, driving into me like I was a spoil of war.

I arched underneath him, and he pinned me down, splitting me open with his rough, angry need. "You are mine," he said. "My boy to fuck. My boy to watch and touch and taste."

I wanted to say no, I wasn't. I wasn't his. If I were really his, he would have had me stay last night, and he would have called me today. If I were really his, he'd want me in every way, not just with my legs spread.

But I couldn't bring myself to contradict him because, at that moment, it *felt* true. Even if it was only true for right now during these stolen moments on my sofa. *I was his.*

"Yes, sir," I said, going loose and open the way he liked, surrendering utterly to his rutting cock. "I am yours."

"Boy," he said, and that was it, but I could hear the need in it. The torment. He was in agony over something, and it was more than his building release.

His hips settled into a brutal, punishing rhythm. His tie caressed my chest as he moved, the expensive wool of his suit trousers rubbed against my thighs. My penis leaked pre-cum, entire pearls of it on my belly, and he

ran his fingers through it, licking it while looking down at me. And then he gathered up the edge of my silk robe, gathering more and more of it in his fist, and he used that fistful of silk to jerk me off.

I won't lie and say I've never used that particular silk robe to jerk off before, but having him do it, having him be in his suit while I was the slut-whore with the undone robe and nothing underneath it...

Having all those inches stroking into me while his cruel fist gripped me around all that silk....

Well, it was like nothing I'd ever felt. I arched my throat and begged my way through the climax as it sawed me in half, ripping me open and sending ropes of ejaculate spilling out of my tip and onto my stomach. James went still, his eyes avid and hungry on the sight of me soiling all that fabric with my seed, and then he followed me, spending inside my channel with a low, vicious oath and several long pulses that nearly felt as good inside me as the thrusts.

And then...

And then it was over.

It was over, and nothing had changed. Nothing had been fixed. We were just stickier now.

I pulled myself free of him and stood.

"Tobias," he said, but I held up a hand, indicating he should wait.

I returned with wet wipes and a towel for him. I'd already cleaned up and tugged on my favorite pair of fuzzy pajama pants and an old T-shirt.

He cleaned himself up and righted his suit, and when he looked over at me in my pajamas, something around his mouth went soft and kind.

"Do you fancy some tea?" I asked as he sat on the edge of my sofa, still staring at me in my pajama pants as though he'd never seen anything quite so endearing.

"No," he said, and then he seemed to snap out of whatever reverie he was in. "No, I shouldn't stay long."

"Then why are you here, if I might ask?"

He ran a hand through his hair. The silver at his temples caught in the

moonlight, and my heart stuttered. What *was* it about older men?

"Gregory has gone to the press," James said finally. He lifted his eyes to meet mine, and all traces of softness were gone. He looked completely and utterly...empty. "My people tell me that the tabs are already printing their versions of the scandal. In the morning, it will be everywhere. You. Me. Us."

I stared right back at him. "So?"

He blinked. "So?"

"So fucking what?"

He blinked again. "Tobias. This is quite serious. This could damage your future, ruin your name—"

I interrupted him. "James, I have a lot of money, and I'm very pretty. This is not the first time papers have been interested in my sexual exploits, and it won't be the last. I'm not afraid. Or ashamed."

He stood, stabbing a hand through his hair. It occurred to me that *I* was being the calm one right now, the one with perspective. *He* was the lost one. And when he looked down at me, there was something so frightened and tender in his gaze. Something so *young*.

"I don't know what to do," he whispered. "This is the end of my career. I might be able to hold on for a few weeks, but if someone seizes this chance to call for a snap election—I have to resign either way. Now, or later."

"But why?" I demanded. "Why can't you just say, 'Yes, I was with my boyfriend in my office, but it was after hours, so it's not like I was shagging him during a NATO call?' Why can't you say, 'Yes, this is my boyfriend, Tobias. He has an encyclopedic knowledge of pre-Saxon timber construction and also an amazing arse?' Why can't you just say, 'Fuck your outdated bigotry, I'm queer?'"

"You don't understand," he said. "It's not that easy. I can't be—I can't do that. I'm not like you. I can't be that person. I'm not that person!"

Finally, I'd had enough. "But you are! Bleeding Christ, James, take a minute and think about the past two months. Has the world

stopped turning since you started seeing me? Has anything materially changed? No. Because it's *okay*. It's better than okay, it's good because you deserve to be with whoever you want to be with. We all do."

He stared down at me as though I'd started speaking ancient Akkadian to him.

"But I can't," he said again, breaking our stare and looking down at the floor. "I'm sorry, because you are wonderful, but I…it's not who I am."

And then it hit me.

This was more than hiding. This was *shame*. And I wasn't better than a lot of things—bad television and those cheese and onion-stuffed rectangles from Gregg's among them—but I was better than shame. And he was too.

A cool, collected calmness filled me as I stood.

"I think you should go," I said. "You came here to warn me about the press, and I appreciate it, but now it's time you left."

"Tobias," he said. "Wait."

I looked at him. At this cold, handsome knife of a man. What an idiot I'd been to fall in love with someone like James Caldron. "What will you do tomorrow? Will you deny everything? Will you stay silent?"

"I don't know yet." He stepped close enough to me to touch, but he kept his hands in tight balls by his sides as though he wanted to grab me but didn't trust himself. "I don't want to hurt you, Tobias, so you tell me what I should do. Stay silent? Claim libel and lies?"

"It doesn't matter because both those options hurt me. But you know what the real problem is? Both of those options hurt *you*."

I started walking toward the door, and he followed.

"No," he said, "they protect you and me. They protect us. Surely you see that?"

"And surely you see that I don't want to be protected if the price is shame." I sighed. "I love you, James."

He started, his lips parting.

"What?" he whispered.

"Which is why this is over now."

"It's not over," he cut in, panic flashing in his eyes, but I kept talking.

"Maybe I could bear being a secret for a while longer, maybe I could even bear it a long, long time just to be near you, but I can't watch you be a secret to yourself. I can't watch you be ashamed of yourself because that means you're ashamed of the man I love, and that's unforgivable, I'm sorry, but it is."

I opened the door to the steps down to the street, where his car waited outside.

"Tobias, wait," he said urgently, pressing his forehead to mine. "This isn't over. I won't let it be. You're supposed to be mine. My boy. And I care deeply for you. So fucking deeply."

I let him kiss me once—a kiss that was fearful and hard and a little angry—before I pulled away. "How can I believe that you care for me if you're only willing to say it in the dark?"

He had no answer to that.

Because there was none.

"If you figure it out, call me," I said. "But that's all I can offer you because I can't stick around and watch you loathe yourself and pretend it's not gutting me."

"Tally," he said. It was the only time he'd called me that, and I hated how still—even now—it made my heart flip over in my chest.

No. Be strong. He's made his choice, and now you've made yours.

"Goodbye, Prime Minister," I said. "I hope Downing Street is worth it."

Chapter Seven

JAMES

It was chaos.

The clatter of so many fingers on computer keys, the sharp yip of raised voices into phones, and the whispered hush of many conversations heavy with the weight of scandal.

The conference room held so many bodies that it was impossible to avoid meeting someone's gaze every time I turned my head.

Disgust, shock, condemnation, and, worst of all, pity lit those eyes up like neon signs. It was impossible to avoid their garish light.

Mona sat beside me, doing her best to keep me distracted as everyone scrambled to figure out some kind of plan to mitigate the scandal stamped on every gossip rag this morning.

Prime Minister of Buggery.

Oh, Dear. The PM is Queer.

Backdoor Politics in Britain.

The headlines were burned into my brain, searing pain still igniting along my synapsis as they circled like a magazine rack in my memory.

Horrible, disgusting headlines that said nothing of my relationship with Tally.

Horrible, disgusting headlines that said nothing positive about being gay.

It was only as I was facing them now, the gross displays of homophobia directed, for the first in my life, at *me* that I understood Tally's reasoning for ending things with me.

We were not this shameful, hateful thing.

There was nothing negative, nothing untoward about my boy.

He was everything good in this life—unapologetically ridiculous, deliciously impudent, smarter than half my MPs, and *fun*.

So much damn fun.

I'd had a long life before Tobias Talbot-Ullswater, but it had been done up in black and white, flat-toned and grim.

For two brilliant months, Tally had brought me purple bow ties, tight pink pants, and twinkling blue eyes. He had splashed his technicolor spirit slapdash over the canvas of my life, and far from ruining it, he had made it bright, beautiful, and worthy of contemplation.

I stared unseeing at the sheaves of paper before me, the words blurred together as my nose itched and my eyes watered.

I felt as wretched as a heroine in a Bronte novel and as ruined as the Neolithic village buried beneath the site at Battle Bridge Stadium that had brought Tally into my life.

"James," Mona said softly, a hand on my shoulder gently shaking me out of my downward spiral. "If you want to go home…we can handle this for you."

A sharp, hollow laugh exploded from my lips. I ran a shaky hand through my hair and exhaled harshly. "No, Mona, the world may be crumbling about our ears, but let's not be ridiculous. If I am not here to stem this flood, if I don't make the exact right statement in front of the press this afternoon, I'm sunk."

Mona tucked a lock of black hair behind her ear and bit her lip. "I

would never have said this before today, but would that really be such a bad thing? I've never seen you so happy as you've been over Christmastime. If it's this boy, maybe it's worth considering?"

My boy, I felt like growling viciously even though she didn't deserve it. Of all the people in my office, I was closest to Mona. Of all people, a happily married lesbian immigrant would understand my plight.

"This is all I know," I admitted quietly beneath the ruckus of voices. "What am I without this?"

"Dare I say, gay and in love?" she quipped with a soft smile.

I laughed. "Sounds like something Tally would say."

"Tobias?" She studied me for a moment. "I think I'd like him, then."

"You would," I admitted. "He's impossible to dislike. To do so would be like hating a puppy."

Mona laughed this time and then did something she had never done before. She dropped her hand beneath the table and reached over to give my thigh a tight squeeze.

"In my experience, anything worth having is hard to come by and even harder to keep. You have to fight for it, work for it, every day."

"Like this damn office," I joked even though it landed woodenly on the table.

Because Mona had a point.

What was worth fighting for?

For my entire life, it had been my country. I loved England. I loved the sweep of fog off the northern moors and the purpling heather gathered in the fields; I loved our endless sheep and the turquoise waters off the coastline. I loved the wild southwest with its salt-crusted castles, and the white cliffs that stretched the entire length of our southern tip like calloused heels. I loved the people, the cultural melting pot of our Londoners, the northerners with their thick accents, brashness, and industry, the southerners with their polite rituals and agriculture, the west with its history, and the east with its memories of war.

I'd wanted to be the leader of Her Majesty's government since I

visited my father in his MP office as an eight-year-old lad.

And I'd accomplished it.

Scandal aside, I'd achieved one of the most successful terms in office since the great Churchill himself. I had taken down one of the most corrupt secret societies in the last five hundreds years, accomplished dozens of important social reforms, and created thousands of jobs.

Did being in love with a man change any of that?

My gaze snared on one of the trashy mags littering the tabletop, and my heart clenched beneath the iron fist of my renewed shame.

It seemed the reporters thought it did.

Did the people, too?

Were we still so backward that loving a man would negate all the sacrifices I'd made for them over my life?

"Let's sort out a statement," I said, rolling my shoulders back and raising my voice so I could address the room as a whole. "Call a meeting of the press for two o'clock. I want a statement drafted in twenty minutes, and I want it done properly."

"Yes, Prime Minister," they echoed as they doubled their efforts.

I sat there amid the turmoil and support like a lonesome king amidst his courtiers, tragic and melancholy because duty would always outweigh his personal happiness.

I'd done it hundreds of times.

Usually, I was nothing more than a marble statue reciting my pre-approved script, completely unflappable in the face of even the most scathing questions.

Not today.

My skin was clammy, my bones ached, and my heart roiled in my chest.

I fixed my eyes to a point beyond the crowd of reporters and cleared

my throat before speaking.

"Good afternoon, everyone. Thank you for being here on such short notice. Though, I'll note, most of you have been camped out on my doorstep since dawn." I slanted them a cool look. "Perhaps one day I'll afford you the same courtesy."

There was a smattering of dull laughter.

They quieted, though, as soon I launched calmly into my prepared spiel.

I am sorry for any reports of an untoward nature...Mr. Talbot-Ullswater and I are good friends...First, you claim I'm too much for the ladies in my younger years, now this, are you never happy (cue laughter)... It's a slow day in politics when one man's story takes control of the media...

It made me sick to speak it. So ill, at one point, that I felt my skin bleach white and my stomach heave dangerously.

Good Lord, let me not lose my breakfast on national telly.

When I finished, I laid a hand on my gut, willing it to settle, and smiled woodenly out at the sea of people letting me feed them this utter rubbish.

A reporter I trusted not to be outrageously inappropriate raised their hand with a question, and I pointed at them, allowing it because I needed a moment to catch my breath.

"Mr. Prime Minister," he began, an edge to his voice I didn't recognize that made my gut clench. "The hashtag #gaygate has gone viral on social media platforms, with many saying that Tobias Talbot-Ullswater, well-known for his sexual exploits, seduced you into indecency."

"Is there a question in there somewhere, Mr. March?" I asked coldly.

"Is it true he seduced you against your better judgment, or are you really, as you claim, '*just good chums?* '"

The reporter cast a quick glance over my shoulder as a few of my staff who stood behind me and I knew this was a part of their tactic. Plant a reporter who would open the door for me to deny my active participation in this affair. Make like Ron Davis and claim this was merely a moment of

pure madness when I'd given in to the witchy charms of a charismatic boy.

Anger burned clean through the anxiety and doubt that had clogged my arteries for the better part of thirty-six hours. My fingers gripped the podium so tightly, my knuckles cracked and burned.

I imagined Tally, maybe at home curled up on his couch in those silly, endearingly adorable, fuzzy green pajama pants watching the news and feeling like shite because I was doing more than keeping him a secret. I was condemning him as the bad guy in the story.

As an immoral slut. A horrific aberration in my infamously contained and gentlemanly manner.

My heart squeezed so tightly, I worried it would never beat properly again.

Tally had said he could wait for me in secret and be mine in the shadows, but he couldn't endure knowing I was ashamed of myself for wanting him.

And suddenly, acutely like an arrow through the chest, I understood that sentiment exactly.

I opened my mouth, and words spilled forth before I could think things through, before I could rein in my gut instinct and my heart's inner song.

"I will not let Tobias Talbot-Ullswater's life be defined by this affair. He is not the kind of man who deserves to be nor enjoys being in the shadows." I sucked in a deep breath and nearly panicked when it brought me no comfort. "I forced him there with my shame and my inability to be honest—not just with you all but with myself. There is only one thing I want to be taken from this entire invasion into my privacy, and that is this…"

I stared out at all those faces, reminded that this was being live-streamed on the 10 Downing Street YouTube channel so people might very well be tuning in internationally as well.

Being prime minister had always been about setting the right example for this country, and I had fallen down on that job in the most unforgivable

way.

"Being gay is nothing to be ashamed of. Certainly, anyone who identifies with the LGBTQIA community should be proud and should never be persecuted for who they love or how they choose to present themselves. In keeping my relationship with Mr. Talbot-Ullswater a secret, I implied that there was something to be embarrassed about when the truth is, knowing him has been one of the highlights of my life." I held up my hand to stymie the flow of questions that came at me. "I will not speak further on my relationship with him. Many of you will be upset with this news, that I have had relations with a man or that I hid it from you. I hope you can understand that though I'm forty-three, you never stop growing, and these past few months, I've learned more about myself than I have in years."

The murmur of the press grew, a rising tidal wave I knew would crash against the podium and take me under any second.

"I would like to believe this country is in a place where we could accept a gay or bisexual prime minister. A man's sexuality, what he chooses to do or be behind closed doors barring he isn't hurting anyone, should be separate from his political acumen and ability to serve his country. I would like to believe this, but only time will tell. Will you castigate me for loving a man? Because the truth is, I do love him. Very much."

"Prime Minister, are you gay?" someone shouted.

My tongue was thick and numb in my mouth, and every inch of my skin tingled as if I'd been poisoned by my reckless words.

But beneath all that, the heart that had beat so dully against the cage of my ribs for years soared into exultant palpitations.

I am brave. I am brave. I am brave, I thought.

I am brave like Tally.

I looked up from the podium and smiled in a way I had never felt on my face. It was wobbly, skewed on the left, and showed too much teeth.

But it was whole.

Warm and vital.

"When the elections are held next month, I will not run for office

again," I said, then louder over the eruption of murmurs and shouting in the press corps. "Not because I am in love with a man. Not because I am afraid of what this country might think of me because of it. But because I have done at forty-three what I set out to do as a boy. I have been honored to serve Her Majesty and this country as prime minister, and I feel my duty is done. Now, I would like to try my hand at living freely for the first time in my life."

"Do you mean with Tobias Talbot-Ullswater?" someone cried over the calamity of voices as I inclined my head in farewell and stepped away from the podium.

A smile flashed over my face before I could contain it and a pap standing near caught the expression perfectly. I would think so when I saw it in the paper the next day with the headline, "*Is There a Happily Ever After In Sight For Our Prime Minister?*"

"Where the bloody hell are you going?" Sylvia, one of my MPs, snapped as I entered the hall.

I ignored her.

I was too focused on winning back the only person I'd ever loved.

A person who happened to be a very delightful, slightly ridiculous boy by the name of Tally.

A boy I pledged right then and there to make my own for good.

Chapter Eight

TALLY

"Mr. Talbot-Ullswater?" the cameraman asked. "We're ready for you."

I nodded at him, and then told my mum I loved her and hung up the phone.

"Your mum, eh?" the cameraman said with a knowing roll of his eyes. "My mum is the same way."

I gave him a weak smile, not bothering to tell him that my mum had called me because she'd just found out—along with the rest of the world—that I'd been fucking the prime minister. Who just so happened to be my stepbrother. She hadn't been upset, though, only surprised. And determined to wash the sheets in my bedroom again.

The story had been everywhere this morning, just like James had warned me. My phone had been blowing up all day—Twitter, Instagram, text messages.

I'd felt numb looking at it all. I hadn't lied to James when I said I'd been a scandal before—although I'd never been a scandal of this

magnitude—so I wasn't much bothered by it. Truly. The paps waiting outside my flat this morning had been annoying, but there weren't too many by the time I left, and I lost them easily enough coming here to shoot a short segment for ITV about the Battle Bridge stadium site. And I was sure people were saying terrible things on Twitter, but I turned off all notifications and simply pretended I was living in 2003, and social media didn't exist.

But then James made that incredible speech.

That speech that sent my pulse racing and my heart twisting and my stomach floating somewhere near my throat.

Knowing him has been one of the highlights of my life.

Will you castigate me for loving a man? Because the truth is, I do love him. Very much.

He loved me. He loved me, and he'd said it.

To *other people*. In *public*.

I'd stood there on the pavement outside King's Cross station while the ITV crew got set up, and I'd watched over and over again the clip of him saying he loved me. And then of course, Mum had called me, and I'd had to explain to her that yes, yes, it was all true, but that James and I had sort of broken up last night so she didn't need to soundproof my room at Ullswater Cottage in preparation for next Christmas just yet.

Because despite what he said today, I still wasn't sure what happened next.

I had hopes, I had fantasies, I knew what I wanted more than my next breath—but after how we left things last night, I couldn't be sure. James had announced the end of his career—

the career that had defined his life, the career he'd dedicated his entire being to—and I wasn't sure how he felt about his choice. He'd said it was because he wanted to live freely and not because he was worried about what the nation would think, but still...

What if he already regretted it?

Regretted me?

I stepped where the producer indicated, and then the journalist interviewing me stood opposite. I was deeply grateful this was for a program specifically about historic areas under threat of urban development and that there wouldn't be an opportunity for her to ask about the prime minister's statement. I could sense she was itching to and I just wasn't in the headspace for it. Not right now. Not when I didn't know whether to be elated or proud or anxious or lonely or what.

"Tell us about the Battle Bridge site," the journalist said, and that was my cue to speak. To be Tobias, the adorable and photogenic archaeologist.

"Many of us Londoners might not realize that we're actually standing on top of a river, the River Fleet, which before becoming an underground sewer was an important waterway for Celts, Romans, and later the Saxons. Boudica herself was said to have fought a battle at this very site..."

I was rattling all this off when I heard the producer say, "Sir, sir, we're filming right now, excuse me—*Sir!*"

And I turned and then I saw him. Framed by the silver light of late afternoon, his eyes a shade of blue usually reserved for painting the Virgin Mary.

I stopped talking. I couldn't think of anything to say.

"Tobias," James said, his voice rough and low. The same way he'd say it if he was inside me.

I shivered.

He strode forward, and God, that stride. It didn't matter if his address wouldn't be 10 Downing Street; he would always be a man of power, a man of cold, intelligent arrogance. He came up to me while I stood there like a prize idiot, and then he took my hand, ignoring the journalist and the cameraman and the still-sputtering producer as if they didn't exist.

"I'm sorry, Tally," he murmured. "I'm so sorry. I have no excuse, but I want to do better. You are worth doing better for, and I know now that I am too."

"I saw your speech, you impetuous twat," I said, my voice quavering. "What were you thinking? And announcing your resignation

too?"

"I was thinking that I love you," he said fiercely. "And I want to spend the rest of my life with you."

I stared up at him, at that stern mouth and those eyes, intense and glittering just for me. "But your work…"

"I'm not leaving it because I'm ashamed or afraid of the public," he said. "I'm leaving it because I realized it's no longer where my heart lies. It lies with you, my ridiculous boy, and nowhere else."

"But—"

"Tobias," he said. "Do you want me to kiss you or not?"

I reached up and ran my fingers over his mouth. The sculpted lines of it softened just for me. "There's a camera," I warned him. "And at least four people with smartphones recording us right now."

"Good," was his prompt, grave reply.

And then his mouth was on mine, demanding and firm. Imperious and just a little vulnerable.

Heaven.

I melted against him, and he wrapped me in his arms, all wool coat and pure, male strength, and I knew I would follow him anywhere. I would give him everything.

"No more secrets," he promised, pulling away just enough to press his thumb against my lower lip. "No more dirty little secrets."

"Well," I said, nipping at the pad of his thumb. "Let's keep the dirty part. *Sir*."

"Always," growled James, and then with another ferocious kiss, he swept me up into his arms.

And in front of the television camera and the gathering crowd, the prime minister of the United Kingdom carried me off into the gray-pink London sunset, kissing me the entire way.

Epilogue

JAMES

"You're being a baby," Tally said, a hint of smug satisfaction in his voice as if the idea of my immaturity amused him.

I snorted. "Hardly. I'm forty-three years old, nearly twenty years your senior. You should respect your elders, boy."

Tally grinned impishly in my periphery as I maneuvered my Aston Martin around the narrow, curving lanes in Wiltshire leading to Ullswater Cottage. We were on our way to visit my father and his wife for the first time since #gaygate, and understandably, I was nervous.

Though, I was unequivocally *not* being a baby about it.

"Maybe you should remind me later just how much respect you deserve," my boyfriend purred as his hand found my thigh and trailed up the length of it to squeeze my cock.

"You're trying to distract me with sex." I noted coolly.

He gave my dick another squeeze and then a nice pat, pat, pat as if it was a beloved animal. "Yes. I rather think it's working from the feel of you hardening in my hand."

"Do you want to get into an accident?" I asked, tugging his hand away from my growing erection. "You know I can't think of anything but you at the best of times, and I'm *trying* to get us to Ullswater Cottage safely."

"So that you can officially come out to your father."

I slanted him a grumpy look, but it was impossible to stay cross when I caught sight of his beautiful smile.

He had been smiling like that every day for the past month. Ever since the scandal broke, and our love came tumbling out of the closet into the open. It wasn't easy, the fallout. Tally was called a slut in the press more times than I could count, though he seemed to find it amusing, especially when he was dubbed the Yoko Ono of politics. People in my own party refused to deal with me, waiting out my time in office silently, or, bitterly, making their homophobic sentiments known in a myriad of creative ways.

It was difficult, but then, as Mona had rightly pointed out, anything worth having was.

And this past month had only succeeded in proving that risking everything for Tally was not only the right choice, but the only choice for me.

I loved him desperately. Almost feverishly.

We simply couldn't get enough of each other.

The sex, of course, because he was a limber, gorgeous youth with a rabid sex drive and a wonderfully kinky imagination, and I was a man who had just discovered the joys of the male body.

But more.

It was the way he shuffled out of bed in the morning, blurry-eyed, hair a tousled mess of feathered curls around his sleep-creased face. He took a full hour to recover his usual spirit, sitting quietly, curled up in a chair with his fuzzy pajama-clad legs held to his chest while I plied him with his tea and toast.

It was the way he touched me always. Little morsels of affection gifted throughout the day with the press of his hand to my back, a kiss to my cheek, fingers trailing down my arm so he could fit his lean fingers between

my own.

It was the way he said my name. *James*. As if I was his king, his Lord and God.

It was the way he made me feel bigger than I ever had before, even as Prime Minister, the head of Her Majesty's government. I felt taller, grander, more capable with Tally because his belief in me was so utterly absolute.

"I love you," I said suddenly, almost clumsily because the shock of it still robbed me of breath most times.

Tally patted my thigh again as if calming an agitated horse. "I know. It's practically impossible to feel any other way about me. I'm incredibly lovable."

"And ridiculous," I retorted, shooting a glance at his soft angora sweater in a vivid shade of turquoise.

"All the best things are," he said breezily, then laughed when we caught sight of the two people waiting for us in the driveway of the cottage. "Oh look, we have a welcoming committee."

Tally's mum held a large cardboard sign that said, "Welcome home, boys!" in rainbow paint and sparkles while my father, standing rather awkwardly, held one that said, "Congrats on coming out!"

I parked the car in front of them but found my body wouldn't comply when I told it to get out of the car. Tally had no such qualms. He bounded out of the vehicle and skipped to his mother, who enveloped him in a long hug before they began to giggle and whisper between them. She slipped her arm in Tally's and urged him toward the house, already forgetting about me.

My father did not.

We stared at each other through the windshield.

I thought of all the moments growing up that had led me to this moment. All the ways my father had made it clear that he did not approve of gay men.

A bit light in the loafers, that one, he'd say.

Of course, he's gay, so you can't expect otherwise.

Never understood how one bloke could choose another man over a

445

woman. Something not quite right with that.

A random memory shook loose. I was nine years old and wrestling in the backyard with a friend. I'd just pinned him, hands to wrists, my body pressed fully down the length of his and our faces close enough to feel the warmth of his breath on my tongue. There had been a small thrill of excitement at the base of my spine and a question I felt in my body more than my mind.

Then my father, shouting from the doorway to get off poor Sam and leave him alone.

I couldn't be sure, but I thought I hadn't been allowed to invite Sam over after that.

Shame curdled the happiness in my stomach as it hadn't done in the month since I'd come out.

My father dropped his sign to the ground and walked around the side of the car, settling into the passenger seat before I could think of a way to tell him not to.

Alone in my little car, both of our long bodies folded up, I realized I hadn't been this physically close to the man since I was a boy.

"James," he said, then cleared his throat. "My son."

"Father," I replied, colder than I might have wanted.

He sighed, his hand shaking as he ran it through his hair. A nervous habit I suddenly realized we shared. "I'm not very good at this...stuff. Never have been. But Figgy, she's told me I've been remiss, and unfortunately, I have to agree with her. I think, well, rather, I wanted you to know that I'm very happy for you, James."

I blinked. "Oh?"

He looked at me then away, fixing his eyes, blue as my own, out the window. "Well, yes. You see, misery recognizes misery. I was very unhappy after your mother passed away. Quite frankly, it gutted me. I was lost without her and lost raising a boy who was too much like me, so driven, so calculated. I didn't know how to talk to you, to anyone really. Stiff upper lip and all that. Now, I know it was unfair of me to leave you so alone because

446

you were miserable too. It seems Tally makes you happy just as Figgy has made me happy. How could I not be supportive of that?"

"Because I'm gay," I said. The words came easier now. Sometimes, Tally caught me saying them into the bathroom mirror, practicing. "Because I'm in love with a man who also happens to be my stepbrother."

"Yes, well..." Nigel made a face. "It's not ideal, but it's not as if you grew up together. It was a shock, you know? Hearing it in the news like that didn't help. But I've known Tally now for long enough to know he has his own kind of magic. He's very lovable."

"Yes," I said, strongly, almost defensively, because I was so tired of seeing or hearing anything bad about the man I loved. "He's everything."

My father turned to me finally, searching my face, reading the resolve and the passion there. And then he did something that nearly made me break.

He reached over, clasped my hand, and smiled brilliantly. "Good. I'm glad. You deserve that, you know? You're a good man, and you've done so much good in this life. You deserve some fun and happiness."

"Thank you." I tried to remain stoic, but Tally had ruined me for it. I blinked away the sting in my eyes and gave my father's hand a squeeze. "I appreciate that from you."

We both jumped when there was a loud knock on the window. I turned to see Tally's nose pressed against the glass, a pink martini in one hand with a maraschino cherry in it.

"Are you done having your Hallmark moment?" he asked impudently. "Mummy's made cucumber sandwiches, and you know those are my kryptonite. If you don't hurry in, I'll eat them all, and I won't feel badly because now, I've warned you."

"You will save some for me," I warned him.

He raised an eyebrow. "Will I?"

Before I could answer, he turned on his heel and walked back into the house.

"He's delightful," Nigel admitted. "Took me a minute to get used to

him, but really, a lovely boy."

"He is," I agreed, somewhat dreamily.

"What will you do now?" he asked. "Now that you're no longer PM."

"You know, I haven't the foggiest," I said, laughter bubbling up in my chest as Tally popped his head out the front door, sandwich in hand, and shoved the entire thing in his mouth. "But for now, I'm very content to live my life with Tally."

He would always be my dirty boy, but I would never again let anything between us be a secret ever again.

The End

ABOUT SIERRA SIMONE

Sierra Simone is a USA Today bestselling former librarian who spent too much time reading romance novels at the information desk. She lives with her husband and family in Kansas City.

www.thesierrasimone.com

ALSO BY SIERRA SIMONE:

Thornchapel:
A Lesson in Thorns
Feast of Sparks
Harvest of Sighs
Door of Bruises

The Priest Series:
Priest
Midnight Mass: A Priest Novella
Sinner
Saint (Coming Summer 2021)

The New Camelot Trilogy:
American Queen
American Prince
American King
The Moon (Merlin's Novella)
American Squire (A Thornchapel and New Camelot Crossover) SEP

Misadventures:
Misadventures with a Professor
Misadventures of a Curvy Girl
Misadventures in Blue

Co-Written with Laurelin Paige
Porn Star
Hot Cop

The Markham Hall Series:
The Awakening of Ivy Leavold

The Education of Ivy Leavold
The Punishment of Ivy Leavold
The Reclaiming of Ivy Leavold

The London Lovers:
The Seduction of Molly O'Flaherty
The Persuasion of Molly O'Flaherty
The Wedding of Molly O'Flaherty

Her Christmas Present

Christmas Present

Present

JADE WEST AND LUCIA FRANCO

Chapter One

LEXI

"Lexi, your ass is grass if Dad sees you dressed like that," Brock says.

A smile tips my lips. Father is known to skip out on family events that don't serve his purpose. To him, watching his youngest toddler of a daughter meet Santa for the first time is not important, which is why I knew I could get away with my outfit. He wouldn't be here.

I hike my little sister higher on my hip. Crystal's legs squeeze me as she holds on tight, jerking my skirt as I walk through the shopping mall with her attached to me. I came straight from cheerleading practice and had an extra pair of bloomers with me to slip on, otherwise my ass cheeks would be hanging out right now. Brock questions my outfit with narrow eyes again but I brush it off. Our stepmom had my outfit made to match the fabric my half-sister I'm currently lugging on my hip is wearing. Only, she screwed up the measurements and ordered European sizes instead of American. The two-piece elf-inspired outfit was delivered three sizes too small *and* several weeks late.

In my eyes, it couldn't be more perfect a fuck up since the rumor at school is that Mr. Vaughn dresses up as the mall Santa every year. How I never knew that blows my mind. Then again, my childhood crush on the teacher next door had always been innocent up until about a year ago, when I caught him buck naked in his backyard jacuzzi fucking some chick for hours. I should've moved away from the window and got myself back to bed, but I couldn't do it. I couldn't tear my eyes away from them. I should've definitely been a good girl enough to stop myself slipping my hands down between my thighs, but no. No way.

Since that night, I've been consumed by it. Every time I look at him in class, I imagine it was me in that jacuzzi with him. Even now I'm thinking about it as I cross the mall.

We come to a stop and stand in line. I look for the Santa guy but I'm too far around the corner to get a good view. All I can see is the top of his hat. My heart is pounding regardless.

"Your underwear is hanging out," Brock mutters.

"They're called *bloomers*, not *underwear*. I wear them to practices and competitions, *over* my underwear."

"What about your tits, huh? What do you think Santa is going to think of them?"

I scowl at him. "I can't help that I was blessed with a decent rack, you idiot. Just like you can't help driving a jacked-up truck to compensate for whatever's in your pants."

Jared giggles and covers his mouth. Brock glares at me. He isn't amused but I can't help it. He's an easy target and I can get away with it because he's my overprotective brother and we're extremely close.

"This is such bullshit," he grunts, shaking his head. "My first day home for Christmas break from college and I have to take this corny ass picture."

I chuckle at his whining. "That's because you're hungover. Should've had the *hair of the dog*."

He eyes me curiously. "What do you know about that?"

"I'm eighteen, dummy. Have you seen how much the parents drink? I've seen and heard it all." I juggle Crystal to my other hip and feel a cool draft breeze past the back of my thighs. She bounces excitedly. "I've been raising this chunky monkey since she was born. I'm not the same sister you left behind. Honestly, while you've been away, I've been more of a parent to her than anyone."

"Yeah, yeah, yeah," he says, but I don't miss the concern that crosses his eyes. Brock turns to Jared to right his clothes. "Ready to ask Santa for a special toy?"

Jared stares at him. "I don't believe in Santa anymore," he says.

"Since when? Lexi still believes in Santa. She's gonna ask him for something," Brock says, spoken like a concerned father.

"Are you?" Jared asks me with sudden bright eyes.

The line moves and we all shuffle along behind. "Yes," Brock says at the same time as I say, "No."

I glare at him and my jaw flexes.

"I am not!"

But I have to do it. If it means for one second that Jared will believe in Santa for just a little bit longer, I'll ask Santa for a gift all day long.

Heat flames my cheeks. I already have it bad for Mr. Vaughn. Sitting on his lap wouldn't be a good thing. The thought makes me nervous as hell and my heart thumps like mad. Nerves and excitement are a crazy wild combination.

There are only a few more families before us. Butterflies swirl in my belly again. Crystal's growing impatient and bouncing rambunctiously on my hip. I follow her gaze and see that she's pointing out the jolly old guy I've been aching to see, only he isn't so jolly and old, not under the fake white beard. A smile spreads across my face.

Oh my God. It's really him. It's really Mr. Vaughn!

"If Lexi sits on Santa's lap, then I will too," Jared claims.

"She will," Brock assures him, and he's right. I will.

My heart is racing, because I'm going to do it. For real, I'm going to

bite the nerves and do it. I can't wait to tell my bestie Jessica how damn brave I am. She's going to flip! Mr. Vaughn is eye candy at the high school and I'm pretty sure he knows it, like the rest of the human populous who's ever seen him. He's got the most gorgeous blue eyes and they're a dead giveaway. Yep, there they are. I'm sure that's him.

Baby sister squeals again and I realize we're next in line. Flashes of light are popping in front of us from the camera, Christmas carols being sung by a choir, and everyone is decked out like they just flew in fresh from the North Pole.

"Next!" the call sounds out.

I swallow thickly and step closer. Jared walks right up to Santa with a big smile. Crap. I have to go too.

Crystal screams in my arms and Santa turns my way. I lock eyes with him, and I know it without any shadow of a doubt. It's definitely Mr. Vaughn.

Whoa. Just WHOA.

My stomach is a flustered mess. Even my ears flame with heat. He's staring at me – at all of my skin that's showing, and my grand idea for doing this suddenly seems so damn stupid, but still, still, I can't stop thinking about what he looks like under those overstuffed clothes.

Santa puts his arms out and reaches for Crystal with a *ho, ho, ho*. I put her on the floor and she toddles on over.

Brock comes over to stand next to me, close enough to whisper. He nudges me from behind and it forces me to step toward the ornate sleigh.

"Go on. Go sit on Santa's lap and tell him what you want for Christmas in that naughty little elf outfit."

"I hate you," I tell him. Playfully, of course. I could never hate my brother. "And for the record, I think I look good in this naughty little elf outfit, thank you very much."

"Come on, Lexi!" Jared says, waving me to him. He's such a kid at heart still. I smile and walk on over.

I bite my lip to push away the nerves. Santa's going to ask me what I

want for Christmas and I'm going to need an answer. I could be respectful, or I could be naughty and pretend that I don't even know it's my teacher.

Which one, which one, which one?

Mr. Vaughn watches as I stride over, and his gaze is focused right on my tits. I take pleasure in seeing what he's looking at. Yep, he's looking. He sure is looking. *Santa* rakes a slow gaze down the length of my body. My lips twitch. Go, elf outfit, go!

"Ho, ho, ho, Merry Christmas," Santa says, trying to be jolly. I paint on a coy smile and grab the end of my braid, standing in front of him, twirling it, trying to be cute.

It works. He's still staring. He taps the side of Jared's arm while looking at me. "Why don't you let your sister get a turn?"

"Sure," Jared says and heads away, taking our baby sister with him and leaving just me and Santa.

Holy shit. Mr. Vaughn is giving me a go on his lap. I'm going to be sitting on Mr. Vaughn's lap. He's staring and I must be beetroot red.

Santa pats his red velvet leg. I take a deep breath. Here is my opportunity to get away with being bad. This is it. My chance. I decide to take it.

"Hi, Santa!" I say and go for it.

I do it. I sit on Santa's knee.

He hitches in a breath under the thick, fake beard and I feel the heat of him. I do my bad girl elf move and spread my knees until I'm all but flush against him. *Please. Please, let him like me.*

From all appearances it must be innocent, just Santa with a girl on his knee, but it feels anything but innocent to me. I feel naughtier than I've ever felt in my life.

Santa wraps his arm around me for the standard hug he gives everyone.

"Well, hello there, little one," he says, trying to disguise his voice. "Have you been a naughty girl or a good girl? Let me guess." He pauses. "A good girl."

Here goes. I actually do it. I pout for him. "I was a naughty girl this year, Santa. I don't deserve anything but coal."

"Oh, I don't believe that. Everyone deserves something," he laughs.

I shake my head and give him puppy dog eyes. "I don't, Santa. I was *really* bad. I saw something I wasn't supposed to see, and I liked it a lot. I'll get in trouble if I tell anyone though, it's very secret."

He laughs a jolly laugh again. "You can tell Santa. There's nothing I can't fix. I don't believe my little elves should wake up on Christmas morning without a present under the tree."

I drop my voice to a whisper. "I watched my teacher have sex outside last winter and I haven't been able to get it off my mind. I couldn't stop watching. Really, I couldn't. I liked it too much. "

Santa clears his throat and the air suddenly feels hot.

"Uh, that wasn't what I was expecting." He laughs nervously and rubs his long beard. His gaze shoots around like he's paranoid someone heard us, but no one did. It's too loud around us for our voices to carry.

"Ah, where did you, ah, see this?" he asks me.

"From my bedroom window."

His eyes widen in surprise. "Your window?!"

"Oh, yes," I say with a smile. "You see, I don't think he knows it, but I watch him quite often. My teacher is my next-door neighbor."

Chapter Two

LEO

I'm Mr. Vaughn, history teacher at Macwood High. I shouldn't be sitting here with my eighteen-year-old student on my knee in Santa's sleigh. I *definitely* shouldn't be sitting here with my student on my knee and my cock straining to get at her through my Santa costume. It's… disgusting.

Lexi can feel it. I know she can. Any illusions I've had about her innocence are done and gone. She knows what she's doing to me. The girl is a sweet little vixen with a horny twinkle in her eyes, fully aware of who I am as she teases me. Her elf costume barely covers her perfect, cheeky little ass. Her tits are perky, on display.

Yeah, she knows what she's doing to me. She's planned long and hard what she's doing to me.

A flood of *holy shit* hits me hard as her words truly soak in. I'm still digesting it with embarrassment and shame – the girl watched me fuck someone for hours on end like a dirty bastard.

I know which someone she's talking about, too. She's talking about

on top of beer. The sassy bitch made a move, hungry hands and a dirty smile, and I'd eaten it up like a beast until I realized just how annoying she was when she didn't have my dick inside her. She was plenty damn annoying.

I still remember her squeals as I moved my cock from her pussy to her tight little asshole, then fucked her like my toy dolly. I stretched her wide and it felt damn good on my dick. I can still hear her begging for more in that sassy little voice of hers. I gave it to her rough.

The thought that Lexi was watching the whole thing through her bedroom window is enough to send a thrill of heat straight to my balls. Yeah, it's wrong. It should never have happened. But it *did* happen. She *did* watch the whole thing through her bedroom window. She saw me taking Betty like I owned her, pushing her to her limits. Fuck, my cock is so damn hard.

I feel like a monster. My *student* saw her *teacher* fucking a dirty bitch's asshole until that dirty bitch was squealing. Then, the best of it, she's keeps it quiet for almost twelve months, being a good girl in class for me, and saying *hello, sir* when we met on our street. I'm wondering why she waited so long when it hits me.

She's kept it quiet until her eighteenth birthday… which only happened last month. I saw her birthday party in her yard through my window. Ha. Yes. Figures.

I try to clear my head enough to be Mr. Vaughn again. The respectable Mr. Vaughn I've been for the vast majority of my time as her mentor.

"Lexi, I'm sure your teacher didn't know you were watching," I tell her, with an edge to my voice. "He'd never have done that if he knew you were watching, I can assure you of that."

She shifts on my knee some more and I know she can feel my hard-on. Her voice is quaky as she replies, "No, I guess he didn't. But I *did* watch him. I watched him… and I liked it. Honestly, Santa. I liked it so much."

She must be shitting herself with nerves, confessing this to me.

Weirdly, that only makes me harder. I like her dirty innocence like a heady scent you can't shake off. I like it a lot. I like *her* a lot.

It feels strange to be sizzling this raw about someone I've known for years. I've never felt like this about any of my other students. They never grow up for me in my mind. I do my job, teaching them as best as I can to prepare them for their life ahead, and then I wave my farewells. They never make the transition to adults in my mind.

After what transpired over the weekend, Lexi is different. She's not my student. She's not the girl I've watched grow up next door to me. Right now, in this place, on my knee, she's different.

"You're being a very naughty girl telling this to Santa," I say, my voice low.

"I know," she replies, barely more than a whisper. "I am a very naughty girl but I don't know what else to do. Telling Santa might be the only way to ever get the present I *need*. I'm eighteen now, Santa. I'm all grown up."

It's the way she says *need* that has my heart racing. She wasn't lying when she said this was all she's been thinking about – that much is obvious. She's desperate as she squirms on me, wanting everything a filthy little elf would want from a bad Santa. She slides closer and bats her lashes at me.

I've been with women as gorgeous as Lexi before, but never one quite so squirmy, or so young, or off limits. The way the heat of her pussy nudges against the tip of my cock tells me she's not quite so innocent as she appears.

"Tell me," I say. "Have you been with any naughty boys already, Lexi? Be honest now."

She shakes her head. "No, Santa. I haven't. I couldn't be with any guy my age after I watched you." She bites her lip and hesitates. "I only want to be with my teacher. I want Mr. Vaughn to be my first."

The confession slams me right in the gut. Hearing her talk like that about me should make me retch, but it doesn't. It makes me even harder and it makes my mouth water. I hate it, but it does.

I should pull myself together and tell her that Mr. Vaughn is her teacher and will never touch her. It would be the right thing to do. So, why don't I say it? Why don't I tell her? Why do I say nothing at all, just sit with the minx squirming on my lap?

Because I fucking like it. That's why.

I'm sitting like a dumbstruck fool when I hear someone call her from the side.

"Lexiiii! Are you done telling Santa what you want? We have to take family pictures and then I want to check out the candy stall!" It's her younger brother, Jared, in his little grumpy voice.

The dirty girl jumps at that, and I do too. She's up on her feet in a flash, trying to pull down a skirt that barely covers her ass while I'm trying to hide my bulge of a damn fucking hard-on. She stays standing in front of me as she waves her siblings over. Thank God for Santa's overfilled coat. All I have to do is move it over my lap and no one will see.

"I'm, um, sorry…" she says, and her confidence has dissipated to nothing. She's just little girl Lexi again, a sweetie in a tiny little elf costume.

Her cheeks are bright pink, and she's caught up in a bluster as she gathers herself for the picture. Mrs. Claus snaps a bunch of them in five seconds flat and the boys are up and she's grabbing her sister from my arm. She's almost out of here when I call her back, a simple *Lexi* that has her spinning to face me.

"Yes, Mr. Vaughn?" Her eyes widen as soon as she says it. "I mean Santa! I'm sorry, Santa, I mean Santa! Not Mr. Vaughn!"

We stare at each other, and we're both horrified in different ways. Her cheeks burn even brighter. It wouldn't matter if she's my student or not at this point since the semester is almost over for winter break, it's the fact that she's my next-door neighbor. Otherwise fuck the consequences. I'd be tearing the elf costume from her and savaging those lovely tits already. Fuck. I'd love every minute of it, and I'd be claiming her right from the start… I'd be her first.

I clear my throat before I answer and act quick since people are watching. I reach down to pick up a candy cane and hold it out to her. The plan works and Lexi steps closer.

I whisper, "Have you told anyone about this naughty Christmas wish, Lexi? Not your mom or dad, I hope?"

Her wide eyes are on me while she shakes her head.

"No, sir. I haven't. I wouldn't."

"Good girl," I say. "Keep it that way."

"I will, Santa," she says, and chances a smile.

"LEXI!" the voice calls from outside again. "LEXI! COME ONNNN!"

It's Lexi who jitters on the spot, nerves jangling louder.

"I gotta go. Happy Christmas, Santa," she says, but she's still hovering, waiting, and of course she would. I'm her teacher. She's waiting for permission to leave.

We're still staring, both of us, because I should dismiss her with a wave and a *ho, ho, ho* after telling her it won't be happening again. I hate myself, but I don't want to. The sight of the beautiful little creature is enough to drive me insane.

"Can I go now, Santa?" she asks me, and now's the time to say it. I should say so fucking much.

I don't. I don't say what I should do, not even close.

"Make sure you're a good little girl until then, please, and maybe, just *maybe*, you'll get your Christmas present."

The shock on her face speaks a thousand words. She's out of the faux sleigh, nothing but a scurry of limbs as she darts away. I almost call her back to try and get out of what I said, but another family is already walking over to me with their little bawling toddler.

Damn it. At least it cures my hard-on in a second.

One last glimpse of Lexi and it only slams in again what a beautiful, young woman my student has grown into. She really is something divine.

I've heard on the usual gossip grapevine that being a teacher gives you

access to, how that boy Marty Harris has been fighting over her with Neil Vine. I guess neither of the senior jocks have claimed her yet. The thought that they won't ever get the chance makes me feel almost noble about being her first introduction to the world of sex. I'd be doing her a favor since the guys are both total jerks and losers.

I get absorbed back into an afternoon of smiles and *ho, ho, hos* but I can't shake it off, not for a heartbeat, not how much that girl has been thinking about me naked in the backyard. I've been her fantasy for twelve months, and I'd live up to that. I know I'd live up to it.

The shopping mall comes to a close and Santa's workshop is wrapped up for another year before I head back home, wired because of Lexi still. Only one more week left of the school semester before the holidays and then it's time for celebrations and tinsel and Christmas songs until the New Year. The houses are flashing with lights as I walk past them, windows bright with action from inside. Families are getting ready for the time out and the world around me is alive with festive cheer. I'm sure the season is incredible if you aren't an independent loner living in a sprawling house on his own. It doesn't bother me in the slightest for 364 days of the year, but Christmas morning makes things feel a little different. It's why I try to participate as much as I can as the local Santa when it comes to holiday festivities.

I'm still wearing my Santa jacket, but my beard has been cast aside and tossed onto the passenger seat. I don't feel anything like a Santa Claus. He's supposed to be a tubby little cute guy with rosy red cheeks. I'm anything but that.

I'm still trying not to think about the dirty little elf when I pull into my driveway, but she has me transfixed. Turning the ignition off, I peer through the trees and look at her house. I can see it's active but that's hardly a surprise since there are two young kids running through the place as well as the older ones. I lift my gaze toward the second story and for the first time I can't help but wonder which of the windows she watched me from that night. It seems the most fucked up but natural reaction in the world is to

head to my backyard to see if I can actually see her. Getting out of the car, I walk around the side of the house and stay hidden in the shadows until I get to my jacuzzi. I take a chance and look up.

And holy fuck, there she is, my dirty little elf girl. Lexi is staring down at me from that very same window, illuminated from the backlight.

I can imagine her there, just the same, watching me that night in the dark. I can picture her crystal clearly, looking down on me while I was fucking Betty like an animal.

We stare at each other for long, slow seconds, both of us speaking volumes in the unspoken silence. Someone calls her name, I can hear them bellowing at her from across the yard. Sounds like her stepmom, in her prissy bitch voice. Lexi scurries away like before and I'm left standing in the cold with a throbbing dick.

The corner of my lips curl at the thought of seeing Lexi in class on Monday.

I just hope I've come to my damn fucking senses by then.

As it turns out, I haven't. I've anything but come to my senses by Monday morning. I've had my dick in my hand for most of the rest of the weekend, thinking about what I'd love to do to that dirty little elf girl.

I've always been a dirty, filthy guy outside of the classroom, with a very definite divide between the two. I've been a pussy hungry piece of filth since I was old enough to get one, I've just never been tempted by girls that I shouldn't be – not until now. Not until Lexi.

I tell myself I'll be doing her a favor and saving her from the idiot boys around school, because that's what she'll get if I push her away like the honorable teacher I've spent the rest of my working life being – she'll get an idiot of a boy popping her cherry like an immature, grunting little jerk, barely able to find her clit. I can picture them. I know exactly who the losers out to claim her are. Fuck them.

So, maybe this is the ultimate Christmas present – giving little Lexi the fantasy she's been having for the past twelve months. She'll be off to college in just a few months, and at least her bar will be raised higher when

it comes to the other guys she'll be letting into her panties on new ground, far away from this town and all the dross that goes along with it.

I'm convincing myself, and I know it. I'm being a dishonorable asshole, and I know that too, and I should stop myself, get a grip of myself, find another sweet pussy to pound in this town and leave Lexi-pretty-elf the hell alone.

I know I won't be doing that the very second I pull up in the parking lot at school. She's too damn gorgeous for that.

Chapter Three

LEXI

Monday morning comes around way too quickly and I'm anxious as heck.

I woke up early and debated if I was going to skip school or actually go today. I opted for the latter, because I'm sure a good little academic when it comes to it.

I don't regret what I said to Mr. Vaughn in his Santa's outfit, I'm just nervous to see him now. Really damn nervous.

Yeah, okay, that's an understatement. I'm about to throw up.

I feel like I should apologize to him for my stupid outburst – a blustering mess of embarrassment. He won't have a fluffy white beard to hide behind today and I won't be dressed up like an elf, just clad in my usual private school uniform like every other day he usually sees me. Fuck.

Taking a deep breath, I tuck my text books to my chest, approach the door to class, and wrap my hand around the handle. I did this on purpose. I came to first period a few minutes early, knowing full well he'd be here after I saw his car pull out of his driveaway this morning. Having his class

first thing sure is a blessing in disguise. At least I can get this confrontation over and done with.

I only realize just how fast my heart is racing as I step into the room and find him sitting there, at his desk, his head tilted down, writing something. He's wearing black, bold glasses, and his green and red plaid tie is loosened at his neck. As per usual, his sleeves are rolled to his elbows, which just makes him so much hotter. All staff follow a dress code, which just about every girl at Macwood High is secretly grateful for. Mr. Vaughn isn't the only eye candy to drool over – but he's the best. In my humble, elf girl opinion, he's the absolute best.

The door closes behind me and we lock gazes. Surprise is written all over his face and I burn up as he gestures me closer.

"Lexi," he says under his breath.

I blink, unsure what to say. I'm mute and lost for it, struggling to pull myself together. Somehow, I manage it. I clear my throat and I smile like I usually do.

"Good morning, Mr. Vaughn."

He glances above my head at the clock then back at me. "Is there something I can help you with?"

I guess he's pretending it didn't happen. That's even worse, I think – the fantasy drying up to nothing in the face of embarrassment. My brave Santa visit could just fizzle to nothing. Not even a hint of a mention for the rest of all time.

Can I do it? Can I push the bravery again and talk about my fantasies some more, in the face of abject terror and humiliation?

My throat tightens as I think about it, and I want to do it. I *need* to do it.

I find my voice.

"Ah, yeah, ah, I wanted to talk to you."

I curse myself inwardly for stuttering as he removes his glasses and places them on the desk.

"What would you like to talk about?"

My fingers tighten around the stack of textbooks I'm carrying. I'm not used to the bite in his tone. I think he's mad at me and it only tosses more butterflies around in my stomach. Shit. I really messed up.

I step closer to his desk. My voice doesn't sound like mine when it hits the air. My words come out in one giant run of a sentence, which is as embarrassing as hell.

"I'm-so-sorry-for-the-things-I-said-and-for-confessing-that-I watched-you-have-sex-I-should-have-never-said-them-to-you-if-you-want-to-have-me-transferred-out-of-your-class-I-completely-understand-but-I-couldn't-stop-watching." I exhale a heavier breath than I intended and blink over and over. Then I add the obvious. "And I haven't stopped thinking about it since."

He can tell that I'm nervous. I reek of it. I don't know what I'm expecting, but I jolt at the sound of something snapping.

Oh, fuck. The pencil Mr. Vaughn is fisting broke in his hand. Hard eyes glare at me.

"You were a naughty girl coming to me like that, Lexi," he tells me. "Very naughty," he says, and his voice is low. "Come here. Now."

I'm a good girl for Mr. Vaughn and step closer.

My lips are parted and my arms are folded so tight that my books are clutched against my chest. I'm holding on to them for dear life. It's a good way to hide my hard nipples, at least.

"Closer," he says.

I shuffle closer at the same time as he wheels his chair forward until our knees bump. Heat flames my cheeks, fuck, fuck, fuck. I take a step back, but he grabs the top of my thigh.

"Stay, Lexi. Be still."

His fingers press into my skin and he tugs me to him, then swiftly grabs the hem of my prep skirt and slips his fingers along my inner thigh.

If I had to make a list of all the ways that I thought this morning would go, Mr. Vaughn's fingers near my pussy wouldn't have even be a thought in my mind. My heart is about to burst from my chest. I hold my

breath and stare down, panicked someone is going to walk in.

He pinches the inside of my thigh and I let out a small gasp, widening my stance. It was a direct shot to my clit.

"Stand still," he orders me. "Don't move. If you move, someone might question us if they walk in. You wouldn't want anyone to do that now, would you?"

All I can do is shake my head. His actions have rendered me speechless and caused my panties to dampen. A grin spreads across his mouth and his lids lower in satisfaction. I like that he's happy.

"Tell me why you would confess that to me?"

My jaw bobs as his fingers inch higher. "It was a dare."

His eyes harden to stone. Mr. Vaughn pinches the sensitive skin on my inner thigh once more and I wince. "Try again."

I can't believe he saw through my lie.

"I don't know. I thought I could play coy."

Drawing a breath, the tops of his knuckles glide over my bikini line. He brazenly slips a finger under the elastic and it pulls one of my pubic hairs. I wince but immediately forget about the pain as my knees automatically bow so he can slide toward my pussy. I'm so unprepared for this that I can't even think straight.

"And get away with it?" he asks. I nod quickly, but he freezes. I frown. "So, was it a lie? Was everything you told me a lie?"

My brows bunch together wondering how he could possibly think that while I was nearly masturbating on his lap? Looking him straight in the eyes, I tell him the truth.

"It's all true. I didn't lie. I watched you fuck that girl through my window." Holy shit. I can't believe I actually said it. "I could hear her moaning from my window every time you pushed into her."

Mr. Vaughn glides his fingers over my mound. My ears are flaming hot and my pussy is swelling with desire by the second. I don't shave, except along my bikini line, because I'm never sure if I should or not or how much. I definitely wasn't going to ask my stepmom, but now I'm

second guessing my decision. I feel embarrassed because it's so thick.

But Mr. Vaughn pets my mound like I gave him the right answer and it sends such a delicious shiver down my spine that I find myself inching just slightly closer.

"Keep going," he demands.

Fuck. I'm playing with a man who is nearly three times my age, but I can't help it. He's so fucking hot and after I saw him have sex with Betty, I wanted him to have sex with me the same way. I clearly didn't think this all the way through but that's because I kind of figured he'd ignore me or pretend it didn't happen. Not touch me like I wanted him to.

Nervously, I say with a sugary smile, "It's the season of hope... and I have hope."

He's not pleased with my response and swiftly grabs the other side of my panties and fists it. He pulls the fabric upward and I let out a sigh at the pressure on my clit. The corners of his lips curl. It feels so good that I want him to pull on it harder.

"Hope for what?" he asks, then uses his other hand to shock the shit out of me and rub my plump pussy lips over my silk panties. He does it a few times and that's all it takes to make my inner thighs shake with need.

"Mr. Vaughn," I say, my voice husky.

He cuts me off by rubbing right where my clit is hidden. A sigh bursts from my lips before I can stop it. "Hope for what?" he asks. "What did you wish for from Santa?"

I'm sweating, my skin prickling on my arms. My hips thrust against his hand and an ache throbs through me. He knows what I wished for and now he's teasing me with it.

"I wished for you to fuck me like you fucked her," I hear myself saying before I can stop myself.

The old, grandfather style clock in the corner of the classroom chimes at every quarter of the hour. It goes off in the silence of the room and I jump, moving to look over my shoulder. I'm so nervous we're going to get caught. Mr. Vaughn gives my panties a good yank and it startles me to look

back in his direction. My books slip from my arms and thump to the floor as I collapse onto my teacher, his fist still clenching around my underwear. I freak out, trying to scramble off him, petrified that we're going to get caught. This was a bad idea.

"Shh…" he says, in my ear. The pads of his fingers stroke over my swollen pussy lips. It feels so good. "I can't stop thinking about you, Lexi."

Using his legs to hold me to him, my back bows at the intense ache shooting through my clit as he grinds his thigh against my pussy. Fuck! If he doesn't stop, I'm going to come and then I'm going to be even more embarrassed than I already am. I try to wriggle away.

"Be still, Lexi." I freeze at the command. "Good girl," he says, petting the side of my face. I lean into his touch. "The staff knows I like my mornings uninterrupted before the chaos begins. No one will dare walk in here."

That explains why he was surprised to see me. Taking his word for it, I nod but I don't move.

"Listen to me."

"Okay."

"We have less than fifteen minutes before class. Sit up and take your backpack off. Face me."

My brain goes haywire. "I don't think this is a good idea in your class," I whisper.

Not because I don't want something to happen between us. I do. I really, really do.

Taking my hand, he guides my palm over the bulge in his pants and shows me how to squeeze him. My eyes widen, feeling the warmth of his cock, how his balls feel under my nails as I press a little deeper.

"It's a little late for that."

The way he says it does something to me I've never experienced before. His voice weakens my body like it's at his will. I had no idea a voice could be so fucking sexy.

Pushing back, I sit up awkwardly in his lap and take my backpack off.

It drops to the floor in a heap. Mr. Vaughn takes me into his own hands and centers me so I'm straddling him. My skirt bunches at my hips and I feel his cock pushing at me through his slacks. Cool air breezes past my butt cheeks.

I grip his shoulders in worry. "What if someone *does* walk in though?"

A heavy, hot sigh blows over my neck. "Already have it covered," he says.

Reaching behind me, he grabs a piece of paper and shows me the prewritten detention slip with my name on it for later today in his classroom. He tosses it back onto his desk then shocks me again.

Mr. Vaughn plants his lips on mine. Before I can think any wiser to stop him, I wrap my arms around his shoulders and lean into the kiss. His tongue thrusts into my mouth and he groans when I wrap it around and tug.

He's thick, warm, and *all* man.

I kiss him back with just as much enthusiasm and feel my nipples harden against his chest. While I've never had sex, I've fooled around with enough boys to know what I think feels good too, and the building pleasure between my thighs tells me I'm headed in the right direction.

He doesn't stop, and I don't want him to. I love that his hands are all over my body like he can't get enough. My hips move against his and I feel his massive erection strain against his zipper. I moan into his mouth and his teeth nip my lips. I can't believe this is actually happening. I've come on my fingers, my vibrator, and I even bought a dildo and imagined it was his strong arms taking control all night. My toes curls inside my sandals and it feels so good on my clit as I shamelessly show how much I want him with my body. He likes it, I can tell, because our lips haven't stopped and his hands are guiding me right where I want him. He's hungry and it only spurs me more. We can't seem to get enough of each other.

He breaks our kiss and pants into my mouth. "You're so fucking sexy when you rub yourself on me like that," he says, still driving his hips into me. "Like a little fucking kitten." My lashes flutter, surprised by his words. My chest falls and rises, and he notices. Mr. Vaughn palms my breasts and

my head falls back, feeling his fingers press into my C cups.

"Fuck yeah," he says, his voice throaty. "You're doing perfect." He groans and directs my hips into his, making sure his dick rubs the wet spot on my bloomers. Pulling his bottom lip into my mouth, I grind down hard and slow, and almost come, just like that.

"Just perfect... fuck, kitten. Where'd you learn to move like this?"

I'm on the edge of bliss, ready to orgasm any second. His thumb rubs circles over my nipple and a loud moan falls from my lips. My hips rise into his and he growls as I continue to rub myself uncontrollably on him. He's like a drug I'm chasing, and my breathing is laboring. I've never been on the brink of desire like this, not when I play with myself, and never with a boy. My panties are soaked and wedged into me, but it doesn't bother me. Nothing could ruin the lust coursing through my blood right now.

"Mr. Vaughn, I don't want to stop this, but we have to!"

He ignores me, staring at my chest. "I love your tits. I came all weekend in my hand, imagining my cock was between them and, every time I came near your mouth, you sucked my dick."

His words are a direct shot to my pussy. At this point he could ask for anything and I'd give it to him. My thighs clench and my body contracts wildly.

"Oh, God. You feel so good," I hear myself saying shamelessly. A whimper slips from my lips. My clit is aching for release and I don't know what he's waiting for.

"But right before my balls tighten up, and I'm two seconds from coming on your face, I shove my cock inside your sweet little cunt and fuck you senseless."

My skin prickles with heat and my eyes lock with Mr. Vaughn's. We're both quiet, breathing into each other while we digest what he just said. He's my teacher, and he's told me how he's imagined having sex with me.

"Oh, Lexi," he says under his breath.

This changes everything.

"Did you like it?" I dare to ask.

Sitting up closer, Mr. Vaughn presses his chest to mine and threads his threads his fingers through my hair, bringing my mouth to his. "I haven't been able to get you out of my mind since then," he says on my lips then kisses me deeply.

Reaching for his hand, I grab his wrist and lift my hips without breaking the kiss. My hand slides over his and I guide him right where I want him.

"Please," I say, sitting on his palm. He growls when he feels my wetness. I shoot a quick glance over my shoulder at the clock to mark the time then look back at him. "Make me come, sir."

Chapter Four

LEO

I'm still in shock that I'm doing this to one of my students. It's insane, and filthy. Disgusting beyond belief, like I've known it would be from the very first moment I considered it. Still, I can't stop myself. I've been thinking about nothing else from the moment the kinky little elf confessed her fantasies to me and stared at me from her bedroom window. I couldn't stop. She's far too intoxicating with that sweet little smile.

I knew she'd been with other boys from the very first second she let herself go in my hands. She knows how to kiss and she knows how to play and she knows how to grind, but there's more than that. There's a little sacred gemstone waiting down deep in her, ready to be claimed.

Lexi is still a virgin.

My sweet little student is still a sweet little untouched flower who hasn't truly known what it's like to be taken.

I'll most certainly be the one to claim her.

I'm still quite surprised by her bravery as she takes my hand and

moves it against her. Not only has she pushed her mouth to its limits by confessing all to Santa on his lap, but she's pushing her body now, moving against me like a horny little bitch for more, more, more.

Yes. Lexi is indeed a horny little bitch.

I can imagine her there at night, in bed, thinking about my filthy jacuzzi time with Betty Richards, with her dirty little fingers working her pink bud of a clit. I can picture her teeth pinching her sweet bottom lip, breaths ragged as she thinks about my dick ploughing another woman like a beast – whichever holes I want to be taking.

Whichever holes of *hers* I want to be taking.

That's the truth of it, too. I'll take every prize she has to offer me, considering just how much risk I'm putting into claiming it.

Her eyes are so pretty as she stares at me, grinding just enough on my fingers to drive herself wild. She wants to come, and she wants me to touch her bare skin while she does it. She's been thinking about this fantasy right from the start, I can see it written all over her. She's been desperate for the truth in it. Desperate for me.

"Touch me the right way," she whispers.

She won't be having me yet though, not until I drive her wild to her limits, chewing her mind over at the thought. Hungry.

"Stop it now, Lexi," I tell her, barely more than a grunt as I push her aside.

Her eyes are wide and shocked, and it's incredible, just how pretty she can look when she's so fucking nervous.

"What, sir?" she asks, and her voice is barely more than a meek little whisper, bravery all gone.

"You're dismissed," I say, and mean it. I point her away. "You're dismissed, Lexi. Go to your desk, please."

"But, I…" she begins, but trails off.

I flash her a smile.

"Who's in charge of you in this classroom, little girl?" I ask her, and her wide eyes are still palpably nervous.

reward is?" I say, and I'm sure my eyes must be twinkling with the filth in my head.

She gives just the slightest nod, and scutters away from me just a tiny amount. It's not far, but it's enough to see just how short that nice little skirt of hers has ridden up her thighs.

I'll be seeing a lot more of her thighs later.

"Dismissed," I say again and take great joy as she flusters, picking up her books and backpack before dropping her sexy ass at her desk.

Her breaths are still ragged and horny as her classmates start to arrive.

The first lesson goes slowly, but purposefully. I shoot her filthy, heavy glances every chance I get, pacing around the room, closer and closer, only to step away again with a smile on my face.

I watch the idiot boys in the room watching her, clearly slavering over the thought of taking her pussy. She's a gorgeous girl, always has been. It makes me feel every bit the playboy inside that I've always been, heading up the line when it comes to men seeking their fill with dirty, hot looking women.

Lexi is a picture of beauty – one of the prettiest creatures I've ever had the pleasure of knowing.

She really is my Christmas present far more than I'll ever be hers… she just doesn't seem to know that yet. What a dirty little angel she is with such meek little scraps of belief in herself.

Lexi's eyes are on me right the way through that hour, fingers tapping a pencil against the desk as her cheeks stay bright, rosy pink. I'm sure she's barely able to focus on the lesson happening around her, her dirty little thoughts on all the dirty little thoughts she's ever had about me… and all the dirty little thoughts about just how good it felt when I touched her.

She leaps out of her seat when the bell sounds for the end of class, nervous enough that she seems to be actually shuddering. She scoops up her things, loading up her backpack before she dares to look at me, eyes wide on me for my next instructions.

I shoot her another smirk before I clear my throat and call her out in

class, nice and loudly.

"Miss Dawson! I've had no homework from you again this week. Do you have any excuses?"

Her mouth drops open as people stare, and I can see that sharp little brain of hers ticking.

"I don't, um..." she begins, and then it clicks into place. Her eyes widen some more. "I'm sorry," she tells me. "I'm really sorry. I forgot it."

"Forgetting your assignments isn't good enough," I tell her. "There is only one option for bad girls who don't respect their studies."

I can hear the ripple of nudges and whispers around her, other students gossiping and laughing. She looks... embarrassed.

"I'm sorry..." Lexi begins to say again but I hold up a hand.

"You can apologize in your after-school detention later," I tell her. "I expect to see you here after the bell, nice and prompt."

Those wide eyes are focused on mine so fucking hard, digesting what I'm doing. Her rosy pink cheeks are rosy red cheeks by the time she slings her backpack over her shoulder and darts out of the room. She's almost through the doorway when she shoots me one final glance over her shoulder, and that's when I see it all over again.

The girl is a desperate, kinky little girl who's been thinking about my dick inside her for a whole damn year. My balls tighten to a fresh new tune as I sit there, at my desk, because I know what I need to do about it, beyond all doubt...

I need to live up to her expectations.

The rest of the lessons through the day are okay, but pretty standard. The kids are the same kids, chattering in the same way, excited about Christmas in the same way they always are at this time of year. I do my job, trying to instil as much knowledge into their festive brains as I possibly can do, while still keeping an eye on the time.

The day goes by so fucking slowly, and my balls get so much fucking tighter. I should've made her suck me off for putting me through this torment.

I'm more than ready for it by the time the final bell sounds out through the corridors and the school springs into end of day life as students get themselves ready for home. There's a flurry of commotion outside my room, students from the last lesson darting right out amongst it as I wave them goodbye with a *homework tomorrow, please* announcement.

The door closes and the room goes quiet. I grab my balls and give my cock a good tug in hopes of letting it breathe a little. The school comes alive and goes to sleep again in one crazy little tornado, and I'm left fucking aching and ready to blow at this point.

All I can focus on is Lexi and what I want to do to her.

I'm right at the heart of it as the world unfolds, and then... a little tap, tap, tapping at my door as a good little girl comes to her after-school detention, just like she's been told.

"Come in!" I shout, and my voice sounds heavy.

Little Miss Dawson is more nervous than I've ever seen her when she steps inside. Her knees look like they've been knocking together as she edges on in and drops her backpack alongside her on the floor.

"I'm here for my detention," she tells me, and I can see the wavering in her, still not quite able to believe this is really going to happen. "I came back just like you told me, Mr. Vaughn. For my detention. My detention, right?"

That's when I can't resist it anymore.

I sit myself down on my desk with my arms folded across my chest and a smirk, nice and dark and dirty on my face.

I look out of the window and watch calmly as the buses gather up their students ready to leave and the school day winds down to nothing, and then I say it. I deliver the truth she is still struggling to believe in my voice.

"You're not here for detention, little girl," I tell her. "You're here so I can fuck you like the dirty little bitch you want me to make you."

Oh, the amazement. The horror. The fascination. The desire.

She struggles to speak. Struggles to do anything but stand and stare. I take a seat in my chair and spread my legs wide.

Clicking my fingers, I point to my lap and she's on autopilot, inching closer with tiny little paces until she's right at my feet, like this morning, but round two. A much harder one.

"You're going to give me every one of your tight little holes, you know that?" I ask her. "You won't just get one Christmas present from filthy Santa, you'll be getting three."

She nods. Even though she's nervous and shocked to all hell, she nods at me.

Her smile is intoxicating, beyond any drink I've ever had.

"Yes, please, Santa," she whispers, her voice husky. "I've been a very good girl who deserves all three."

Oh, her voice. The twinkle in her eyes.

It turns out that Lexi Dawson really has been playing out some fantasies in her mind after all.

Her panties have soaked through to her thighs already by the time I slip my fingers underneath her skirt.

Chapter Five

LEXI

My lips part in surprise.

I want him to slide his fingers over my clit and stick them inside me while I ride his palm into oblivion. I inch closer hoping to get what I want.

"Please," I beg, his knuckles skimming higher up on my thigh. He doesn't stop and I whimper, hoping he gets the hint. His thumb glides over my panties in a tantalizing way and he rewards me with a groan.

"Have you been like this all day?"

"What do you mean?"

His thumb circles over the top on my pussy then strikes a swift flick to my clit. I gasp, my hips rearing back on their own accord, delighting in the pain it caused to ricochet through me. He grabs my thigh and brings me back to him to stroke my clit again. My heartbeat rises and I gasp in pure rapture as heat zips down my spine.

"Your clit is sticking out."

Mr. Vaughn's words flame my cheeks and cause my pussy to drip.

I knew it was because I'd been horny for my teacher all day long and I couldn't do anything about it. I just didn't know he'd feel it and know why too.

Pouting my lips, I frown before I attempt to ask him a question when he says, "This pleases me. Tell me, which hole do you want me to fill first?"

Oh, man. I thought he'd never ask.

Instead of telling him, I reach between my legs and grab a hold of his wrist, guiding him to my pussy. He hisses under his breath at the wetness and cups me hard. A moan vibrates in the back of my throat and that earns me a good, hard rub on my sensitive clit. My knees weaken and they almost buckle.

"Jesus fucking Christ. Your cunt is so swollen."

Before I understand what's happening, Mr. Vaughn is dropping to his knees and dipping his head under my skirt. I hear him draw in a breath as his hands grip my hips and yank me to him. Jagged teeth scrape up the center of my pussy and a jolt goes through my pelvis. I thread my fingers through his hair, squeeze, pull his head into me.

"Oh, Mr. Vaughn," I moan and lift my knee to give him access. His tongue slips out and drags a wet trail up my pussy until he's stroking my clit with the tip of his tongue rapidly over my cotton panties. I want him to move them aside with his tongue and lick me indecently. It'd be so daring and hot. "Don't make me co– " I sigh, unable to hold back any longer and feel myself leaking down my ass. The pleasure is too good already that my body is simmering on the edge. My leg comes down on his shoulder and my other knee gives out. I'm not used to feeling like I'm soaring in the air from foreplay.

Mr. Vaughn is quick though and slides me up onto his desk he already had cleaned off before I walked in here. Hungry hands push my skirt up my waist as he takes a seat in his chair. I lift my knees and place my heels on his wooden desk, shocked this is actually happening. He leans between my legs and inhales the air like it's some type of magical potion.

"I've been dying to taste your pussy and feel you on my tongue."

My eyes go round. "You have?"

His thumbs massage my swollen lips as he stares between my legs. I can hear the wet sounds my pussy is making.

"I'd go to jail if I ever admitted how long I've wanted you."

His admission shocks me to the core. I had no idea he felt this way.

"How come you never tried to be with me before? I've lived next to you for ever. It would have been so easy."

A groan leaves his throat like he's lost in thought. Reaching inside one of his desk drawers, he holds up a pair of shiny scissors. My brows crease together and I frown, wondering what the hell he's doing.

"I've imagined unwrapping your untouched body many times..." he says, and I'm absolutely speechless. "But I had to wait until you were eighteen because I knew once I got a hold of you, that I'd want more and I wasn't going to chance that. Now hold still. I've been waiting a long time for this moment."

Swallowing thickly, Mr. Vaughn brings the scissors to my waist and cuts the elastic on my panties. He doesn't stop there. He keeps going until the cool blade is moving over my mound and toward my pussy. My lips part as a breath lodges in my throat. I don't move as he angles the blade over my slit and down my ass. He cuts the fabric at both hips and a gasp of air bursts from my throat. I watch as his blue eyes flash with lust and his nostrils flare. I have a pretty dark and full bush that I was debating on shaving and now I wish I had. It looks massive and slightly embarrassing. My knees try to pull together but he stops me.

"Hold still, I said," he bites out, and I don't move. "Spread your legs and let me get a good look."

My heart is bursting against my ribs, ready to jump from my chest at any second. Swallowing thickly, I say with a shaky voice, "I've never been so... exposed before."

His eyes flash to mine, narrowing. "What do you mean?"

"Ah, just that I've never sat in front of a guy with my legs wide open this close to his face."

Mr. Vaughn's eyes lower and a curl twists at the corners of his mouth. I feel the warmth in my belly spread. "No one has seen your pussy," he corrects. I shake my head and pull my lip in and bite down.

"No," I whisper.

"No one's licked your cunt." It's more of a statement. My cheeks are bursting with heat and I shake my head. "Have you ever had fingers inside here?" he asks, teasing my slippery entrance. My lips pout and I nod. "Whose?" he asks angrily. I like it.

"Only mine," is a whisper on my lips. "I was too shy to let anyone down there."

The dreamiest smile splays across his lips that has me glowing. He's pleased I've never let another guy touch me.

"I've only ever played with myself," *while thinking of you* I want to add. Pausing to take a breath, I admit, "I wasn't sure if I needed to shave to, so I, ah, just never went any further because I was embarrassed."

His fingers form a diamond over my pussy and he spreads my lips wide open. I gasp, on the edge of humiliation and desire. Cool air assaults me and I clench, puckering up.

"Don't you dare touch a thing. All I need to do is move the hair out of the way and a present is waiting for me... like now."

My back bows in response. His words are enough to send me over the edge. "Mr. Vaughn..."

"I can't wait to fuck you, Lexi. But first, I need to know what purity tastes like before I darken you with my touch."

A moan falls from my lips and I nearly whimper, lifting my hips to him. He chuckles under his breath and closes the distance.

His lips touch to my pussy and he sucks. I yell out, unable to control myself. I've never felt anything so good in my entire life that I weaken in seconds. My hands find his head and rub his hair, pushing his face into my needy pussy. His large hands hold my thighs down as his tongue glides along each side, up the hidden slits and down to my entrance before he's French kissing my clit like a fucking expert. I yank on his hair, feeling my

heart in my throat and take a deep breath, twisting and turning under him.

Pulling his head back until he breaks free from me, Mr. Vaughn finally comes up for air from between my legs. His mouth is glistening and there's fluid on his facial hair. But it's his eyes that pull me in. He looks downright maniacal, and it unlocks something in me.

"I want you to put your fingers in me and lick me at the same time. I've always wondered what it would feel like."

Without a word, he leans forward. I can't help it and lift my hips up to meet his thirsty lips like I'm offering myself up. I feel his thumb push against my entrance then slip inside. Suddenly I'm pumping quick and hard, eager to come as I feel the impending orgasm start in the tips of my toes. I'm on the brink of when his teeth strike my tender clit. I sigh, unable to hold back my vocals. Mr. Vaughn doesn't stop me as I thrust against his mouth like a wicked animal. A moan falls from my lips and I whimper in bliss over and over forgetting that I'm on school grounds. I'm so close and almost there when he pulls away again and a gust of cool air blankets my pussy.

Lifting my head to question him, Mr. Vaughn takes a moment to spread my legs as wide as he can to get a good view.

"I've been such a good boy this year," he says, his eyes on my pussy.

His mouth is covered with my juices now and he's breathing hard like he's about to blow in his pants when he leans in and plunges his tongue into my entrance, stroking around my virgin walls. I moan with divine pleasure, my eyes rolling shut. He uses his tongue like a spoon to scoop me out. It reminds me of someone eating soft serve ice cream.

"Oh, oh, oh…"

"The first time you come, is in my mouth," he says, then brings his hand up.

Before I know what he's doing, Mr. Vaughn slaps my clit with his palm and covers my mouth with his other hand. I yell against his palm and my hips raise and meet his mouth. He sucks my painfully hot clit between his teeth while he penetrates my entrance with two fingers. I explode in

his mouth and his lips suck tighter to my pussy as I orgasm on his tongue. Silver stars dance before my eyes. My legs come down and lock behind his neck as my body takes on a rhythm of it's own, riding his mouth with unbashful vigor while his fingers reach as deep as they can go. I can't control myself and he seems to like it by how he's, quite literally, eating me out.

"Oh, God, don't stop, don't stop, don't *ever* stop," I say, my voice taking on a husky note.

My thighs squeeze around his neck as my hips roll against his face. I hold my breath and feel the most intense orgasm ripple through me, wondering if this is what sex is going to feel like. My toes curl in absolute pleasure and liquid seeps from me but I'm drowning in the best vibrations to care.

Tapping the side of my thigh, something tells me to loosen my legs. I can't process it though and keep rubbing my pussy on his tongue, falling into the sensations his fingers are creating inside of me. I'm panting heavy and, without realizing it, another orgasm rocks through me and I'm nearly crying in tears from the pleasure.

My legs finally loosen as I come down from the best high of my life. I'm positively dripping when he lifts his head to look at me. His hair is dishevelled and his eyes are glossy. He doesn't seem like he can focus and his shirt has wet marks all over it. My brows furrow as it dawns on me that the wet spots are… from me.

"You're a squirter."

I clench my eyes. I've heard of this after watching pornos, but I've never had that happen before when I touched myself. "I didn't…" Do I say I'm sorry?

Mr. Vaughn, much to my surprise, rolls his chair closer to the desk. My fingers are still tugging on his salt and pepper hair when he sticks his tongue out and gently licks my thighs clean before moving to my sensitive pussy while I catch my breath. The sound of him slurping up anything left leaking from me echoes throughout the room. The man has no shame. Turns

out neither have I.

I release the hold on his head and sit up just as he's standing. His hand snakes out and grips my throat. I gasp just as his lips crash onto mine. His kiss bruises my mouth and I'm hungry for it. Mr. Vaughn is a dirty kisser, licking my lips, my tongue, his hot breath breathing into me, all the while commanding I follow his lead without so much as saying a word. I can taste myself on him, and it's erotic. I kiss him back just as hard and moan into his mouth. He bites my lip.

"You're a bad girl for not telling me you can squirt. Do you know what that does to my cock, Lexi? You taste so damn fine in my mouth."

His words are dark, mysterious. My eyes light up. Taking my wrist, he guides me to the center of his hips. I palm his massive bulge and my lips part in bewilderment as I stroke the tip of his dick, feeling the crown. He feels really big. Almost too big.

"You're not mad I made a mess?"

"Mad? I'm hard as a fucking rock and all I can think about is splitting you in two because I want to fuck you until you can't walk. All that gorgeous pussy did to me is make me want you even more, right now, right here, Lexi. I'm not mad, I'm turned on all to hell."

I'm still rubbing his package and getting worked up again when he presses his lips to mine and says, "Now it's my turn to come… in your mouth. Get on your knees and open up wide."

He helps me from the desk and I do as he says like a good girl, quietly and with a smile. I just hope I can make him feel as good as he made me feel.

The floor is cold and unforgiving. I undo his belt and pull the zipper down with eager fingers. His cock springs free and I marvel at the view before me. I palm him, observing his erection like he's a precious gift. He's a throbbing purple color and straining like he's in pain. Shoving his pants down further, I take hold of his tightened sack and roll his balls in my palm.

It's definitely not like the dicks I've seen in pornos, all shaved back

and skinny, raw and pink from too much unnatural sex. Mr. Vaughn has girth and length. *Hair.* He's also a man's man, and not some college kid trying to cut it. He's got a hot body that packs a punch. The meaty crown looks both intimidating yet erotic as hell. A tingle sparks between my legs and I rub my thighs together hoping for it to go away.

I look up at him and say in all honesty, "That's not going to fit inside of me. This was a mistake."

He grins, massaging my jaw to open. He watches as his thumb slips between my lips and I suck on it. He swallows thickly, his Adam's apple bobbing. He pulls his thumb out and wipes it on my cheek.

"It will fit," he tells me, "Which is why I plan to stretch you out all week, just in time for Santa to bring you your Christmas present."

He lifts a brow. Just before I take him in my mouth, I ask one more question. "Mr. Vaughn, but what does Santa want for Christmas?"

"Santa likes when his elves make it snow on Christmas morning." Still not following completely, I have another question but he cuts me off. "I'm about to come on your face if you don't start." Leaning forward, I wrap my lips around his cock and start licking him. "Suck me off good and don't let any cum slip out of your mouth or you won't get my cock again."

Chapter Six

LEO

This pretty little thing doesn't know what she's doing, but it's delicious. She's hungry for my dick and it shows in her ambition. She's trying so hard it's beautiful to see, eyes open wide as they dare to stare up at me.

Her spit strings from my cock to her mouth as she pulls away enough to retch a little. Overly ambitious. I like that. I like it enough to take hold of her sweet, soft hair and guide her back to me, thrusting my length into her mouth and giving her more.

She takes it. She takes it well.

This is some kind of detention for this horny little girl.

I hold back over and over, keeping my cum from her to make her work for it. Her eyes are watering when I jam myself to the back of her throat. She holds her breath until I pull away, controlling every gasp.

This is indeed the best kind of introduction to a hungry student. Throw them in deep, right from the beginning. They get so much further in their studies.

We are way past the detention cut off when I finally let my balls tighten and blow.

"Get ready, Lexi," I tell her, and then I shoot my load, thick and fast into her wide-open mouth.

"That's it," I say. "Show me your tongue."

She pokes the pretty little thing right out for me.

I wonder if the taste of me is everything she dreamed of. I can only imagine it's quite a shocker since it's her first time.

"Swallow," I grunt and she swallows everything.

I tell her she's a good girl with a smile on my face, gliding my thumb across her cheek like the proud teacher I am. The way she blooms with happiness is magical.

"What now?" she asks me, with a meek little voice. "Will you take me now?"

Oh, it's magnificent to see the surprise on her face when I say no.

"No?" she pushes.

"No," I say. "Not yet."

"Not yet?" She frowns.

My dick gets hard again seeing how she doesn't want to let me down. Lexi probably thought that if sucked me off good that I'd fuck her for it. Oh, she did and I wanted to. She sucked my cock like a champ, took me down to the root, like she wanted to ace her final exam. But she's not ready for me to fill her yet.

Her shoulders sag and I act quick. I don't want her to doubt herself. "Be a good girl and don't talk back to your teacher again or I'll have to give you another detention." She pauses, a blush creeping up her cheeks. "I want you to play with that pretty little clit of yours and think of me."

She lets out a giggle. "I won't be able to think of anything else but you."

Fuck, how I love to hear her say that.

She's flustered as she leaves the classroom, looking every bit the good student she is as she tugs her bag up onto her back and shoots me a shy look

over her shoulder as she opens the door.

"Thank you, sir," she says, and I smirk harder.

"You're very welcome, Lexi," I reply, proud as she closes the door behind her.

I watch her leave the school yard before pulling up the classroom blinds. Taking those tight holes of her is going to be a gem of a pleasure. I'm going to have to restrain myself not to claim the prizes all at once.

And I do manage to restrain myself… for the most part. I'm fucking human after all.

Every day after school she's had detention for talking back. She's purposely been a troublemaker in my class and it just ramps up my need for her. Of course I don't report her to the office. I crumple the paper and toss it into the garbage, keeping that little titbit to myself. That way, every day I can hold her back after classes and suck her clit until she squirts for me. I fucking love that she does it. If she doesn't, then I'll make her come again until she's ripping out my hair and begging me to stop. After school, I fuck her mouth until she gags and tears are running down her cheeks. Every day at school, I make her assure me of just how much she's thinking of me in bed at night.

Every night in my bed, I think about what a filthy man I am for doing this to one of my students, but it doesn't stop me. I want her too much for that. She's become an addiction in the best way.

The semester finishes with the students loving the looming holidays. I dismiss her early that day, but I pull her aside and give her the instructions before she leaves.

"I'm going to call your stepmother and tell her how I'm offering extra tutoring. I want you to assure her how much you need it as it accounts for a large portion of your final grade."

Lexi blinks, then her cheeks flame rosy. She knows what I'm saying. "Of course, Mr. Vaughn."

I ruffle her hair, smiling down at her before I gesture to the door.

Lexi follows through. I call her stepmother that very afternoon and she

is dismissive. She asks me if Lexi is doing poorly in her studies. I say no, just a little under par, but that I'm sure an extra bit of study with me will put her right before the new year."

"Yeah, thanks," she says, and that's all she cares.

Her lack of attention will sure make it easier to bring my plan to fruition. It's the very first morning of the holidays that I call her stepmother up on her cell.

"Please send your daughter around this afternoon," I say, and get a simple *sure* in response. Lexi was right. Her stepmom doesn't give much of a shit about her.

Lexi's knock at my front door is meek and mild. She looks divine in her sweet little skirt, trying to look like a sexy slut in a tight top, even in the cold weather. It works. She looks like the sexy little seductress that she is.

I'm right at work when she steps over the threshold and shuts the door behind her. I bundle her into my living room, making her gasp as I press my lips to hers and invade her wet little mouth with my tongue.

She loves it. She groans for more.

I give her more.

I throw her down onto my sofa and pin her hard, grinding my thumb against her needy clit through her panties. I'm not going to hold back this time. I'm about to claim my prize and give her hers, and I do it.

I tug her panties off, splay her thighs nice and wide and I say it. Palming my cock, our eyes lock. Two simple words in a voice that lets her know how serious I am.

"Take it."

I thrust inside her in one hard plunge, one that she will remember for all time, and grab her hips to steady her. She's a good girl and she takes it, crying out in little gasps as I pound into her like she claimed she wanted. She's tighter than I thought she'd be. So fucking tight that my dick is already aching to explode.

"Oh," she says, trying to cover up her pain. "Mr...." she sighs this time, unable to finish. Her thighs are quaking and her nails are digging into

my forearms.

"That's right. Keep taking all of me, you little slut. Spread your legs and give me this cunt or I'll find another whore to take my dick."

She gasps, her pussy clenching around my cock. Thank God my girl likes the dirty talk. I continue with the filth, watching her lips part further in pleasure.

My hips rear back and I drive in without shame. I make her take it hard until I let her take it slow. It's the only way I'm going to break her in right. She's wet for me as I ease up my hips and change my angle, knowing full well I'm going to find her spot. I do find it. I find the tender place deep that has her gasping to a whole different tune.

Oh yes, I've got her.

"Tell me harder," I say, and she whimpers, nervous.

Her hips answer before her mouth does.

"Harder, please..."

"Relax into it," I grunt, and she nods.

I lean back enough to circle her clit as I grind myself in. Her hairy pussy is a delight for both of us as it adds another wave of pleasure. I love it that way.

I know she's tensing up, reaching her peak, and I want to match and come inside her, but I don't dare. I can't plant my seed in that forbidden cunt.

"Come for me, you dirty bitch," I say, and she lets herself free, circling herself against me as her breaths come out sharp and fast as I pound into her. "You're a dirty, dirty bitch for watching me fuck Betty Richards from your bedroom window. But it's what you wanted, right? For me to fuck you like I fucked her? You know what happens to whores like you? They get fucked harder, deeper, longer... better." I take a moment to catch my breath before I say, "Your cunt is mine."

"Yes," she moans. "Yes, I wanted..."

She can't even finish her words, let alone make sense. It's fucking magnificent to watch her come with my cock inside her sore little hole.

I let her collapse, catching her breaths when I pull out of her. I barely give her a moment before I grab her hand and wrap her fingers around my length, thrusting myself against her.

I angle my cock across her swollen pussy and shoot my load in that bush of hair, loving how it streams and glistens. She gasps, fixated as my thick cream drips down her raw, pink cunt.

It's when I pull away further that I see the gorgeous smears of blood on her thighs. My cock jerks at the sight, hardening. It's a brilliance when she smiles at me, letting out a giggle right from her heart.

"What do you say, Lexi?"

She takes a moment to think.

"Thank you, sir," she tells me, and I know she thinks our session is over. Showing her it's not, I bend down to clean the blood from her thighs with my tongue, slurping her up. She becomes lax in seconds and I reward her with a swipe over her very tender clit.

"There's a long way to go this afternoon before you give me your thank you. Our lesson is far from over."

Chapter Seven

LEO

Far from over was right.

I spent the afternoon getting acquainted with Mr. Vaughn's cock. Once he got inside of me it was like he didn't want to leave. He couldn't control himself, grunting and biting me, all the while teaching me how to make a man feel good.

I hadn't even stepped over the threshold when he was tearing my clothes off and shoving his fat cock past my virgin barrier. He pumped his hips without remorse until he got seated where he wanted to between my thighs. I had a feeling he took me hard to prove a point, hitting the back of my cervix to rid me of pain and allow the beauty of pleasure to thrive between us.

God, I wanted to scream out in agony from how intrusive he was from the first thrust. It hurt so bad that I tore from it. Luckily, I have a vivid imagination and I've seen plenty of pornos to know what I like. All I had to do was imagine a camera up close and personal watching us have sex. I *like* seeing a cock thrust into a pussy, and I imagine I'm watching our own

porno and a warmth ignites through my belly. It didn't take long to warm up to Mr. Vaughn's animalistic ways and my pussy to surrender to his mercy.

Yes, Mr. Vaughn. He's already instructed me to not call him by his first name while I'm riding his cock.

Sir or Mr. Vaughn is the only acceptable way to address him. I made a deal and said I'd submit to his demands if he continued to degrade me.

I wish I could explain why it feels so fucking good to be called a slut while this man is deep inside my pussy, fucking me like a cave man, but it does. The way his broad back hunches over me, how his thighs press mine to the bed and his arms cage me in, makes me soaking wet. My desire drips down my ass and spreads to the bed. I swear I feel his cock swell inside of me the deeper he reaches. He treats me like a ragdoll, flipping me around and manhandling me at his will, confident I would like what he gives me in the end. He wasn't wrong. He even made me slip in and out of consciousness while he choked me.

I. Was. Hooked. On. Him.

So when my stepmom told me I had another tutoring lesson this evening after dinner, I was surprised. Mr. Vaughn hadn't said he was going to ring. It was Christmas Eve and already late. But it was my dad who said it was my last session for the year and insisted I go.

They weren't going to get an argument from me. My plan was to sneak out once they fell asleep anyway, knowing they wouldn't wake up from their drunken haze. Now I wouldn't have to, and I could give Mr. Vaughn my Christmas present without the fear of getting caught.

I ran upstairs to change my clothes and grab my studies, stuffing them into my backpack along with the special outfit I handmade to wear for him. My parents watched me walk across the lawn, waving goodbye when my teacher opened his door.

He had the door slammed shut and me slammed up against the wall with his lips pressed to mine in a matter of seconds. His scruffy beard prickled my skin as his tongue plunged into my mouth.

"I couldn't handle going another day without you," he says, breaking

the kiss. He's breathing heavy and staring me straight in the eyes. I tell him I was going sneak out to surprise him, his eyes light up. "You've already driven me fucking wild," he says. "I'm already addicted to you, Lexi."

My heart melts, taken aback by his admission. A smile splays across my face. I reward him with a slow, sensual kiss by making sure I stroke the roof of his mouth. A vibration rumbles against my chest. I'm a good student – he's taught me well to know when to take control with my tongue to set the speed. His cock hardens and a thrill runs through me. This must be what it feels like to be in command all the time. It's intoxicating… and he's letting me experience it too.

"Sir," I say, my turn to break the kiss. "I have a present for you." His baby blues twinkle under the hall light. "I need to go change into it though. Meet me in your room?"

His brows shoot up this time. He chuckles then smacks a kiss on my lips before letting me go. He bends to pick up my bag and hands it to me before standing tall. I forgot how he towers over me.

"Hurry up. Don't keep me waiting."

A grin spreads across my puffy lips. Mr. Vaughn's kisses are a mark that I willingly take. I skip away toward the bathroom and giggle as he slaps my ass.

I step into the bathroom and shut the door. It doesn't take long to slip into my present – all I'm wearing is a sheer black thong with a huge red bow sewn into the fabric right before it disappears between my cheeks. No top. No shoes. Nothing else but the panties and my hair resting in soft curls over my breasts and down my back. Glancing at the small bows I made for my nipples, I decide not to wear them and stuff them away.

Expelling a breath, I take one more look in the mirror and blink in surprise from the glow on my face. I have my teacher to thank for that.

"Lexi, come along," I hear through the door.

"You sound like you're in pain," I say, chuckling.

Turning the light off, I push the door open and step into his room. His eyes take me in, starting at my toes. Mr. Vaughn rakes a wicked glance up

my body that makes me shiver in anticipation.

"Fuck me," he says to himself and sits up when he sees me.

I giggle again. "I was hoping *you'd* fuck *me*, sir," I say then slowly spin around on my tiptoes. Our eyes meet again and he sees the truth behind them. But just in case, I tell him as I reach his spread thighs and lean in. He goes to pinch my nipple but I brush his hand away and offer him a teasing smile. His need for me fills the air between us. He's on the edge... and I like it like that.

"I wore the bow because it's my present to you. I want you to take my last hole like you said you would." I pause then say, "And I want you to do it in the jacuzzi. I want you to fuck my asshole the way you fucked my pussy. Get the pain over with. Fast, quick, no taking your time."

He flips me over onto my back on his bed and looms over me. "I don't think you know what you're asking for. It's not the same kind of pain, baby, it's going to hurt at first, much more."

I trace his lips with my tongue. He breaths out a heavy breath and I say, "Pour me a double shot of tequila then get me good and hot for you. I trust you to make me feel like I'm floating on a cloud. You always do."

His eyes gleam and it excites me. Within seconds he's got me thrown over his shoulder and carrying into the kitchen where his bar is set up. He sets me on the counter as he prepares our shots. We clink glasses and down them together before he's whisking me outside and stepping into the hot water with me in his arms.

"I have a present for you," he says surprising me. Mr. Vaughn reaches around to the other side of the tub and produces a box. I take a seat on the steps and wait with my teeth digging into my bottom lip. "I thought this would be helpful the first few times I break you in." He opens it for me and I frown.

"Why would I want a dildo if I have the real thing?"

"Because it'll help when I fuck your ass, baby. It's waterproof."

"Oh," I say, intrigued. Then I say it again, my voice heightened when I realize how he's going to use it. A blush heats my cheeks. "You're going to

fill both holes at the same time, aren't you?"

A slick grin curls the corner of his lips. "Merry Christmas. Now get that ass over here and let me untie the bow. I want my present."

Chapter Eight

LEO

The girl has no idea how rough taking my cock in her tight little asshole is going to feel, and her naivety is beautiful. I can't wait to be the one to enlighten her.

She's a sweet little mermaid in the jacuzzi, glowing like a princess, no doubt from being a part of the fantasy she's been living with for months.

"Show me that dirty little hole I'm going to be taking, then," I tell her. She gives me a little giggle before she slides over my way.

She turns her back to me and hitches her ass up onto my lap, presenting her cheeks under the bubbles. My hands find her nice and willing. I guide her to stand up, and she does, showing me that gorgeous butt of hers. I slide down her sexy thong and she lets out a gasp, nervous.

She has every reason to be nervous.

She hisses as I splay her ass cheeks as wide as they will go. Her little asshole puckers up a few times and I'm sure that I come a little in the water. Jesus, I'm so going to enjoy taking her ass.

But first, my tongue is a beast as it laps up her crack, digging its way

into her delicious little hole. I knead her ass cheeks and hold her to me as her knees give out under her. She yells out and whimpers, falling into my hands.

I don't give her much time to settle in before I wrestle her smoothly over the side of the jacuzzi. Her ass is in perfect position when I slide my thumb in nice and deep.

"Ahhh," she cries out, but she's a good girl and pushes back against me.

"That's it," I tell her. "Take it."

Like always, she takes what she's given. A thumb works up to two fingers, slowly as she groans for me, and then two fingers squirm and work up to three and Christ my cock is hard as hell as I spread that tight little hole.

I'm good with her clit, teasing just right when I need to, taking away the intensity of her ass. I use the jets to my favor and have them vibrate viciously on her clit. She's enjoying it, a panting little minx when I decide it's time to use the dildo on her. I'm gentle as I work it in, giving her the chance to work back onto it before giving her the first proper fuck that she needs.

"That's... hard..." she says to me over the hum of the water, but she doesn't stop moving. In fact, she's building up speed, her fabulous pink tits splashing in the water. She gasps, her chest rising. I'm sure she's feeling the burn now and just doesn't want to admit it.

"It will be a lot harder when it's my cock," I tell her next to her ear, and give her the dildo a little bit harder.

She doesn't protest, just shoots me a glance back over her shoulder, telling me with no uncertainty that she wants everything I have to give.

"Please, sir," she says when the dildo is fucking her nice and deep. "Please, give me you now..."

It's dark around us, Christmas Eve reaching its close. I'm still surprised that nobody gives two fucks about what she's doing from her household, but seemingly they don't. There is no sign of life next door.

She sees me looking at their house.

"They aren't even awake now," she tells me, still panting. "Once their heads hit the pillow, they're out cold until the next morning. They're just pleased I'm getting one on one tutoring. Didn't care that I wouldn't be coming in until late."

Yes. I was right. They are dickheads.

I guess I'm one, too. Fucking a student in my jacuzzi on Christmas Eve.

Reaching to the side, I turn the jet bubbles on high for maximum force.

"Get ready for it," I tell her, but I barely gave her the chance this time.

My balls are swollen hard, desperate, dick throbbing as I position myself up close. Working her up only made my cock so desperate, it won't take long for me to bust.

I take hold of her hair like a pretty little slut when I claim my prize, adoring how she tenses up just perfectly when I slide my cock right the way into that tight little asshole.

She cries out and I aim her pussy toward the jet to disguise the intrusion. It works and she cries out in sheer bliss.

It is absolutely. Fucking. Divine.

Lexi is everything I'd imagined she could be. She winces and whimpers a little, struggling with short sharp breaths, but then she shifts, and I feel it, feel her enjoying the grind.

I had a feeling Lexi would enjoy taking cock in her ass after the things she said to me the first night.

"Tell me you want more," I grunt, and she nods her head, even though I have her hair in my fist.

"MORE, please!" she squeals and I give it. I give my pretty little princess everything she wants.

I fuck her deep. Rough. Hard. I slam her tight hole with so much damn force that the water bubbles around us. She asked and I aim to deliver.

Right before I sense her release, and with just the tip of my cock in

her asshole, I ease the dildo into her tender cunt and almost come when she grits her teeth and takes the stretch with a grunt.

"Fuck," she says and it's enough to set me off.

I slide that dildo deep at the same time as I push my cock all the way home and I fuck both holes at once. The jet sputters to a different rhythm over her protruding clit and she goes off like a rocket, coming undone. It is heaven. She is heaven.

That's when I know for definite I'll never be able to let her go.

This isn't just about Christmas. This is about for ever.

"I'm going to come in your sweet ass," I tell her, leaning forward to grunt right in her ear.

"Yes, please!" she hisses. "Please!"

I pull my cock free and then slide the dildo from her puffy cunt, my balls tightening all the more at the sight of her juices dribbling from her.

"Please," she says again, "please, sir, just..."

I grab those soapy ass cheeks and her head drops as my cock nudges her asshole.

She's panting, wanting, waiting, and I can't hold back any longer, my groan matching hers as my cock plunges all the way deep.

It doesn't take long for my balls to burst, which is probably just as well considering the noises she's making. I'm a growling beast as I shoot my load inside her, my ears ringing raw with the thrill. Fuck. She sucks the seed from my balls in a way I've never known. She sucks me well and truly dry, her ass winking and spitting cum back out as I pull away, spent.

She recovers with a grin, endorphins running high. Her smile is everything to me as I hold her close and kiss her forehead, loving just how beautiful she looks in the aftermath.

"It must be Christmas Day by now," I tell her. "Happy Christmas, Lexi."

"Happy Christmas, Mr. Vaughn," she says, "And thanks for giving me the best present ever."

She lets out a sigh soon after, shifting herself away from me like she

knows she's done with her lesson.

I can see it in her face. She really thinks this was a lesson, nothing short of a cheap little fantasy from me to give her what she wanted.

She's almost out of the jacuzzi when I call her back.

"You think this is done, don't you?" I ask, and she looks nervous, embarrassed.

"Well… yeah…" she says. "I thought this was a bit of fun for you, you know?"

I do know. And she was wrong. Very wrong.

I beckon her back over with a smirk, holding my arms open wide.

"Our fun has only just started," I say when she throws herself back into my arms with a smile. "You'd better get ready for a whole world of new lessons, little girl. I'll be giving them whenever they're wanted from here on in."

Her giggle is a delight as she straddles me.

"I'm ready for my next lesson, sir," she says, reaching for my cock.

Happy fucking Christmas to us both.

The End

ABOUT JADE WEST

Jade West has increasingly little to say about herself as time goes on, other than the fact she is an author, but she's plenty happy with this. Living in imaginary realities and having a legitimate excuse for it is really all she's ever wanted.

Jade is as dirty as you'd expect from her novels, and talking smut makes her smile.

If you want to check out more of her work, here are a good couple of starters:

Sugar Daddies
Bait

ABOUT LUCIA FRANCO

Lucia Franco resides in sunny South Florida with her husband, two boys, and two adorable dogs who follow her everywhere. She was a competitive athlete for over ten years - a gymnast and cheerleader - which heavily inspired the Off Balance series.

Her novel Hush, Hush was a finalist in the 2019 Stiletto Contest hosted by Contemporary Romance Writers, a chapter of Romance Writers of America. Her novels are being translated into several languages.

When Lucia isn't writing, you can find her relaxing with her toes in the sand at a nearby beach. She runs on caffeine, scorching hot sunshine, and four hours of sleep.

Her novel can be found at all online retailers. Find out more at authorluciafranco.com.

Standalone Titles
You'll Think of Me
Hold On to Me
Hush, Hush
Say Yes

Off Balance series
Balance
Execution
Release
Twist
Dismount

Forbidden Flaws

PEPPER WINTERS

Prologue

IFE.

The privileged existence we all enjoyed.

Some squandered it. Some adored it. Others tried to destroy or hoard it. But no matter how hard we tried, we were merely passengers travelling through time.

I thought I'd built the perfect life for myself: a career I was proud of, a body I was comfortable in, and a husband who worshipped me. My life was the perfect illusion of happiness. No one saw the flaws hidden beneath the polished veneer. No one saw my heart breaking as the truth smashed through the lies. And no one was there to save me.

Life.

I almost lost mine.

But fate decided it wasn't done with me.

Fate gave me him.

Not once, but twice.

The first time, I didn't know the gift I held.

The second, I was too broken to deserve him.

Chapter One

"CRAP, WHERE IS IT? Where is it?" I screamed, tearing around my dark hotel room.

When I'd arrived six hours ago, I thought the space-ship shaped coffee table was fashionable, the thick ruffled curtains ideal, and the oversized walnut desk perfect. Now, I found them instigators to my demise.

"Dammit, where the hell—"

Beep. Beep. Beep.

The smoke alarm tore through my ears, just like it had torn through my sleep. My brain shredded with the noise.

Run, Saff. Leave it.

Common-sense told me to abandon my worldly possessions and save my life, but my heart didn't want to leave behind the eight hundred page script I'd just earned, or the freshly signed contract, solidifying my spot in an A-list movie in freaking Hollywood. They were priceless. They signified winds of change—of luck and happiness coming my way.

I won't leave them behind. I won't!

I ran blindly, wishing like hell that the lights worked. The room was pitch black, worse than a tomb or crypt because I wasn't dead yet, but might be very soon if I didn't run.

Tripping over a large slippery bag, I cried out as carpet burn singed my knees. My heart plummeted, remembering the insanely expensive, and not able to afford yet, shopping spree I'd indulged in. I'd had such fun…was it only a few hours ago? Shopping in the streets of Brisbane, spending money that I had yet to be paid, designing my new life based on recommendations by couture and *Vogue*.

Beep. Beep. Beep.

My stomach rolled. I had to stop being so stupid. None of this stuff would matter if I were dead.

Grab the laptop. Leave everything else.

Clambering to my feet, I inched as fast as possible with my arms outstretched and eyes completely useless in the dark. Where did I put it?

I fumbled over to the desk for my computer. The only thing with a lifetime of photos on it. The only thing left of my parent's smiling faces. I was such an idiot not to upload the images onto a secondary device while I had the chance.

Beep. Beep. Beep.

The shrill siren tore through my determination, sending spiders scurrying down my back.

It was too late. I had to go.

I had to leave everything behind.

I gritted my teeth and shuffled as fast as I could through the foreign room. Colliding off the wall, my fingertips followed the corners and smoothness of the perimeter, making my way as fast as possible.

Beep. Beep. Beep!

Passport!

Shit. I stopped, my heart hurling itself against my chest at a hundred miles an hour. My passport. Freshly minted and locked in the safe with my one-way ticket to Los Angeles. The hotel assured me it was the safest place

for such precious items—now, it was my worst enemy.

Just leave!

Beep. Beep. Beep.

My lungs sucked in air, panic whizzing in my blood. The superficial part of me wanted to stay, to guard everything that poised me for a better life, but instinct finally roared into being, kicking my ridiculous butt and propelling me toward the exit.

Beep. Beep. Beep!

I found the door and wrenched it wide, falling into the corridor.

I blinked. The lights were off; only the emergency exit sign cast its eerie green glow, illuminating the thick gold carpet and the gorgeous aboriginal paintings of the fourteenth floor.

There was no smoke, no flames or screams or burning.

Doesn't mean the building isn't on fire.

Trying to calm my breathing, I jogged down the corridor toward the glowing sign. My blonde hair bounced and tickled my exposed back with every step.

The closer I got, the louder the sound of pounding feet echoed in the stairwell. Glad to know it wasn't just me taking their sweet time to escape.

Beep. Beep. Beep.

God, I wanted to cover my ears—the alarm almost made my ears bleed from shrieking.

Yanking open the exit door, I darted down the first flight of uncarpeted stairs. The rough concrete stung the soles of my feet but now was not a time to be precious.

Grabbing the banister, I shot down the next flight, almost careening into a man dressed in boxers and a t-shirt.

He looked over his shoulder, his brown eyes immediately dropping to my chest.

I flushed with horror.

Oh, my God!

My underwear!

The man smirked, jogging down another few steps, never taking his eyes off my very sexy, and entirely too revealing, lingerie.

"Must say this alarm had pissed me off, but now I'm rather happy." His face crinkled in a smug grin. "Nice get-up."

Beep. Beep. Beep.

I wanted to slap him.

My arms wrapped around my breasts hidden just barely in the scantily sheer Provocateur lace that I'd purchased after my audition. The G-string was silver and black, and hid exactly nothing of the fresh Brazilian wax I'd suffered all in the name of Hollywood perfection.

Mortification painted my cheeks. "Stop looking."

Beep. Beep. Beep.

He laughed. "Shouldn't wear something like that if you don't want blokes to look." Giving me a wink, he turned away and disappeared down the stairs with a tsunami of people pouring in from the other levels.

Half-naked and fully dressed bodies swarmed around me, all descending as fast as possible.

I knew I should move, but my legs were frozen. I couldn't go outside like this!

Beep. Beep. Beep.

You're in a burning building with the smoke alarm repeating that your life is in peril. Leave, Saff, for God's sake.

Hating myself and the idiocy of my knickers, I hurled myself down the next flight of stairs. There were no drapes or upholstery to snag and hide my indecency—there was nothing left to do but run.

My toes gripped the concrete; I tried my hardest not to think of people watching my mostly naked butt.

The stairwell echoed with the mind-splintering alarm and people's urgent voices. The walls hemmed us in, closing heavier and heavier with claustrophobia.

I wanted out. I wanted fresh air and safety. Lengthening my stride, I took two steps at a time—my bare feet nimble.

Beep Be—

The alarm cut off—strangled, leaving blistering silence in its wake.

I looked up to the ceiling, expecting to see flames attacking the warning system, but there was nothing—just a pure white ceiling.

Then I was blinded as bright fluorescents switched on, drenching the non-descript stairwell and perspiring guests with light.

The intercom clicked into life.

"There is no cause for alarm. We apologise for the inconvenience. We repeat, there is no cause for alarm."

Static and crackle interrupted the speaker before continuing:

"Please, return to your rooms at your earliest convenience. There is no fire, just a faulty connection with our electrical system. We repeat, the local fire station has assured us it's a false alarm. You are encouraged to return to your rooms. We apologise again for this inconvenience."

"Inconvenience? A mad run at three fucking a.m.? That's more than a damn *inconvenience*," a man with a beer belly growled.

A woman with two snivelling children scowled. "Bloody fantastic. We have a flight in three hours. No way will I get them back to sleep."

Grumbles and curses rose from the displaced and rudely awoken guests.

My own annoyance sat heavy on my chest, but in reality, I would've preferred the mad dash than burning alive in my bed—half-naked or not.

Shuffles and footsteps changed direction, trading jogging for an angry plod back up to their rooms.

Wives stalked past with bleary-eyed husbands, their curled upper lips shouting just what they thought of my attire, while their husbands did their best not to get caught gawking.

Keeping one arm around my chest and the other pointed between my legs, I swallowed my pride and turned around, following the herd upstairs. So what—children and fat men could see my G-stringed butt. In a few months, my breasts would be broadcast on every movie screen around the world. Fellow actors would touch me in places not many people had,

producers would order me to make my 'cum face' more believable, and old high school friends would witness the full frontal that I'd agreed to do to land the role.

Embarrassment had no room in my world anymore—not if I wanted a successful career.

It's just skin.

Cocking my chin, I dropped my arms, and climbed the rest of the stairs with shaky confidence.

Chapter Two

The moment I charged through the heavy fire door and back onto my floor, I grabbed a glossy magazine—the only thing on the skinny side table—and fanned the pages against my chest while striding toward my door.

Sure, it was only skin, but I had to cultivate my confidence. Baby steps.

I couldn't expect to be the sleek, poised actress I portrayed at my audition overnight. After all, I came from a small town a few hours from Sydney. I'd been on my own for six years, since my parents died in a horrible bush fire, and used the measly life insurance to pay for a course in drama.

Every day had been a struggle.

Every day I ached for company.

And every damn day I looked at the poster of Los Angeles and vowed that I would make it.

The day my parents died, I died, too. I cut myself off from friends—

removed myself from the human race—and spent my time as a hermit. It wasn't until I realised I'd been acting impeccably when asked the question 'how are you' that my coping mechanism had given me a way to freedom. I could create a world where I'd become different characters with different problems and heartaches—I would be safe from feeling the truth.

I would be a chameleon.

Reaching my door, in the regiment of other doors, I pressed down on the handle.

I frowned as it didn't budge.

I pressed on the handle...

Shit!

Of course, it's locked. And where was the key? In the stupid switch that permitted lights to turn on—*inside* the room.

"Great," I groaned, pressing my forehead against the smooth veneer. Not only was it three a.m., but I now had to head to reception and ask for a spare key.

I peered at the magazine. Perhaps I could make a dress type thing or even a micro skirt out of its pages—would that be better than flashing my feminine charms?

At least life decided it had tormented me enough as no other guests entered the floor. I was alone. For now.

What should I do? Wait till most of the guests were back in their rooms, then make my way stealthily to the lobby? Could I use the lift, or did I have to walk the stairwell of shame again?

A small laugh escaped me. "God, this is just the beginning I needed."

My head snapped up as the emergency exit slammed open and a couple dressed in flannel pyjamas siphoned into the corridor.

Flannel. *Of course.*

Next to their buttoned up floral and striped goodie-two-shoes flannel, I looked like the hotel whore.

I pressed my back against my door, fanning out the magazine and positioning it over my breasts.

"Evening," the husband said, his eyes flickering between my gaze and my sheer knickers. His wife scowled, picking up her pace and fishing a key card from her pyjama pocket.

Damn, what I wouldn't give for a key. I had sanctuary behind me. One tiny piece of plastic had the power to end this night of horrors, but no—I had to leave it behind and grant myself more misery.

"Evening," I muttered as the couple drifted past. The wife stabbed the key into the lock, waited impatiently for the blinking green light, then disappeared into the room a few doors down. The husband shrugged, giving me an awkward smile. "Um, have a good night."

The wife reached out and jerked her man inside, slamming the door like a vicious slap in my face.

"Great," I muttered. "Everyone thinks I'm a home wrecker just for some scraps of material."

If only they knew how completely wrong they were. First impressions were always dangerous. Up until four days ago, I hadn't had a haircut in six years, worn make-up in four, and preferred baggy track pants and my father's tatty t-shirts over Victoria's Secret.

The girl people saw today was a perfectly crafted persona of a successful actress with the world at her feet. I meant to live the role so brilliantly that even I believed the lie.

But it would take time.

My nails might be buffed and my body plucked and waxed within an inch of being bald, and I might wear clothes that any respecting girl from my hometown would turn her nose up at, but it was the part I had to play.

A part I had every intention of embracing.

Spinning around, I tried my door again. Why? Who the hell knew? Maybe leprechauns had somehow granted me a reprieve.

My skin broke out in goosebumps. The hotel's air-conditioning had sprung into action, fighting imaginary fire with arctic gusts.

Keeping my grey eyes trained on the exit, I waited to see if any more stragglers would appear.

Two minutes passed.

Three minutes.

Good enough.

Flattening my arms over the magazine like a shield, I pushed off from my door and made the decision to dash. My toes sank into the plush carpet as I trotted toward the lift in my three hundred dollar underwear.

The buttons of the elevator glowed, welcoming me with every step. So close.

The emergency door opened.

Shit.

I slammed to a stop as the exit spewed forth a man dressed in a suit with lipstick marks on his white collar and pink smudges on his cheek.

Classy.

His eyebrow twitched, a smirk twisting his lips. He couldn't have been more than mid-thirties, and the wedding band on his finger hinted it might not have been his wife mauling him.

"Well, aren't you a pretty sight. If I knew a fire alarm brought out creatures like you, I would've set the thing off myself." He stopped, eyes slithering over my body.

Gritting my teeth, I turned the magazine sideways, earning a few extra inches to hide behind. Not that it helped. I either had to choose between exposing my nipples or the freshly waxed landing strip between my legs.

"Waiting for someone?" he asked, moving closer.

I backed away, plastering myself against some unfortunate person's door. If they opened it, they'd get my backside in their face. Tilting my chin to stare into his brown eyes, I nodded. "Yes, as a matter of fact."

The man looked left and right, waving a hand at the empty corridor.

Of course, it was empty *now*. Heaven forbid anyone else arrive when I actually *wanted* more eyes on me to ensure my safety.

He ran a hand through his messy black hair, smiling as if he were God's gift to women. "Want me to keep you company while you wait?"

Narrowing my grey eyes, I said, "No, I don't. How about you scurry

along to your wife…or your mistress? I'm guessing the lipstick might not be your wife's colour?" My blonde hair stuck to my nape with a sudden flush of nerves.

He froze, anger darkening his face. "Clever. But I wouldn't be so cocky if I were you." He took another step.

I stood my ground. What could he do? We were in a busy hotel with guests within screaming distance.

"Not cocky, just sleep deprived. I suggest you leave before I get mean."

He leaned closer. "I like mean."

God, he was an idiot.

"Go torment someone else. I'm not interested."

"Any woman wearing see-through underwear is guaranteed to be interested." He laughed. "Don't treat me like a fool."

"I'll treat you like a rapist and scream if you don't bugger off."

He frowned. "That's a bad word to use, pretty girl. Anyone ever tell you—"

"Back. The. Fuck. Off."

Both the creep's head and mine shot up, searching in the direction of the growled command.

My heart instantly tripped over itself; my eyes drank in a man wearing a white terrycloth dressing gown with the hotel's emblem on the front. He was tall—taller than the asshole pestering me—and towered over my dainty size. I noticed all the usual traits—grim full mouth, dominant blue eyes, and bone structure bordering on the rugged line of perfection—but it was the things I *felt* that froze me to the spot.

Something strong and eager unfurled inside me.

He wore an effortless cape of violence, cascading off his shoulders like some superhero. His bare feet were gorgeously formed and symmetrical. His hands were fisted by his sides, while every muscle stood out in preparation for a fight. Not to mention the shaggy dirty blond hair or the minor bruising on his cheekbone, turning him from roughly delectable

to dangerously unpredictable.

I clutched my magazine harder as his eyes landed on mine. Time slowed to a never-ceasing whisper as his gaze trailed from my mouth to my breasts to my stomach and swept down to my toes.

I forgot all about the creep as I remained locked in his powerful stare. He stood as if he were used to the world bowing at his feet. He moved as if he had every right to be smug and self-assured because he'd beaten life into submission and won.

I wished I had that confidence. I wanted to steal it from him. I wanted to duck under its protection.

Shit, get a grip.

Blinking, I glared at the newcomer. He glared right back, sending shivers down my spine.

"Who the fuck are you?" Creep asked, facing his newfound opponent.

The man didn't tear his blue eyes from mine; his nostrils flared as if seeing past my choice of undergarments and seeing the real me.

The real me!

In a split second, I shed everything I knew and stepped into a new role. The role of a woman who belonged to the man breathing shallowly and oozing with violence—the woman who'd been waiting for her lover in the corridor on the fourteenth floor.

"David! Damn, you took long enough." Throwing the magazine at Creep, I strode confidently and purposely toward the man I'd decided would be my ticket to freedom. He didn't blink as I threw my arms around his waist.

It was like hugging granite.

The dressing gown gave no comfort or softness to the insane strength and rigidness of masculine muscles beneath.

Damn, what did this guy do for a living?

He didn't move for an interminable second, then, as if we'd scripted and played this part all our lives, his arm came up and wrapped lovingly around my shoulders. "Lace, I told you to go back to the room." The weight

of his hold pinned my head in place, trapping my blonde hair.

I fluttered my eyelashes, looking up into his deep blue gaze, while cursing my racing heart. "I know. But then this gentleman decided to detain me."

Swallowing, I commanded my nervous system to calm the hell down. My stomach was a riot of frothy bubbles, my heart full of moth wings and palpations.

He *affected* me.

I wanted to hate him for that. But I couldn't. How could I hate someone who gave me back a smidgen of life just by existing?

His fingers dug into my arm as his embrace tightened. It wasn't romantic or protective—purely possessive and aching with the urge to harm. "Oh, did he now?" His eyes narrowed at Creep. "Care to tell me why you *detained* my woman when she clearly said she wanted nothing to do with you?"

My woman.

I'd always hated the caveman mentality of mine, yours, belonging— so why did my knees feel a little less substantial than they did three seconds ago?

Creep scowled. "Look, man. Any woman wearing shit like that attracts attention." His eyes landed on my thigh, searing into my skin like a brand. "It's a fucking invitation."

Oh, shit.

I didn't know this man I clung to—I had no idea of his temperament or morals, but I knew not to antagonise him. I was just a stranger to him, yet his entire body stiffened with undiluted rage.

"What the fuck are you implying? That every woman caught in a fire alarm wearing sexy as hell lingerie has a sign on her forehead saying 'please fucking rape me because I'm gagging for it?'"

My heart stopped beating. His voice dripped with menace and threats.

I squirmed under his heavy arm, trying to get free. The pressure of an imminent attack clouded the corridor with testosterone.

I didn't want to be the cause of anyone's pain—regardless if Creep had been a douche-bag. He was partly right, I supposed. Strutting around wearing practically nothing could be seen as inappropriate, and to those with loose convictions, an invitation.

Guilt swarmed me for causing this mess.

"David, it's fine. Just a misunderstanding." I patted my saviour's chiselled granite chest, shaking out the tingles in my fingertips from touching him.

The man never tore his attention from Creep's.

"No, Lace," he growled. "It's not. He disrespected you and any other woman wanting to wear something hot. That's not fucking okay."

My stomach tangled with my heart, turning me into a pretzel. His voice sounded as gruff and thick as any Neanderthal, but intelligence shone bright in his eyes.

Interest and fascination spread fast through my body.

Who is this man?

Creep took a step back, his hands flying up in the universal sign of surrender. "Fuck it, man. Keep the slut. I can get plenty more."

My eyes closed. *Fantastic.* There was the line, and he'd just waltzed right over it.

David's arm crushed my shoulders, moulding my form to his until I was sure I'd be forever glued—like a piece of lichen clinging to unmovable rock.

"Don't—" I said, fighting against a mouthful of dressing gown.

David didn't pay any attention. This was no longer about keeping me safe—but winning. He bristled with the urge to hurt, and Creep was his target.

"Let it go, man. You don't know who you're messing with." Creep walked backward, one hand fumbling in his pocket for a room key.

David chuckled, the baritone echoing through his chest straight into mine. "Funny, I was just going to say the same to you." He dragged me forward, stalking Creep down the corridor. "*You* don't know who *you're*

messing with."

I did.

David was a man intent on pain. A man who was an expert at delivering it.

How did I know? Instinct mainly, and the sight of bruised and scraped knuckles. He'd been in another fight this evening.

I inhaled sharply. His smell trickled up my nose, clouding my lungs with all things peril and ferocious. He smelled of soap and…was that watermelon?

I wriggled, pushing against him.

Every step of his, I took two, awkwardly skipping by his side, closer and closer to Creep. I wanted to close my eyes, but morbidly, I couldn't look away.

Creep turned sharply, stabbing his plastic key into a lock and pressing frantically on the door handle.

He wasn't fast enough.

David tapped him on the shoulder, and never letting go of me, ploughed his fist right into his face. "Don't harass another woman who says no, you fucker."

I winced as the crunch of a broken nose and the wet splatter of blood sprayed across David's dressing gown.

"Ow, you motherfucker!" Creep swung up, his eyes watering with pain. The fist swung in my direction. I squeaked, burrowing into David's chest.

The strike never connected.

The stomach curdling sound of another fist hitting home sent Creep from consciousness to dream world. He sprawled in a suit-tangled pile at David's naked feet.

Oh, my God.

"What did you do?" I breathed, looking frantically up and down the corridor. "Hotel security will have seen that. We better go."

Squirming again, I said, "Let me go."

His grip tightened, then released—his large arm draping off my shoulders, leaving me feeling tiny and cold without his immense strength and heat. "Stay."

Stay? Like a well-trained poodle?

No chance.

What other choice do you have? Stroll nonchalant to the lift and ask reception for a spare key? What if I came across Creep Number Two?

While my brain charged after useless thoughts, David stooped down, pinched the key card laying beside his unconscious victim, and inserted it smoothly and unhurriedly into the lock.

The light turned green, and he opened the door, backing in and keeping it wide with the aid of his foot.

With an effortless yank, he pulled Creep's body inside and left him in a crumbled heap.

I stared at the bloody man on the floor as the closing door hid him from view. "Don't you think we should tell someone what happened? He might need a doctor."

David didn't reply.

Instead, he checked the door was locked, then in a flash grabbed my wrist with extremely long and exceptionally powerful fingers.

"Hey!" I tugged on his hold. "Let me go."

All thoughts of thanking him for his help flew out of my mind. What the hell was he doing?

He cocked his head. "I've seen a lot of women in various states of undress this morning, but none as fine as you."

I narrowed my eyes at his messy blond hair and the five o' clock shadow bristling on his jaw. His eyes were rich—a blue that seemed depthless—like a puddle that led to hellish temptation. "I appreciate what you did for me and for playing along, but I need you to let go."

"No."

"No?" My heart bounced uselessly around in my chest. "What do you mean no?"

He scowled, striding down the corridor, further and further from my room. "I mean exactly that. No, I will not let you go."

Shit.

I looked over my shoulder, willing another Good Samaritan to appear from the emergency exit and save me. This damn underwear. Never again. I would stick to tatty t-shirts and torn shorts.

"You can't do this."

He just kept walking, carting me away as if I were a balloon drifting demurely behind him.

Slowing, he pulled a key card from his pocket and slotted it into the reader. The instant the green light flashed, I snapped. Twisting in his grip, I used the element of surprise to break away and bolt.

"Fuck," he muttered. The soft footfalls of his steps gave chase. I didn't get far.

In a second, he caught me, yanking me to a stop and clamping his large hands on my shoulders. "Stop, will you?"

Breathing hard, I struggled in his hold. "Just because you saved me from that guy, you think you can get what he was after?"

His lips pursed, leaning over me until his face was mere inches from mine. "No, I'm not a fucking cunt like he was."

I stopped breathing as ferocity rippled around him. I preferred it when that anger was directed at someone else. Taking a deep breath, I tried to stay calm. "What do you want then?"

His thumbs moved, tracing circles on my shoulders where he held me. "Do you want a truthful answer or a lie?"

I froze. What sort of response was that?

He watched me as if he could see past my smoke and mirrors. Did he sense I wished I had more of what he did? More of his confidence? His commanding control?

What does he want?

"The truth. Give me the truth."

One hand fell from my shoulders, moving upward to sweep the messy

hair that'd flopped over his forehead. His other thumb never stopped its ceaseless torment of caressing circles. "First, you can answer some of my questions. Then I'll decide if you deserve the truth."

I swallowed hard as he inched closer, his bare legs flashing beneath the wrap of his robe.

Oh, God. Was he naked under that thing?

Dropping his voice from angry to alluring, he murmured, "Where exactly were you running off to in your—I must admit—sexy as fuck underwear?" The corner of his lips twitched, showing a side I hadn't seen. A side that had the potential potency to sweep the world from under my feet and deliver me into corruption.

"Fire alarm," I breathed. Clearing my throat, I tried again. "You know—the loud shrieking noise that promised our imminent doom if we didn't flee the building?"

His lips twitched a little more. "I heard it. And I get that part." His eyes trailed from mine to my cleavage, a steely glint entering their blue depths. "What I was asking was, why are you practically naked?"

My mind went blank, eyes landing on the hotel emblem on his robe.

He followed my attention, his voice dropping to gravel. "It was hanging on the back of the bathroom door. I'm guessing every room has one." The intense interest in his gaze pinned me to the floor. "Either you didn't see it, or decided against it. In which case, that leads me to believe two things about you."

My heart stole all my energy with its over beating thrum. "Really? And what's that?"

He smiled lopsidedly. It transformed his face from scary fighter to charming seducer. "That you're either unobservant or secretly wanted men to look. Wanted to see how badly they'd react to a fucking gorgeous woman when blatantly faced with nipples as tight as yours and a pussy as inviting as the one hidden behind that ridiculous lace."

My breath caught at such crude conversation. It flowed from his mouth like aged port, reeking of time-mellowed barbarianism.

He licked his lips, running his hand expertly from my shoulder to the nape of my neck. His fingers closed around the base of my spine, keeping me in place, sending shockwaves of need right to my toes.

I'd never been held like that and never by a complete stranger. I'd never been talked to that way or watched like I was delicious prey. And I certainly never thought I'd stand by and permit it.

The urge to scream wasn't there. The instinct to run mysteriously absent. He'd tied me up with mystery and sex appeal.

When I didn't respond, he murmured, "Which is it? Innocent or temptress?" The muscles in his neck tensed as he swallowed, giving away a flicker of knowledge that his words were weapons, but I wasn't the only one turned on.

What did he hide beneath that robe? How affected was he standing so close to me with no one around and no rules to obey.

My mouth opened but no sound came out.

He tightened his hold on my neck, moving me closer until my body pressed against his. "Want to know what I think?"

I bit my lip as something hard and most definitely male pressed against my lower belly.

"I think you're completely clueless. You have no idea what you're doing, or how you look dressed like that. You're more afraid of yourself and what others think of you than how much danger you could invite being dressed like an untouchable whore."

Fire flashed through my system. "I am not a whore."

He nodded. "I know that; I've figured you out."

No, you haven't.

His eyes gleamed; a pink tongue ran over his bottom lip. "You ran from your room when the alarm woke you up, probably more focussed on your belongings rather than safety or dress code. You bolted without thinking of taking your key, and now have the dilemma of being stranded with no way of hiding and trapped by a man who has no self-control, decency, or the pretence of being a gentleman."

I should've been scared, terrified—but instead, I felt exposed and desperate for more of his insight. He read me so well. I couldn't permit that with my new world. I couldn't let others see past my projection and guess what a fraud I was.

"What gave me away?" I honestly wanted to know. For some reason, I lost the sense of danger and sought his help to hide the things I wanted to keep hidden.

His eyebrow rose. "What?"

Looking into his deep blue gaze, I said, "You were right. About everything. How did you know?"

He chuckled—the sound existed between sin and seduction. "Okay…" His fingers massaged the back of my neck, drawing me back a little to look at my breasts. "This is how I knew. You don't have storage for a key, and as perfect as your tits are, I don't see a key card stuffed between them." He smirked. "You wear uncertainty like a perfume, you move as if you're only just getting used to being a woman, and you're scared shitless of being seen."

Leaning closer, he whispered, "I smell it on you. The doubt. The lack of confidence."

My heart broke. "Really?"

Shit, everything I thought I'd achieved in the past few days came toppling down in lies. How did I land the lead role if I'd been so transparent?

His fingers released me, dropping from my neck and leaving me bereft. He nodded. "It's a gift. I sense others' weaknesses." Lowering his voice, he added, "I catalogue them, so I can use them against my opponent. No one is what they seem."

He'd shown my biggest fear. The terror that I would get to Hollywood and someone would point and expose me. That my dreams of living other characters' lives and not having to confront mine would explode in my face.

Something fierce and hot glowed in his eyes. "By the way, my name isn't David."

The switch of topics slammed me back to reality. I laughed quietly. "It was the only name I could think of at the time." Suddenly wishing for the protection of the magazine I'd thrown at Creep, I added, "My name's not Lace."

"Pity, it would've been rather convenient if it had." His gaze narrowed, temper etching his face. His voice turned husky and dark. "It suits you, though. That lacey bra is doing my fucking head in." He ran a hand through his hair again, trying to tame the mess of blond. "You can't see past your issues, but I can assure you, you have more power than you think."

Something sparked and tingled in my belly. It was beneath me to fish for compliments, but after what'd happened, I needed to hear something good.

"What power?"

He made a guttural noise in the back of his throat. "Fuck, woman. You might be naïve, but you're not stupid. Do you want me to describe the affect you and your barely usable lace is having on me, or would you rather see evidence?" His hands shot to the white belt wrapped around his hips. "After all, fair's fair. I see you. I should return the favour."

I gulped.

Oh, my God. He *was* naked under that thing.

The image of his muscular body being on display, along with the tantalising guess of whatever equipment he had between his legs, stole my breath.

Slowly, his fingers undid the knot, never taking his eyes from mine. "What's it going to be, Lace?"

"You're naked beneath that?" I didn't mean it as a question, more of a statement. I didn't need a response—it was obvious with the way the material tented out where the hardness I'd felt hung like an unsheathed sword.

"You already know the answer to that," he murmured.

Dammit, did he have to be so intoxicating? I should've fetched my

key and been cocooned in the safety of my room by now. I shouldn't be talking to a complete stranger who admitted he found me…sexy.

He finds me sexy.

He was right. That was power. Delicious power. Exhilarating power.

I drank him in—taking in the arrogant way he stood with his legs slightly apart and hands ready to pull aside his robe. Cuts marred his knuckles, intermingled with yellowing bruises, and there was a faint swelling beneath his left eye.

In the fluffy robe, he looked like a wolf in sheep's clothing. No older than late twenties, he seethed with restrained energy and savagery. The sexual glint in his blue eyes was the final touch to a man who was dangerous, capricious, and so far out of my league he might as well have fallen from the stars.

I took a stumbling step backward. "I'll take your word for it. I don't need to see."

If I do, I have no idea what sort of woman I will become.

He paused for a moment, his nostrils flaring as if sniffing my lie. Slowly, he retied the belt.

Taking a few steps backward, he leaned against the opposite wall, creating a chasm between us.

His lips pressed together as he blatantly drank me in, doing nothing to disguise the lust glowing on his face. "You haven't run from me yet, so I take that my honesty isn't freaking you out." He lowered his head, watching me from beneath his brow. "Here's another truth for you, Lace. You've got a fucking killer body. Curves in the right places—muscle where it's needed. I want to touch every inch and see if you feel as good as you look."

Shit, I was in serious trouble.

My heart gave up beating and switched to fluttering manically around my chest. I'd never been so thankful for the torturous sessions of Bikram yoga I'd been doing in preparation for my audition. I'd been living my character for months. I didn't really like the heat, let alone doing some stupid downward facing camel in a sweating room, but I did it to live

someone else's life.

The character I was to play was a traveller who owned a yoga business, hopping from country to country, training rich debutantes and billionaires. Amongst some hot scenes with sexy actors, I'd get to travel, be the lead in a romantic suspense, and get to work with the highly acclaimed director Felix Carlton.

But none of that mattered. Standing before a mountain of a man who made me wet with need and power, I didn't care about anything else.

"You're very bold," I whispered.

He crossed his arms, smiling coyly. "Not bold. Just honest. Will you be honest with me?"

Honesty. Truth. A painful path to a past I wanted nothing to do with. *Yes. No.*

Balling my hands, I nodded.

His muscles went taut; his voice quivered in the air like a visible force. "Are you turned on hearing me say things like that, or does it make you want to run?"

My chest rose as I tried to formulate my answer. He wanted honesty? What was the harm? There was no one else to hear me. We existed in the witching hour before dawn where whatever I admitted could stay in the dark and never encroach on my real life.

Straightening my spine, I said, "Yes. I like it."

"Are you wet thinking about me? Does it make you hot to know my cock is rock hard and my fingers ache to touch you?" His gaze tightened. "Be honest."

I'd never admitted to such things. But this was unique. A once-in-a-lifetime occurrence. The moment the sun rose, it would be over, and the opportunity to step into the shoes of a woman I would never have the strength to play again would leave. "Yes."

"Yes, what?"

"Yes, I'm wet. And yes, my fingers ache like yours."

He pushed off from the wall, sending my heart exploding with

pinpricks of fear and desire. "Are you seeing anyone, married?"

I had so much to say—so much to hide. A single betraying word fell from my lips. "No."

"I hoped you'd say that."

I blushed. "And you?"

"And me what?"

I gritted my teeth. "Stop playing with me. You know what I want to know."

A flash of heat filled his face. "No. I don't do relationships. We each have traumas and ghosts, Lace. I just hide mine better than everyone else."

Anticipation and impatience clogged my throat. I'd never had such overwhelming curiosity about another person before. Never truly cared to know what they hid behind their smiles or anger—too wrapped up in my own secrets to enquire.

"Do you believe in fate?" he asked.

A chill froze the twisting heat inside. I knew the answer to that. No. Definitely, no. I refused to believe fate decided to burn my parents to death, or leave me alone on my sixteenth birthday. I couldn't stomach the thought of life being so cruel.

"No," I growled.

We both flinched at the passion behind my answer. I hadn't meant to show another one of my flaws so soon. It didn't stop the lust blazing in his blue eyes, though—if anything, it amplified it. He watched me with a need so deep it was like a black hole, sucking me closer and closer to him, reaching for my light—determined to draw me into his corruption and devour me.

And I was powerless to stop it.

"Interesting answer," he whispered. Closing the distance between us, he reached up slowly—his touch hitching a few times with uncertainty. I shivered as his fingertips brushed a lock of blonde hair behind my ear. Sensations bolted through me, heating up dark recesses of my soul I'd never had the courage to explore.

"What's your name?"

My cheeks pinked as my traitorous blood heated. My core twitched, confronted with how virile and strong he was. The look in his eyes was… predatory.

"What's yours?" I deflected.

His lips quirked. "I have two. And I'll allow you to pick which one you'd like to scream out when I make you come."

Did he truly just say that?

My mouth parted.

His finger swooped beneath my chin, pressing up and closing my lips. "Two options, Lace. I'll let you choose."

Oh, God. I didn't trust myself to make the sensible decision. He was potent—an ambrosiac invitation.

My voice wavered. "What are my choices?"

He hemmed me against the wall, planting his hand by my head on the door. His body heat scalded. "Choice number one: I'll ignore my fucking hard on and be the gentleman. I'll head to the lobby to retrieve a spare key for your room. I'll save you the journey of wandering around in your underwear and bid you a good night." His eyes flashed. "The minute you step inside your room, you'll never see me again. We'll both continue our lives as if we'd never met, and after I jerk off to the fantasy of you bent over the bed and screaming my name, I'll forget all about you. We'll remain perfect strangers."

My stomach flip-flopped. All I could concentrate on was the image of him stroking himself while picturing me doing naughty things—things I truly wanted to do. What a delicious vicious circle to be trapped in.

Surrender melted my muscles, saying farewell to my good girl convictions. The sun wasn't far from claiming the night, I was on the cusp of my new life and identity—what better way to celebrate than with him? This man, who made me tingle and throb just by looking at me?

Forcing myself to speak, I said, "They won't release the key to you. The security here is over the top." I knew, because I'd paid with my credit

card with my real name: Saffron Duncan, but used my new movie role—
Lucy Larson—as my nom de plume. Why? Who the hell knew.

I didn't really care, until I had to explain to management why I wanted
to check into a room under a name I had no identification for.

"Yes, that could be a problem." His eyes crinkled as he smiled slightly.
"I could always offer you my robe, but then you'd see everything I want to
show you behind closed doors."

My cheeks pinked.

Shit, why did his voice have such an effect on me?

"Either way, Lace, you aren't going to the lobby on your own."

"Why?"

His eyes narrowed. "Why? Because I'm completely against the
thought of anyone else seeing you dressed like that. I'm jealous at the
thought of others looking at you, and I don't even know your name."

His voice dropped to a whisper, "Another truth for you, Lace. I'm one
second away from spinning you around and showing you just how fucking
tempting you are."

My skin broke out in goosebumps. "You're making me
uncomfortable," I whispered.

He sucked in a breath, visibly clawing back some of the tension
echoing in his muscles. "*I'm* making you uncomfortable? What about me?
Fuck, woman, you have no idea how hard it is to just stand here with you
looking like that."

Ignoring that and clambering for safer subjects, I murmured, "What's
my second option?"

He bent his head, his lips stopping a whisper breadth from mine. "You
allow me to help, while at the same time helping me with a little problem."
His eyes hooded, once again taking liberties of my scantily clad body.
"Come with me—to my room. You can call reception for a key. You'll be
safe from prying eyes…apart from mine. And you'll be able to return to
your belongs with no other problems."

Disappointment sat heavily. I tried to hide it but my voice rippled with

unspent need. "That's it? A phone call and safe haven while I wait for a replacement?"

The air thickened between us as his face darkened. I felt as if plummeted head first down a black chasm, falling and falling with no end or conclusion, destined never to find the bottom or truth.

He shook his head, blond tangles kissing his forehead. "No. If you take that option, a key will be delivered, but I personally guarantee you won't want to leave. You'll allow me to undress you, lick you, touch you, *fuck* you. You'll permit a perfect stranger to use you. I'll never forget about you. You'll never forget about me. We'll take everything from each other."

His hand moved, fisting my hair with slow winding fingers. "You chose option two, and you'll live the rest of your life comparing lovers to me. We'll both walk away with pieces of our souls missing, but fuck, it will be worth it."

Holding me immobile, his body pressed against mine. His knee wedged between my legs as his hand tilted my neck back, arching my spine. I trembled in his hold—completely in his control.

"Say yes," he whispered.

Words stuck to my speechless lips like silent begs.

"Say yes to the best fucking release of your life."

I sucked in shallow breaths. "A rather cocky thing to say to a woman you've only just met."

His white teeth flashed as he smiled slyly. "It's not cocky if it's the truth. And I can be honest with you."

"Why?"

"Because there's nothing to hide. No future to tarnish or past to twist. Just the present. Just *now*."

I moaned as his lips suddenly crashed against mine. The shock of his hot mouth claiming mine rendered me mute and frozen. Then life swamped me with its passionate lava cascade.

I forced myself harder against him, jerking my hair in his hold. He trapped me against the wall, smothering me with huge robe-covered

muscles. His tongue licked the seam of my lips, demanding entry.

I surrendered.

He groaned as I opened my mouth, welcoming his violent intrusion, tasting this stranger for the first time. I didn't know his name, but I did know he tasted of suffering and sex, wrapped up in the sweetness of watermelon bubble-gum.

His hand fisted harder in my hair, forcing me to open wider. His knee shot up between my legs, thrusting against my swollen and extremely needy core.

Holy hell...

Then the kiss ended, leaving me panting, flushed, and upside down in a reality I no longer knew.

"Give me an answer, before I lose my mind." His hips pulsed, forcing his hardness into my belly.

My eyes fluttered.

What are you doing?

I bit my lip, searching for an answer that would justify the craziness of what I wanted.

I'm learning to live again.

The soul-deep reply rendered me dumbstruck. I'd never acknowledged how functionary I was—how detached and mediocre my feelings had become. There were no spikes of joy or caverns of despair. No blips of laughter on a flat-line script of life.

This was my blip. My one chance to re-enter the world and live *my* life rather than hiding behind a character.

"What is it, Lace? I need to either get as far away from you as possible or drag you into my room. My control is about to fucking snap." His lips landed on the corner of my mouth, his teeth nipping with fraying restraint.

Panic took hold.

My life was planned and organised. In two days, I would leave for a career in the States. I had a one-way ticket. I'd fought for this all my life. I couldn't.....*I can't give that up.*

I shook my head. "I—"

"Stop. You were going to say yes before. I saw it." Grabbing my chin, he held me tight. "Get rid of the bullshit in your head. Life is too short. Way too fucking short not to take pleasure where you can. I'll ask you again. Yes or no?"

"I—I..."

A quick dart of pain crossed his features before he blocked his emotions. He smiled, unsuccessfully hiding the strange look of losing something precious before he'd even owned it.

The look of sudden vulnerability sent my heart winging, blowing away my panic and fanning the flames of desire.

"Ask me again," I breathed.

He stiffened. "Option one, we forget. Option two, we fuck."

Do it. Trust. Leap. Give in to spontaneous madness.

"Option two. I choose option two."

"Fucking hell." His mouth stole mine again in a passionate kiss. The back of my skull bumped into the wall from his pressure. His tongue swept into my mouth, stealing any doubts that I would regret this.

As suddenly as he'd kissed me, he released me.

Grabbing my hand, he tugged me toward his room, whisking me away from my old life, changing the whole dimension of my world.

If I had known how thoroughly he would change me, I would never have agreed.

I would never have given him my soul.

I would never have put myself on a trajectory of calamity.

Chapter Three

The moment the door shut, his fingers uncurled from around my wrist.

Rubbing the tingling sparkles from where he'd touched, I asked, "Confident I won't run?"

He smirked. "Confident I can catch you."

My stomach somersaulted. Every inch of my body strained toward his. My fingers wanted to uncover every ripped muscle and my mind wanted to tear past the impenetrable outer shell and find out just who this enigma was.

His smirk transformed into a teasing smile. "Didn't like this room before. Now I do."

His room was identical to mine, only reversed. My feet moved forward on their own accord, stalking him as he quickly grabbed a black shirt and a pair of faded blue jeans from the desk, and threw them into the open suitcase on the floor.

Sneaking a look into his belongings, I frowned. "You're an athlete?" Tank tops and workout gear filled the case, along with mesh shorts with a

large waistband with a name stitched in gold thread. I couldn't read what it said—a sock rested over the middle, obscuring it.

He grabbed the top of his case, slamming it closed. "I'm going to give you another choice."

My eyes shot to his. "What other choice?"

He prowled forward, closing the distance until his heat prickled my skin. I fought the urge to back away—it would only end up with me splayed against the wall and him pressed against me. If he touched me now, I wouldn't be held responsible for my actions.

Locks of messy blond danced over his forehead. "A choice and a promise. I promise I'll use your body like no other man before. I'll give you everything you've ever wanted from sex." Reaching up, he stroked my bottom lip with a confident thumb. "Have you ever been disappointed? Looking forward to fucking someone only for it to be a huge let down?"

My scarce romantic past shot before my eyes. There'd been Carl from school, who'd taken my virginity, Patrick, my ex-friend's brother, and a few years ago, Cameron from my drama class. I had no scale to judge, but neither man had rocked my world, nor shown me the supposed bliss of carnal joining.

"I take it from your lack of response that you're either too polite to complain about past lovers or don't have the necessary experience in which to judge."

"Stop doing that." I moved out of his reach, unnerved by his ability to read me so well.

He cocked his head. "I'm right, though." One stride and he caught me again. His hands landed on my hips, holding me firm. "I promise you, you won't be disappointed."

I couldn't control my racing heart. "Again, so cocky. How can you be so sure? How can you be so sure *I'm* not going to be a huge disappointment to *you*?" I hated to admit it, but there was no doubt in my mind he'd had more conquests than me and more of a scale in which to judge.

His eyes narrowed, filling with sapphire sex. "I know because

I haven't wanted a woman as badly as this before. It's all a matter of chemistry, not skill."

"We have chemistry?" Is that what the spitting electricity arching between us was?

"Hold up your hand," he ordered.

Biting my lip, I obeyed. My breathing was shallow as he raised his, placing his palm a centimetre from touching mine. Our hands hovered together, so close but apart. His fingers were so much longer, the span of his palm made me look positively doll-like.

I shuddered.

Something fierce and undisputed jolted from his non-existence touch to mine. It spooled through my blood like a comet, exploding into blistering shards in my core.

His chest rose and fell as his breathing lost its composure, matching mine for shallowness. "See, Lace? Chemistry." He swayed toward me, bringing more of the intensity until even my pinkie toes ached for more. "It's rare—true chemistry. That's why I couldn't let you walk away without fucking you—without indulging in something we might never find again."

My mind tripped. Was he talking about lust or love at first sight?

Don't be ridiculous.

He wasn't talking about love. He'd already warned me that this would be a one-night deal. He didn't do relationships, and well, neither did I. I would be leaving forever in forty-eight hours. He didn't factor into my new world.

My brain scrambled as I dropped my suddenly extremely warm and heavy hand. "My name isn't Lace. Don't you think we should introduce ourselves before we…"

He chuckled. The sound was positively decadent with intoxication and brutality. "I haven't finished laying out your choices, but fine…" Tilting his hand, so it changed from chemistry deliverer to handshake introduction, he said, "Pleasure to meet you…" His eyebrow rose, waiting for me to give up another part of myself.

The peace offering hung between us, slightly awkward, completely sexual. My body hummed from being so close.

I was tempted to lie—to give him my character's name—Lucy Larson. But only the truth was welcome in this strange connection. Only truth.

Slowly, I placed my hand in his. The intensity of touching him sent another full body flush through my system. I bit my lip as his fingers wrapped smoothly, imprisoning me completely. "My name is Saffron Duncan. And it's a pleasure to meet you…"

His eyes smouldered. "Cas. Cas Smith." His cocky smile dropped as he sucked in a ragged breath. "I woke up to that fucking smoke alarm thinking I'd sue for lack of sleep, but now I want to write the hotel a thank-you note for planting you in my path." His voice dropped a decibel, whispering around my nipples. "You're like every wet dream I've ever had."

I tugged my hand in shock. There was no appropriate response to that.

Rushing for a topic, I said, "You mentioned before you had two names…why?"

His fingers twitched. If I wasn't so in tune and throbbingly aware of his every motion, I would've missed the flash of wariness on his face. "The why is purely a professional hazard. The second name is Ghost."

"Ghost? Like the movie?"

He grinned, but it didn't reach his eyes. "No…like Casper the Friendly Ghost. They got it wrong on both accounts. I'm neither friendly, nor dead."

My eyes widened. "So your full name is Casper?"

He sighed, the openness in his blue eyes fading faster and faster. "No. It's not." His shoulders straightened as he gritted his teeth. "Back to the choices. However, I've just made the choice for you, so it's really more of a rule."

My heart tripped at the torn emotion in his voice. He sounded closed off—so different to the confident, cocky fighter from the corridor.

I didn't want rules. This was supposed to be spontaneous and fun—not ruined by lines we couldn't cross.

"Do we have to have rules? Can't we just enjoy this for what it is?"

He scowled. "That's why we need them—just one—to ensure tonight is exactly what we want. Pure delicious sex and nothing more."

His fingers inched from my hipbones to the small of my back, pulling me into him and pressing his erection against my stomach. "I told you we'd lose a piece of our souls. I fully intend to keep that promise, but I refuse to give up any more than that, and I don't want to steal what I don't deserve."

I couldn't keep up. This man was too intense for me—too much life, too many demands, too much of everything. Dropping my eyes, uncertainty filled me. "I don't know—"

"You already gave me your word. You're not leaving." Grabbing the back of my neck, he jerked me hard. I fell against him, my mouth parting in surprise.

He took full advantage.

His lips landed on mine, devouring my excuses and drowning out any denial that this wasn't what I wanted. Once again, the heady combination of watermelon and sin swept down my throat, twisting my heart and soul.

My clit swelled, begging for the same attention that my lucky lips received.

Cas groaned as he backed me up against the wall. His hands fumbled for my wrists, yanking them above my head and slamming them against the hard surface. His tongue danced with mine, licking and worshipping in the unique way of a male taking and giving all at once.

He corrupted me completely.

I cried out as he bit my lip, sucking the abused flesh into his mouth. My body bowed, trying to rub against his, needing friction, needing *him.*

Breaking the kiss, he rocked his hips into mine. "Fuck, you taste divine."

My wrists burned in his violent touch. I licked my lip, wincing at the tenderness from his teeth. "I could say the same about you. Watermelon?"

A smile broke through the dark intensity of his gaze. "A habit. I chew bubble-gum when I'm between fights. Gives my body something to do,

while easing the blows to my jaw."

He fingers tightened around my wrists, eyes widening.

I got the impression he hadn't meant to give me that strange but endearing piece of information.

Fights?

He did that for a living?

Kissing me again, his tongue dived into my mouth, making me drunk. With his lips pressed against mine, he breathed, "You don't get questions. You get to obey. Take my body, take my come, but don't take anything else."

My back bowed as he thrust harder against me. His lips were an aphrodisiac, his words even more so. "No guessing about who I am. No wondering about my life, my past, or trying to turn this one night into more. You do that, and I'll promise the same."

I shuddered as he kissed me deep, his tongue sweeping and dragging a moan from my chest.

Sucking my bottom lip into his mouth, he let me go with a nip. "I want your body. I don't want your mind."

Ouch.

My heart smarted with reprimand. I'd never been complimented in such a confusing way. He wanted me—never wanted another as much as he wanted me—but he wanted nothing to do with me. He only wanted a release.

Nothing more.

But that's what you want, too…isn't it?

Well…yes. His rule made perfect sense. It meant I could relax and board my plane with memories of an incredible man named Cas Smith and never think back on what could've been. Because there never could be more than what was.

But what does he hide to be terrified of simple questions?

Letting my wrists go, he stepped back. His lips glistened from kissing. "Use the phone. Call for your spare key before I drag you to bed."

He pointed at an invisible watch on his wrist. "Time, Saffron. We have a limited amount of time, and I plan on a lot of fucking."

I shivered as my name fell from his lips.

Up until now, my name had been a curse—a fairly unusual one that kids at school loved to mock. But in one moment, he'd turned it into an expensive spice—just like I was named after. Amplifying the threads of red and passion, mixing with his intoxicating voice.

Without a word, he headed toward the super king bed.

I swallowed hard, taking in the crisp white sheets as he threw himself backward, going from standing to reclining. Propping a hand behind his head, he relaxed into fluffy pillows. His dressing gown parted, revealing powerful thighs with a splattering of dark hair and the delicious shadow of what existed higher.

My belly clenched, thinking of him sleeping there, alone—only a few doors away before the fire alarm brought us together.

His eyes latched onto mine.

"Every second you stand there, you're denying yourself pleasure from my tongue."

My breath caught, gaze drinking him in. The tangled comforter was shoved to the bottom of the bed and there was a trace of blood on the pillow case.

Blood?

I frowned, moving closer to the bed. "Are you hurt?"

Surprise filled his eyes, then annoyance. Sitting upright, he followed my attention, glanced at the blood, then flipped the soiled pillow upside down. "No."

"What happened? Are you okay?"

A noise of warning rumbled in his chest. "Don't, Lace. No questions. Remember?"

I knew what I'd promised, but I couldn't stop myself from peering closer, searching for the origin of his wound. His five o' clock shadow had inched from sexy to slightly scruffy, the bruise beneath his eye was

diminishing, so what caused…

Then, I noticed.

His bottom lip was split. I hadn't felt it when he kissed me—in fact, it was mainly healed, just slightly red. "You were in a fight."

Suddenly, everything clicked into place. Just like he'd been able to read me, I saw a little of what he wouldn't say.

Bubble-gum after fights.

Something about his jaw.

"You fight—I'm guessing for a living. That's why your knuckles are a mess, and you have boxing shorts in your suitcase. You—"

"Yes. I fight." He sat up, swinging his legs over the side of the bed and spreading them the way men do. Locking his hands between his thighs, the hotel robe spread wider, granting the barest amount of discretion. "I fight. I hurt others for money. I've been doing it for a while, and I'm fucking good at it. You going to judge me, Lace?"

Lace.

It seemed my real name wasn't good enough when he was pissed at me.

Waving his hand at the door, he growled, "Go. If you're too much of a fucking princess to sleep with a guy who is good with his hands, then go. I won't stop you. It's you who'll regret walking away, though. Not me. I don't look back. Ever."

The animosity washing off him both thrilled and terrified. Beneath the strength and cocky confidence existed fractured morals and a broken sense of self-worth.

The flash of vulnerability—just like in the corridor—lashed me to the spot. I couldn't leave. But I also couldn't sleep with him. He'd already taken more than just my sex drive. If I let him use me, give me the pleasure I knew I'd feel, I didn't think I'd be strong enough to forget.

I wasn't very good at forgetting. Hell, even now I still held onto the blind belief that my parents had made it out of the fire somehow. Their remains hadn't been found—I had no closure. Hope was a never dying

enemy sitting painfully on my heart.

"I'm not leaving," I whispered.

You're not? But you just...

I shut my internal voice up. I'd come here with one goal. I wouldn't back down. *I'm not a coward.* I wanted him. I wanted to live with no regrets.

"I won't ask any more questions, and I'll leave when we're done. We'll both walk away from this as we began."

"What does that mean?" Cas asked, his voice dark.

"It means we'll stay strangers. We'll fuck as strangers. We'll part as strangers. That's what you want, isn't it?"

My heart poised mid-beat, hanging onto a small thread of hope. It smashed to dust as he nodded. "Yes. That's what I want."

"Good." Breaking eye contact, I turned for the phone on the desk.

Running my hands through my blonde hair, I cursed the appearance that'd landed me into this mess. The lingerie was one culprit, but I'd also lavished attention on my other attributes. I'd splashed out a small fortune to have golden low-lights and ash highlights put in my hair before the audition. I'd learned how to tame the thickness into soft curls—so much nicer than my mousey blonde straightness from before.

I should've thought of the consequences of looking confident when in reality I still nursed the orphaned sixteen-year-old.

Picking up the phone, I dialled one for reception.

Cas smiled, leaning back and spreading his legs on the bed again. His confident pose could be taken either as a lewd gesture or overtly sexual. I tried to ignore him but that was as impossible as ignoring an asteroid plummeting to earth.

"Reception. How may I help you?"

Cas's eyes took full advantage, latching onto my breasts. The way he ogled made the expensive underwear between my legs grow shamefully damp.

"Hello, Mr. Smith. Are you there?" the chirpy female voice prompted

in my ear.

Mr. Smith?

Ah, yes. The stranger I'd agreed to sleep with.

Tearing my eyes off him, I said, "Yes, hi. I seem to have locked myself out of my room during the fire alarm. I need another key."

"Oh, I'm sorry, this isn't Mr. Smith?"

"Do I sound like I'm a man?" My heart fluttered. "Sorry, that came out a bit rude."

The receptionist giggled. "No, ma'am, you don't. Sorry for the mix-up. Do you mind advising me of your room number, so I can confirm the necessary details?"

I hooked my hand over the mouthpiece. For some reason I didn't like the thought of spilling my privacy—now that we'd established the 'rules', it seemed like an invasion—not to me but for *him* to listen.

"Ma'am? Who is the room registered to?"

There was no way around it. "The room is under Lucy Larson."

The gentle sound of sheets rustling behind me made the hairs on the back of my neck stand up. Was he wondering why I'd given him one name but used another? Too bad. He'd lost the right to ask questions when he decided he wanted to remain clueless.

The tap-tap-tapping of computer keys came down the phone. "I'm sorry, ma'am, there is no room under that name. Is there another name perhaps?"

I slouched in the chair. They must've amended the guest name after the problem with my inability to provide identification.

I looked over my shoulder at Cas. He sat upright, curiosity blazing in his eyes. He didn't hide that he was listening.

"Ma'am? Perhaps you can come down to the lobby to confirm the correct details?"

"No, that's not possible."

There was a pause. "Um, well, we really need to confirm your identity before we can approve a new key. Are you sure you can't come—"

"The room might be under Saffron Duncan."

A soft shuffle from the bed as Cas shifted to the edge. His jaw clenched, eyes dark.

Every thought shot from my head. Damn him for being so distracting.

"And the room number?"

"1346."

I couldn't concentrate—completely obsessed by the seething sensuality of the man behind me.

I glared at Cas, who was now perched on the end of the bed, his fingers steepled in front of his lips, blue eyes narrowed and sharp.

What was his issue?

"Look, can you just send housekeeping or something with a spare?"

Silence for a moment before the woman said, "I'm afraid our housekeepers are dealing with another issue. We'll have another key coded the minute the problems have been fixed."

"Problems?"

My heart skipped, thinking my credit card had declined or something dreadful had happened. What if she saw through my façade and was about to say I would be kicked out on the street in ten minutes?

Cas inched closer, invading my personal space with his intensity.

"Our computers are down due to the electricity short that set off the fire alarm. I won't be able to use the software to key your card until it's up and running again."

I sighed heavily, looking over at Cas. His eyes were hooded, never rising from my scantily dressed hips.

"How long?" I whispered.

"I'll call you the moment it's complete. In the meantime, I'll send up some complimentary champagne and some desserts, to apologise for the inconvenience. Please let me know if there is anything else I can do."

She hung up before I could tell her exactly what I thought of the inconvenience.

Cas frowned as I put the phone back on its cradle. "What's going on?"

"Apparently you've scored some champagne and desserts, while I have to intrude on your hospitality for an indefinite period of time due to the hotel's technology being non-operational."

He chuckled. "It seems you wouldn't be able to leave even if you had second thoughts. I call that fate."

"It's not fate," I hissed.

He tilted his head. "Ah, yes. You don't like that word. Call it divine intervention, then. The universe planted you in my path and kept you at my mercy because it wants us to fuck. It's meant to be."

Holy God, every word lashed me with delectable torture. "What if they still haven't given me a key by the morning? Won't that mean I'm intruding on your life? Crossing boundaries you don't want crossed?"

He shook his head, plucking me from the chair with possessive hands. "No, Lace. It just means I get to fuck you tomorrow as well." Pressing his forehead against mine, he growled, "Now get on the bed. I'm hungry to find out just what those useless pieces of lace are hiding."

I tottered on my tiptoes as he guided me the short distance to the mattress. Every inch I travelled, nerves thickened my blood. "Wait—um, don't you have something important tomorrow? Are you working?"

Working?

He fights for a living.

His lips twisted into a coy grin. "Yes, I am *working* tomorrow." He shrugged. "I've fought on worse circumstances. Besides, nothing a can of Red Bull won't fix."

His head lowered, his teeth nipping at my throat. "Fuck, I've been hard since I saw that asshole talking to you. I'm in serious pain, Lace. I'm looking to you to save me."

Save him?

Why did I get the feeling he hid so much behind his bottomless blue eyes? So much unsaid—to anyone?

His tongue licked where his teeth had bit, sending a wash of sensitivity to my core. I swallowed, hating the power his voice had over me,

but loving it, too. My insides turned into a billowing volcano, erupting with steam and washes of hot lava.

"What do you want me to do?"

He shuddered, pulling me close. "Whatever you want to do to me."

The innuendoes in that one sentence sent the room rippling with sexual tension. I wasn't equipped to play these games.

He pulled back, lips parting. The damn robe spread even further, not just between his legs but his torso, too—showing a very well defined chest with splatterings of dark hair and muscles etched in shadow.

My heart stuttered. I should run. I should stay. I wanted to disappear. I wanted to jump him.

His fingers whispered across my cheek, drugging me better than any other substance. "I want to own every inch of you."

His mouth crashed against mine.

My God, what's happening to me?

My lips swelled beneath his, aching to be devoured. His tongue pressed hard and fast, massaging with slippery heat. Gone was the taste of watermelon, replaced with pure lust.

I melted in his arms, giving in completely. I wanted him naked. *I* wanted to be naked. I wanted to revel in being naughty just once.

Grabbing his gaping dressing gown, I panted, "Fuck me, Cas Smith. Throw me on the bed and—"

The door knocked, dispersing the magic weaving between us, slamming me back to reality.

Chapter Four

I locked myself in the bathroom.

A mirror image of my hotel room, the space was completely untouched save for the body wash bottle left on the rim of the over bath shower.

Cas chuckled through the door. "If you're running from me, you know you can't hide—*especially* after saying 'fuck me, Cas'."

Why do I let him speak to me like that?

And why do I secretly love it?

I panted, grateful for some space before I combusted. Every inch of me burned. "I'm not afraid of you," I whispered under my breath, staring at myself in the mirror. Oh, God. I looked like I'd been kissed within an inch of sanity—my expression was completely glazed with lust.

Saff, you look demented.

And wild.

Rubbing my hands over my face, I wished I still wore the makeup the movie producers had put on me. The fine micro minerals that made

my cheekbones look like sculptured blades, the soft as silk foundation that made my skin glow like honey, and the pouty pink lipstick that made me look as if I'd been adored by some sexy prince.

I must've scrubbed up pretty well because the director couldn't take his eyes off me. In his mid-thirties, Felix Carlton was said to be the next Spielberg, and the fact they'd been able to secure him for a romantic suspense was the best thing that could've happened for the production.

"You're Saffron?" he'd asked, letting himself in, unannounced, to the changing room I shared with three other prospective actresses. We'd been shortlisted from the hundred or so interviews that morning.

I stood, dressed in the aquamarine ball gown my character wore in the final scene when her lover catches her cheating on him with one of her yoga client's husbands.

Felix Carlton was one word...dashing. Straight from a Jane Austen period drama, he wore pleated grey trousers, a white shirt with no tie, and a shiny grey waistcoat. He even had a handkerchief peeking from his shirt pocket.

His dark hair was cut into a modern style with short back and sides with the strands longer on top to flop gallantly over his forehead. His face was kind, fierce, dominating, and understanding, all at once. And those eyes—the calculating brown that hadn't missed a thing in every shot, that directed with effortless skill and intelligence.

"You were really good," he'd said, coasting to my side and looking me up and down. He'd completely ignored the other actresses. "I think you'd play a murderous Lucy Larson."

I'd kept my head straight, and heart full of business. "Thank you very much, Mr. Carlton. That means a lot."

He'd smiled, showing white perfect teeth and a dimple in his strong chin. "Please, I have a feeling we'll be working a lot together. Call me Felix."

I jumped as Cas slammed a fist against the door. "Lace? You can't hide in there all night. We now have a room full of sugar and alcohol, but

I personally guarantee I'm not going to enjoy them nearly as much as I'm going to enjoy you."

I shook my head, shoving all thoughts of Felix Carlton from my mind.

Pointing a finger at my reflection, I murmured, "Don't let this ruin you. Take what he gives you and don't look for more. One-night—remember that."

Please don't let me get hurt.

Turning to leave the bathroom, I noticed another terrycloth robe hanging on the back of the door. There were no toiletries other than the hotel-supplied shampoo and body lotion, and the only sign of Cas's existence was blood on a hand towel and crimson tissues in the metal basket.

How badly had he been injured when he returned from wherever he fought? Who was there to make sure he opened his eyes and survived after losing?

I doubt he's ever lost.

The memory of the way he moved when we first met—that cold calculation of knowledge that he punched life in its face and won, sent awe filling my heart. To have that confidence...

"I'm counting to three. If I have to come in there, the first time will be for my pleasure not yours. But, hell, you might actually like that."

My stomach flipped.

His finger tapped on the door. "One..."

Shit!

Grabbing the spare robe, I shrugged into the thick comfort, and belted it against my Agent Provocateur underwear.

What are you doing, Saff?

No amount of clothing would save me—just added more of an incentive to strip me as quickly as possible.

"Two..." Cas growled.

"Thr—"

I wrenched the door open before he finished. He paused, hand raised.

His eyes fell to my hidden body, a laugh tumbling from his mouth. "Fuck, I didn't think I'd find you any hotter, but damn, woman, I think I just came."

My eyes flared. "What?"

He wrapped an arm around me, moulding me to his chest. With one hand, he grabbed mine, and with no foreplay whatsoever, wrapped my fingers around his cock. It didn't matter it remained hidden—barely—by his dressing gown, or that the material was thick and hid the silky heat of him—my core detonated with tiny sparks.

"You're trying to hide what I already know is under there. It makes me fucking hard." The agony in his voice couldn't hide behind lust. He was honestly in pain with need.

Fisting my blonde hair, he tipped my head back, forcing himself into my hand. "Like what you feel?"

His lips landed on mine before I could reply, kissing me hard, possessively—so damn thoroughly, I couldn't breathe.

He thrust into my palm.

My fingers tightened around his erection. "Yes, I do like what I feel." My voice turned breathy. "A lot."

He groaned, kissing me harder, forcing my mouth wider. I submitted to his control, moaning as his hands roamed, fingers digging into my skin.

Yanking me from the bathroom, he trapped me against the wall again. His breathing stuttered and tripped. "I like what I see—" His fingers tugged my belt, undoing it with one pull. The gown gaped, revealing the black and silver lace of my bra. "I love the shadows of your nipples through this material." His neck bent; I cried out as his mouth settled hot and fierce around the throbbing bud. His tongue swirled, drenching the bra in saliva and need.

My heart plummeted off a cliff as he pushed aside the remainder of the gown, nudging my legs apart with his knee. "And I love the glimpse of your cunt through these delicious panties." His strong fingers cupped me boldly, holding me as if I belonged to him.

Which I did, in that moment. Utterly his.

Wetness melted faster and faster. He didn't move or stroke, just held me as I trembled in his grip. "I can feel your heat. Fuck, I want to be inside you."

His lips stole mine, his head tilting to kiss so deep. I sucked in a breath, drugging myself on his flavour.

His fingers drifted sideways, inching toward the side of my G-string.

I froze, desperate for more, terrified of what was to come. I would explode. There was no other conclusion to the build-up twisting inside.

My knickers came away, eased open by his mind-numbing touch.

Just as his finger grazed bare flesh, he broke the kiss, panting, "Just so I'm not breaking any laws…how old are you?"

How *old* was I?

He expected me to remember when his finger was fractions away from claiming me?

He teased me, fluttering his touch over the entrance to my pussy. I moaned, my eyes snapping closed.

"Answer me, Lace. I'm struggling to restrain myself. The minute I drive my finger inside you, it's over. You'll be naked, and I'll be driving into you until we both combust."

"I'm—I'm—"

His finger pressed in a little, stealing my ability to stand. "What are you—twenty-one? Twenty-two?" His voice was guttural—as affected by touching me as I was.

Growling with frustration, he withdrew his finger.

Squeezing his cock, that still rested in my hand, I rushed, "Twenty-two! I'm twenty-two."

"Thank fuck."

He seized my mouth again and I screamed as his finger shot upward, driving deliciously hard inside. "Oh, *God.*"

My lips bruised, his teeth punishing the tender flesh.

"Goddammit, you're wet." His finger pulsed, rubbing the perfect spot, making me buckle and writhe.

His mouth never unglued from mine, annihilating my thoughts. His tongue dove in time with his finger, thrusting deep, retreating, then taking me all over again.

Gasping against my mouth, he muttered, "You're young enough to do something reckless— " he kissed me deep and swift "—but old enough to know the consequences."

I narrowed my eyes, fighting against the crest of pleasure. I didn't like the way he said it. "Why does that sound as if it's a threat and a challenge all in one?"

He grinned, lips wet and swollen. "Maybe it is." He kissed me again, shoving aside words in favour of taste. His proximity burned like a naked sunbeam against my already hot flesh.

"Tell me what you like." His finger curled inside, rubbing my G-spot. Spasms shot from my core and down my legs. I couldn't do anything but take what he gave.

Driving his hips into my hand, his cock swelled. "Feel what you're doing to me. Fuck, just touching you makes me want to come."

I gasped as he drove particularly hard inside. "I don't know what I like—"A moan wrenched from my lungs as he hooked his finger, pressing another one deep. The luscious feeling of being stretched sent my mind washing with white noise.

"You like that?" His teeth captured my bottom lip. "You like my fingers inside you?"

I shivered, my knees buckling. *"What are you doing to me?"*

He groaned as I rocked on his hand, seeking more from his stupefying touch. "Chemistry, Lace. It's not me. It's something that's fucking magic between us."

I'd never put much stock in lust or connection, but shit, he was right. I didn't know him. I didn't care what his favourite food or colour was. I didn't care, and I didn't *need* to care. My body was the leader in this interlude, and my mind...all it had to do was *feel*.

His lips stole mine, kissing while thrusting his cock into my hand. I

tightened my fingers around him, giving him friction. My heart clamoured in my ears as his tongue stole the rest of my sanity. I'd never been kissed like this.

Never been consumed.

He was right. When this was over, we would be walking away missing a tiny piece of us—a tear that would forever whistle in the winds of time— never to be repaired.

His thumb circled my clit while he mimicked the action with his swirling tongue. Everything he did stripped me of worries, drenching me in his enviable confidence.

Shoving aside his robe, I gasped as my hand dove between his legs and found his bare cock. It scorched my fingers, jerking with angry need.

"Fuuuck," Cas grunted, throwing his head back as I pressed a thumb against the tip and encircled the rest with eager fingers.

Power surged through me, sweat beaded between my breasts, and my mouth watered to taste him. I wanted to kneel before this unique stranger and give myself completely into his control.

Cas's eyes flashed with black desire, his messy blond hair ruffled as if it suffered an overload of electricity. His face contorted as I stroked him. "You're going to fucking kill me."

His head bowed, lips crashed, tongues danced.

We kissed.

We rocked.

We drove each other to the pinnacle of lunacy.

Then he pulled away. His cock slipped from my grip. My hand throbbed with the phantom feel of his hard heat.

I flinched as his fingers left me empty. With a gentle smirk and blazing eyes, he linked those same wet fingers with mine, pulling me from the wall.

Silently, he guided me toward the bed.

Awareness for more than just his mouth and fingers reminded me that room service had been delivered. I'd totally forgotten.

On a large tray at the foot of the bed rested two dishes covered by

silver covers. A chilled bottle of champagne perspired in a blanket of ice in a black bucket by the bedside table.

My heart couldn't calm down. How quickly my life had deviated off course. An hour ago, I was running for my life from a fire. Now, I was ruining myself with a stranger who fought for a living.

Not ruining.

Evolving.

I needed experience to draw on for the erotic scenes I would be made to play. If I could recall tonight as acting material, I would be forever hailed as the best sex-scene actress ever.

Cas leant over the tray. His robe hung open, flashing me hidden hard flesh. I shivered in anticipation as he inserted his finger into the hole of a silver cover and whipped it off.

"That looks incredible." My mouth watered at the scrumptious cheesecake with chocolate curls and raspberry coulis.

Cas looked up, his eyes dropping to my flushed body, no longer hidden by the fluffy gown. I'd let it fall from my shoulders, puddling onto the floor. I didn't need it. I was too hot. And besides, I planned on being very naked in the next five minutes.

"Looks sweet, but not as sweet as you," he murmured. With a soft smile, he removed the next cover. A three-tiered ice cream sundae with strawberry, chocolate, and vanilla and a single glazed cherry on top. He smirked. "Could have potential."

I swallowed, my body making it known that'd been hours since I'd eaten and every cell was dust thanks to the incinerating lust this man caused.

"Looks delicious."

"Probably are," Cas whispered. "However, I'm sure a mix of you and sugar would be better." Sticking a finger—the same finger that'd been inside me—he scooped up some ice cream and sucked it slowly. His eyes flashed. "Mm, I was right. Saffron and vanilla—my new favourite combination."

I stood frozen to the spot. My suddenly dry mouth hankered for some crisp champagne. He had no shame, no guile, no filter.

I loved it.

My eyes flickered to the ice bucket.

Cas noticed.

With a low chuckle, he strode forward and grabbed the neck of the bottle. With sexy eyes—fiercely intelligent and cagey, he whispered, "You want some of this?"

What will he do?

I nodded.

Coming closer, he smiled. "I think you deserve a reward. Open."

When I didn't move, he frowned. Placing a tingling hand on my shoulder, he turned me around and backed me toward the bed. With conquering pressure, he pushed me into a sitting position on the mattress.

"Open," he repeated, towering above.

He looked like a menace, a God…a demon.

My pussy clenched. Slowly, my lips fell open.

He bent to grab my hair. His fingers looped with my strands, tilting my head back. With intensity echoing off his body, he raised the ice-cold bottle of alcohol and splashed bubbles into my mouth.

I flinched as coldness trickled down my throat. Missing my lips, a path of champagne cascaded down my chin, running a swift path to my cleavage.

Cas ducked, his tongue lashing out to lap up the mess. I moaned as he followed the trail, capturing a nipple in his intoxicating mouth. I didn't need alcohol to become drunk. I already was—on him.

He stood upright, eyes burning into mine. "What do you prefer?"

"Prefer?"

His lips twitched. "Chocolate or vanilla?"

My attention darted to the ice cream sundae.

"As a rule I don't eat things that are bad for my health." He ran the tip of his finger from my bottom lip, down my sternum, over my belly, before

stopping on my core.

I gritted my teeth as he pressed against my clit, pleasure thickening my blood.

"However, I plan on eating you, and if I'm going to break rules, might as well do it thoroughly."

His finger pressed harder, sending shooting stars into my womb. I panted, "And why would eating me be bad for your health?"

He shook his head slightly as if amazed. "You already know, Lace. My tongue will never taste the same way once I've licked you, and my cock... well, that might just be ruined forever once I fuck you."

My heart catapulted around my ribcage, careening into bone. "You can't say things like that."

"Like what?"

I sat up, looking directly into his endless blue eyes. "Like that. It confuses me. I know whatever is going on with us will only last a few hours. I—I want you, but I don't want you inside my head."

Pain shadowed his eyes then disappeared. Bending over me, he kissed me fleetingly. "I'm already in your head, Lace. Just keep me out of your heart and you'll survive." Lust blanketed him again, hiding the snippets of vulnerability.

Who is *this man?*

"Time for dessert." His voice whispered into provocative darkness. "When this is over I want the bed smeared with chocolate and cream and you painted in cum and cake."

Holy shit.

My mind filled with images of him smearing me with chocolate and licking it off. I wanted that way too much.

What's happening to me?

I'd become a nymphomaniac.

The conundrum of a dirty talking fighter, coupled with flashes of whatever lurked in his soul, undid me. I'd come into his room as a knotted string. Knots upon knots all tied tight and unchangeable. But every moment

I spent with him untied each one until he forced me from string to unbound ribbon.

Still holding the bottle by its neck, he drank deeply. His throat contracted once, twice, as he gulped down chilly bubbles. His wet lips glistened in the soft lighting. "Take off your bra."

Breathing hard, I reached behind and fumbled with the clasp. It snapped open, relaxing around my chest with a sigh as if it couldn't wait to be thrown away.

Holding out his hand, he ordered, "Give it to me."

Biting my lip, I held out the bra, replacing it with my arm and hiding my nipples. Self-consciousness was a curse I couldn't avoid, no matter how wanton he made me.

His jaw clenched, but he didn't reprimand or demand I stop hiding. With hungry eyes, he looked to my knickers. "Take them off, too. Unless you'd rather I bite them off."

My core clenched at the dark promise in his voice. Slowly, I reclined on the bed, dropping my arm from my nipples.

Cas sucked in a breath, his body tensing with anticipation and need.

Hooking my fingers into the waistband and saying a silent prayer that I wouldn't regret giving myself to a stranger, I tugged them down.

The second I dropped them on the floor, Cas stumbled forward. With a look of sheer gratefulness, he collapsed to his knees before me. Placing the champagne on the floor, he grabbed my knees—one hand ice cold from the bottle, one burning hot with lust—and forced my legs wide.

"Fuck me." His eyes shot from blue to black, drenching in desire.

The way he studied me sent a trickle of wetness between my legs, now unhindered by knickers. I flushed, embarrassed to have him witness how much he turned me on.

He groaned, his teeth clamping around his bottom lip. "Christ, woman, you're fucking perfect." Tearing his eyes from my pussy, he tried to grin, but it came out as a grimace.

I knew how he felt. That pain he mentioned crippled me, too. It

throbbed in my clit. It screamed in my nipples. I wanted him to touch, not look. I wanted him to bite, not lick. And I wanted him to fuck me.

Now.

His face etched with restraint as he sat up on his knees, reaching for the ice cream sundae. Stabbing the rapidly melting ice cream with a spoon, he scooped up a blend of flavours and hovered over my pussy.

His tight smile was wicked. "I'm going to give you a reward—just for being so fucking beautiful and having the guts to give into me."

"What sort of reward?"

His tongue stuck between his lips, flat and proud, hinting at exactly what my reward would entail.

"Oops," he whispered as he turned the spoon upside down, dribbling the freezing cold ice cream onto my pussy.

I jolted, muscles tensing against the frigid pleasure-pain of ice. His hand landed on my sternum, pushing me harder against the mattress. "Don't move." His lips curled at the corners as he yanked my hips toward the edge of the bed and bent over me. "Let me feast, Lace. Let me do what I wanted to do the moment I set eyes on you."

His head dropped.

I cried out.

His tongue—shit, his tongue.

He was a wizard, a voodoo master—conjuring a lightning bolt to snap and crackle in my core. He lapped at the dripping ice cream, licking directly over my clit. Hot and *cold*. Ice and *wet*.

The combination drove me wild.

The flat pressure of his tongue and hotness of his breath dragged my soul from its tomb of grief and straight into living.

"Christ, you're better than chocolate, vanilla, or strawberry." Each word disappeared inside me as he panted and licked. His teeth grazed my clit, sending my heart rabbiting.

"Please…" *What am I begging for?*

His tongue turned harder, invoking the lightning bolt to return and

snap around my womb. That—*that* was what I was begging for.

The perfect brewing storm that would shatter me when it broke.

His fingers dug into my hips, holding me down as his mouth latched harder on my pussy. The ice cream was forgotten; his tongue went from flat to spear, driving inside me with no warning.

I arched upward, my legs fighting to scissor together to avoid the visceral overload. But I couldn't. His wide shoulders wedged me open, while his hands kept me spread on the bed. Another thrust of his tongue, his nose inhaling deep. The wet noise as he ate both me and dessert twisted my mind into something dirty and wrong.

I left the realm of sanity, spiralling straight into desire.

"Cas—please!"

Breathing hard, he stopped licking. With jerky muscles, he pinched a piece of cheesecake between his fingers. Climbing over my body, his cock brushed tantalizing against my hip. The wetness of pre-cum smeared my skin; I'd never wanted anyone as desperately as I wanted him.

"Eat it," he ordered, his face tight and dark.

Opening my mouth, I obeyed. I moaned as richness touched my tongue, sending sugar racing through my already overloaded system.

Cas looked at the remaining sweet on his fingers. With a glint in his eyes, he pressed them against my throat, smearing the deliciousness down my cleavage.

The moment he'd painted me, he swooped down to lick it off.

Hot saliva turned cold as he blew on the glistening trail he created. I shivered, my nipples peaking to pebbles.

With a shaky arm, I reached for the closest dish. Using my forefinger, I scooped up a piece of cheesecake, bringing the dessert to Cas.

He paused as I presented my finger.

"Eat," I whispered.

The room thickened with passion and obedience as his lips parted and I gently placed the decadence on his tongue.

He groaned, sucking my finger deep and hard until blood sparked

in the tip. I squirmed, completely turned on by his swirling tongue and supreme dominance.

Shrugging out of the robe, he tossed it to the ground. "Don't think we need that." He twisted to gather more sugar but paused. With a heavy sigh, he scooted off the bed, heading to his suitcase.

My mouth fell open seeing his naked form for the first time. His feet weren't the only perfect thing about him. His calves were well defined, his quads wide and firm, his ass was narrow and concave, showing no body fat, while his back rippled with too many muscles to count. The planes of strength cushioned his spine and the messy blond on his head made him seem wild and completely untameable.

Reaching into his suitcase, he pulled free a foil packet and spun to face me.

Holy mother of all that's holy.

My mouth hung open. "Wow."

He shifted on the spot, incredibly suffering a bit of what I did— shyness. His stomach was a playground of muscles, his chest broad and chiselled like rock. His shoulders might've been too wide if it weren't for the almost elegantly sculptured arms. No tattoos, completely bare and virgin skin.

His eyes glowed. "If you're hungry, Lace, go for the cheesecake."

I wanted to laugh, but I couldn't. My lungs were empty as I sat gawking at his cock. It hung majestically between his legs. Too big and long to stand fully even though it was rock hard.

For the first time in my life, I found that part of a man attractive. It wasn't something that could be called beautiful—but Cas Smith was. Undeniably.

Sitting up on my knees, I opened my arms. "Come here."

He smirked, crossing the small distance to stand just out of touching distance. "I take it you don't want the cheesecake?" His voice wobbled between lust and uncertainty.

What in the hell did he have to be uncertain about?

"You were right. I'm completely ruined for other lovers." Sitting taller, I boldly grabbed his cock.

His jaw clenched as I fisted him, thrilling at the way his body locked down and fists curled.

"Chemistry, Lace. Just chemistry."

I shook my head. "No. Not just chemistry. I'll fight to forget about you the minute this is over, but you'll live forever in my dreams."

He pressed closer, allowing my hand to trace the length of him until I cupped his balls. His head fell back as a groan tore from his mouth. "Dreams? Pity that isn't somewhere accessible."

I worked him with both hands, stroking and squeezing all at once. "Why?" I breathed.

His eyes flashed dangerously. "Because I'd find you and fuck you every night."

My heart froze.

Just the hint of being able to see him again enticed me way too much. We hadn't even slept together, yet, but promises and rules of a one-night stand seemed to be shredding fast.

"You're getting greedy," I murmured, squeezing hard until he almost collapsed to his knees. I adored having such power of this massive, dangerous fighter. One touch and he was mine.

Fisting my hair, he jerked me from my knees to almost standing on the mattress. His mouth crashed on mine, his tongue stealing my protests. "Fuck, how are you doing this?" His mouth worked harder, kissing me frantic then slow, then erotic, then brutal. "What the hell is happening to me?"

I shuddered as he pressed his hard cock against my belly, toppling me backward onto the bed. I cried out as he scooped up more sticky cheesecake, letting it fall into my belly button. My stomach heaved as my breathing galloped out of control. His teeth captured my taut flesh, biting down until fear laced with desire at the thought of him marking me.

Then he let go, sucking up the cheesecake and swirling his tongue in

my navel. The pull resonated directly with my core; I bucked beneath him.
Shit!

I didn't think I could stand too much more of this. My body was boneless, existing with lightning and the roiling storm clouds he conjured.

Pushing his large shoulders, he understood what I wanted and flopped onto his back. The bed shuddered with his muscular weight, his hair flopping over one eye.

Tenderness filled me and I brushed it away, cupping his cheek. He froze, his nostrils flaring, as I bent over and kissed him.

It was the first time I'd kissed him, and I relished in it. I took my time, waltzing my tongue with his, faster and faster until my lips stung with rawness. His hips twitched unconsciously, never stopping their relentless pursuit of more.

Lying beside him, I grabbed the champagne bottle from the floor and drank. The crisp alcohol did nothing to steady my nerves, only made my inhibitions fade faster.

"I want some," Cas growled, his eyes fixated on my throat and the residual smear of chocolate between my breasts.

Wiggling closer, I tipped the bottle just like he had, splashing too much into his mouth. My stomach flipped, my heart erupting in a sunrise as he chuckled and pulled my head to his. "Lick me, Lace. How dare you get me wet."

"Lick you here?" My tongue flicked over his five o'clock shadow, capturing wayward droplets.

He moaned. "More."

"How about here?"

His throat elongated as his head dug into the pillow, giving me complete access to his neck. I didn't wait for another invitation.

Grabbing the spoon he'd used to cover me in ice cream, I scooped up vanilla—my favourite—and hovered it over his cock.

His eyes remained closed as my fingers twisted his nipples. My lips trailed down his stomach.

With a flick of my wrist, the melting goodness covered his shaft.

He jolted upright. "Fuck!"

Throwing my legs over his quads, I shoved him back down again. "Fair's fair in war."

His eyes blazed. "Nothing's fair in the act of love, Lace." His large hands landed on my hips tensing to throw me off.

I gripped him with my thighs. "This isn't love. This is…what was that word you used?"

He smirked. "Chemistry?"

"Yes, that's it. What's fair in chemistry?"

His jaw tensed. "Fair is taking everything and giving all in return. Fair is fucking destroying each other."

Taking his wrists, I plucked his fingers from my hips and in the boldest move of my life, brought them up to wrap in my hair.

His eyes flared as I leaned forward, scooting down his body until my mouth hovered above the melting ice cream and his throbbing cock.

His fingers fisted, tugging on my strands. "Who the fuck are you?" he murmured, his breathing shallow and uneven.

Curling my tongue, I licked up the entire length of him, tasting musk, man, and vanilla.

"Christ!" His body seized, stomach rippling. I pitied his opponents when faced with such a mountain of masculinity. Nothing could beat him. Not even life itself.

"I'm nobody. Just a girl you found in a hotel corridor."

My scalp smarted as he shoved my face into his crotch. I didn't care— in fact, I revelled in his vicious need. "You're more than that but you're driving me mad. Suck me. Fucking suck."

With pleasure.

Opening my mouth, I fitted my lips over him.

Shit, he burned. Beneath the coldness of the ice cream, he smouldered.

His cock jerked the second my tongue swept over the head. His hands tightened in my hair, tugging and making my eyes water.

Sliding further down, I drank his taste.

My soul became drenched in his flavour as I licked away salty pre-cum; my mouth watered at the sweetness of vanilla ice cream. His skin was silky and priceless satin—living stone twitching to fill me.

My jaw ached as I bobbed up and down, but Cas kept my head locked between his legs. I couldn't look up, I couldn't see. But I knew the longer I sucked him, the more he unravelled.

His hips matched my rhythm, driving up as I sank down, fucking my mouth possessively. He didn't try to choke me. He didn't drive past my gag reflex. He took what I gave and nothing more.

Finally, his hands tugged on my hair, yanking my head up.

My eyes watered, and my tongue was numb from granting him pleasure. His fingers drifted to grip beneath my arms, hauling me up his chest. The moment our slippery, sticky bodies sandwiched together, we shivered. His cock had its own heartbeat, thrumming against my lower belly—so damn close to filling me.

"I want more than just tonight," he growled. He swallowed, panic fireballing in his eyes before being devoured by endless blue.

His confession sent my heart ablaze. I couldn't speak.

Shoving me off him, he sat up. As if he'd never uttered the previous words, he growled, "I need you hard and fast, Lace. Tell me if that's going to be a problem."

I shook my head. "No. I want that, too."

"Good. Get on all fours."

Scrambling in my haste, I did as he asked, looking over my shoulder at the powerful man behind me. With shaking hands, he tore open the condom wrapper and sheathed it over his extremely large cock.

My legs trembled. A body-clenching wave swept through me. I worried for my pussy. I worried for my mind staying in one piece when he finally made me come. I worried about so many things.

Grabbing the champagne from where I'd placed it on the bedside table, he swigged it, then rested it by his thigh.

With a cold smile, he positioned himself between my legs, nudging my soaking entrance with his overheated cock.

We both groaned at the tantalizing friction.

"Fuck."

"I need you." I moaned, arching my back, forcing my hips against him.

He tapped my ass. "So impatient."

I screamed as a waterfall of chilled champagne upended on my back. The second the coldness hit my burning skin, his cock no longer nudged my entrance but buried itself inside me.

Oh, God. Oh, *God.*

Too many reactions. Too many sensations.

It felt so good.

It felt so *wrong.*

I sobbed with delirium as he bent over me, turning the cold champagne into a blanket of bubbling heat. His mouth sucked up puddles dancing on my spine as his hips pressed harder, driving deeper in a satisfying glide.

"Cas...shit. More...give me more." My voice failed as he obeyed, thrusting deeper, filling me completely and truly with every inch of him.

The moment my body claimed his, he began to move. His knees moved closer, his hands gripped tighter. "God, you're responsive."

I moaned as he withdrew and thrust, again and again. I gripped the sheets, trying to anchor myself against pleasure.

The storm in my soul grew, swirling with wind and sonnets.

"Yes," I moaned as he reached forward, flicking my clit. My head lolled forward as I gave into his magic.

His fingers bit into my hips, pulling me back, thrust after thrust. His hip bones bruised my ass with every pound.

I lost myself to the rhythm of being taken. I gave up everything.

Nothing else existed—not the sounds of him fucking me or our out of control breathing. Only his body deep inside mine.

"God, I can't stop it. I can't—"His cock swelled, stretching me even further as his pace turned crazed with need.

Every stroke drove me to the pinnacle, up and up, clouds and clouds. The thunder of his groans added to the crash of lightning in my soul.

"Come. Make me come!" I begged. My mouth parted as twisting spindling pressure built in my core. I needed to combust. I wanted to let go.

"Come, Lace. Fucking come while I fuck you."

His filthy words stripped me of power, shoving me headfirst into the storm.

I couldn't hold on any longer.

I came.

The skies opened and torrents of rain drowned me as my orgasm crested and exploded. I had no umbrella, no safety net as I was washed away by the brightest, demanding release I'd ever had.

Cas bellowed, his pace turning wild as he gave himself to my rhythmic milking, following me into paradise. His cock spurted with every thrust, his body spasming with every clench.

On and on he fucked me. His thrusts fierce and jerky as his body drained completely.

He made a delicious noise between a satisfied grunt and agonised groan as the last band of his orgasm left him dry.

His hips still pressed in a never-ending rock, but it was blissfully gentle after savage taking.

I shuddered as he ran a gentle hand down my spine, scattering droplets of champagne. My hair was damp, my skin covered in sex—I could barely remember my own name.

But him.

I remembered everything about him. I would remember until the end of time. Stamped on my soul for eternity.

Falling to his side, Cas took me with him. His cock remained deep inside. I knew I should move, the condom needed to be thrown away, and a shower was definitely in order, but I never wanted to wriggle from his

embrace.

Words seemed to be an archaic way of communicating while our bodies spoke and soothed.

I sighed deeply, hushed and protected in his arms.

The phone rang, shattering our post-sex glow, reminding us that life was still there and we weren't untouchable in our perfect dream-world.

Cas groaned, reaching behind him to pick up the receiver by the bed. Somehow, he still managed to keep his cock inside me. "What?"

Silence.

"Okay. I'll tell her."

He hung up.

Snuggling into the pillow created by his arm, I murmured, "My key is ready?"

He took a while to answer, his breathing soft and warm on the nape of my neck. "Yes."

My heart hurt at the desolation in his tone. "Do you want me to go?"

His arms tightened before he forced himself to relax. "Do you want to go?"

I stifled my smile, loving how this big scary man had changed. He'd softened and lost the edge of anger, from either being intimate or still inside me—he throbbed with tenderness rather than aggression.

"No."

He let out a soft breath. "Good. I don't want you to go either." Pulling me tighter against his chest, he murmured, "I know what I said—about not wanting to know you. But, perhaps I don't have to forget you so soon… this…it's different."

"More than just chemistry?"

He sighed. "I don't know. But I want…"

When he didn't continue, I murmured, "Want?"

"I want you to stay. Spend the day with me tomorrow. Come and watch me fight."

My heart leapt. I nodded without thinking. "I'd love to."

"Good." Tension ebbed from his muscles and almost as if a switch turned off in his brain, he went instantly to sleep.

My heart glowed while every inch of me burned from sexual use. My lips were sore, my body sticky and sweat-dewed. But I couldn't remember a time when I'd been happier in six years.

I lay there in his embrace, very aware of his cock growing flaccid inside me.

What had just happened between us?

Did this happen to everyone who met their perfect other? Did you just *know*? Or was it merely a crazy infatuation between two lonely people who looked for more than what existed?

I didn't know, but I wanted to find out more than anything.

My heart plummeted.

More than anything?

More than a career I'd fought for? A new life that I needed?

Fear cannonballed through my system.

I looked at the curtains, noticing for the first time a sliver of light as the sun welcomed the dawn.

You're leaving tomorrow.

Forever.

My heart shrivelled into cinders.

I'd forgotten.

Somehow, this singular man had made me forget. Made me forget my grief, my goals, my dreams—all in one night of passion.

How had I *forgotten*?

My skin went ice cold.

His power over me was too strong. His allure far too dangerous.

He could ruin my future. Ruin everything I'd run so blindly toward.

I couldn't stay.

I couldn't spend the day with him tomorrow.

I had to follow my dreams.

I have to leave Cas Smith behind.

That was the first time fate put him in my path.

But not the last.

Cas was right about one thing—he'd stolen a piece of me that night—a part I would never get back; something that would forever belong to him, binding us forever.

So I ran.

Did I choose the right path?

Did I follow the right dream?

I thought I had at the time.

But in the end, the truth came out, revealing the road I'd chosen—the one glittering with fame and fortune—was the wrong one.

I chose the road covered in filth and deception.

I chose the path filled with treachery and treason.

And by doing so, I made sure I would never deserve the one person who could've saved me.

But fate wasn't done with us.

Cas wasn't done with me.

Love would ensure we'd end up together, somehow.

The End

ABOUT PEPPER WINTERS

Pepper Winters is a NYT and USA Today International Bestseller. She wears many roles. Some of them include writer, reader, sometimes wife. She loves dark, taboo stories that twist with your head. The more tortured the hero, the better, and she constantly thinks up ways to break and fix her characters. Oh, and sex... her books have sex.

She loves to travel and has an amazing, fabulous hubby who puts up with her love affair with her book boyfriends. She's also honoured to wear the IndieReader Badge for being a Top 10 Indie Bestsellers, best BDSM series voted by the SmutClub, and recently signed a two book deal with Grand Central. Her books are currently being translated into numerous languages and will be in bookstores in the near future.

To be the first to know of upcoming releases, please join Pepper's Newsletter (she promises never to spam or annoy you.)

Pepper's Newsletter

Or follow her on her website
pepperwinters.com

You can stalk her here:

She loves mail of any kind: pepperwinters@gmail.com

WOULD YOU LIKE REGULAR FREE BOOKS?

Sign up to my Newsletter and receive exclusive content, deleted scenes, and freebies.

OTHER BOOKS AVAILABLE FROM PEPPER WINTERS

FREE BOOKS
Debt Inheritance (Indebted Series #1)
Tears of Tess (Monsters in the Dark #1)
Pennies (Dollar Series #1)

BOOKS IN KINDLE UNLIMITED
Destroyed (Standalone)

Goddess Isles Series
Once a Myth
Twice a Wish
Third a Kiss
Fourth a Lie
Fifth a Fury
Sully's Fantasy
Jinx's Fantasy

Dollar Series
Pennies
Dollars
Hundreds
Thousands
Millions

Truth & Lies Duet
Crown of Lies
Throne of Truth

Pure Corruption Duet
Ruin & Rule

Sin & Suffer

Indebted Series
Debt Inheritance
First Debt
Second Debt
Third Debt
Fourth Debt
Final Debt
Indebted Epilogue

Monsters in the Dark Trilogy
Tears of Tess
Quintessentially Q
Twisted Together
Je Suis a Toi

Standalones
Destroyed
Unseen Messages
Can't Touch This

With this Ring

NATASHA KNIGHT

A PREVIEW

Prologue

SCARLETT

The lace veil falls across my face. It's yellowed over the years and the smell that clings to it is musty. Old. But it's my mother's. The one she wore on her wedding day.

Baby's breath and discarded lilies litter the stone floor as the woman grumbles behind me. She's annoyed at having to work with the old veil when a brand new, prettier one sits unused in its box. I move my foot, crush the delicate baby's breath, impaling the fallen petal of a pale pink lily with my heel.

Funeral flowers for a wedding. An omen.

Not that I need one.

The stink of them turns my stomach. This isn't how I imagined my wedding day.

"Finished," the woman announces.

I stand, the petal sticking to my heel. I don't care. I look up to meet my reflection in the mirror.

"He won't like the veil," she says. She's a blur beside me.

I shift my gaze, letting my eyes focus on her. She's plump and short and has a wart on the side of her face with a thick black hair growing out of it. Don't judge a book by its cover has nothing on this one. She is as much a bitch inside as she looks on the outside.

"I guess he'll have to get over it."

"You should wear the one he sent."

I don't bother to answer her, although I agree. The veil was a gift from my brothers.

Gift.

No, not a gift.

Just another cruelty to make me wear my mother's veil for this sham wedding.

She snorts, turns to gather up the dress, the keys jangling on her belt. I could take them. Overpower her. That part would be easy. It's the men with the guns outside the door who'd be the problem.

Noisy footsteps on the hundred stairs announce the approach of soldiers to my tower room.

A tower. They locked me in a fucking tower. My own fucking brothers.

From the sound of things, they're expecting me to put up a fight. They'll take me kicking and screaming if I do. Besides, I know better than to waste my energy on them. I'll need it after. For the wedding night.

A man says something, another one laughs, just before I hear a loud crash, like something smashing hard against the wall.

It's then that it happens. Gunfire explodes just beyond my room. A bullet splinters its way through the thick wooden door and shatters the mirror, breaking my reflection into a thousand pieces, sending me backward into the stone wall.

The woman with the wart screams.

I right myself. Touching the back of my head with one hand, I somehow still to keep hold of the lilies. Suddenly, the door is kicked in, banging against the wall as heavily armed men in military fatigues raid

my room. A cloud of smoke follows behind them, seeping into my circular tower.

They fan out, a dozen of them and I don't recognize a single one. These aren't my brothers' men.

The woman is on the floor blubbering something, sobbing.

I just stare at the door as another set of footsteps approach, quieter now. This one isn't in a hurry. And I know the instant he steps into my line of vision that he's in charge.

He's the one to worry about. The only one who's masked.

He stops just inside the room, surveys it, eyeing every soldier, every stone, every cobweb. And when deep blue eyes land on me, a weight drops in my belly, a hundred-pound cement block.

The woman with the keys stands, tripping over her words as she walks toward him. He looks down at her like he's irritated, and she doesn't get far. An echo of bullets shuts her down, splattering blood like paint on my neck, my face. The shots put her back on the floor.

Fuck.

I don't spare her a glance. I don't need to, to know she's dead.

The man's eyes return to mine. They narrow. And when he takes a step toward me, I take one back, knocking the chair behind me to the floor, panicking then. Animated then.

I turn to run but see a dozen sets of eyes staring back at me. The masked intruder, the biggest of them all, blocks the only exit. I can't even jump from the window. They're barred. Suicide was never an option, not for my brothers. They needed me.

But something's gone wrong.

And before I can decide what to do, before I can make up my mind to try to charge him, to risk bullets putting me down like they did the woman on the floor, he's got my wrist in his right hand and he's squeezing it.

My hand opens. Flowers scatter to the floor. I watch them, then watch him lift my hand to his face. His thumb comes to my ring finger where the hideous diamond catches the waning sun. For a moment I think he's going

to break my finger. But he twists and forces it off. It's tight but he manages. He pockets the ring then shifts his gaze to mine again.

I swallow hard.

He cocks his head to the side, one hand still locked around my wrist. He spins me around.

I scream as he jerks me to him, his body a solid wall at my back.

He releases my wrist and bands his arm beneath my breasts. With the other, he pushes the veil off my neck, his hand rough against my skin, fingers digging, bruising. I think he's going to snap my neck. One quick twist is all it would take. He's a fucking giant.

But he doesn't.

Instead, the moment I turn my face up to his, he squeezes and instantly, my knees give out. My arms drop uselessly to my sides. He shifts his grip and as I slip, he lifts me up, hauling me over his shoulder, turning the room upside down before it goes black.

Chapter One

SCARLETT

I feel like I'm going to vomit. The smell is musty and damp, like an old basement. Cold is seeping into my body, making my muscles ache.

"Get up!"

Pain in my right side. I curl away from it, but it comes again. I groan.

"Fucking get the fuck up!" It's Diego. My brother. You'd think I'd know the feel of his boot by now.

"That's not going to help," another voice says.

Angel. My other brother. The slightly less insane one.

"There's no way out," he adds, voice oddly resigned.

"There's a window," Diego says before digging the toe of his boot into my ribs. "Up you fucking worthless piece of—"

"Leave her alone, you idiot."

I blink my eyes open, roll my head and stop instantly, the pain sharp at the back. I bring my hand up to touch the spot, feeling the bump as I try to remember.

Lilies and baby's breath on the floor. Shattered shards of the mirror crunching underfoot as I ran. Or thought about running before he grabbed me.

I look at my hand. The ring is gone. He pocketed it. I'm glad. My wedding day. My forced wedding. It never happened.

I push myself slowly up to a seated position. The musty smell, it's not only the room. It's the veil somehow still on my head.

The room spins and I close my eyes until the dizziness passes. When I open them again, a dark shadow looms over me. Leers down at me.

Diego.

"About fucking time."

I look past him to see Angel sitting across the room, his back against the far wall. Noah's head is on his lap.

"Hurry up, untie me," Diego says. He's been beaten. His lip is cut and there's blood and numerous bruises on his face. He crouches down with his back to me.

I see that Noah's hands are bound and Angel's must be too. They're behind him. I'm the only one they left unbound.

The white satin of my dress is smudged with dirt and blood, the hem black and the skirt ripped. I reach up to pull the lace off my head, the sound of hairpins dropping to the ground too delicate in this dungeon room. That's what this is. A cell in a dungeon. With three stone walls, the fourth a wall of bars. The window my brother mentioned is about the size of a shoebox and too high to reach. That's where the light is coming from. A too-bright square in the otherwise darkness. Daylight. I've been passed out since last night?

I wonder where we are. In the cellar of the compound where I was first imprisoned in the tower? I prefer the tower.

"What the fuck is wrong with you?" Diego barks, spittle landing on my face as he cranes his neck. I'm sure if his hands weren't tied, he'd have slapped me a dozen times by now.

I meet his dark, hateful eyes.

Without a word, I reach to untie him. Ever obedient. Christ. What the fuck is wrong with me?

I look over at Angel. He's younger than Diego by a year. He looks sad, and like I heard in his voice, resigned. He's also got bruises along his jaw and dried blood by his nose, but his face isn't as bad as Diego's.

"Is Noah okay?" I ask. Noah, our youngest brother, is still passed out.

"Yeah," Angel says, looking down at him.

"Not for long if you don't get these fucking ropes off me," Diego interjects.

I look at the knot, shift my gaze back to Angel.

"What's going on?" I ask.

"We were betrayed."

"Marcus?" My would-be husband?

He shakes his head.

"Lover-boy is gone," Diego tells me. "Ran away like the fucking coward he is."

"He's not my lover-boy. I hate him."

"Well, that makes two of us. Move." He gestures to the knot.

I'm about to focus my attention on it, when I hear the sound of a door clanging open nearby. Light falls into the space outside the cell. Heavy footsteps follow and I hear a man's voice. Another one that I recognize. One that makes my skin crawl.

"Fuck," Diego mutters, awkwardly getting to his feet as the men come into view.

Soldiers enter first, automatic weapons on their shoulders. Three of them, one carrying a heavy-duty flashlight. They insert a key into the lock and open the door of our cage just as my uncle comes into view. He's grinning like a fucking jackal.

His eyes fall on me first, skim over me. It would make my skin crawl if I wasn't so afraid. His gaze bounces off each of my brothers. He's clean-shaven, hair neatly combed back slick with gel. I can smell his signature overuse of cologne from here.

"Fucking traitor," Diego mutters and spits in his general direction. It doesn't touch him though.

My uncle looks at him, his lips turning down in disapproval. "Isn't that what we all are?"

More footsteps.

I look beyond my uncle as he steps aside. Two more soldiers, another man I know isn't a soldier just from the casual slant to his stance.

And then him. The one in charge. He's no longer masked but I know it's him. I'd recognize his eyes anywhere. I will never forget those eyes or the way they looked at me.

He stops just inside the cell, big frame taking up the whole of the entry, sucking up more than his share of oxygen.

My heart races at the sight of him.

The man I know isn't a soldier slides his hands into his pockets. He leans toward the one in charge and says something too low for me to hear. He's speaking Italian from what I can make out. I'd have known these weren't Cartel men anywhere. He's wearing a white button down and jeans. Casual beside the suited man who took my ring and somehow knocked me out.

The suited one scans the cell, taking in each of my brothers in turn and it takes all I have not to shrink away when his gaze fixes on me.

Instinctively, I touch my neck as I take in his head of dark hair, the shadow of a beard. The scar along his right cheek does nothing to take away from his features. The opposite. He's dangerous, this man. Deadly. I'd know it even if I saw him out on a normal day in the normal world.

Not that I've ever lived a normal life in a normal world.

And even though I don't know who he is, my brothers do. I see it in their eyes. Feel it in the anxiety coming off them, their fear stinking up the room.

"Look who's risen from the dead," Diego starts, taking a step toward the man like the idiot he is.

The man's lip curls upward, and it takes the most minute gesture of his

head to have a soldier on my brother, pushing him roughly to his knees.

The man's eyes shift to me again as if he's curious. He holds my gaze momentarily before scanning Angel and Noah, who is still passed out. What did they do to him?

"The boy," he says. They're the first words I hear from his mouth. His voice is deep and low. Quiet, but without a doubt, in control. I get the feeling he doesn't waste words.

A soldier moves toward Noah, boots loud, echoing. I wonder how vast the darkness beyond our little cell is. In the distance I see glimpses of light. Windows like the one in our cell, I guess.

"He's breathing," Angel tells the soldier when the man bends to check if Noah's alive, I'm guessing.

The soldier checks for himself, straightens and nods to the one in charge. He looks different out of his camo. Deadlier. His hair is a little wet. I guess he took the time to shower.

He nods to the soldier, shifts his gaze to me once more before turning to my uncle.

"Get it done," he tells him.

Jacob, my uncle, nods and reaches behind him to where he must have had his pistol all along.

"What's happening?" I cry out, a new panic taking hold of me even though guns aren't new to me. I live in a world of violence. It's my inheritance. It will be my legacy. I am the princess at the heart of it. Or I was when my father was alive. Since his murder I've become a pawn.

I pull my legs back, readying to stand. I'm barefoot, I realize. I must have lost my shoes in transit.

All the men turn to me.

I only look at the one in charge. He appears taller than before but that's because I'm still on the ground. He steps toward me. I scramble backward, my hand falling on the rusting metal frame of a cot. I pull myself up to stand, willing the nausea to subside. Willing my fear to.

I realize I still have my mother's veil in one hand. It's bloody too.

Probably from the woman his men killed in the tower.

He stops when he's only a few feet from me. He's taller now than he appeared in the tower room. I've lost the four inches my shoes gave me. I have to crane my neck to look up at him and my gaze moves from his deep blue eyes, to the scar on his cheek, to his mouth, his neck. Another scar there. The edge of one. It disappears beneath the collar of his shirt.

This man has been through war.

"Kneel, Scarlett," my uncle calls out from behind him. "Show some fucking respect."

I shift my gaze from that scar on his neck back up to his eyes. Someone chuckles at my uncle's command.

The man's gaze skims my face, then down. I follow it, see how the blood had splattered over the torn bodice of my dress, too. I don't know why I'm surprised.

I reach to put my hand over it and cover myself.

"Do you know who I am?" he asks in the same quiet tone he used to tell his soldier to check on Noah.

My gaze snaps back up to his. I don't know him. I've never seen him before in my life. I study him, shift my gaze to the other one who's watching me, hands still in his pockets, but nothing. I shake my head.

"Grigori," he says.

Grigori?

That isn't right. They're dead. The whole family massacred.

I swallow, feeling the blood drain from my face. Because I know what we did to him. To them.

He smiles at that like he sees inside my head. Sees what I'm thinking.

"Say my name," he commands.

Grigori. That's their family name. My brothers attacked them after turning on my father.

"Say it."

I swallow, lick my lips.

He waits patiently. But if he's alive, he's had time to learn patience.

It's been ten years.

Grigori. I do the math. He must be in his late twenties. I glance to the other one. See the resemblance. He's younger though.

"Grigori," I try out the name. "Cristiano Grigori."

I don't know how he hears me. My voice is barely above a whisper, but he gives the faintest smile and a slight bow of his head.

"Scarlett De La Cruz." His gaze shifts down to the swell of my breasts above the ruined gown. "All grown up. Shame you have to die."

My mouth goes dry. I'm speechless as he closes his hand over my shoulder, his grip slightly less painful than it was earlier as he forces me to my knees.

He leans down, brings his mouth to my ear.

I'm caught off guard by the tickle of the scruff on his jaw.

"Don't look," he warns, and I know what's coming. I know I'll have to look.

He walks away from me. I watch him from my place on the hard ground. He stands before my brothers as my uncle gives the order for Angel to be made to kneel beside Diego.

I can see their faces from here. See how when Cristiano crouches down in front of Diego, a dark patch blooms on the insides of Diego's trousers. My brother pisses himself. My all powerful, ruthless brother pisses himself.

I would laugh but it would be insane when we're all about to die.

Cristiano doesn't miss the expanding dark spot.

In my periphery I see Noah just starting to move. Will they kill him too? He's a kid.

"Where is Rinaldi?" Cristiano asks.

"How the fuck should I know? That mother fucker set us up. He's the one who orchestrated—"

"That's not what I asked you, is it? Do you know where he is?"

"Fuck no, you think I'd take the fall—"

"Then you're of no use to me," Cristiano says and straightens. He

steps back and gives a nod. Just a nod. And my uncle points the gun between Diego's eyes and pulls the trigger. It's so fast, no hesitation, no time for Diego to beg. No time for me to even process, though I knew it was coming.

The sound reverberates off the walls. Why don't they use a silencer? Blood and pieces of my brother's brains splatter across the wall, and my face.

I wince, wipe it away, but I don't scream. And I don't look away. I watch instead. Watch Diego as his body twitches, still kneeling as if not realizing he's dead, before finally dropping to the floor with a thud.

I don't feel a thing. Not an ounce of emotion.

We're all monsters, the De La Cruz family.

When I shift my gaze from my dead brother, I find Cristiano watching me, that curious expression on his face again.

Angel is looking at Diego motionless on the floor, half of Diego's head missing. He's next. He knows it. I know it. And he begins to whimper as Cristiano takes hold of his hair and forces him to look him in the eyes, while my uncle prepares the next shot.

"Where is he?" Cristiano asks. Same question.

Angel drags his gaze from Diego. He's shaking. My two brothers, both cowards when they're outgunned and outmanned.

I only wish it lasted longer. They deserve to suffer. Doesn't he know that? Doesn't he want that?

"Where. Is. Rinaldi?" Cristiano asks again. It'll be the last time he asks. I know it.

Angel glances sideways to Diego momentarily before shifting his gaze back to Cristiano, then to my uncle. He's trembling now. He used to laugh at me when I trembled.

"Please," he begs.

Cristiano releases him with a disgusted expression on his face and steps back. I guess he doesn't want to get his nice suit dirty. That alone is the signal my uncle needs to pull the trigger again, killing his other nephew.

His godson, this one.

He's never been much of a family man, but I didn't realize he was a killer. Although I'm not surprised.

Cristiano's eyes fall on Noah who is sitting up now, looking dazed, shocked. His head is probably spinning like mine was, jarred awake to witness this scene. This massacre of what remains of his family.

"Bring the boy," Cristiano commands. Two soldiers move as if it would take them both to lift my fifteen-year-old tall but scrawny baby brother.

"No!" I'm on all fours then, scrambling toward Noah, the wedding dress slowing me down.

In my periphery I see my uncle raise his gun and aim at me. Then I see Cristiano's hand close over his forearm and point the gun down.

Would he have shot me? God. Would he have shot me, too?

I throw myself between Noah and the soldiers, spread my arms out Christ-like. "No!"

One comes to shove me out of the way, but Cristiano makes a sound. A tsk. The man stops, steps backward. They're like dogs, his soldiers. Well-trained dogs.

Cristiano moves toward me, my uncle on his heels.

"He's a boy!" I scream, pushing my back into Noah in my attempt to shield him.

"Boys grow up to become men."

"Please. He's only fifteen. He was five when it happened. Five."

My uncle cocks the gun, drawing all my attention.

"Look at me," Cristiano says.

I blink.

"Me. Look at *me*." He steps fully between my uncle and me, so I'm forced to. "How old were you?"

"What?"

"You. How old were you?"

I'm confused. I open my mouth, see my uncle's impatient face move

611

into view beyond Cristiano's shoulder.

"Twelve," I say to Cristiano, forcing myself to block my uncle out.

"One of my brothers was twelve. The other eleven."

"We didn't...Noah and I..." I shake my head, panicked as I see Angel and Diego's bodies. Unable to block them out. "We weren't part of that."

"Hmm. But you would marry that Rinaldi bastard?"

"What?" It takes me a moment to process. "You think I had a choice?"

His response is a grunt but it's something.

"Did you notice the fucking door you broke down was locked? That I was *locked in*?"

"The boy," he says calmly to his solder, opposite my frantic tone. He holds my gaze as he speaks.

"No!" I'm on my feet and lunging for the soldier in the blink of an eye, fingers like claws, nails digging into flesh. But big hands grab me from behind and peel me off.

Cristiano turns me to face him and I get one good scratch down his face before he can stop me. He mutters a curse as he twists my arms behind my back, gripping both wrists in one hand. With the other, he fists a handful of hair half in-half out of the twist the woman had just painstakingly pinned my mother's veil into. He forces my head backward making me look up at him.

"Please. Not him," I plead, tears finally coming. "Please."

He studies me, eyes narrowing.

"He's a boy. Just a boy," I try.

"Like I said, boys grow up to become men."

He releases me and gestures to my uncle with a nod. My uncle moves. Noah's up on his feet, back pressed to the wall.

I drop to my knees at Cristiano's feet, hugging his legs as he's half-turned away. "Please. God. Please don't kill him. Please!"

The gun is cocked. The echo is deafening. It's surreal what's happening and all I can think is, we're all going to die. He's going to kill us all.

But when I look up, I find Cristiano staring down at me with a look I can't quite name. Disbelief? Curiosity? Confusion?

I open my mouth to beg again. "I'll do anything. Anything you want. Just please—" my voice breaks.

My uncle mutters something, some sound of annoyance as he steps forward.

"Stop," Cristiano says.

I stare up at Cristiano.

He lays his hand on my head and I feel a glimmer of hope.

"Cristiano," my uncle starts after a moment of silence. I can hear irritation in his voice. "You need to kill them both. Like you said, boys grow to be men and she's a liability. Bear in mind, they didn't spare your mother."

I see from here how Cristiano's jaw clenches. How the hand at his side fists. He turns his head slowly toward my uncle.

"Maybe I should kill you too, then. Just to be sure." His words are a whisper. A hiss. The threat is unmistakable.

Someone chuckles. It's the casually dressed man. The sound is so out of place. When I look at him, he meets my eyes. Inside, I see hate. He hates me. Probably hates all of us.

I turn back to the two before me and see my uncle's throat work as he swallows. It dawns on me. He's afraid of Cristiano.

But hell, who wouldn't be?

Cristiano shifts his attention back to me and he does something strange. Unexpected. He rubs the bump on the back of my head like he's just noticing it.

When I stagger to my feet, he lets me. I go to my brother and take his hand.

My little brother is crying. My gentle brother. He was born into the wrong family. How Diego would have taunted him for his tears.

I look at Diego's body. See how that dark stain on his pants is bigger. He pissed himself in fear. And he got better than he deserved.

When I look back at Cristiano, he's watching me.

"Clean this up, Jacob," he tells my uncle then moves toward the exit. "Get them off my island."

Island? Where the fuck are we?

"I don't want their bodies on my land," Cristiano finishes.

He stops before exiting and turns to glance at me once more. Then, directs his attention to a soldier. "Put the boy under guard in another cell and bring the girl."

My uncle follows him to the door, grabs his arm to stop him. "This isn't what we said. What we agreed."

Cristiano stops, looks down at where my uncle is touching him. Looks back at his face.

My uncle lowers his gaze, drops his hand and moves back.

Cristiano steps toward him, his body, his whole being a threat. "You do as I say. Period."

My uncle nods.

Cristiano turns his back on him.

"Bring the girl," he barks at the soldier and walks away.

Chapter Two

CRISTIANO

Fucking Jacob De La Cruz is a piece of shit. A petty, opportunistic piece of shit.

The girl is arguing something, but I don't stop to listen. I don't care. They'll figure it out. She's safe, for now. So is the kid.

"Are you going soft, Brother?" Dante asks me.

I don't dignify the question with a response. He knows better. Or he should, at least.

I strip off my jacket, toss it aside when I walk into the main part of the house. I've only been back a few times since my return from the dead. Couldn't take a chance on being seen. Not before I interrupted that wedding.

Dust cloths are still strewn over most of the furniture and I stop to glance at the pieces that have been uncovered. At the paintings of my family. Another of my ancestors. The ancestors are easier to look at. I didn't know them. They don't mean much to me. But I move to the one of my mother. My father commissioned it when they got engaged. Or so I'm told.

I look up at her blue eyes. I inherited them but that's where the physical similarity ends.

Her blonde hair only one of my brothers and my sister inherited. They're all dead now apart from Dante.

The blood of the De La Cruz brothers crusts on my skin as I stare at the painting, undoing my tie, willing myself to remember.

Bear in mind, they didn't spare your mother.

And therein lies the problem. I don't remember. I don't remember a fucking thing. My own mother and looking at this painting she's a stranger to me.

"Is it done?" Charlie asks. He's talking to Dante. Dante is the reasonable one. I'm a fucking walking disaster.

"The girl and the kid are still alive," Dante mutters, obviously annoyed by the fact.

I force the anger I feel at not remembering down into my gut, to a place I can manage it. Barely. I move past the painting, through the living room toward the dining room. I stop between the pillars that hold up the vaulted ceiling.

"Are you okay?" Charlie asks when I don't speak.

Charlie Lombardi, an attorney with a penchant for uncovering details most want to keep hidden, was a friend to both of my parents and a man my father trusted.

I nod, take in the large windows, some still devoid of glass that let in the sun.

"Diego and Angel De La Cruz are dead," I say.

He studies me. I'm sure he wants to know why they're not all dead.

"Good," he says.

"You should have killed them all. Finished it," Dante says.

I turn to my younger brother. Just one year between us. Every time I look at him, I think how grateful I am that he's not dead. That he wasn't here when it happened.

"I'll finish it my way. In my time. This is up to me. Not you."

Dante snorts. "I'm going to get something to eat." He disappears into the kitchen.

Charlie gestures to the men working at the windows. "This project will be finished today, I'm told. You sure you want to be here?"

"It's where I belong."

The house has been in my family for generations. The bigger windows are an addition my father made at my mother's request. It was too dark for her otherwise. Even here, in southern Italy on her own island, she needed more sunlight.

My uncle told me that. Said she always hated the dark. Got depressed in winter and on the rare rainy summer days.

And so, my father had the windows made bigger, but he fucked up. Sealed our fate. Gave his enemies an easy target because the bullet proof glass that was to be put in wasn't. Another betrayal.

I killed them too. The pigs who sold him that glass.

I will kill every mother fucker who betrayed us. Who had a hand in my family's massacre.

"We'll meet representatives from the families tomorrow. Everything is arranged," Charlie says.

"How did they take the news?" The news that the Grigori family wasn't wiped out as Marcus Rinaldi would have you believe. That they missed two sons. The ones who will avenge the murders of our family.

Charlie smiles wide. "They're thrilled the Cartel is out of the picture and that you've returned to take your rightful place," he says, the note of sarcasm in his tone subtle but unmistakable.

"I bet."

"We know the two who sided with Rinaldi. We still have the majority of support on our side."

I nod, walk toward the stairs. "They're either with me or against me. There will be no middle. Not this time."

He doesn't reply. But this is where my father went wrong. This is where he made the mistakes that cost my family their lives.

"I'm going to change. Are you staying for dinner?" I ask.

He checks his watch. "No, not tonight. I'm meeting with a few people."

"All right. I'll see you soon."

I head upstairs and walk into the master bedroom. It's one of the few rooms that's ready. I toss my tie aside, unbutton my shirt and tug it out of my slacks. I look down at it. Even on black, blood shows. Luckily it was never my favorite suit.

There's a knock on the door and I turn to watch a soldier manhandle the girl into the room.

Scarlett De Le Cruz.

Only daughter of Manuel De La Cruz.

Her uncle is right. I should kill her. But there's something about her that's got me curious and I can't quite put my finger on it.

I look her over. Even in the bloody, destroyed wedding dress, she's gorgeous. A fuck should take care of it. Sink my cock into her warm pussy and then I'll be over my curiosity. Be rid of her.

"Fucking brute," she mutters, stumbling when the soldier releases her. He did have a pretty firm grip but I'm sure it was because she asked for it. She seems like a woman who'd ask for it.

He looks at me, waits for my nod, then goes. He'll be outside. Not that I need him to manage her. I can handle Scarlett De La Cruz with one hand tied behind my back.

We study each other and for a moment, I see her on her knees at my feet again begging me to spare her brother. Not a word about herself.

She's out of breath from the haul up the stairs or from her fight with the soldier. Not very smart if she wasted her energy on that.

I continue to strip off my clothes, undoing my cuffs and two buttons on the front before pulling it off over my head. I follow her eyes as they take me in, her eyebrows knitting together momentarily, forehead wrinkling. Not sure if it's at that tattoos or the scars, but either way I stand there and let her have a good look. While she does, I do the same. I

study her because there's something in those honey-colored eyes I don't understand. Something that goes against everything I have learned is true.

But fuck that shit.

Pretty girls are a dime a dozen. There's nothing special about this one. She makes my dick hard. That's all I have to worry about.

"Take off your dress," I tell her.

Her eyes narrow and she cocks her head to the side. She's petulant. A pain in the ass.

But a nagging voice tells me there's more than those things. It'd be simple if she were just those things. And I know exactly what it is. She's loyal. A trait not easily come by in my line of work. She humiliated herself, threw herself at my feet to save her brother.

It's too bad she's loyal to the wrong side.

"Are you hard of hearing?" I ask.

She just glares.

I gesture to the gown. "It's dirty. You're covered in blood and brains. Not to mention it's fucking ugly. I don't want you to dirty my things."

Her eyebrows rise on her forehead. "You don't want me to dirty your things?"

"Correct."

"I want my veil. Your goon wouldn't let me get my veil before he dragged me out of there."

I snort at that, take off my shoes and socks, undo my belt and pants. I turn and walk toward the bathroom, stopping at the door to look back at her momentarily.

"I thought you were forced to marry Rinaldi. Isn't that what you said? Or was it a lie to save your neck? So why in hell would you want any remembrance of the supposedly forced nuptials I interrupted."

Her gaze drops to the unzipped crotch of my pants and she's not quick enough to turn her head away as she clears her throat.

I was right. Just a dirty girl thinking dirty thoughts. Good. Dirty is good.

"It has nothing to do with him. The veil is my mother's." She stops, gives a shake of her head. "It *was* my mother's. And I want it back."

I watch her face. Watch her try to mask her emotions. "She's been dead a long time. Why would it matter?"

"You don't forget people you love. Unless you're some kind of monster, of course."

Her words hit their mark.

I grit my teeth.

She doesn't know. She's just throwing words at me. Just words. She lost her mother weeks before I lost mine. Parents killed by those two assholes lying with half their faces blown off downstairs.

I turn into the bathroom and strip off the rest of my things, then switch on the shower and step under the flow.

"Hey!" She's at the door.

I look at her.

She glances down then quickly away as her neck and cheeks flush with embarrassment.

"I want my veil. I mean it."

"I haven't even decided how long you'll live yet, and you want a stupid veil from a wedding you were forced into?"

"I told you, it belonged to my mother."

"It's got your brothers' brains all over it. Ruined. Like the dress. Get it off and get in the shower." I switch off the water and step out, grabbing a towel to wipe my face, very aware how red her face has turned. "Please tell me you've seen a dick before."

"Fuck you."

I give her a smile I don't feel in my eyes. "I will. As soon as you've got that shit cleaned off you."

Her mouth falls open.

I wrap the towel around my hips and when I move toward her, she scurries back. Passing her, I walk into my closet, pull on briefs and choose another suit. I hear the bedroom door open then close. I'm sure that's

Scarlett thinking she can just walk out of here. I chuckle as I step into the slacks and slide my arms into a button-down.

When I return to the bedroom, she's just walking back into it.

"You looked," I say, dropping the suit jacket over the back of a chair as I button up my shirt.

"What? I'm not looking at you." Her face gets that pink hue again as she folds her arms across her chest and makes a point of not looking at me for all of a second.

"I mean you watched your uncle kill your brothers. You knew what was coming and you watched."

Her eyes darken to a deep caramel and suddenly, I'm taken back. Caught off guard.

Burnt sugar. The smell from the kitchen. Mom standing over the pot, swirling it. Smiling. We're standing beside her, watching in awe as she makes caramel.

I give a shake of my head. The image is gone as quickly as it came—a split second of memory. It leaves a void in its place and has me wondering if it's truly a memory or something I was told.

Focus.

Scarlett grits her teeth, jaw tensing.

"Why did you look?" I ask.

"Is my brother going to be okay?"

"Why?"

"Because he's my brother."

I walk toward her, and she backs up until the backs of her legs hit my bed. I catch her before she falls onto it, straighten her, taking her jaw in my hand, putting my thumb over her lips. "You like playing games? I'd be careful playing them with me if I were you." I release her and turn to walk across the room. "Do not sit on any of my furniture until you get that dress off."

Opening a drawer, I look at the array of cufflinks. My dad's supposedly. Fuck. Again. Nothing. Not a god damned thing. The only

thing I recognize is the engagement ring I tossed in here after taking it off Scarlett's finger.

I choose a pair of cufflinks at random, closing the drawer a little harder than I need to.

"Why did you look?" I ask again as I turn to her, slipping the links into their slots.

"Because they deserved what they got. Actually, they deserved worse. You were too easy on them."

"Hmm." I study her. See a hate in her eyes I find familiar. That's good. That's what I need to see.

"Why did you have my uncle do it?"

"Why did I have him kill them?"

She nods.

"A test of loyalty."

She snorts, rolls her eyes.

"He failed. But to be honest, he'd have failed either way. Kill your own blood and I know you're a traitor. Don't, and you're not loyal to me."

She's confused, her forehead wrinkling.

"The reaper stands at his door either way." A knock at the door interrupts us. "Yes."

The door opens and my uncle, David, peeks his head inside. When he sees the girl, I see a flicker of surprise in his eyes, but he's quick to catch himself. I'm sure he'd agree with Dante. I should have killed her and the boy, too.

"Ready?" he asks.

"Two minutes."

He glances at her again, nods to me and leaves, closing the door.

I turn back to Scarlett, look her over and close the space between us. I give her credit for not backing away.

"Get that dress off. Get showered."

"Can you just tell me if Noah's okay?"

"He's fine."

"Is he going to stay fine?"

"For now. Get showered. I'll have food sent up. You don't leave this room."

"Why? Why didn't you kill us?"

"Yet."

"What?"

"Why haven't I killed you *yet*. That's how you should ask that question."

She swallows, worry making her face go pale.

"You may be useful."

"What does that mean?"

"It means I'm going to need something to fuck when I'm back."

Shock registers on her face and her mouth opens into a perfect O. I give her a minute to process.

"I will not be fucking you," she finally says, tone a little quieter.

"Face down ass up is my preference. So I know my options. Be sure to be in position—"

She raises her arm to slap me. Instinct or stupidity. Jury's still out.

I catch her wrist. "You're an angry little thing, aren't you?"

"You can fuck yourself, Cristiano Grigori. I will not be fucking you."

I chuckle.

She raises her left arm to do what the right couldn't. I catch that wrist too, my opinion leaning toward stupidity rather than instinct.

"Don't think what I did for you was a kindness and don't ever think to strike me. If you get rough, I'll get rough and you've seen what I'm capable of."

"Giving the order to kill you mean?"

I squeeze her wrists, walking her back to the wall. "The only thing keeping your brother and you alive right now is the warm pussy between your legs. Once I'm done with it, all bets are off, so I'd try really hard to ingratiate myself if I were you." I lean in so the tip of my nose is touching the tip of hers. "I'll make this simple so you can follow. Do not fuck with

me. Am I clear, Scarlett?"

She grits her teeth I assume to stop herself from opening her smartass mouth.

I press her wrists into the wall and squeeze. "I asked you if I'm fucking clear?"

She winces, eyes wide. What does she see in mine, I wonder? Rage. Fury. A monster.

I raise my eyebrows. "Do I need to dumb it down some more?"

"I'm not stupid and you're fucking crystal clear."

"I'm glad to hear it."

She calls me an asshole under her breath. Not stupid enough to say it to my face at least.

"What was that?" I ask, cocking my head to the side.

She keeps her lips sealed.

"Did you fucking say something, Scarlett?"

"No."

"Good."

I look down at her blood-crusted dress, shift her wrists into one of my hands and grip the bodice.

"What are you—"

The dress makes a glorious ripping sound, cutting her off. It exposes her bra, her flat belly. I shift my gaze back to hers. Her eyes have gone wide, mouth still open.

"Get it off. Shower." I release her wrists and walk to the door. "Alec." The guard turns to me. "Keep an eye on Ms. De La Cruz," I tell him, glancing at her. "She doesn't go out and nobody comes in."

She's wordlessly cursing me to hell and back. All I have to do is look at her to know. Her hands are tight fists holding the remnants of her dress together.

"If she does anything stupid, don't touch her. Punish her brother."

"No!" she calls out.

I walk out, then stop and turn back to her. "Remember what I said.

Face down, ass up."

She loses what color remained on her face. Good. She'll heel. Because the tables have turned on the De La Cruz family and I decide whether she and her brother live or die.

I hope you enjoyed this preview of With This Ring by Natasha Knight. Read the full story today, available on all platforms!

ABOUT NATASHA KNIGHT

Natasha Knight is the *USA Today* Bestselling author of Romantic Suspense and Dark Romance Novels. She has sold over half a million books and is translated into six languages. She currently lives in The Netherlands with her husband and two daughters and when she's not writing, she's walking in the woods listening to a book, sitting in a corner reading or off exploring the world as often as she can get away.

Write Natasha here: natasha@natasha-knight.com

Check out her books here:
https://natasha-knight.com

Sign up for her newsletter here:
https://bit.ly/3heleGN

Connect with her here:
Facebook Page→ http://bit.ly/29q3s4b
Facebook Fan Group → http://bit.ly/2xvnZO5
Instagram → https://bit.ly/2MeoPKk

Tyrant Stalker

ISABELLA STARLING

A PREVIEW

Chapter One

DOVE

I will never be as beautiful as I was before my face was ruined by a madman.

It's a hard truth, a bitter pill to swallow, but one that I've come to accept. My fingertips glide over the puckered scar. My reflection stares back, judging my appearance. I was pretty once. Years ago, before he cut me. I was pretty, careless, young, and stupid. I'm none of those things now.

"Dove, are you coming?"

"One second," I call out, untucking the dark strands of hair and allowing them to fall over my cheek, covering the scar. Like this, I look almost like I used to. I'm not the innocent nineteen-year-old I used to be. I'm twenty-seven now. I'm on a new path. I have a new life. A different kind of life. Sometimes I wonder if I would've been happier without the scar. But it's a dangerous path to go down. Better to focus on what I have than what could never be.

"Dove!"

"Coming!" I peel myself away from the mirror, sighing as I tuck my

hair behind my ear again. There's no point in hiding the scar. They all know it's there. It's the reason I got this job, after all.

I leave the bathroom, exiting into the studio where the bright lights blind me. I groan inwardly. Why the hell did I agree to do this again? Because of Robin, I remind myself. Because I'd do anything for my brother. He's all I have.

"Where do you want me?" I ask, standing awkwardly in the middle of the brightly lit space.

Raphael glances up from his camera, shooing his assistant. His brows knit together when he sees me. "You messed with your hair."

"I'm sorry," I mutter, fighting the urge to play with it again. "It was too perfect."

He approaches me, critically examining my features as he toys with the strands of hair framing my face. He doesn't touch or mention the scar, and I'm grateful for it. I know how hard it is to ignore.

"It looks better this way," he finally says, more to himself than me. "You'll have to take the robe off, though."

"Sure," I nod. "What am I wearing?"

Raphael returns to his setup, making sure his camera is connected to the computer screen. He doesn't look at me, fiddling with the cables as he says, "Nothing."

"Nothing?" Panic seizes my body in a deathly grip, my heart nearly jumping out of my chest at the thought. I do my best not to show it. I don't want to spoil this for myself. "What do you mean?"

Finally, Raphael glances up from the screen. "This is a nude shoot. Didn't I mention that?"

Wordlessly, I shake my head. The lump in my throat is getting bigger and bigger. What the hell did I get myself into? Damn Robin. He never mentioned this little detail. I wonder if he knew. My hands shake as I tug on the tie holding the black silk robe in place. I don't want to take it off, but what choice do I have? Raphael Santino is a world-renowned photographer. Booking this shoot was an honor. I can't let him down now.

"Sit on that chair," he says, staring through the lens of his camera as he points me underneath the bright lights. They all point at the chair, and I walk over there. It's hot under the lights, but not hot enough for me. I thrive in the heat. The cold always reaches my bones, making me feel more alone than ever. "Robe off, Dove."

I glance at everyone else in the room. There are two assistants, a lighting guy, as well as the makeup artist and hairstylist. I want to ask if they're all staying for the shoot, but I'm too embarrassed, not wanting to show just how inexperienced I am.

"*Pronto*, Dove," Raphael sighs, then follows my gaze to the rest of the people in the room. He seems to have picked up on my nervous energy. "Would you be more comfortable if we were alone?"

I contemplate his words. It would be easier to have just one judging pair of eyes on me instead of five. But out of all the people here, Raphael is the most intimidating by far. The Mexican photographer is gorgeous. Messy black hair, the most intense dark gaze and a body that looks like it's carved from stone. I've seen his Instagram feed. Even his selfies look like works of art, and he has beautiful models throwing themselves at him all day long. So what the hell does it matter? It's not like the guy's interested in me, anyway. He doesn't care what I look like. I'm not his girlfriend – I'm just his inspiration of the day.

"Yes," I finally manage.

He clicks his fingers and my watchers file out of the studio while casting curious glances at me. I can tell the hairstylist, Katya, is jealous. She was eating Raphael up with her eyes earlier. She must be hating this. The thought gives me a sick kind of satisfaction, yet I'm dreading what I'm about to do.

"When you're ready," Raphael says, returning his eye to behind the lens.

I get to my feet, the bright lights unforgiving, my hands trembling as I tug on the tie and the robe comes undone. I let it fall off my pale shoulders, gathering at my feet in a pool of silk. I can feel Raphael's gaze on me as he

drinks in my body, and shame threatens to burn me up from the inside.

But the photographer doesn't mention any of my imperfections. Not the fact that I'm painfully thin, emaciated. Not the tiny cuts covering my body, scars from years ago and some as fresh as a few days back. He doesn't talk about my visible rib cage, or the hip bones painfully protruding through my pale skin. Doesn't mention the scabbed scars on my thighs. And it's a welcome relief.

This is who I am. This is what I look like. If he doesn't like me, that's fine – I just hope he's quick and as painless as possible when he turns me down. But the words never come. Instead, I'm blinded by the flash of light as he snaps a photo.

"*Hermosa*," he mutters, admiring his own work on the screen. "Just fucking beautiful."

It's been a long time since I've been called beautiful.

For the next three hours, I work hard as Raphael's muse. He positions me in different ways, neither of us stopping for a second. I'm naked for the entire shoot, but it doesn't feel icky like I feared when Raphael first mentioned it. He doesn't look at me like a sex object. He looks at me almost impersonally, as though I'm a work of art he's been sent to capture. Like a true artist.

By the time he finally announces we're finished, I'm feeling exhausted.

"Do you want to see the photos?" he asks as he stares intently at the computer screen, scrutinizing our hard work. "I think they came out—"

"No, that's okay," I cut him off. I don't want to hear the ending of that sentence. "As long as we're done here, I'd like to head back home."

"Of course." He gives me a curious glance. This time, he doesn't look at me like I'm an object. He looks at me as a woman, and his gaze lingers on my puckered nipples, on the black trail of hairs leading down to my neglected center. I flush, letting my hair fall over my face to hide the traitorous blush in my cheeks. Picking the black silk robe off the floor, I put it on as fast as I can. Once I'm covered by fabric again, I can finally

breathe.

"Thank you for this opportunity," I say, my gaze meeting Raphael's. "I'm really grateful."

"Of course you are," he smirks. Cocky. But why wouldn't he be? "It was my pleasure, honestly, Dove. We have something amazing here. I'll be in touch in a few weeks with the final selection."

His eyes drink me in again as I head to the clothing rack where the clothes I came in are still hanging. I rummage through my purse first, seeing a couple of missed calls from my brother. He's probably anxious to know how everything went. I didn't expect for the shoot to take this long.

I smile to myself. Robin's way too protective, but I'm grateful for it. I can't trust my own judgement, never could. Robin makes sure I'm okay, and not getting into too much trouble.

"Unless..."

"What?" I turn back to face Raphael who is still staring at me intently. "Unless what?"

"Unless you'd like to see me before then." He smirks. The cockiness would be unbearable on any other man, but Raphael has a certain kind of charm that makes it impossible to hate him for being so forward. "I like you, Dove. You're... different."

Not special. Not beautiful. *Different.*

But it's a compliment, nonetheless. I stare back into the photographer's gaze, pondering his words. There's no way I can live up to the flock of picture-perfect, barely legal models that decorate his arms at public functions. I'm not as pretty, and I'm too broken. But maybe that's exactly why he likes me.

"Are you asking me out?" I wonder out loud, and he laughs.

"You're really straightforward, aren't you?" he asks, and I shrug in response.

"No point in pretending. I am what I am," I reply.

"I like that." He sets his camera down, grinning at me. "I *am* asking you out. Have dinner with me. Tonight."

"Tonight?" I shake my head. "No, I can't tonight."

"Got another hot date?"

I think of my plans. Dinner with Robin, then curling up in front of the TV, binging the same TV shows for the thousandth time. "You could say that."

"You're a popular girl, Dove Canterbury," Raphael smirks. "I'll settle for tomorrow then. And don't give me another excuse. I want to see you again, soon as I can."

I weigh up the pros and cons. The negatives by far outweigh the positives, but despite that, I find myself nodding in response to Raphael's question. I grab a pen from his desk and scribble my address on a pink Post-It note, handing it to him.

"Pick me up here. Eight p.m. tomorrow."

"Do I get your number too?" He raises his brows, obviously amused. I hesitate, but then scribble that down, too. "And your social media? Instagram? Facebook? Do you have Twitter?"

"No," I reply firmly. "I'm not on social media."

I neglect to mention my Instagram account, but I don't want him to know about that. Not even Robin does.

"You're an enigma, Dove Canterbury," he mutters. I ignore his words and change in the studio while his gaze swallows me up with curiosity. What's the point of hiding now? The guy's already seen me naked from every angle.

"Well, you got yourself a deal. I'll pick you up tomorrow. Say hi to your brother for me, alright?" Raphael says once I'm back in my baggy clothes that hide a multitude of sins.

"Sure." I smile awkwardly and grab my purse, hoisting it on my shoulder. "You have a good day."

I exit the studio into the office area. The hairstylist glares at me, but I ignore her, saying my goodbyes and heading outside while ordering an Uber on my phone.

I wait outside. It's warmer here than it was in the air-conditioned

studio, but still not enough to warm my cold bones. Nothing can stop the cold spreading from the inside.

As I wait for my driver, I scan the passersby for any sign of trouble. But no one pays me much attention. I'm invisible like this, in my all-black, baggy clothes, natural makeup, and my hair covering half my face – the ruined half.

But then a mother walks by, holding a little girl's hand, and my heart jumps. The girl is cute, wearing a pink tutu and light-up pink sneakers. She must be about four. Really freaking cute. I smile at her, and she gives me a curious look while her mother impatiently tugs on her hand.

Tucking my hair behind my ear absentmindedly, I push my tongue out and make a face at her.

Her eyes widen as she notices the scar on my cheek. I almost forgot about it. Almost.

But as the little girl's smile changes into a grimace, I know I can never forget.

I'm ruined. A monster. And nothing will ever change the fact that Parker Miller destroyed my life eight years ago. I hate the bastard.

Chapter Two

NOX

*L*ittle bird is not so little anymore.

I raise the cigarette to my lips and suck on it, inhaling the smoke. It's hot out here. Outrageously fucking hot. I hate it. Hate being in this heat. It doesn't agree with my body, but Dove doesn't seem affected by it at all. My eyes follow her into the office building. I don't know what the fuck she's doing there, but once she disappears inside, I use the opportunity to scour the metal plates with business names on them.

Raphael Santino Photography.

Bright Idea Marketing.

Sweet Buns Bakery.

What the fuck is my little bird doing here? Not knowing is driving me fucking crazy. But I don't have a choice – there's no way for me to find out what's happening here, not unless I can get a hint somehow. All there's left for me to do is to wait for her to be done. And fuck me, it's taking forever.

I linger in an alleyway close to the building, keeping an eye on the revolving door. People come and go. Some carry sticky buns in

brown paper wrapping, from that bakery I saw mentioned on the plaque. Others carry briefcases, wearing smart business outfits. Nothing like the misshapen, baggy clothes little bird wears to hide her true beauty.

For the life of me, I can't figure out what the fuck she's doing in there. The tension of not knowing bothers me, and my nails dig into the palms of my hands, forming red crescent moons of pain.

I wait. I loiter. No one notices me. I'm invisible in my all-black outfit, the hood of my sweatshirt pulled low over my face to hide it. It's not like anyone would recognize me here, anyway. LA is a long way from home. My past is in New York City. But Dove is my present and my future. She just doesn't know it yet.

Finally, what feels like hours later, Dove emerges from the building. She looks different than she did when she went in, and it pisses me off. Her hair's doing some weird curly shit. It looks as glossy as always though, and she's still wearing the same clothes. The light makeup on her face enhances her features but does nothing to hide the scar on her left cheek. I smirk at that. It pleases me.

I watch her interact with a little girl. I see the pain on little bird's face when she sees the kid's fear. I make a mental note of it. As she waits for her ride, I realize I'm being watched, too.

The girl's mother has left her outside, disappearing into the building Dove just came out of. What kind of fucking idiot leaves their kid on a busy street like this? My hands form fists. That woman needs to be punished.

I allow myself to sink into a dark place where I can take out my anger on the girl's mother. I imagine carving her, putting welts into her body as she screams. It doesn't matter what she looks like or if I'm attracted to her. All that matters is taking out my fucking rage on something.

A moment too late, I realize the girl is watching me. When I do, she's already coming toward me. I can't risk Dove noticing me, but I see her Uber's just pulled up, and she's getting into it right when the little girl comes to a stop before me.

"Hello," she says softly, and I groan as I watch Dove's ride drive

down the street. *Fuck.*

"Move it, kid," I hiss at the little girl.

"What's your name?" She stares up at me expectantly. The dumb little thing feared my little bird because of her scar, but she doesn't even flinch in my presence. She doesn't know a monster when it's staring her in the fucking face. "I like your jacket."

I decide to humor the kid. I kneel next to her, waving my hand in front of her and producing a red lollipop out of thin air. The girl gasps as I hand it to her.

"How did you do that?" she asks with wonder in her young voice.

"Magic. You like cherry flavor?"

She nods. "My favorite."

"Enjoy it, kid." I pull away from the shadows of the alley, ready to follow Dove. I'm guessing she went back home. She rarely leaves the apartment, so her little outing today is fucking inexplicable to me.

"Where are you going?"

I turn to face the little girl again, glancing at the building her mother disappeared into. "Where's your mom, kid?"

She smiles. "She's getting us some sticky buns. She says I have to wait here."

"Why wouldn't she take you with her?"

The kid shrugs, rubbing the hem of her pink tutu between her fingers and drawing lines on the asphalt with her toe. She's kind of cute, and I feel bad for leaving her alone on the street. The desire to keep following Dove is strong, but I do my best to fight it. My conscience may be nearly non-existent, but at least it's strong enough so I don't abandon this girl in the middle of the city, unlike her fuck-up mom.

"She likes a boy that works there," the girl mutters. "She says I'll spoil it for her if I come along."

My blood boils with rage. This poor kid. I have a soft spot for children with fucked up situations at home, obviously. And now I can't leave. I'll think about the kid all fucking day if I do.

With a groan, I lean against the wall. I'm fighting the urge to pull out another cig, but I don't want to be a bad influence on the girl. Talk about being a fucking hypocrite.

"I'll wait with you," I mutter carelessly. "But don't tell your mom about me. She'd probably be pissed, right?"

The girl nods with a conspiratorial smile. Knew I fucking liked her.

"Mommy says not to speak to strangers."

"Mommy's damn right," I grunt. "You don't know what's hiding in people's heads, kid. Humans are unpredictable. *Dangerous*."

"I like you."

I laugh out loud, fighting the urge to tell her off. She's not my goddamn kid and I sure as fuck won't be the one to discipline her. But then I see her mother exiting the building, holding a greasy paper bag. This is my last chance to give the kid some life tips. I kneel next to her once again.

"Don't trust a soul, kid," I tell her. "People suck."

"I know," she smiles widely.

"Good girl." I smirk and pick myself back up, leaning against the wall so I'm hidden by the shadows again. "Your mom's back, you better run along."

She nods and smiles up at me before walking back to the office building. She doesn't say goodbye, and I like that. Goodbyes are too fucking final. Maybe I'll see her again someday.

I watch her get scolded for wandering off by her mother, who doesn't even notice me. Stupid goddamn bitch. She should be thanking me, but she doesn't even know I exist, which is better for her, really. If I get too close to people, I end up hurting them. *Physically*.

As they pass the alleyway, her mother is oblivious to my presence, but the kid finds me in the shadows and waves. I wave back.

Hours later, I'm lingering in the street where Dove lives. I know she's

home – the lights are on in her apartment. She's alone for now, but I figure her brother will be dropping by soon. He always does on Fridays.

I kind of like Robin, as jealous as I am of the guy. He's a year older than Dove and has an insufferable girlfriend called Elise. She's some kind of Instagram influencer, obsessed with perfection. I hate girls like her.

But Robin's a good fucking guy. He cares about Dove, really cares about her. He visits her almost every day, bringing food, because he knows she doesn't eat, and little, thoughtful gifts because he knows she needs a distraction from her shitty life.

Glancing at Dove's window, I make sure the lights are still on as I light another cigarette. I raise it to my lips, my eyes still on the building until I see a red car pulling up in front of it. Like I suspected, Robin is back again tonight.

The guy gets out of his Corvette with his hands full. He's got a bag of takeout that I know Dove won't touch, but he's as hopeful about his sister eating something as I am. In his other hand, he has a potted plant. It's not elegant like an orchid. It's barely even green anymore, all dried up and kind of rotten at the same time.

I watch him ring the doorbell, getting myself ready for the moment my little bird appears on the doorstep. A moment later and there she is. She looks tired today. Her little venture into the outside world must've taken its toll on her. Still, Dove's face lights up as she sees her brother and invites him inside.

The door closes, pissing me off. I want to be privy to their conversation, but I can't fucking hear it from here. I need to figure out a better way of keeping an eye on Dove. Maybe I can bug her apartment. Then she really wouldn't have secrets from me.

I watch brother and sister unload things in the kitchen, Dove shaking her head when her brother offers her some Thai food – her once favorite. She keeps shaking her pretty head and Robin keeps telling her off, until he finally gives up. He should know better than that. My little bird doesn't eat in front of other people. In fact, she barely eats at all.

I watch them head into the living room next and settle in front of the TV. They put on some shitty sitcom I've seen them watch a thousand times and settle into a comfortable silence. The potted, half-dead plant is on the windowsill in the bathroom. I have no doubt it'll be thriving in no time. Dove has green fingers.

They spend hours together just like they always do. From my vantage point, I can see Robin glancing at his phone every few minutes. No doubt his vain wannabe model girlfriend is blowing it up with notifications. She's so fucking jealous of Dove. I can't stand her. And it amuses me that Dove hates the girl, too. Little bird doesn't hate a lot of people, but she can't stand Elise.

Finally, Robin makes an excuse to leave Dove for a moment. Since she doesn't have a backyard, he heads outside to take a phone call in the street, and I smirk. He's so weak. That Elise woman needs putting in her place and some bruises to go along with it. I watch him argue on the phone with her before he heads back inside and feeds Dove some bullshit lie neither of them believes.

It's interesting how I can imagine their conversations going without ever hearing them. My resolve to bug Dove's house strengthens. I want more of her voice. I want more of *her*.

An hour later, a shiny bubblegum Porsche pulls into the street, and I smirk to myself, halfway through my sixth cigarette since I got here. This'll be fucking good.

Elise gets out of the car, her yapping Yorkshire terrier barking from the safety of her Louis Vuitton handbag at *every-fucking-thing* they pass. Robin bought the dog for her a few weeks ago, and she complained because it wasn't a more expensive breed. Fucking bitch.

It's weird, knowing so much about people who don't even know I exist. Well, I suppose they do, they just think I'm long-fucking-gone.

Dove relishes in the belief that I died years ago. I bet she's shed some tears over my supposed death, though. After all, she was fucking obsessed with me back then, up until I carved her pretty face.

Sometimes I regret doing it. Not because of the scar, but because I frightened her off. It took me fucking years to realize Dove was it for me. Years after being blind-fucking-sided by my bastard twin brother and his slut bride. June Miller, née Wildfox, was never the one for me. But her former mini me is.

I watch Elise press the doorbell down for so long she nearly breaks one of her talons. I lean back against the wall of the alley and smirk. This ought to be fucking good.

Chapter Three

DOVE

"Hey, kid."

"Robin!" I let him kiss my cheek and step aside so he can follow me into the apartment. "You're late. What happened?"

"Elise happened," he says. "I had to walk Pepper for her."

I groan. That freaking yappy little dog is the bane of my existence, but I choose not to mention it, focusing on something else instead of picking a fight the first few minutes my brother is here. I ignore the bag of takeout he brought and focus on the half-dead plant in his hand. "This for me?"

"If you can save it." Robin sets the food down on the counter and we inspect the plant together. "I don't know what I'm doing wrong. Every plant I get dies. And even worse, it's taking me less and less time to kill them."

"Good thing you have me," I grin, reaching for my watering can of tepid water and carefully pouring some into the plant's cute cat-shaped planter. "I'll have it back to life in no time. You gonna let me keep this one too?"

"Why not?" Robin laughs. "It's not like you need another plant, but at

least it won't instantly die in my house."

He's right. My apartment is like a jungle. I can't resist a pretty plant, and I somehow always come back with something new, leafy and green when I leave the house. Even if I don't, Robin supplies me with his castoffs more often than not. At this point, I'm pretty sure he's killing them on purpose so he can cheer me up with a new addition every week.

"So?" he asks, the excitement clear in his voice as we settle on the sofa in the living room. "How did the shoot go? You didn't say anything earlier."

"I wanted to tell you in person." I pick up the TV remote and click on play and one of our favorite shows starts to play out on the screen. We both know it by heart now. Half of the time we spend together is just quoting the freaking show to one another. "It went well, I think."

Robin reaches for the remote and pauses the show. He's always afraid he'll miss something if we talk while we watch it, even though we've both seen every episode a thousand times. "Well, tell me everything. I got a text from Katya. She said the photographer couldn't stop gushing about you."

I laugh out loud. Katya, one of my brother's ex-girlfriends, who he stayed in touch with – much to Elise's dismay – was the hairstylist on set. She's the one who told Robin that Raphael was looking for unique models. And then Robin wouldn't leave me alone for weeks, begging me to go through with it. He thought it would be good for me, and as hesitant as I was about the whole thing, it ended up working out.

"Well, first of all," I start, narrowing my eyes at him. "You didn't tell me it was a nude shoot."

He laughs, nervously scratching the back of his dark-haired head. "I figured it would be. But you're cool with that, right?"

Robin knows I'm nowhere near cool with that. Not that nudity is the problem. No, it's being exposed – all my scars plainly visible for the viewer. But I find myself nodding now, as if it isn't a problem at all.

"It was actually kind of fun," I admit. "And really exhausting. I must've been there for five hours or even more. Two to do the makeup and

hair, and then another three of shooting."

"So, what's Santino like?"

"He's..." I struggle to find the right words. "Intense. Interesting." Freaking hot as sin, I want to add, but I force myself not to. Although Robin knows me so well, I'm pretty sure he can tell what I was going to say next. "I'm glad I went, anyway. Thanks for making me go."

"You're welcome," Robin beams before waggling his brows at me. "Heard the guy asked you out."

I groan. "Katya really can't keep her mouth shut, can she?"

"Nope." My brother's grinning from ear to ear. "So, how'd you turn down this one?"

Despite the scar, I've been asked out a fair few times in the past few years since I moved out to LA. But I almost always turn down people who ask me. After a few disastrous experiences – including one where my date turned out to be a plastic surgeon and spent half of dinner explaining how he could fix my scar – I've pretty much sworn off dating altogether.

"I didn't," I finally say. "We're going out tomorrow."

"What?" Robin's mouth gapes open. "You agreed to go out with him?"

"Why not?" I shrug weakly. "I haven't been on a date in almost two years. Figured I might as well try again before I fully commit to being a green-fingered spinster."

"Cute." Robin stares me down. "So what are you doing on your date?"

"Dinner," I blurt out, my cheeks flushing a deep shade of red as I feel his penetrating smile on me.

"Dinner," he repeats. "Wow. You must really like this guy."

Robin knows as well as I do, I never do dinner dates, because I hate eating in front of other people. It's always awkward, and I don't want to deal with their prying questions about why I'm just picking at the food on my plate and not actually eating anything.

"What are you wearing?" my brother asks next and I shrug.

"I don't know. The usual?"

"Nuh uh, no way." I groan as I look into his determined eyes. "Why don't you borrow something from Elise? I'm sure she'd be happy to lend you something, and you're the same size, too."

We're only the same size because his tiny girlfriend starves herself on a daily basis to fit into a size zero. But then again, am I not doing the same thing? Even though it's for different reasons, I'm no better than Miss Instagram model/resident bitch Elise Howard.

"Fine," I finally groan. Elise will fucking love this. For some unknown reason, she's obsessed with me. She constantly offers to do my hair and makeup. To take me shopping, to get my nails done. I've fought it off successfully for the past year she's been with my brother, but I guess this is my freaking breaking point. She'll be thrilled.

"Perfect," Robin says. "I'll shoot her a quick text to let her know."

He pulls out his phone, narrowing his eyes at the screen.

"Trouble in paradise?"

"She's texted me twenty-seven times in the past ten minutes," Robin groans.

"God, how do you put up with it?" I shake my head. "She's *so* possessive. It's just as well she likes me. What the hell does she do when you're around other women you're not freaking related to?"

"You don't wanna know," Robin mutters, his fingers busy as he types a reply. For the next few minutes, he glares at his phone. "She's not replying."

"Maybe she's driving," I offer, which is a lame excuse, because we both know Elise texts while driving. "I'm sure she'll get back to you soon."

Just then, the sound of the doorbell rings out through the room. We exchange glances and get up from the sofa, both heading for the door. I open it, and of course, Elise stands on the doorstep in one of her bubblegum pink outfits to match her Barbie car, Pepper barking his head off at us from her designer purse – no doubt another one of my brother's gifts.

"Dove!" she exclaims, giving me air kisses on both cheeks as that insufferable dog barks and barks. "So good to see you, darling."

"What are you doing here, Elise?" Robin asks before I can reply, and his girlfriend gives him an innocent look. "We agreed to meet up tomorrow, not today."

"Well, you weren't answering my texts, honeybear," Elise pouts. God, that fucking nickname. It's so hard not to laugh at my brother when she uses it. "I thought something was wrong."

"I told you, I'm spending the evening with my sister," Robin insists. Why do his words make me feel so guilty? I feel like I'm taking away from Elise's time with him, and guilt threatens to swallow me up whole. "I don't have time to hang out today."

"Why can't we all hang out together?" Elise whines next. "I won't even complain about watching that stupid show again. Please? Let me come in. Please."

She's practically begging at this point, and I can tell my brother's resolve is weakening.

"Why don't you just go back to your place?" I suggest. "I can handle a night on my own, Robin."

"Absolutely not." Sigh. It was worth a try. If only Robin weren't so overprotective. "We'll all stay in tonight."

He steps aside to let Elise in. I groan inwardly. The last thing I want is to spend an evening with the woman, but it looks like I have no choice. The blonde walks inside with a triumphant smile and sets her purse on the floor. Pepper jumps out, stopping to growl at me before raising his leg at a plant I've barely managed to save from dying. Just fucking perfect.

Elise doesn't even scold him, and we all file into the living room. The silence would be awkward, but there isn't any. Elise is desperate to fill every second of the time we spend together with her ramblings. It's almost worse than the dog's constant yapping.

My brother tells her about the date I have the next day, and I cringe inwardly when she shrieks and tells me we must meet up the next day to do some maintenance. I don't have a clue what *maintenance* means, but by her critical gaze as she examines me up close, I'm guessing it'll take up most of

my day. I'm already dreading it, but Robin's always so desperate for me to be close with Elise, I find myself agreeing to meet her in Rodeo Drive the next day.

I think of my mom then. I don't like to think about my parents very often, but I know she'd love that I'm going on a date. As annoying as she can be, I'm actually looking forward to our obligatory weekly call this time. At least I'll have some good news to tell her.

Robin insists on staying until midnight's come and gone. I'm grateful Elise is here though, because I know Robin understands I won't want to eat in front of her. While they feast on the Thai takeout he brought, nobody forces me to eat, and I'm grateful for it. I watch Elise picking at her vegetables – she's pescatarian on Tuesdays and vegan for the rest of the week – and wonder where her issues with food came from. I know exactly why mine are present. It all stems from my mother's belief that I'm damaged goods.

When they finally get up to leave, I'm grateful for the peaceful night ahead. Robin shows me all the leftovers, including an untouched Pad Thai they left for me, and I promise him I'll have some, crossing my fingers behind my back. I walk them out and wave them off as they drive away in their separate cars and then I lock the front door.

My tummy is rumbling, but I pay it no mind. It's not worth the trouble to eat. I pile the leftovers and the untouched food into a brown paper bag and head outside again. The street is colder than earlier, but the night is pleasant. I walk down the street to the alleyway where Sam is already waiting.

"Robin come over again today?" he asks with a wide smile.

"You know it." I hand him the paper bag. "It's Thai today. I left the plastic cutlery in there. And I got you some sweet buns when I was in town earlier. Those are in there, too."

"Thanks, Dove." He gives me a bright smile. "Heading back already?"

"I have to," I say, winking at him. "Got a hot date tomorrow."

"A date?" Sam laughs out loud. "Who's the lucky guy?"

"That photographer I met today," I admit. "He was kind of cute, actually."

More like unbearably-fucking-hot, but I'm not about to admit that to Sam. He'd never stop making fun of me.

"I'll see you tomorrow?" he asks, the hope obvious in his voice, and I have to shrug apologetically.

"I brought you the buns because I'll be away for most of the day," I explain. "But I'll drop by the day after with some food. You need anything else?"

He shakes his head, even though we both know there are a lot of other things he needs.

"You want to come in the day after tomorrow? You could take a hot shower. I can brush your hair." I grin at him. His hair is a rat's nest, but he refuses to let me pay for a barber.

"No thanks, Dove," he replies firmly. He never wants to come into my house, no matter how many times I suggest it. I'm desperate to do more for him, but it was hard enough to get him to accept the food. Maybe with time, I can help him some more. "I'll see you the day after tomorrow, yeah?"

"Of course." I blow him a kiss and he laughs, retreating to his makeshift bed on the sidewalk.

I wrap my black cardigan tight around my body as a chill blows right through me. I've done everything on my to-do list now, but the night stretches ahead, promising hours of insomnia.

Maybe if I could finally catch a wink of sleep, things would be different. But as I lock the door behind me, I know it's not an option. Not with the shadow of my past hanging heavy above me with every step I take.

Pre-Order Tyrant Stalker today!

ABOUT ISABELLA STARLING

Isabella Starling is the USA Today and Amazon bestselling author of Pet, Peep Show and more. Isabella lives in the capital of a small, picturesque European country with her partner and three furbabies.

She describes her books with three words: dirty, dark, and forbidden. Isa loves writing dark, twisted stories with possessive heroes and the women they love.

Stalk me, I love it!

MY FAVORITE BOOKS I'VE WRITTEN

Pet
Peep Show
Tyrant Twins
Box sets
I'm Your Daddy Now

Standalones
Teach Me Daddy
Daddy's Girl
Confess
His Brat
His Doll
His Muse
Daddy Dearest (FREE)

Christmas books
Mistletoe Kisses
Sugar Plum

Elite of Eden Falls Prep series
A Hurt So Sweet Volume One
A Hurt So Sweet Volume Two
A Hurt So Sweet Volume Three
A Hurt So Sweet Volume Four

Rose & Thorn series
Blush Pink Rose (FREE)
Blood Red Rose
Pure White Rose
Last Broken Rose

Thank you so much for reading TALES OF DARKNESS AND SIN!
This has been such a fun project for us to put together and we hope you
enjoyed and love our stories. We hope to do this again!

If you want to hear more from us - join our Facebook group! You'll find
plenty of giveaways, exclusive stuff we share, and readers like you who
enjoy all the dark, forbidden, and sinful books!
Queens Of Darkness And Sin